Younger Thinner Blonder

By Sue Watson

RICKSHAW
PUBLISHING

A Rickshaw paperback
www.rickshawpublishing.co.uk

First published in Great Britain in 2013 by Rickshaw Publishing
Ltd, 102 Fulham Palace Road, London W6 9PL

A CIP catalogue record for this book is available from the British
Library.

ISBN 978-0-9565368-7-7

Printed and bound in Great Britain for Rickshaw Publishing Ltd by
CPI Group (UK) Ltd, Croydon, CR0 4YY

FT
Pbk

RICKSHAW
PUBLISHING

Acknowledgements

This book has taken me to a very far flung place and, like my heroine, I've had ups and downs, but on the whole it's been a fabulous ride. And though they may not have realised it at the time, many of my family and friends were travelling alongside me on that bumpy journey, providing the support, encouragement, deep chocolate cake and rich humour that drives me on.

I'd just like to say thank you to a few of them here.

Thanks to all at Rickshaw Publishing and an extra special thank you to the divine Jo Doyle, my editor, who does the literary equivalent of wiping my eyes, tidying up my mess then making a nice cup of tea!

To Maya's mummy, an inspirational woman who really 'showed' me Nepal, through her lyrical descriptions and amazing insight into the place and the people...Thank you, thank you. And a special thank you to my friend and former colleague Claire Davies-Hobbs for introducing us.

Thanks to my great friend Liz Cox, my sounding board, literary lovely and (for this book) the font of all things designer and Swedish. Her delicious phrases, profound knowledge of high-end splash-backs and in-depth data on profanely priced interiors are all present in the novel. But most of all, a million cream and jam topped Devon scones to her for giving me Astrid on a plate, well a smorgasbord, actually!

Big hugs to my girls and lunchtime legends, Alison Birch and Louise Bagley. Our glamorous suppers, retail lunches and relentless pursuit of the perfect nude shoe are a constant source of hilarity and inspiration. Their support, humour, and genuine friendship mean so much to me and are a wonderful antidote to my sometimes lonely writing life.

I couldn't have continued on this bumpy book journey without my lovely literary ladies, Sarah Robinson, Jan Holman, Diane Tilley, Jackie Swift, Sheila Webb and Sarah Douglas, who make up 'The Bodacious Book Club.' Their continued support, intelligence, humour and capacity for wine is truly appreciated – our Book Club evenings are as raucous as they are literary – and long may it continue!

Thank you to Jeannette and Cyril Watson, for their kindness, faith and support and for sharing their own funny stories which often inspire mine (but theirs are far crazier)!

To my dearest friend Lesley McLoughlin, thank you for always being there, never doubting me and keeping my glass full (literally) with the best Lime Daiquiris this side of Cuba.

I couldn't even have started on this writing journey without my wonderful mum, Patricia Engert, who has always told me anything's possible. Her advice and candlelit suppers sustain me through all life's journeys, literary or otherwise!

A special hug and thank you to my daughter Eve Watson, one of the funniest people I know, and whose lines I shall continue to steal for my books, until she is old enough to write her own.

This book is dedicated to Nick Watson,
who makes it all possible.

1

Psychosis and Cellulite

"So, tell me, just how many women have you made pregnant?" I muffled angrily through toothpaste foam.

Silence.

"Go on... Say something. You're supposed to be the big man..."

I spat toothpaste into the sink with unbridled venom, stopping briefly to take a glug of mouthwash. The bracing mintiness stopped me in my tracks and I inhaled deeply. "Aah...and don't try to deny it, the evidence is...here."

I slammed the bright green bottle onto the side. The relief from that much-needed oral frisson had stopped me mid-rant again. I had to word this carefully – I didn't want him to walk off – so I flossed firmly, whilst giving it some thought.

It was 5am and as always I had been woken by the sound of crazed birds from my alarm clock. I think it was supposed to be soothing, conjuring up a morning scene of country meadows bathed in early sunshine. Problem was, it was faulty and couldn't be relied upon. To be woken at dawn by gentle birdsong was one thing, but it is quite another when the bloody thing sets off at 2am, all flapping feathers and menacing squawks like a scene from Hitchcock's *The Birds*. I couldn't get rid of it because it was a gift from Nathan and he was sensitive about stuff like that.

"...Don't play the innocent! It takes two, or in your case, five, at the same time!" I carried on, shouting through the bedroom door. I could hear Nathan snort and turn over in our huge bed. I sighed and checked the clock. I had precisely one hour before my driver picked me up to take me to the studio – and I hadn't even got to the part with the mother yet. A response from Nathan would really have helped at that moment – *The Truth with Tanya Travis* aired in five hours and I wanted to cover every angle before my confrontation with the nation's great shagging, drug-taking, DNA-testing unwashed.

Still in my underwear, I approached the mirror for a quick inspection.

"Jesus! Look at the state of my bum!" I moaned, finally causing a slight stir under the duvet. Nathan pulled the covers over his head, so all I could see in the dimness was a few tendrils of dark blond peeping out from the top. I smiled in spite of myself; I did love his tousled, tangled mane – though it also made my fingers itch for a comb and a bottle of Serge Normant Velour Conditioner.

"Nathan, you wouldn't believe the spectacle of my thighs... Don't look, you might never fancy me again," I said, thumping my bottom cheek in disgust.

"Tanya. It's 5am, give over with the shouting," he muttered.

"I'm sorry Nathan, but if you saw what I'd just seen in the mirror you'd shout too," I shouted, again. It was OK for him, he wasn't on television. Every extra pound, every fine wrinkle was up there for scrutiny, and TV was so unforgiving – especially now I was in HD. But of course he didn't understand because he was male, and on Mars they've never encountered the horrors of cellulite.

"I can't believe it. I've detoxed, toned and lunged for most of my adult life," I muttered, waggling the flesh around my buttocks. I'd never been Elle Macpherson, but my thighs hadn't expanded in such an alarming and unforgiving way before.

Until now controlled eating, vigorous daily sessions down the gym with Zac – my personal trainer – and my pre-show morning run had always kept me at a size ten. But there was no getting away from it: I was now over 40 and the gym alone couldn't cut it. As I wiped each thigh with cream made from the umbilical cords of unborn calves, I contemplated the pain, cost and inconvenience of liposuction but saw no other way. I rummaged through my BlackBerry for the number of Donna's surgeon of choice, in the hope he could squeeze my thighs into his tight schedule immediately and make me younger, firmer, better. Donna was my agent and she always said that 'Dr Lipo' (Len to his friends) could turn a fat girl thin in a lunch hour, often waxing lyrical on his 'sucking technique'.

I couldn't find the number and I wasn't seeing Donna until lunchtime. Christ, by then my thighs would be like *Quartermass* – swelling until they'd taken over the world. "You are disgusting... five women in a night. You are nothing but a male slag...a...tart..." I said absently, still scrolling through my BlackBerry in the hope that the number would magically appear.

"Turn off the bloody lights, I'm trying to sleep!" came a grumpy voice from the bedroom.

"Go on. You have to tell the truth," I continued, ignoring him. "Shit!"

"What now?"

"I've definitely lost the phone number of the fat sucking surgeon who takes ten years off and turns fat into fit," I said, crossly, "and I need emergency surgery now!"

"No you don't." A response: at last.

"Ha! Try telling Donna that. She said yesterday that if I don't get work done, I've got another two years – max – before they send me to the retirement home for ageing presenters. Mind you, I reckon she's on commission from Lipo Len."

"Ah, stop fretting, you're beautiful, come back to bed. We could get warm together."

"No. You're not part of my pre-show regime." I shouted through with a smile, not prepared to make myself late. I washed my hands again, turning the tap up so it drowned out thoughts of early morning lust. I washed them once more, thoroughly this time.

"Donna would insist you have a complete surgical makeover if it meant you'd stay in work longer and earn more money for her," Nathan said as I padded back into the bedroom. I could just about make out his toned silhouette in the darkness, propped up on one elbow, watching me. "She's a bloody pimp."

"She's not! You don't even know her."

"I know enough."

"Donna's been a good friend to me," I said, picking up my trainers.

"Anyway, stop interrupting me... I've got to finish the script before my run. I have the evidence in my hand so there's no point denying it..." I started.

"Tanya I..."

"Here are the results of the lie-detector test. We're about to find out exactly what's been going on during those visits to your 'dentist,'" I announced dramatically. "It seems you've been getting more than a scale and polish on your nocturnal visits to Doctor Cavity!"

I left it hanging. I was trying for Jeremy Paxman but in an attempt at BBC Two gravitas, I was developing a scary German accent. My style was becoming less 'serious interview' and more 'SS interrogation'. I stopped myself, before the compulsion to goose-step around the bed took over. Not a good look in M&S midi-pants, especially considering the current wobble of the derrière.

"Tanya, just keep the noise down," said Nathan with a sigh. "We don't all have to be up at dawn."

"OK, Mr Grumpy," I leaned over the bed and kissed his warm, sleepy cheek, wishing for a second I could stay with him under the duvet.

I mentally ticked off 'serial impregnator,' on my script. That was only the beginning: there was plenty more on the menu that morning and I moved swiftly on to my personal favourite, the cage-fighting psycho drug dealer... Where did they find these people?

"When not in your cage having a fight, you were bagging up household cleaning products and passing them off as coke and smack!" I shouted, my outrage building; "So you think it's OK to flog Bold Bio and Persil Automatic to a teenager for a tenner a gram? Apart from the obvious, it's a waste of good detergent," I huffed indignantly.

I stood for a few seconds in the darkness, waiting to see if I'd get a reaction but Nathan pulled the pillow over his head and turned over.

"So you aren't up for role-playing the sex-fuelled skin head, or cage-fighting psycho detergent-drug dealer then?" I asked, a little sulkily.

"Oh you don't need me – you're Tanya Travis." He said, with a sigh.

"Yes, I am Tanya Travis," I responded in my best TV voice while lining up the jogging playlist on my iPod, "but even a queen needs her king."

I sat on the edge of the bed and rubbed his back. "I may be Queen of Daytime, but if you're lucky I could be your queen of night-time later," I said softly.

"Yeah... That would be great Tanya, but I might have to work tonight," came the muffled response.

"Work?" I couldn't quite contain my surprise. Nathan was a great musician and wrote wonderful songs, but had so far had no commercial success.

"I'm so pleased for you Nathan. Is it music work?" I asked, wanting to encourage him and practice being the supportive, 'rock-star' wife. One day I would be Trudie Styler to Nathan's Sting, all tasteful interiors, raw wholefoods and tantric sex.

"Don't get excited, Tanya. It's only a chat with a guy from an indie label," he said, pulling himself up onto his elbows again and squinting at me in the half-darkness. "It probably won't come to anything, so don't go on about it."

"I won't." But I couldn't help myself.

"I hope it's a good meeting, though. Wouldn't it be fab if he likes some of your songs," I said, pushing his dark fringe out of his face and smiling encouragingly. "Your talent deserves to be acknowledged, and if someone famous sang it, the royalties could mean big money..."

He frowned at me.

"Oh, so you think I should earn some money? God Tanya, I thought you understood!" He lay back down and stared at the ceiling. "I just don't need this kind of pressure."

"I do understand, Nathan. I didn't mean..."

"Oh, forget it. You're so obsessed with materialism! It's all about what you can buy next -how much does this cost, how much can we afford... Look Tanya, if I'm a drain on your shoe resources, just say. I can go."

"Don't be silly! I don't want you to go anywhere." I reached out for his hand and he moved it back under the duvet.

"Oh come on, Nathan, I didn't mean to upset you. I just meant, well, if someone like Rihanna wanted to sing one of your songs, the sky's the limit..."

But he didn't want to discuss Rihanna or royalties. He shuffled back down in the bed and closed his eyes, obviously a bit upset, so I crept quietly out of the bedroom.

TWEET: @TanyaTruth Just rehearsed today's exciting show at home with @NathanWells my lovely man! Thanks babe. Heart!

2

Organic Vomit and High End Splashbacks

I slipped out through the front door, eager to run off the morning's angst. It was late August, but the dawn chill tingled on my face, reminding me that Autumn was on its way in more ways than one...I might need another trip to 'Doctor Botox'. Some days it felt like I needed a year off, just to fit all the doctors in – by which time I'd be a year older with a year's more fat and wrinkles. It was a never ending fight staying young, like painting Blackpool Tower, my mum used to say. I'd lied when I told Piers Morgan the British climate was the only reason my skin was firm for 42. My run was always the first task of the day, I never, ever missed it – I couldn't. In the absence of Zac, who joined me when he wasn't putting some other poor sod through their paces, my iPod was my enabler for this daily ritual. The iPod kept my jogging to exactly 40 minutes, as mapped out with the 'morning run' playlist. Each milestone had to match the music, starting with George Michael's *Fast Love* for a gentle, flirty spurt in the first few minutes, to warm up and feel that 90's vibe. I had loved the 90's, when I was single with no pressure, plenty of time in hand, younger, thinner and on my way up the career ladder.

Cruising past the post box on the second corner by Delaware Road at seven minutes 23 seconds, I would pant hard as the pace was pumped up by *The Black Eyed Peas* singing *Tonight is Gonna be a Good Night*. This was followed by a tear-inducing (on many levels), thigh-pounding rendition of *M People*'s *Proud* while whipping past the new Italian deli at exactly nine minutes 45 seconds. Nathan laughed at my musical taste and said I had no soul, but he was wrong; I loved music, I just didn't like the stuff he liked. My musical tastes were eclectic and though I might not enjoy techno-vibe garage, ambient-house stuff (whatever that may be) I embraced all extremes. Good God I was positively experimental – my repertoire covered *Take That* to *The Gypsy Kings*.

Arriving home, my morning marathon now completed to time, with the correct tunes played and landmarks passed, I took some time to stand on the doorstep and fill my lungs with cold air. Breathing in I had that fleeting, wonderful feeling of clean, and about 15 seconds spare to enjoy it.

Walking into warm, thick, carpeted stillness, I crept gently upstairs. The clean feeling had vanished as soon as I'd walked into the house, so I took a quick shower in the en-suite so I didn't disturb Nathan then went to get a suit from the navy section of my wardrobe. Rushing from the sparkly white bathroom into warm, bedroom darkness I caught a glimpse of the lump still lying in the bed and softened. A wave of guilt swept over me: I really ought to give him a bit more attention and not be quite so work-obsessed. I dressed quickly in my freshly-laundered, pre-show tracksuit and pulled by damp hair back from my face and tied it, ready for hair and make-up at the studio. I padded downstairs, all negative thoughts forgotten as I sashayed into my brand new Mark Wilkinson kitchen and shivered with delight. I had grumpy boyfriend, scary thighs and a tussle with a skinhead high on smack that morning. But my kitchen rocked.

I ran my clean palm along the pristine work surface; smooth, gleaming and hard as diamonds. Here, in my sleek, white kitchen (with minimalist oriental undertones) I contemplated the orgiastic collision of white serenity, perfect calm and high end splash-backs. I took the Blue Mountain coffee from the fridge and scooped it lovingly into my Pierro Lissoni espresso maker. Several errant grains dared to land on the snow-white counter – but not for long. I wiped vigorously with a damp cloth, working up quite a sweat and restoring pure, white innocence. Then steaming water hit rich, aromatic grains and the world was clean and white again. Carrying the steaming cup in both hands across the kitchen, I held it to my face, breathing deeply as Doctor Nicholas Mason, (the after-care medic who worked on my show) had taught me. I drank the beautiful liquid, looking out of my kitchen window at the emerging shadows of the late summer trees in my perfectly manicured garden.

Suddenly, the doorbell ripped into this warm blanket of peaceful whiteness. It was Arthur, my driver. He always knocked early to make sure I was on schedule, so I now had 15 minutes exactly before I was due to leave. With this in mind, I quickly moved on to the next section of my morning schedule. Blending an apple, some ginger and a handful of organic carrots, I created an 'effortless, body-cleanse, detox breakfast' that apparently worked miracles. It was called 'Organic Voltage,' or 'OV' and I'd found this secret to eternal youth on *HotYoungThing.com*. I hadn't tried the recipe before and pouring the lumpy orange liquid into a tall glass, convinced myself that it had to taste better than it looked. I wiped the recipe card, put it back in my recipe file and strolled through to the orangery to enjoy my drink.

My thoughts returned to Nathan. The downside of my success meant that some days it was impossible to find space in my diary to even talk to him. I wasn't home until late afternoon or early evening and as I was often busy with my script for the following day, then early to bed, Nathan liked to pop out for a drink. I was hardly ever able to go with him and I knew I had to do something about this sorry state of affairs. I decided I would cook that evening and create a lovely, romantic atmosphere for us both... surely that would bring us together again. That night I'd create my signature (and only) recipe, Thai chicken. My fragrant thighs and sticky rice had won him over once before and would only take about 45 minutes in total to prepare. We would open a bottle of white too. I didn't normally drink wine on a show-night, but needs must – it would loosen me up and perhaps after I'd worked on my script, exfoliated and flossed and before I went to bed we would have about seven minutes left for sex.

I checked my Roland Cartier and I now had five minutes before I had to leave for the studio. Arthur would be sitting in the Merc, reading his *Sun* from cover to cover and not expecting me until post-crossword, pre-TV listings. So I was OK for time – in fact, I could live a little and allow myself a couple of minutes to relax and appreciate my bespoke, real-wood orangery by David Salisbury, furnished of course by Marston and Langinger.

Settling down, I took a good glug of Organic Voltage. The only thing that stopped me spitting it out was that it might permanently stain the real-oak floor. The taste made me gag and it crossed my mind that OV would more accurately stand for 'Organic Vomit'. I swallowed hard; I'd always had a high reflux but it was worth the retching if the end result was a sparkly-clean colon.

I sat back in the oversized wicker chair and gazed though the glass towards the garden. It was hard to make out in the dimness of early morning and my un-made up reflection stared back at me. Looking away, I saw the *Hello!* magazine on the coffee table. At the sight of it my heart leapt into my mouth and I felt dizzy.

William and Kate gazed back all regal and perfect and spoiled. Nothing was going to burst their bubble, with a beautiful royal baby to keep them occupied. *Hello!* was giving me palpitations, but not because of the sycophantic prose about 'our royal 'new mum' it was because shortly, the latest copy would land on my doorstep – and it featured me...me and Nathan, to be precise. And whilst Nathan was happy to be photographed with me spread across our vanilla sofas in White Company lounge-wear, he wasn't actually present when I did the interview with the journalist, and I may have got slightly carried away.

I pushed the magazine under the pile of *Country Living* and *Elle Decoration* and steadied myself. I had to think positive, put all thoughts of *Hello!* magazine aside and concentrate on the show. Daylight was weeping through the trees and the garden was slowly emerging from the clutches of night. It wasn't easy to reconcile my daily plunge into sink-estate stardom with these undulating lawns and chaste, parterre triangles leading to the brimming, beautifully-kept vegetable garden. Here, canes stood in strict lines and fat slugs never dared taint my perfect dinner-party leaves with their slimy presence.

Thinking about slugs and soil made me want to wash my hands, but first I had to finish my detox and cleanse my insides so I lifted the glass, my whole body now braced for an internal superfood scrub.

The juice was truly disgusting and trying hard to swallow, my eyes watered with the effort. Holding my nose between two perfectly OPI-manicured fingers, I closed my eyes, thought of England and swallowed. Not for the first time.

TWEET: @TanyaTruth Just had delish detox breakfast smoothie fresh raw vegetables. Yum! #LoveVeggiesLoveLife #HotYoungThing

As the car purred outside on the drive and Arthur checked out what he and Pat would be watching on TV tonight, I had two minutes to complete my morning preparation. I'd been slightly cavalier with timings today and left things a bit tight; I still needed to scrub the kitchen surfaces, wash my glass, clean the gritty blender and make certain no Organic Voltage had gathered around my electricals.

Cleaning thoroughly before I left was an absolute necessity because Astrid, my so-called cleaner, didn't actually clean. All she had to manage were a daily dust, a good vacuum, order a weekly Jane Packer floral extravaganza for the hall table and a little artful spritzing of Jo Malone here and there.

Not too much to ask, but Astrid had no soul. It was my own fault – I'd only employed her because the agency told me she was Swedish and I was reading Steig Larsson at the time. I'd also decorated using washed-out woods and shades of white and felt that a moody, blonde Swede would look good against the paintwork. I had been working long hours and my regular cleaner had quit, so after a rather stern call to the agency, they sent Astrid straight round. When had I opened the door, a sweet little blonde girl with a huge smile had stepped in.

"Mrs Tanya?" she said.

"No... Well, yes, I suppose so" I replied, ushering her inside.

"Thank shit for that!" she said, putting down her bag. "I am thinking, this is big fuck-off house, I am liking that I live here now!"

I was a little taken aback by her directness – not to mention the swearing – but I was desperate and in thrall with all things Swedish, thanks to Steig. Plus, the third book in the *Girl with the Dragon Tattoo* trilogy had yet to be translated into English, which gave me an idea.

"Can you read the third Steig Larsson book to me, in English?" I asked, hopefully.

"That will be no problem. It is shit-hot ending!" She said.

So, later that week I held a reading group for a few select guests, who were all excited about hearing the final instalment of the series before most of the English-speaking world. However, I hadn't accounted for Astrid's 'theatrical licence' and along with other expletives, I was rather surprised at the many different ways Larrson had appropriated the word 'shitting' as an adjective in his final work. "There's a lot of child-like anger in Larsson's third book," our floor manager Tim had said, shaking his head, when Astrid paused reading to make everyone tea.

"Yes," added Judith; "that poor guy was working through his rage writing this one. He's used the phrase "big old shithead" fifteen times – and we're only on Chapter Four."

I smiled stiffly and brought the evening to a close as quickly as I could.

Despite causing deep embarrassment and the end of a burgeoning book club, the reinterpretation of Larsson wasn't the most immediate problem with Astrid. In her capacity as cleaner, it surprised me that she'd never seen a duster, ignored the vacuum and insisted on filling the house with nasty plastic daisies and cheap air freshener. Astrid wasn't a cleaner, she was a bloody chemical warrior and the hit took me by the throat every time I walked into the house.

So I continued with my morning ritual and having cleansed and spritzed and wiped, I opened the front door and looked back at my fabulous hallway. I sprayed another veil of Jo Malone's Basil and Verbena and took one last, heaven-scented breath. I turned to leave, trying not to inhale the dirty world outside, and stepped onto the cold, crunchy gravel.

"Good morning, Miss Travis," Arthur's familiar voice sang as he clambered from the Merc, almost bowing as he took my bag. Now in his sixties, Arthur was much older than me but as I was over forty and on the telly, he treated me like he would a dowager aunt.

Greeting him with a smile and a regal pat on the arm (Arthur didn't do showbiz air-kissing, thank God), I climbed into the thick, expensive interior. The car moved off smoothly and as I settled back, I was suddenly reminded of the first time Nathan had come with me to watch the show. We'd only been together three weeks and he was keen to see where I worked and meet the people I spent my day with. Despite his musician-cool and constant references to

'Tanya's daytime-pond-life-talk-show,' he was quite impressed. He had allowed himself to be seduced by Arthur's butter-soft, leather-scented nirvana and swigged beer like a rock star while nodding slowly with reluctant approval. He gazed around him, a half-smile playing on his lips and announcing after a low whistle; "This is some shit, Tanya Travis."

In the driving seat, Arthur didn't say much, as usual; that's why he'd been my driver for years. The TV channel kept him on a retainer – just for Tanya Travis – and despite cutbacks everywhere, it was a testament to my popularity and viewing figures that the TV company was willing to give me the driver I wanted. It made sense, a happy presenter was a good presenter and I needed quiet concentration in the lead-up to every show.

So I was understandably annoyed when my mobile cut through the smooth silence as we purred along the early morning roads. I was going to ignore it but thought it might be Nathan, so scrabbled in my bag and answered it.

"Hello, Nathan?" I said, breathlessly.

"Guess again, sweetcheeks," came my agent's Brooklyn drawl. "It's Mama. And don't say I never call you".

Oh great, just what I needed: a pep talk from that crazy bitch right before a live show.

"Donna, why are you calling me now? You're normally sleeping off the Stoli until at least 10" I said, tartly.

"Now, now, don't be so scratchy with Mama Bear, little Miss Snappy. I've got good news, but if you don't want to hear it..."

"What?" I said, irritated, hoping this wasn't about some third-rate charity event or Z-list store opening.

"I had a call this morning – well it was the middle of the night, actually. From the Beeb."

"Oh?" I said, sitting up.

"Yeah. They have plans for a new prime-time, Saturday-night format – wondered if you might be interested?"

My heart leaped. "You are kidding! You are, aren't you?"

"Me? Kid you? Why would I do that? It's not signed or sealed, so no sound of champagne corks popping just yet but we're in early talks prior to a pilot. They want someone new and fresh who can do live – they need a presenter with experience but not too much prime-time exposure. So they called me."

My head spun, all thoughts of today's show temporarily tossed aside.

"Wow – the BBC! So what happens now?" I asked, trying hard not to get my hopes up because TV could be so fickle. We'd had a few near misses in my career and I was keen not to let such a fantastic opportunity escape.

"All we can do is wait," she said and I heard her pause briefly to light her breakfast cigarette. "But I can tell you they are VERY keen. Mum's the word."

"What's the format?" I breathed, desperate for details.

"It's a prime-time show dealing with sensitive issues – broken people, shattered hearts, sick minds, the usual blah," Donna never did sympathy very well. I suppose you had to feel it and she never did.

"It sounds just up my street," I said, wanting it badly.

"Oh, it is. And they are under the impression that you are right up their street. And of course you are – but we don't want anything turning up from your past and ruining our hard work do we my little scandal queen? I hope you're still keeping 'mum' on that and not blubbing and blabbing to anyone who'll listen?"

I bit my lip.

"So my sweet, it's early nights and clean living for you until we hear anything."

"As if I ever do anything else," I answered, rolling my eyes.

"Well, you'll need to hold off the Class A drugs and sex with One Direction – one of them has a weakness for older women like you. Oh and keep the bestiality and the child sacrifices to twice a week for the foreseeable, by which time we should have it in the bag and you can shag who or whatever you like."

"Lovely. I'll look forward to that."

"Joking aside Tanya, you need to be extra careful," she said, turning all MI5. "If we get this gig it will rely on your good reputation and caring, sensitive manner. Nothing – I mean NOTHING – must spoil this."

"Now who's being the drama queen? What are you talking about Donna?"

"I'm talking about your so-called partner's little indiscretions..."

"Nathan? Oh Donna, I've told you before. It's not Nathan, it's the press – you know what they're like, they hound him."

I heard her sigh.

"What a crock... He's a gold-digger – and he knows I know. That's why he hates me."

"No he doesn't," I flared, "and there's a flaw in your great gold-digging theory: I don't have any money. As you're always telling me, I spend it as fast as I earn it."

"Yeah, but now he's spending it as fast as you are and when it's all gone and you're homeless, he'll be gone too."

Donna looked after all my finances so I couldn't hide anything from her.

"I only *lent* him the money for the studio, which doesn't make him a bloody gold-digger, Donna."

"You will never see that money again, you know."

"It's a few thousand, when he makes it big he'll pay me back. You're obsessed with money and what I can and can't afford," I said, echoing what Nathan had said to me earlier.

"Hmmm. I hope you're both happy when you're living in your car and on welfare."

"Donna, please, I don't need this lecture now...I'm about to get to the studio." I snapped.

"Go on then gal, go get the pond life, tits and teeth, tits and teeth – or should I say, tarts and tattoos?" she guffawed at her own joke. "I'll see you for lunch after the show." She hung up and was gone. There was never a goodbye with Donna.

Slumping back into the softness and fixing my gaze hard on the window, I tried not to think about how much I wanted the BBC job. We were pulling into the home straight now, Arthur expertly guiding us towards the studio. There would be no need to ask him not to repeat our conversation; he was the soul of discretion. Thank God for Arthur, his safe driving skills and his deep social reticence.

TWEET: @TanyaTruth Just heading for the studio + chatting away with Arthur my driver about the great show we have in store for you today! #TheTruthWithTanya

3

Post-Op Transsexuals and Pageant Queens

I finally arrived at the studio where *The Truth with Tanya Travis* posters lined the corridors. Entering the building I glanced at that sharp-suited TV star, staring down in her pensive, firm, but caring pose. The familiar thrill of seeing myself up there – larger than life – still snaked through me, after 15 years at the top. It was now 7.22am exactly: right on time. Waiting by the studio door, Starbucks in hand was my personal angel, Georgina. Cool and blonde, with a degree in Quantum Physics and a body to die for, I should have hated her – but I couldn't. She was so efficient, tidy and loyal. In fact she was everything anyone could want in an assistant.

"Good morning, Tanya," she said with a smile, flashing her perfectly straight, white teeth and proffering my double-shot, tall, extra-hot, skinny latte. "I hope you slept well. We've got a great show lined up today!"

I smiled and handed her my suit bag as we set off down the corridor together towards my dressing room, nodding at crew members and the production team as they scurried about in the usual pre-show activity. We walked quickly, the air alive and jangling with pre-show nerves as people worked on scripts, cameras, and trailing wires – each of them excited and anxious about their own vital role before we went live on air at 10.30am, in just under three hours' time.

Georgina opened the door for me and as usual, I left the mad bustle and entered deep calm. My face creams, antibacterial wipes, extra scripts and laptop were all laid out for me. The laptop – as always – was already logged in and waiting, the creams precisely ten minutes out from the fridge: not too cold for comfort, but cool enough to tighten those fine lines and refresh my skin. I sometimes wondered if Georgina had some kind of sixth sense, because she always did everything just how I liked it, before I'd even thought to ask her.

She handed me the running order. "Here is the latest version," she said, passing me the freshly printed-out sheets.

"As you can see, there's been a slight amendment, but obviously nothing you can't deal with, Tanya" she said, sincerely.

"It's now the post-op transsexual, followed by the drug-dealing cage-fighter who's made at least five women pregnant, then the six year-old pageant queen, and a mother-in-law from hell; in that order."

"Well, that's clearly the work of Ray." I said, irritated, flicking through the pages. Ray was our boss and lately had taken to meddling with almost every aspect of the show.

"He's so keen to get unusual sex and the under-forties on the Daytime agenda, he's losing sight of the bloody goal post," I sighed.

Georgina nodded: "Yes, and it's affecting the kind of contributors we get. Today for example, we're talking aggressive, unattractive, monosyllabic and animalistic."

"Oh, no! My viewers don't want to watch an inarticulate, aggressive, psycho cage-fighter..."

"No, not the psycho cage-fighter – he's a sweetie. I was talking about the Pageant Queen. She makes Honey Boo Boo look like Snow White."

"Honey who? Oh. don't bother – as long as you know who she is, you can tweet that I do. I can't keep up, Georgina, there is so much going on in the world and online. One minute, I think I know the latest bands, the coolest models, the highest technology...then suddenly, the rug's pulled from under me and I'm like an OAP at a rap convention." I rubbed my temples.

"Don't ever think I don't appreciate how you have transformed me in cyberspace." I said to Georgina, seriously. "Which reminds me, I popped a little thank-you from 'Crème de la Mer' on your desk."

"Tanya, you shouldn't. I'm just doing my job, but thank you – it's lovely of you to do that," she said, with a big smile.

"Actually it's a bribe... Don't ever leave me for another presenter," I squeezed her arm affectionately.

My 'online presence' was fabulous through Georgina. She gave me a youth and vitality I didn't really have. She'd tweet that I was at parties or trendy 'gigs', when I was really tucked up in bed with a cup of lavender tea. As I chewed on a celery stick and slurped a big glass of Chablis, she'd tweet photos of 'my delicious, healthy home-made suppers' (which she'd found online somewhere). My hip but healthy life was so bloody convincing that Donna was in talks with a publisher for me to write my own 'Hip, Healthy and Hot' cookbook. When she was being me online, Georgina used youthful words, implying that I was down with the kids, giving me a whole new persona who not only had an amazing social life, cooked fabulous meals and always had 'friends round' – but also apparently found time for 'great sex with Nathan – or at @NathanWells' as he was known on Twitter. I'd look at my Facebook or Twitter timeline sometimes and be amazed and almost envious at the crazy, loved-up, youthful forty-something I virtually seemed to be. I managed the odd tweet myself, once Georgina had shown me how, and she was always careful not to contradict anything I had shared within the Twittersphere.

I patted my face with the warm flannels Georgina had ready for me, (they prepared my skin for the La Mer moisturiser, which promised to 'penetrate deeply, renew and energize.')

"I've checked your online diary and booked your Prada dip-dye highlights with Guido Palau for Wednesday," she said, referring to her perfect notes, "then you have a manicure with Marian Newman..."

I stopped patting the flannels and looked at her in the mirror: "What? Georgina... You've booked Kate Moss's manicurist – for me?" She nodded. I gave a little cry of pleasure.

"How in hell did you get that?" I was holding the flannels so tight they were dripping.

"She's here for Fashion Week. I told her you were a fan and she was cool. She says it's all about nail tips... and it's only burgundy this season."

"That's fantastic Georgina, thank you," I carried on patting and spotted that my nails were neither 'tipped' nor burgundy. I wondered how I would survive pink and 'tipless' until my nail communion with 'La Newman'.

"Now, I've taken the liberty of booking you in for a Fresh Lift Facial too. Hope that's OK, Tanya? Its Jet Peel 3 system uses a non-invasive water jet to deep clean and exfoliate then..."

"Oh, keep talking Georgina, I feel ten years younger already..." I unscrewed the moisturiser and gently applied it, imagining the Fresh Lift Facial in all its Jet Peel glory -whatever that was.

"Then prescription serums are pushed deep into the skin for maximum effect and voila, Tanya Travis is 21 again. Let me know if anything crops up and I can change any of the appointments – except of course Marian. Lady Gaga has her on speed-dial and she could be whisked away anywhere at any time."

"Sweetie, I'd cancel my own show before I'd cancel Marian Newman, manicurist to the stars." I breathed, standing up.

Georgina handed me my blouse and I began to dress for the show.

"Oh yes and I have tweeted, blogged and updated your Facebook status, Tanya."

"Oh great, what am I?"

"Happy," she smiled, "but nervous (serious face) for the amazing guests who've been through such a lot and are here to talk about it on today's show... And you've been tweeting all morning about how 'awesome' they are."

"Awesome – I like that word, makes me sound young." I smiled, fastening my blouse buttons and taking my skirt from her outstretched hand. She smiled back and gave me a little wink.

"Is my blog interesting today?"

"Oh yes, you are contemplating the old nature-versus-nurture chestnut."

"Ah, that old thing...great," I smiled.

"Yeah, but don't worry, you've updated it of course to look at current findings on parental influences. You were saying the other day you wanted the show to go more upmarket?"

"Absolutely."

"So, Tanya you are considering behaviour-genetic designs, augmented with direct measures of potential environmental influences..."

"Am I?"

"Yeah. Hope that's not too obvious."

"Well, no. Not really..."

"Good, because you go on to suggest that current findings provide more sophisticated and less deterministic explanations than earlier theory and research on parenting did."

"Ooh, do I? How fabulous."

I didn't quite know what to add to that so I took a huge gulp of steaming latte, to stop myself saying something silly.

"Tanya, it is rather 'in-depth' but I think it will pitch you to a new, potentially more intellectual, sophisticated viewer. I can alter the blog if you'd rather look at studies distinguishing among children with different genetically influenced predispositions in terms of their responses to different environmental conditions?"

"Oh no I think what you said before is all – just gorgeous."

"And of course, I've multi-platformed it and shared links with all the networks."

"Absolutely."

The daily, pre-show ritual was now complete – my face creamed, my suit on and my second coffee drunk, we set off down the hall to hair and make-up.

At this point, Judith the Producer joined our race along the corridor. All frizzy hair and waving arms, Judith pounded the corridor in sync with me, while trying to link my elbow. Georgina fell discreetly behind by a few steps.

"I see from the running order that Georgina's just given me that you're going against my wishes and putting the post-op tranny on first?" I said, trying but not succeeding to soften the irritation in my voice.

Judith rolled her eyes; "I know Tanya, I'm so sorry but Ray's screaming for a tranny."

"Not for the first time."

"Yeah," she said with an uncomfortable giggle. "I know you think we need to get mad mother-in-law, then psycho Sid, the sex-addict cage-fighter and the tranny before ending with the Pageant Queen and pushy mother, but..."

"Exactly – that's exactly what I want. So why is Ray insisting it's the other way round? The cage-fighter is a one-stop shop – Christ, he's a psycho and a drug dealer who's made at least five young women pregnant!" I shivered. "How many issues can there be in one contributor? It's bordering on abuse, the tranny isn't a story and we're not offering him any advice, we're just looking at a big butch man dressed up as a woman, it's not a bloody freak show! Ray has no idea... What the fuck's he doing getting involved again?" I levelled a glare at Judith.

"Tanya. Erm... I wasn't trying to overrule you or anything," Judith's hands were wringing, face pleading, hair frazzled. "It's just that we're getting pressure from the fourth floor to make everything sharp, current – you know, Tanya?"

"I know," I softened. "But current? What do you mean by current, Judith?" I affected my amused, Paxman-style incredulous eyebrow raise. Despite my confident stance, a twinge of worry was creating a well in my stomach: she hadn't answered me.

"Judith, are you trying to tell me something? That the powers that be aren't utterly delighted with my award-winning show? Is someone, somewhere implying I'm not 'current'?" I spat. I stopped walking and stared straight at her.

"No, noooo... Not at all Tanya, they love you and the show and..."

"I should think so. Please remind them that I'm the official 'Daytime Darling'... and I have the award to prove it."

She nodded, smiling weakly.

"So what do you mean exactly by 'making it current', Judith?'

"Well...I don't...know...It's just the fourth floor..."

"Ah, the mysterious 'fourth floor'. Spoken of like a living, breathing thing. The lift never stops there and some have been known to visit and never to return," I said sarcastically.

"Yeah. It is a bit like something from The Twilight Zone," she agreed, nodding vigorously now. I decided to let her off. The new running order was fine, who was I kidding? It was a freak show, however we presented it, despite my best efforts to make it less like one.

"Never mind, Judith. Let's allow Ray to have his little way, I need to choose my battles. Now, how was your weekend?"

"Good, yeah." She said, with a sigh of relief. "Rain was home from uni."

"Oh that's nice. Did you do anything special?"

"Yeah, we lit a fire in the garden."

"Great. I bet Om enjoyed that?"

"Yeah. You know Om, he loves fire."

"Mmm, he's always enjoyed lighting stuff with Mum's lighter hasn't he? I bet he enjoyed his big brother coming home too?"

"Yeah. It was good to be together again as a family."

"All sitting round the fire."

"Yeah."

"Chanting?"

"A bit...yeah."

She grabbed a couple of bottles of water from a trolley handing one to me. I took it and opened the door to Make-Up, Judith gesturing for me to go first. Georgina gave me a smile and a little wave and slipped off down the corridor. Georgina never came into the make-up room with me, it was too fraught. She once upset Sally-Make-Up by suggesting that a slightly 'less fussy' hair style would make me look years younger. Sally could barely contain her anger as she pulled and heaved my bob into a more natural, face-framing shape as directed by Georgina. I was headsore by the time she'd finished, but that day everyone said how lovely my hair was and how much younger I looked. Sally hated her after that.

"Look Judith, I'm not having a go at you," I said, feeling guilty as we walked in. She was a sweetheart really, all she wanted was happy kids, world peace and enough tofu to go round.

"I know when Ray gets a bloody bee in his boxers you all have to jump," I started, about to embark on one of my famous Ray diatribes, "I mean Ray's such a weak, bullying, sordid little tosser..."

"Aah!" she said, like she was in pain, staring at me to stop. "Here's Ray... I mean hi Ray..."

"Hey girlies, how are we this fine morning?" Ray waddled in, all short, fat and sweaty, in his trademark ill-fitting suit. He was rubbing his hands together nervously.

"Hey Tanya, how's today's show shaping up? Have you got something super scratchy for me today?"

"Yes I've got something very scratchy, Ray," I stepped forward, air-kissing him on both cheeks. "In fact just thinking about it is making me come over all itchy," I smiled, knowing he was too busy hearing his own voice to spot the sarcasm in mine.

"Now Raymondo, I have it on good authority you've been fingering my running order, you naughty boy," I said, waggling my finger at him.

"Oh Tanya, I am but flesh and blood and can't keep my fingers off your tight little running order," he replied, clasping both of my hands in his. They were sweaty as usual and I didn't know where they'd been (though I could make an educated guess). I was desperate to pull away and run to the bathroom to scrub, but that might have seemed rude.

"Well Raymondo," I continued, giving him the eye, "you should ask a lady before you go rifling through her show."

"Oh Tanya, forgive. But as ever I am being sat on heavily from above…"

"Not the dreaded fourth floor again, Ray… What on earth are they asking of you now?" I said, mock surprise on my face.

"The fourth floor are asking for street-fighting, bitch-slapping-Jerry-Springer style action" he said, rubbing his sweaty palms along my hand.

"How much more do they want? I sold my soul to the fourth floor 15 years ago Ray- I already do street-fighting and bitch-slapping. Is it not enough for them, do they think I'm Jerry Springer?" I snapped.

He laughed nervously.

"No of course not…they know exactly who you are, you're Tanya Travis, Darling of Daytime." There was an awkward pause. "Well, onwards and upwards!" he said abruptly, letting go of my hands and making for the door. "I need to catch a train to the Big Smoke, I'm off to see Dickie at The Ivy. He has big plans for Daytime and I've got a throbbing head, my arteries are clogged – and I'm not sure if my ticker can take it." With that, he left, shaking his head like he had the world on his shoulders as he left the room.

"What was that about?" I said to Judith.

"Something about Dickie and his throbbing ticker?"

"No, the bit about being sat on by the fourth floor?"

"I don't know, Tan. Just crazy Ray-speak," she carried on marking her script and studiously ignoring me.

"And who's Dickie? And why is he throbbing? Or was that one of Ray's euphemisms?"

Sally Make-Up giggled.

"Dickie's about to take over as the new head of the channel. I saw an interview in *the Guardian* and man, he's one tough dude," Judith looked up from behind a hundred years of hair.

'Have you ever tried Frizz-Ease, Judith?' I wanted to ask, but managed to keep my mouth shut, whilst manoeuvring myself into the make-up chair and trying to blank my mind. Sally Make-Up pushed a button so I could lie back, but being prostrate didn't help. My rising pre-show panic had begun and the last thing I'd needed was Ray going on about new talent and Dickie's 'throbbing'. I'd now have to fit in another thorough hand-washing session before rehearsal, thanks to Ray. In the meantime, I slathered my hands in Sanihand, my favourite brand of cooling, antibacterial gel. Inhaling the sharp, lemony scent and breathing deeply, I counted to ten.

"What are we doing with this bloody freak show?" I sighed. "What happened to our plans for a Book of the Month, Judith?" Sally Make-Up let me rant on as she began my transformation into glossy Goddess of Daytime. "What happened to the treatments we offered up about Mum of the Month, Perfect Partners, Children of pissing Courage, Judith?" I snapped, from under Sally Make-Up's skilled fingers; "What has happened to all those lovely plans we had for our show? What are the fucking fourth floor doing about *them*?"

Judith looked at me with a pained expression, twisting one of her many rings round and round.

"The fourth floor don't seem to be interested at the moment..."

"But we worked so hard on that. Judith, you are bowing under the weight of Ray and God forbid, I don't mean that in the physical sense."

"Oh no, that would be too freaky," she muttered, under her hair.

"I suppose it's all about ratings these days, Tanya," Judith continued. "We need viewers, if we don't have them we won't have a programme."

"I check the ratings from the previous day as soon as they come out. I check them every morning when I come in. There's no ratings problem, Judith." I knew in my heart there was nothing to worry about but...

"You're right, Tan, we do have good ratings but the fourth floor don't want us to be worthy do-gooders when the satellite channels are doing live STD tests on teenagers and sex addicts."

"Ooh no, Judith! Perish the thought that we may actually be making a difference here. I don't flatter myself that my show could even begin to compete with a swab of streptococcus taken from a teenager's genitals live on air."

She bit her lip and I made a mental note to ask Donna to arrange a schmooze meeting with Ray. I suspected that Donna had intelligence on Ray Potter and wasn't afraid to use it. She had something on everyone and he'd no doubt roll over like a puppy once he got a whiff of Shalimar (Donna's signature scent) and the sound of her size-seven killer heels approaching. She'd do her job, scare the hell out of him with unreasonable demands and find out exactly where those bodies were buried.

Sally was dabbing my face with something cool and wet that smelt of roses while Judith regaled me with background on the day's guests. She talked convictions, fighting, sexting, sex-changing, slapping, jacking up and blow jobs whilst I relaxed into Sally's cool hands. Asking me to look up as she did every morning, Sally applied lower eyeliner while I counted the squares on the tiled ceiling, stopping as always at 24. And in the low bubble of chatter and thick, sweet smell of cleanser I felt a fizz of happiness.

"It's now exactly 22 minutes to rehearsal and I'm channelling Oprah," I announced, sitting up. Sally smiled like an indulgent parent, finishing with a soft fluff of tickly powder to set my camera face. This ritual was followed by the blow-drying of the hair, like watching a magician at work as she pulled and straightened and shone, turning my dreary, dyed, coarse curls into a gleaming straight, caramel-highlighted bob.

Stepping back to admire her work, Sally smiled, searching for my reaction in the mirror.

"Thank you, my love. You have performed yet another miracle," I squeezed her arm, turning my head left and right, amazed as always at the daily transformation. "I don't know how long you can hold up this forty-something face but you're doing a great job, Sally."

"Is that incorrigible sex-bomb Tanya Travis in the building?" It was 8.30am, two hours exactly until transmission and Tim the Floor Manager's camp voice emerged through the radio chatter, on cue and as always, right on time. I nodded, smiling with my eyes and looking in the mirror, my hair moving like a short, shiny curtain, my lips quivering with sugar-pink gloss. I stood up and swept through the make-up room.

"Tanya is here, baby," I called to Tim, "and boy is she ready for her close-up." I was now in full Gloria-Swanson mode and taking his hand I reached the door where he was standing, all gorgeous and muscular and gay. My young white knight lead me safely over wires, and twisted cables, delivering me to my first pit-stop for a ritual hand-washing, then on to my throne on the studio floor. After discreetly handing me a small but thick pack of bacterial wipes, Tim checked my mic. I wiped and tested, then wiped again; "Tanya Travis is now in the building."

TWEET: @TanyaTruth We've got gr8 show 4 u today. Lots of lovely guests who need my help ☺ #TruthWithTanya

4

Love, Betrayal and Donner Kebabs

"So, you attacked your son-in-law with a Samurai sword at the Royal Kebab House?" was my opening gambit with Brenda, the final guest, whose label 'the mother-in-law from hell' wasn't even beginning to cover it.

"Yes I BEEPING did get him with me Jap sword, but he can BEEP off, he's nothing but a BEEPING BEEPER!" was the ageing blonde's considered response.

I was on the home straight and I was buzzing. I'd warmed up on the tranny, almost strangled the obnoxious Pageant Queen, perfected scorn and derision on the rampant cage-fighter, and now Tanya Travis was ready to tell Brenda just how it was.

"Brenda, please take us through that particular evening – without swearing – so the audience and our viewers at home can understand exactly what happened."

She looked at me as though I'd just addressed her in Mandarin Chinese.

"So Brenda, you were enjoying a glass of wine with friends when..."

"That BEEP threw a BEEPING pint of beer over me and called me a BEEPING BEEP!"

I threw my hands in the air. As I'd feared, Brenda's vocabulary didn't go beyond BEEP and I now had to piece together the whole sordid yet complex betrayal/kebab-shop/Samurai-sword story for the viewers myself. How I longed for that Oprah-style Book Club or a whole series dedicated to little children's courage and middle-class super-mums.

"So, Brenda," I said, eyeballing her sternly. "You are telling me that you were in the local pub with your daughter Chantal and your son-in-law, Karl."

"Yeah I BEEPING well was, I needed a BEEPING drink after I found out that BEEP..."

"Indeed Brenda." I interrupted. "You had just found out you were to become a grandmother, is that right?"

"Yeh," she said, slumping back into her seat and scowling at Karl, "and I don't want our Chantal ruinin' her life. She's got to dump him and get rid of it."

"Why are you trying to stop your daughter from becoming a mother? I think you should let her decide what to do with her own body, her own baby?" I glared at her.

The audience started to mutter their approval.

Brenda waved her bingo wings at the world and continued to describe – in no uncertain terms – her feelings for her BEEPING son-in-law Karl, the BEEP. I let her rant for precisely 10 seconds, before I cut in.

"Brenda. Is it true to say that you hate Karl so much because you used to have feelings for him? In fact," I said, pausing to build the drama, "you hate him because he dumped you for your own daughter?" The audience collectively gasped. Chantal leaned forward in disbelief and gaped at Karl. He shifted in his seat and looked at the floor, lips pursed, scowling. This tattooed teenager with no job, no future and – it has to be said – no teeth, was a knight in shining shell-suit to skinny, seventeen-year old Chantal and this had come as a revelation to her. The researchers on the Tanya Travis show were nothing if not thorough.

"That BEEPING BEEP!" said Brenda, jumping to her feet. "He said he loved me! Then he shagged our Chantal! He's a BEEPING BEEP and I'll BEEPING well BEEP..."

I held up a hand to silence her. "Well, Karl?" I said, looking sternly at him. "What have you got to say for yourself?"

He shot Brenda a filthy look. "It were a one-night stand, I were BEEPING pissed!"

Brenda jumped up and lashed out at Karl, but the guys from security were on hand (for drama and safety, in that order) and they stormed the stage, grabbing Brenda and holding her back.

"Brenda, I think it would be true to say that you're an alcoholic and a bad mother," I heard myself cut in over her, positioning myself between her and lover Karl, who was glaring so hard at the floor he could have melted a hole in it. "You need to take responsibility for your actions Brenda, stop blaming the past and start putting your child first. You will never resolve your deep family divisions with ancient Japanese weaponry."

The audience cheered. There were now three minutes and 20 seconds to go – and it was time for Tanya to start bringing it home.

"I don't care about Karl, because he is poison." I announced over Brenda's incoherent BEEPing. The audience fluttered their approval.

"Chantal, your mother is an alcohol soaked old BEEP who's wrecked her own life." I said, turning to face the audience, who cheered in response. I waited a beat, held it there and let it build, like an orchestral conductor. "And if you don't get out, she will wreck your life and your baby's life if you decide to go ahead with the pregnancy," I said, with the certainty that 15 good years in the job brings. The audience were now roaring with outrage, clapping loudly, safe in their seats and lives, delighted I was telling Brenda exactly what they thought too. Brenda was poor, uneducated, ignorant, alcoholic and not surprisingly, pretty aggressive. This audience weren't asking why or looking for solutions, they were seeking blame and Brenda was in the stocks.

"What I do care about, Chantal," I said, turning to the traumatised teenager, "is that you want your baby. And if that is what you want, I personally will make sure you have support. But you need to get your stuff and get out, now." Whoosh! Thunderous applause and a standing ovation came from the audience. A rush came over me and I knew I was about to say something wholly inappropriate for daytime. "Your mother Chantal is a BEEPING BEEP and I for one will not share a stage with her. BEEP OFF Brenda and take that little BEEP Karl with you!" The audience rocked on their feet, hollering and shouting in approval. I stood looking out at them, jeering and shouting at the unfortunate Karl, passing their combined judgement on the little family group in front of them.

With minutes to go, Brenda began yelling at Karl over the head of the silently weeping Chantal. Fortunately, the audience were making too much noise to hear the expletives coming out of her mouth and Karl finally rose to the bait and jumped to his feet with an angry snarl. As they squared up to each other, I yelled at them to sit down but we were drowned out by the sheer racket as the bear-baiting reached its climax. Karl took an angry step towards Brenda and she broke free from security and leapt towards him. There were a few seconds of violence, just enough to give the audience what they wanted, then in a flash Chantal's mother and Karl were escorted off the stage by the big men in black T-shirts. Chantal was left sitting alone on a chair, her head bowed and her thin shoulders heaving. She looked at me through her tears, with dribble on her chin, her mascara in rivulets down her cheeks.

I strode purposefully across the stage towards Chantal, arms outstretched. She rose from her seat and fell into my embrace, sobbing. Judith was in my ear: "Tan, 45 seconds, no more swearing we're now live, final sound bite please."

I braced myself for the grand finale. I pulled Chantal away from my chest and gripped her by the top of her arms, looking intently into her face so the camera could get a close-up of the dampness and sincerity in my eyes.

"Chantal, that baby comes first. You must cut your family off. Our aftercare team – all part of *The Tanya Travis Show* – will take good care of you."

"Counting down now...nine, eight, seven, closing titles..."

I looked straight into Chantal's eyes, "We're your family now."

She nodded, tears falling silently, and flung her arms around me again.

The Director's voice: "Close-up on hugging, tight on the tears. Hold it... Going to a wide on camera three – and out. Great stuff! Well done everybody fab show, see you in the pub!"

I looked down at the woman-child, still clinging to me like a limpet and hugged her back. We stood together, holding each other until the credits ended, but after two whole minutes in that position I wondered when someone would take her away. I had a lunch meeting with Donna – I couldn't stand there all day, where was the bloody so-called aftercare team? They were all over the show when the cameras were on, but as soon as cameras were off and the credits rolled they were in the pub, having a cheese and onion pasty and a pint of bloody Guinness.

I looked down at Chantal, still clinging to me like a baby monkey would its mother and as I waited for someone to come and detach her from me, I thought about what a big decision she had just made, live on air. I saw family disputes day in, day out and it was easy to forget that what happened on the show was quite literally life-changing for some of the contributors. Chantal was going to stand up to her mother and have her baby. It would be lonely and hard, but she was going to do it. I felt myself tightening my grip around her shoulders. As her sobs continued, I allowed myself to imagine her situation – for all of about ten seconds. Then I felt a burning desire for a Saniwipe and I didn't want to hold her anymore.

I managed to catch Judith's eye and she rushed over and led the still-sobbing Chantal off the studio floor. I watched her go, my last words to her ringing in my head: *'We're your family now.'*

TWEET: @TanyaTruth Gr8 show today. I talked with Chantal 4 hours after. We'll support her. She's gonna have baby. ☺ x #GoChantal #TheTruthWithTanyaTravis

5

Kerry Katona's Cast Offs

"I blame the Bacardi Breezers," I said to Donna over lunch at Nobu later that afternoon after the show.

"Bacardi Breezers, my fat ass!" she responded, far too loudly.

"Forget alcopops, I blame the lubed-up little tart, she clearly couldn't say no to the first hormonal hoodie that showed her his dick!" Donna was oblivious to the fact that she'd alerted the whole restaurant to the contents of that day's show. She was like an obscene audio version of *The Radio Times*.

I cringed inwardly and there was a faint murmur as diners shifted in their chairs, repositioning for a clear but discreet view. Donna's decibels always held the promise of impromptu lunchtime entertainment, which was free. In complete contrast to the sushi, which definitely was not. Arthur had driven me from the studios in Manchester to Mayfair straight after the show and we were having a late lunch in Nobu Berkeley Street. It could take up to four hours to get there from Manchester, but that was part of the joy. I could get away from the studio and all the guilt and grime. Besides, I loved the restaurant on Berkeley Street as it was known for being the younger, spirited and more casual sibling to the original Nobu on Park Lane.

During Donna's rant, Nathan texted to say that the guy from the Indie label couldn't meet him until 10pm so he'd be very late that night. I was disappointed – I was looking forward to squeezing in Thai chicken thighs and sex – but this was about Nathan's future.

"Anyway, who cares about another pregnant teen... What about that tranny?" Donna screamed into the silence. "Jesus, I never saw a five o' clock shadow like it... and the hands, the size of his fucking hands!"

"He... She was troubled," I added sternly, speaking in a hushed tone, desperately hoping Donna would follow suit and keep her big Brooklyn voice down. But she was shaking her head vehemently, about to make all the other diners aware of her feelings on this matter. "For Chrissakes, Tanya, it's not natural! Twinset and pearls on a 6 foot 4 truck driver – give me a break!" This was followed by her shrieking laughter as she slammed down the wine menu and ordered a bottle of Chablis.

"I do feel like I'm running a freak show sometimes, Donna." I admitted.

"Yep, that's because you are, my little primadonna. Freaks...they are what they are... so let's round em' up and clean the streets!"

I grimaced as the food arrived, looking down at the tiny, perfectly cajoled morsels delivered in lines on sparkling white plates. Sitting here restored my faith in beauty, tasteful interiors and cleanliness. Nobu was an expensive-but-necessary antidote to my morning.

"So, to continue our conversation: I reckon we can squeeze the channel for another few thousand." She announced into the silence, tearing at her yellowtail sashimi like it was still alive and might just bite back.

"Really? Is it wise in this financial climate? Even prime-time presenters are taking pay-cuts."

"Your stock's on the rise babe. Tanya Travis is the Daytime Darling again... Do you realise you've won the award for ten years running? You're the heroine to toddler's mums and the truant-playing, trailer-trash, benefit-scroungers of Britain!" She raised her brows and glugged the rest of her Chablis.

"No-one's ever completely safe though, are they?" I said.

"No honey, it's the nature of this goddamn awful business. But that's why you've got Donna. I can out-snake a snake babe and I smell danger well before it bites."

I was relieved she had it covered. And she was right: while I had Donna for an agent nothing could touch me – but as Judith had inferred earlier, we mustn't rest on our laurels.

I sighed and put down my chopsticks. "I'm starting to get a bit fed up, Donna. I don't mind if they reject my Book of the Month idea but they won't even let me be 'Tanya Travis: Saviour of the Great Unwashed'. Lately, things have changed, and now we bring them to the show, push them onto the studio floor, make a spectacle of them and send them home. They take whatever happens back with them; at best it's the baggage they came with – at worst it's a whole new set of baggage. No-one does anything for these people, once the cameras are off, and they're back in their horrible lives."

"Look, it's not your job to wipe up their blood and snot – you're the fucking *star*! Where's the aftercare team?" she yelled, like they were hiding behind the bloody menu. I rolled my eyes.

"OK fine, Miss Middle-Class-Guilt, here's a plan," said Donna with a sigh. "Let me speak to Ray. I'll work my tits off, negotiate loads more cash off the back of all our hard work... and if it makes you feel better you can give it to a teenage tarts and trannies charity." She made speech marks with her fingers and shook her head in disbelief.

I shook my head. "You are missing the point, Donna. They come on to the show to get help, but they don't actually get any once the show is off-air."

"Then give 'em the number of the Samaritans, hail a taxi and send 'em packing. Trust me, sweetcakes, they know what they're doing, they're manipulative."

"Do you really believe that? I disagree. It bothers me that a year after our guests appear on *The Truth with Tanya Travis* nothing's changed and we drag them back for a bloody *Tanya TV Special*."

"Which proves my point. They don't change. They are their own worst enemy and will stay on the same treadmill throughout their loser lives."

"It must be easy to be you, Donna and have no conscience," I smiled, shaking my head.

"I do have a freaking conscience – I also have a job as your agent. I don't care what you do with your money, Tanya," she spat, getting angry now, "but we've both worked our asses off for years to get you to this point and I'm bored of you whining on about the poor bastards who star in the show. Trust me, they love every minute of it."

"I'm not 'whining', I am just saying that..."

"Stop kidding yourself, Tanya. The night before they come on the show they get a free stay in a chain hotel with full abuse of the mini-bar. They're in hog heaven, some of them have never even seen an en-suite. JESUS, some of them never even saw a bath! A Travelodge on the M62 is the fucking Ritz to the likes of your 'guests'!" she yelled.

She emptied her glass and banged it on the table causing another ripple of Shalimar perfume and disapproving whispers.

"Now, let's get down to business and talk about the offers on the table, my little People's Princess," she said with a twisted smile, clutching a wad of papers from her briefcase.

"Offers?" I said, my heart leaping a little. "Is this what you phoned me about earlier, the programme for the Beeb? The prime-time slot?"

"No, sweetcheeks, they are still considering that. They need to decide whether someone of your veteran TV status will last at the helm."

"Veteran? What do you mean, Donna?"

"Listen, honey," she said, avoiding the question, "the offer I am talking about is just as good. And it's prime-time too."

"Right...." I discreetly took a wipe from my handbag.

"It's foreign travel..."

"Ok?"

"It's working with other celebrities..."

"I'm listening."

"And it's sleeping under the stars."

"No. No. No!"

"You haven't even heard what I'm going to say, Tanya."

"I don't have to – I refuse to be hurled from a plane into the bug-ridden Aussie jungle with a bunch of Z-list nobodies to eat kangaroo dick."

"There was a time when you used to DREAM of kangaroo dick!" she shouted, alerting everyone in the vicinity to my apparent former predilection for marsupial genitals.

I cringed and took a large mouthful of wine.

"No, my little nut-job, it's not *I'm a Celebrity Get Me Out of Here*. You won't be partying with Ant and Dec this year. Oh no – this offer is much, much better."

"So, what is it?" I was irritated now, Donna was toying with me. It was going to be a long afternoon. I ordered a coffee.

"Donna, don't drag it out – just talk me through the offer, then you can have your cigarette." I said, noticing her long fingers were starting to tap on the table, a sure sign she needed a nicotine hit.

"OK. Here's the deal" she said. "We have here a written document, offering to pay you seventy-five thousand pounds, a presence in five European countries with an option on the US. AND, my little fairy-tale princess, all the outrageous expenses your agent can claim on your behalf," she glared over her bifocals.

"Go on, I'm still listening... I'm just concerned that there's something you're not telling me."

"All above board," she rummaged in her black patent YSL just to make me wait a little longer.

"Donna, what's the show? Don't keep me in suspense."

She curled her lip. Holding a fag in one hand and a contract in the other, she was like a baby with a comfort blanket, calmed just from holding the things most precious to her.

"Ok sweet cheeks, it's like this. You want a slot on prime-time, and I want a cut of seventy-five grand. So make Mama happy and agree."

"Stop dragging it out and tell me you twisted bitch... What is it?"

"You will love it ...here's a clue... my little spa queen."

"Spa? A luxury spa show?"

I held my breath.

"It's *Celebrity Spa Trek*" she said, holding out her arms like she'd just offered me a prestigious documentary series for the BBC.

I stared at her in horror. "Donna, I watched the first episode of that last year and couldn't face the rest of the series. It isn't a luxury spa! It's Guantanamo Bay!"

"Look, before you say no, three things. Money. Exposure. Prime-time. It will give the viewers a chance to see a different, softer side to you. You can cook for them all and cry about how you miss your agent. The Beeb will be banging your door down after it."

"No."

"Think about it."

"I have. And I am not doing a downward dog at the top of a bloody mountain on live TV. And I'm definitely not doing it next to a skinny blonde, twenty years my junior with a flexible torso. Oh, and just in case you mistake my reluctance in any way for 'yes,' the answer's a definite 'no.' I will not 'perform' – even on prime-time – with a sad gaggle of reality-show, bitchy, has-been C-listers." I snarled.

"Enough with the C-word," she muffled through the unlit fag now dangling from her mouth. "We're all one show away from the C-word. One bad day, one email with low audience figures and C is your status."

"It's not about status. I hate camping and dirt and... It would be madness. Where is this travesty of a programme taking place?"

"Nepal."

"Oh, fuck off!" I snapped loudly just as the poor waiter approached.

"No... Not you!" I called after him. But he'd gone. I was definitely turning into Donna.

"I can't go to the Third World... it's dirty, there's no running water and... and I have my show."

"Show, shmow," she spat. "Look, you haven't had a holiday since you started. Ray owes you some time off. They can get someone to cover for you for a couple of weeks."

"No Donna, I'm not doing it."

"I can't discuss this anymore until I've had a ciggie," she barked, unfurling her gaunt, six-foot frame. She wouldn't look at me, just pushed her Chanel glasses over her head and staggered off to inhale her fag on the patio where, according to the website, cutting-edge design blended seamlessly with attention to detail.

Nathan had recently described Donna as the love-child of Janet Street-Porter and the American model, Janice Dickinson. As I wiped my hands and watched her stagger onto the distant patio like an elegant, disgruntled giant, I smiled at the sheer accuracy.

Seven minutes of calm later, she was back – for round two.

"Think of your karma," she yelled. "You were only talking about your karma the other day." I put my finger to my own lips in a desperate but polite gesture for her to shut up. I really didn't want any more of my business blasted across the pristine interior of one of London's most fashionable eateries.

"It's all about Ayurvedic and Amchi..." she continued, flopping into her seat: "It's about Buddha and ...well my little piggy ...it's about losing ten pounds and gaining seventy-five thousand," she sniggered, deliberately looking me up and down in a critical fashion.

I ignored her.

"It's for charity... you *love* charity, you're always banging on about it."

"There won't be any toilets!"

"Look, filming starts next week and they are looking for seven celebrities to be hauled up hills. The goal is to firm thighs and change lives, forget toilets."

"Next week? And they are only just asking now?" I stared at her. She scrutinised the table top.

"Kerry Katona dropped out," she muttered.

"Oh, great, so I'm not even first choice? Forget it!" I said.

"Well it's not just about you, Tanya Travis. If you don't want to change your life, just think of those poverty-stricken peasants, their arms outstretched... every mile you trek spares them another night sleeping in the filthy gutter."

"I couldn't do it. I'll just donate instead."

"You'll have no money to donate to anything if you keep saying no to work," she said crossly. "Remember, I see your bank balance and trust me, what's coming in ain't covering what's going out. You live way beyond your means; you always have. You give money away like a man with no arms to anyone who asks and you need more money than the show pays."

"I refuse to bare my soul or my cellulite to ten million viewers. I'm funny like that!"

"Look hon, if you want the Beeb job, there's work to do and you are going to have to show the nation a softer side. Plus, if you don't get out of Daytime now, you never will. We always wanted prime-time, didn't we? It's what we've worked for all these years, God knows we've both made sacrifices along the way."

I bit my lip. Yes there had been sacrifices for my success – and we both knew mine had been greater than Donna's.

"No, Donna."

But she wasn't giving in; "Look, my little Prime-Time Primadonna, it'll be worth you taking a couple of weeks off your show. The Beeb will be gagging for you and so will Ray and Dickie who'll probably up your money when they realise how even more fabulous and sought after you are. So even if the Beeb thing doesn't work out, it's a win-win."

"The answer's still no." I said, firmly.

Always quick to anger, especially when someone didn't do as she told them, Donna slugged back the last of her Chablis. Throwing a wad of cash on the table, she gathered up the *Spa Trek* documents, and punched them into her bag.

"I don't have time for this, Tanya. I have meetings with my other clients – who *want* to take my advice. Time's running out – call me. In a few weeks I may be able to get you a gig with a well-known stair-lift company ... or not!"

She hugged me roughly and stomped off, almost knocking the beleaguered waiter over in her haste to leave.

Once outside, I climbed into my car and Arthur set off for Manchester and home as I relaxed into the peace and quiet without Donna. My phone beeped as we sped away from the capital: it was Nathan.

No meeting tonight after all so dinner somewhere nice? Let me know where u are and what u are up 2. Miss you.

I read it out loud, aware that my face was producing a large, involuntary smile and sent him a text back.

Was planning a night in with my fragrant thighs, like 2 join me?

The phone soon pinged a response:

Delighted to Miss Travis. See you later. Ps needed 2 buy that new kit 2 day so borrowed your card like u said. Hope that OK. C u later sex kitten x.

I smiled and slumped back into the comfortable car. Calm washed over me as I wiped my hands and thought of a relaxing evening at home, with Nathan.

As we travelled back up north through the rainy city streets I thought about the evening to come and felt a rush of warmth.

Donna thought Nathan was only with me for the fame and the money but I knew our relationship was based on more than that. The real problem was the Press, who loved to torture older women with the audacity to think they were still vaguely attractive enough to be on the telly. Poor Nathan kept getting caught up in it all and we were constantly reading lies implying he was cheating on me with younger women, usually blondes. He was only a couple of years younger than me and if I'd been the man and he'd been the woman we'd have been considered the same age. It must have seemed incredible to the rest of the world that a man as good-looking as him could be with someone less than stunning and older than 25.

Driving past the housing estates on the outer edges of the city, I gazed through the car window, imagining other lives. Running home in the rain, oven chips, children's voices, hot baths and homework all played against the backdrop of crockery clatter and teatime news droning on the telly. In this world, there was no pressure to perform, stay young, keep 'current', just to live your life and love your kids. It was something I might have had if things had turned out differently. And despite the fabulous home, designer clothes, and glittering awards, in that moment I felt a longing for what might have been. Given the chance, I would make some different decisions to those I had made when I was younger... when anything was possible. I'd just been too young to know.

TWEET: @TanyaTruth Heading home after a delish + relaxing lunch at Nobu with my uber agent + best friend @DonnaAgent #BestFriendsForever

6

Fantasy Weddings and Flagrant Tights

Arriving home after my meeting with Donna, I put all thoughts of the past aside. As the car pulled up in front of my beautiful house, calm washed over me. After all, ratings were good for the show, the Beeb were chasing me and Nathan would be home tonight. I was also quite flattered to be asked to do *Celebrity Spa Trek*, though I wasn't letting on to Donna because it was sure to be a C-list nightmare halfway across the world and Hell would freeze over before I said yes.

I unlocked the door and walked into the house, which smelt of air-freshener and warm garlic. I'd called Astrid from the restaurant to ask her to buy chicken thighs for tonight's seduction dinner and it smelt like she'd made a start.

"So, I put bastard thighs in bowl with lemon-stick shit?" she said, looking up as I came in.

"If by that you mean, you marinade the chicken thighs with the lemongrass, then yes, Astrid," I said, walking into a messy kitchen that made me itch just looking at it. My Kashmir granite worktops were sprayed with red paste and Astrid was about to drip coconut milk over the polished floor. I leapt forward and made a save with some kitchen towel because I knew she wouldn't.

Judging by the amount of coconut milk she was adding, they were way past marinade – drowned would have been a more appropriate term.

I grabbed my apron from the utility room and without even taking off my suit, made a rescue attempt on the seduction dinner. I moved in next to her to keep a close eye as she studiously followed the recipe on the laminated card. It was my signature dish – well, I always claimed it was mine, but a gay hairdresser from Norwich made it on *Come Dine with Me* and I stole it from him.

"Not too much milk, Astrid." I instructed, as she slopped it all over the place. "And be careful with the chillies, we don't want to blow our heads off – just a gentle kick."

"You are a cock, Tanya," she said, ignoring me (and apparently, the recipe) and opening another tin.

"What ...?" I said, distracted, suddenly spotting a pile of post on the table.

"Cock, you are the big old cock."

"Yeah...that's right... I am..." I monotoned, my stomach lurching at the sight of the unpaid bills and demands on the side; I swept them into a drawer. Then I realised what Astrid had just said.

"What do you mean, I am a cock? I've only just got in, Astrid, and I've had a long day. That's not very nice," I remonstrated, I absently picked up the magazine-shaped brown envelope, pleased it didn't look like yet another final demand. Then I realised what it was. Oh God, it was worse than a bill – it was this week's copy of *Hello!* – with me in it! I held it to my chest, afraid to open it.

I gazed through Astrid, imagining the horror of what was inside the unopened envelope. She frowned, then her face split into a smile and she started laughing.

"Oh Tanya, I tell you that you are cock ...that's so funny..."

"Well, I don't think so." I said holding the envelope tighter. This was all I needed right now.

"Tanya... It's IS funny, you think I call you man's willy when I say cock?"

"Well, I suppose you've called me worse, Astrid." I said, and put the envelope on the side where it glared at me, willing me to open it.

"No. No. No... Not cock! Kok – k-o-k. This doesn't mean you are a big man's willy! In Swedish it means cook. You are big old cook, Tanya."

"OK. Fine. I'm just popping to the bathroom, Astrid," I said, absently. Astrid was guffawing loudly at the translation from Swedish to English while kneading the thighs very roughly. They would be escalope of thigh by the time she'd finished – but I didn't care, I had a more pressing matter to attend to. Once in the downstairs bathroom, I ripped opened the envelope, then chewed at the plastic package with the urgency of a wild beast eating its prey. It was at times like this I was glad I'd turned down the offer to go on *Celebrity Big Brother* – imagine how this bathroom scenario would have played out on secret cameras! Eventually, after much gnawing and tearing, and swearing, the bloody thing was liberated from its packaging and I was staring at myself, dressed in cloud-grey cashmere and wrapped around Nathan. The cover picture was good, airbrushed well, giving me a dewy, thirty-something look I approved of. But oh – the headline, the headline: *'Tanya Travis Exclusive: Her Wedding Plans Revealed!'* It screamed.

'Tanya invites us into the beautiful Cheshire home she shares with gorgeous rock musician Nathan Wells and reveals all the details of her big day!'

My blood was now boiling water, coursing through my veins. Why, oh why did I have to let my imagination run away with me? The journalist was so sweet, and during our chat she revealed she was getting married herself. We started chatting about her venue, and before I knew it I was describing the dream wedding I so desperately wanted for myself in graphic detail. Her eyes lit up and she started taking notes but I didn't care, I was on a roll. I had planned it all in my head for so long, it was wonderful to actually share it with someone. She looked at me, all young and bright-eyed at the end of the conversation and said, "So, when is this all going to happen, Tanya?"

This had flustered me slightly. "Oh, well, he hasn't *actually* asked me yet..." I started. She looked at me quizzically. "But," I hurried on, "between you and me, the proposal is imminent. Let's just say it could be any day now." She broke into a beam again, and after exchanging a few more pleasantries, she left. It was only when I received a crate of Bollinger and a *'congratulations from the team at Hello!'* the following morning that I realised she might have read too much into what I had said.

I was sure Nathan and I would walk down the aisle one day, he just needed time, that's all. I'd played it all so well for four years with not even a whisper of white lace so as not to frighten him off and it worked, he'd stayed with me. The last thing he needed now was a full-blown, six page special of the thing that scared him most..

Of course I know how it works and as the journalist left I'd had a horrible feeling my non-existent wedding would feature in the story, but I never imagined this – not a front page exclusive. *'Wedding Plans Revealed'* – Christ! I sat on the toilet seat with my head in my hands – Nathan was going to go ballistic when he saw it.

"Tanya! Tanya! The flagrant tights are burning."

I hastily stuffed the magazine under a pile of books in the toilet and rushed into the kitchen to rescue the thighs, and Astrid.

When Nathan came home later that evening, he grabbed me roughly for an embrace as soon as he walked through the door and my legs turned to jelly. I melted into his chest, inhaling the sweet, slightly musty smell of the pub which clung to his clothes. He looked casually gorgeous in his Levi's and checked shirt. "Hello, Miss Travis," he said with a twinkling smile, brushing my hair out of my face, "something smells good."

I smiled at him and led him through to the dining room, where I was slightly surprised to see three places set. Having a third person at my romantic meal hadn't been part of my seduction plan, but Astrid was clearly proud of her efforts in the kitchen, and she dished out three plates and plonked herself down at the table with us.

"Tanya, we missing Embarrassing Dr Christian tonight while we eat your thighs," she said, taking a huge mouthful of steaming food.

"Well Astrid, we wouldn't be offended if you want to watch *Embarrassing Bodies* in the sitting room. You could eat yours on a tray in front of the TV," I suggested tactfully.

"Oh no, Tanya. You silly cow, tonight the bloody doctor looks at skin – I don't want to eat these thighs of chicken and watch stinking flesh covered in scabby old ..."

"Ooh, I think we get the picture thank you, Astrid," I smiled, holding up my glass in a cheers gesture. I smiled indulgently for Nathan's benefit, pretending I wasn't bothered about the programme, but I had the inner security of a woman with 'Catch-Up TV' technology.

We ate in silence and when we'd finished our 'romantic' meal Nathan suggested we go into the living room and listen to some of his latest music on the laptop. Astrid hated Nathan's music so she went off to her room to catch up with Dr Christian and his *Skin Lesions Special*.

Nathan and I cuddled up together on the sofa and he proudly opened the computer and played me his latest tune. He searched my face for a response as I listened to the rather jarring and slightly erratic sounds coming from his laptop.

"Oh, it sounds great," I enthused, trying hard to tap my foot in time with the music and rub his back at the same time.

"I'm glad you like it, Tanya. It means such a lot to me."

My heart melted. "I'm glad, Nathan. How could anyone not love your music?" I looked up to see Astrid passing to go into the kitchen.

"It's big shite," she mouthed. I averted my eyes.

He leaned back, his long legs stretched out, his whole body relaxed, losing himself to the music. I studied him, drinking him in, wanting to kiss every part of him starting with his face, which was beautiful and unshaven. I leaned in and kissed his prickly cheek, inhaling the warm, manly smell of aftershave and sweat. I reached up running my hand through his squiggly fair hair, staring into those blue eyes and feeling like a very lucky lady.

"Yeah...I'm pleased with it. It's even better than the track I laid down last week."

"Oh definitely," I nodded, not able to tell the difference.

"It's the new kit. I got a new Mesa rectifier head and a better guitar amp."

"Oh. That sounds good. Really makes a difference," I gently nodded my head to the music and all I could think was, 'what is it and how much did it cost?'

He smiled, staring ahead, tapping his fingers on his thigh. "The sound quality is just amazing."

"Yeah. Did you buy it... at the usual place?"

"Yeah."

"Did you... Er, did you use the credit card?"

"Yes, is that a problem? I didn't think you'd mind. You know I'll pay you back."

"Yes, of course. No, I don't mind ...it's just that I'm not sure how much credit is left on it..."

"Oh there you go again!" he said, sitting up and pushing my hand away. "Money, money, money. It doesn't matter that a few quid here and there turns my music into something special, something moving and ground breaking. All you're bothered about is 'How much, Nathan?' He said this last bit in a whiney voice; I suppose he was mimicking me, which stung. I felt my chin tremble.

"Nathan, please don't take it the wrong way. I'm so pleased you're happy and it's just a fabulous sound. I just worry about money sometimes, that's all. Stupid I know, because it's the music that matters."

"Yes, it is. Now come here," he said, his voice suddenly husky with lust as he leaned towards me, pushing his hand under my skirt. We began kissing and within 40 seconds his shirt was off and I was burying my head in his furry chest, licking the salty skin, longing for him to take me there and then.

"If this... is going... to continue," he whispered; "I will need to go to the bathroom first." I smiled and emerged from his chest and he clambered up to go to the bathroom.

"Don't go anywhere," he joked, pointing at me as he left the room.

I sat back, feeling relaxed and happy and on hearing the toilet flush, I arranged myself on the sofa in a more flattering pose for his return. The bathroom door closed and I waited, hearing his eager feet almost running up the hall to me. I sucked my stomach in and lay back slightly so my face would defy gravity – or look like it had.

"Have you seen this?" he yelled.

I gasped.

He was standing in the doorway brandishing the copy of *Hello!* I'd hidden in the toilet.

His face was white with anger and shock. "I don't believe it, Tanya," he opened the magazine at a random page. "Have you seen what they've written? It's all bullshit, you're gonna have to get lawyers involved this time."

I sat up, my stomach twisting. "Nathan, I know it's not what we expected." I said, looking up at him. "But...it's not really their fault."

He looked at me, open-mouthed.

"What the hell do you mean, it's not really their fault? Whose fault is it, then?"

My heart was hammering in my chest. I took a deep breath. "Nathan, I did actually say some of those things." I blurted. "Well, all of them. I didn't actually say that we were engaged – but I did tell them my plans for our wedding. One day," I offered, hopefully.

"Our wedding? You told them we are getting married? I am fucking speechless, Tanya. I can't believe this!" he shouted.

"Nathan, I'm so sorry," I said, trying not to cry. "It wasn't fair of me to say all that without talking to you first – but it's what I want most in the world, and once I started, I couldn't stop."

"Yeah, I can see that! You even told them you've been going for dress fittings with bloody Vera Wang, whoever she is!"

I burst into tears and looked away from him, staring resolutely at the floor.

"Tanya, is that true too?" he asked incredulously. "Tell me it isn't. Have you been going for bloody fantasy wedding-dress fittings, like some demented spinster?"

"The... the dress is in the wardrobe in one of the spare rooms Nathan..." I choked. "I met Vera at a party, and one thing led to another... It's beautiful Nathan. If you saw it, you might just..."

He was shaking his head and pacing the room.

"Might just what? Propose? What's the point? The world already thinks we are engaged, thanks to this!" he said. "I have no say in my own life any more – I'm just your accessory. You don't need a groom, you just need a 'yes' man!" he yelled and hurled the magazine at the sofa.

"You're too much, Tanya." He went on. "You rule my life, you're so controlling about money ... and now this. I can't take it anymore. I won't." he looked up, spittle on his chin from the shouting.

"Nathan, no. Please don't say that. I don't want to control you, I'll call *Hello!* and tell them it was all a big mistake...I love you."

But it was too late. Nathan was walking out of the front door. And slamming it.

How could we go from candles and kisses to door-slamming so quickly? Why did being in love have to be so fucking hard? I fell from the sofa, crumpling down onto the floor, huge sobs heaving in my chest, my heart in pieces around me. I sobbed and banged my fists on the floor until I heard Astrid's voice and looked up to see her standing over me, holding two steaming cups.

"Tanya, you will drink lingonberry tea and stop the floor-banging. We will watch the Embarrassed Bodies on Channel 4 – don't cry for Nathan, he is shit-head." She sat down and pointed the remote control at the TV with great precision and a very serious face.

I wiped my eyes and joined her on the sofa, as Dr Christian welcomed another patient into the *Embarrassing Bodies* clinic.

"Now Nathan has gone – you lucky lady – you are free to marry Doctor Christian Embarrassed Body man," she said, gasping with admiration as Dr Christian opened a patient's bottom cheeks to reveal a large, protruding cluster of pus-filled boils.

Once Astrid had gone to bed, I sat up waiting in vain for Nathan to return home to me. I tried his mobile, texted him and left messages apologising, asking him to call me and let me know he was OK, but nothing.

By 11.37pm, I realised there was nothing I could do and I had a show in the morning. I was already two hours and 37 minutes late for sleep so I reluctantly went upstairs, not before taking one last look out of the windows and checking my phone for a message. Climbing into the shower, I spotted my naked body in the mirror, a horrifying glimpse of orange-peel skin and rice-pudding thighs, which depressed me even further.

When I'd asked Donna about 'Lipo Len', she'd said he offered his celebrity clients the utmost discretion and so as to avoid a pap-fest outside his clinic, he liked to keep visits down to a minimum. Therefore, in the first instance, to save a visit and any press intrusion regarding my thighs, I had to email a close-up shot of my cellulite directly to him so he could 'evaluate' my 'persistent subcutaneous fat.' I didn't have his email address so after a boiling shower and another phone check to see if Nathan had called, I tried Donna, but there was no answer; she was probably asleep – or pissed. I couldn't wait for her to wake up or sober up, this was now an emergency, so I did the only thing I could do and called the divine Georgina for help.

"No problem, Tanya," she said, sounding as bright and breezy at ten past midnight as she always did. "If you send the photos to my email address, I'll find Dr Len's details from somewhere and I'll make sure he gets the pictures before start of play tomorrow."

Making a mental note to give Georgina the new Prada Spazzolato Colorblock Bucket Bag I'd just been sent by a PR company, I went to the bathroom, took candid shots of my vile cellulite and tried not to cry over Nathan.

I called Georgina back in less than five minutes; "OK sweetie, I'm sending the pictures over now."

"Great Tan... Hey, were you ever going to tell me?"

"What about?"

"The wedding? I was checking the social-media sites earlier and I read that *Hello!* have revealed your wedding plans! I didn't even realise you were engaged!"

"Oh... yes... well, it's..."

"Fabulous. That's what it is. Oh Tanya I'm so happy for you!"

"Thank you, but..."

"So I wrote a short post on your blog."

"Oh no..."

"Don't worry, I haven't give away too much. I just wrote something along the lines of: '*we're excited, delighted and in love – watch this space, Tanya and Nathan.*' Oh, yes, and I tweeted some '*engagement announcements*' on Twitter – *hashtag excited*."

"Ah...Great! Goodnight," I whispered, putting down the phone... *hashtag horrified*.

TWEET: @TanyaTruth Can't believe I'm going 2 be a bride! Thnx 4 all your good wishes. Nathan + I r so happy! #Excited #Vera Wang #TheCakeFairy

7

Rising Gizmos and Big Burritos

I woke up the next morning with a space in my bed and a rock in my stomach. I checked my mobile as soon as my eyes opened – Nathan hadn't called. I pounded out my frustrations with my ritual run, but it just wasn't doing it for me that morning. Being at work didn't help either – everyone at the bloody studio was congratulating me about the engagement all morning. I went through my show on autopilot, not even flinching when a vicious fist fight erupted between a gypsy bride and a jealous drag queen. They were fighting over a man and it had all the ingredients; sex, betrayal, outrageous frocks – but it meant nothing to me. Nathan was all I could think of, and how stupid I'd been to fuck it all up.

After the show I fled the studio and shut my dressing room door behind me, leaning on it so no-one would come in. Longing to nurse my bruised heart and check my Blackberry, I turned it on. There were two voicemails. *Oh God*, I thought, *he's trying to get hold of me and I haven't responded*. Just as I was accessing the voice message, there was a knock on the door.

"Tanya, it's Judith. Great show...are you OK?"

"Yes... Yes, Judith," I reluctantly opened the door, leaning on it as I did so, my body barring the way if she should even contemplate coming in.

"Thanks for this morning, Judith. It's always good to have you in my ear, talking me through. Sorry if I was a little out of it today, I just have a lot on my mind."

"Oh I'm sorry to hear that, Tanya. I thought you'd be happy ...with the engagement and everything?"

"Well, it's not quite... I mean Nathan isn't sure any more about getting married," I said, with a lump in my throat.

"Oh dear. Well... perhaps it's a good time to focus on work, then. The...the fourth floor are talking about making changes to the show and it would be good if you're across them."

I opened the door. "What?"

"Well, I think some things are changing and we..."

"Come in, Judith," I ushered her through. What was she trying to tell me? "I've always put my career first, Judith. The show's doing so well, I actually thought that perhaps it was time I put Nathan and my personal life first." I said with a fixed smile. I wandered over to the sink and began to wash my hands.

Judith smiled at me awkwardly and started twisting her rings round her fingers.

"Yes of course, I understand that Tanya. We should always put our loved ones first. I suppose I just worry about getting older, really, and when the fourth floor start talking about changes it makes me nervous. Do you know what I mean?"

"Judith, Judith, Judith," I sighed, stopping at the fourth hand wash, taking a seat and gesturing for her to sit on the sofa. She'd obviously come for a Tanya counselling session. Poor old Judith was as paranoid as ever about losing her job. After her last lover left, her self-esteem had hit an all-time low and she was still finding it hard to cope, with all those younger wannabe producers snapping at her heels.

"Now, I want you to stop worrying, Judith. You go home, relax, forget about it for a while and have a bit of 'Judith time'," I smiled. I made a mental note to buy her a floral remedy next time I was shopping at Bach: Aspen from their Fear remedy collection might be the answer. I'd read on the website that it promised to 'help those with an apprehension of some unknown future event.' It might do something for those split ends too.

She hugged me gratefully and left the dressing room. Still smiling serenely, I picked up my phone again, desperate to hear Nathan's voice... but just as I was dialling voicemail again, another knock.

"Tanya, are you decent?" It was bloody Ray.

"Come in, Raymondo," I sighed, placing the phone back on the dressing table.

"Great show today, Tanya. Just thought we could have a bit of a chin-wag... Shoot the breeze, skim a few stones over the water."

"Absolutely," I said, gesturing for him to sit. I didn't relish another encounter with Ray but I'd wanted to talk to him for some time about how we would move the show forward and he was never available. I was a grown-up -not some love-struck teenager – and I tried to be professional, placing thoughts of Nathan firmly to one side for the moment to put my work head on.

He sat down heavily on the sofa.

"Are you happy with the show, Ray?" I asked, waiting for the oily compliments and gushing platitudes about my brilliance.

"Ah yes...We're getting it right, the recipe is coming together, all those ingredients are turning into a perfect sponge cake every morning."

"That's good to hear. And guess what, Ray? I have some ideas to make it even better." I offered, joining him on the sofa.

"Definitely, definitely – all thoughts welcome on board, Tanya T. But you won't get better than yesterday's show... Chantal and her boyfriend: a perfect recipe. And, an example of how a couple of troubled teens who are easy on the eye" he gave a nudge and a wink at this, "can cause the ratings to zoom. The fourth floor are loving young people and sex."

"I'm sure they are, Ray, but let's admit it, you didn't want the mother-in-law from hell, did you? But it was she, the woman over forty, who had them tuning in..."

"Come, come Tanya... Yes, the mother made good telly, I'll give you that, but Chantal -well, she is a lovely young girl. Such flawless skin, such slender young..."

"Yes Ray, but it's not just about the guests, is it?" I interrupted, before he got too carried away. "You have said it yourself; it's Tanya who is the catalyst. Without me wringing all that emotion from them, the show would be nothing." I reminded him, with a sickly-sweet smile.

"Yes. Yes. Yes. Of course. And our guests are the filling in your big, daytime burrito, Tanya."

"Look, Ray" I interrupted, before he could take his revolting analogy further and include the guacamole and sour cream. "I think we both know that *The Truth with Tanya Travis* is a cutting-edge talk show. It's about feelings, about real people with a story to tell. But we need to commit to our guests and continue to help them when the show's over."

"But we have the aftercare team." Ray shrugged.

"Look, forget aftercare, whoever, whatever and – more pertinently – wherever they are," I snapped; "we're in serious danger of turning into a freak show that provides merely spectacle – not solutions – and none of us ever wanted that did we Ray?"

He pulled an 'I'm-not-sure' face, pulling his mouth down and turning his head on one side.

"Ray, indulge me; I'd like some guests who can actually speak without swearing, people who understand words of more than one syllable. Go on, really spoil me Ray; give me some guests with teeth? I suppose what I'm asking you for is more talk and less low-life sex..."

"Ha... I bet you say that to all the boys," he said, relieved to find a loophole out of this uncomfortable conversation.

"Judith mentioned the other day that there's been talk on the fourth floor about show merchandise, mugs and T-shirts and – well, I don't want to seem ungrateful, or not 'current' but moving forward, I was hoping for more... gravitas?" I said.

"Gravitas? Ah...yes, you have that in spades, love. But I'm not sure it translates very well with the 19-to-27-year olds."

"If you really think mugs or T-shirts with my name or face on them would translate better with the youth then I will have to move with the times I suppose, but I can't help feeling it's tacky. And before we know it, the programme will be turned into some heavily merchandised, sleazy sex-circus."

"Stop right there!" he said, holding up his hand. "Sleazy will not be on the Daytime agenda. Not on my watch, Captain, no sir. Though hearing you say it out loud, I am rather fond of the alliteration... sleazy sex circus has a certain ring to it... Perhaps we could work it up as a late-night format?"

He stopped talking when he saw that I was neither amused nor interested.

"Ray, forget late night sex circus formats – I'd like to develop my Daytime format into something better... more useful." I tried again. "We talked once about a book club, didn't we? An Oprah-style book club."

The hand was up again, in the stop sign; I was sorely tempted to push it up his bloody nose.

"I have a gizmo, Tanya, in my office, which tells me when the ratings rise. It shows a sharp increase when an interesting item comes up on the TV and gets viewers twitching – and let me tell you, NOTHING is twitching OR rising at the mention of 'Book Club.' Throw in a pretty young girl, a rough, hunky guy and get them talking about their sexual problems, sexual proclivities, sexual diseases, sexual..."

"I get it, Ray."

"...Then there's plenty of twitching, a huge rise – it's positively...tumescent."

"I don't doubt it."

"As for the merchandise, well, it's a wild card, blue-sky thinking on a rainy day. Don't worry – we won't put your face on anything like that, love."

"Good. Don't get me wrong, Ray. I can see that you might want to make the most of all my 'Darling of Daytime' awards, but I just wouldn't be happy with merchandise."

"What, not even some 'Darling of Daytime' Frisbees?" He winked.

"I have a busy afternoon, Ray. Lots to do." I said, standing up. "I just wanted to make my point." I picked up my bag, ready to leave.

"Tanya, all those years ago when the country lost Diana, its 'Queen of Hearts,' it took you, Tanya Travis, to its bosom." he sighed, leaving a theatrical pause while heaving himself to his feet. "We may have lost her in a Parisian tunnel but we found you on ITV, five mornings a week. And for fifteen years you have offered a special brand of solace and advice..."

"Ray..."

"... Just like she did." His eyes were twinkling. "Diana wouldn't have shied away from live STD tests and DNA results."

"I beg to differ, Ray. I think we can safely assume that STD tests were never on the Princess of Wales' royal itinerary."

He lurched towards me, taking both my hands in his. "Tanya Travis is television's 21st century 'Queen of Hearts'. I want you to be remembered for..."

"Frisbees with my face on?"

"No, not Frisbees, Tanya. What I'm saying is that Diana changed her image, from 'fluffy' to 'landmines'." I frowned at him, not sure what he was getting at.

"Tanya, who knows, perhaps we can in the future look at placing you in something with the gravitas you dream of – documentaries, political interviews... Diana's Landmine Legacy?"

"Oh yes Ray... That would be great. That's what I really want. Something that will have a effect, make a difference. I could still look at difficult situations and human relationships in my own way, but in a more serious format. A close up on child trafficking? An in-depth on HIV? 21st century slavery? I'm not scared of real life, Ray."

"Oh I know. But in the meantime, let's just hang on in there and stick with the teenagers, the trans-genders and the traveller brides." He licked his full lips. Ray didn't want to hear about the real world, only the one where women wore bunny ears and no-one ever died from having sex.

I stood up again, to encourage him to leave. He continued to talk and I watched his mouth move over words like 'intimate,' 'gushing,' 'probing' and 'sexual satisfaction.' A deep heat was surging through me and rising up my neck. If I didn't get out now I wouldn't be able to resist the urge to wipe Ray vigorously with a damp facial flannel.

I eventually evicted him from my dressing room and finally, finally checked my voice messages. I thought my heart would stop when that stupid female voice said, "You have two new voicemail messages. To listen to your messages, press one."

"Yes, yes I know!" I said, pressing one and waiting, agitated, my head about to explode.

"Hey honey, it's Mama Donna. Have you thought about that fabulous offer of foreign travel and prime-time exposure? *Celebrity Spa Trek*... You know you want to."

So, Donna was still trying to wear me down on the reality show? I pressed one again and the second message started: "Oh... and before you ask, no I haven't heard from the Beeb and yes I have put calls in to them." Fucking Donna, again! I stared at my phone, disappointed.

Within 10 minutes I was tucked into the back of the car with Arthur at the helm. I felt war-torn, beleaguered and old. I had never been so glad to be going home, where I could be alone with my thoughts of Nathan, the pain of his departure duetting with the tantalising possibility he might already be there, waiting for me, ready to forgive.

TWEET: @TanyaTruth Gr8 show 2day! On way home 2 spend evening with @NathanWells + early night. #TrueLoveIs

8

Vodka Cocktails and Love in the Clouds

Arriving back at the house I climbed out of the car on shaky legs, trying desperately not to build my hopes up that Nathan might be back. I waved goodbye to Arthur, opened the front door and walked into the silence. No-one was home. My heart dipped as I took off my shoes in the hall and padded through to the kitchen. I put the kettle on, took my rubber gloves from the drawer and was just about to begin a vigorous tile-scrubbing session when I heard a creak upstairs. Perhaps I wasn't alone, after all? The hairs on the back of my neck stood up.

I left the kitchen and walked into the hall.

"Astrid, are you there?" I called, taking the stairs cautiously. Once upstairs, I opened the door to my own room and called out again.

"Astrid, is that you?" There was a muffled sound, so faint I could barely hear it. What was it? Giggles? Cries? My heart jumped a little.

"Who is it?" I called again. "Nathan... is it you? Are you there?" The noise seemed to be coming from Astrid's room, so I stepped towards her door on soft carpet, calling her name as I did. I leaned gently against the door frame to try and hear what it was. "Hello? Hello?" I tried again, knocking gently, panic rising in my chest.

Suddenly there was rustling and movement and I was tempted to throw open the door. *But it might not be an intruder*, I thought, *it might actually be Astrid in her room.*

"Astrid?"

"Yes, yesss, I'm here. I feeling a bloody little head-aching Tanya – I stay here and do some of the sleep."

"Oh, I'm sorry, I didn't mean to wake you," I tried, hoping she'd come to the door so I could see into her room. She definitely wasn't alone. *But who was in there with her?*

"Shall I make you some tea?" I asked, planning to bribe my way in with her favourite lingonberry brew (which should have been more appropriately named, 'Swedish Cat Pee'). This wasn't the first time I'd heard noises coming from Astrid's room recently and what worried me was her reluctance to let me in. I stood there for a few seconds more but she didn't answer me, so I left her to her headache.

I went back into my bedroom, washed my hands eight times and hung that day's Armani jacket and skirt on soft, padded hangers. I placed them high on a rail in the black section of the walk-in wardrobe and stood back to admire the view. A Gucci jacket in French navy and a pristine, white silk blouse waited in the wardrobe wings, ready for the next day's show. I smiled; smooth suits, good, straight lines, colour-coded, clean – all in their place. I stood for a few minutes, enjoying the deep pleasure of clothes hung according to shade, running my hands along the pleats of fabric, from the blackest Jean Muir to the lightest, pastel Chanel. I pulled on my robe and just as I was brushing my hair, there was another noise on the landing then movement on the stairs. I leapt out and to the top of the stairs, just as the front door closed.

"Astrid?"

"Yes?" she staggered up the stairs, breathless.

"Was someone at the door?"

"Yes. I opened door for shithead postman, but he's gone. What a dick's head he is."

"Yes, isn't he?" I responded absently, thinking *the postman never comes in the afternoon. Who just left*?

Another hand-washing session calmed me slightly, but I couldn't be as thorough as I liked because I had to check the next day's running order and make notes. I also had to call Georgina about my blog, phone Tara, my sister in Australia and text Nathan again. I couldn't do anything until my hands were absolutely clean and the more I thought about wasted time the more I had to wash. Suddenly hand washing wasn't enough, so I climbed into the shower and turned it up, as hot as it would go. Discovering a bottle of extra strong, delicious, Flash All-Purpose in Crisp Lemon in the cubicle, I grabbed it, slathered it all over me and worked it in with the scrubbing brush. Pinpricks of blood emerged on my thighs, upper arms and neck. I caught my breath as my flesh protested at the wire brush and the searing, citric detergent. Flash may not smell like Jo Malone but it eradicated the day's filth and life's pain in a way her White Jasmine and Mint oil never could.

I finally emerged from the spray, rubbing myself vigorously with a towel, hoping that would be enough for that day but knowing in my heart that it wouldn't.

After my shower, I checked my phone for the hundredth time. Damn, he'd called while I was washing. "Damn, damn, damn!" I hissed to myself through the bathroom steam. I was excited and delighted he'd made contact but filled with anguish and regret that I hadn't answered. I immediately called him, desperately hoping he'd answer this time. It rang and rang and rang... and just as I was about to pass out, he answered.

"Hi, Tanya."

"Hello Nathan? How are you? I've been so worried about you, darling."

"Yeah. I'm sorry. I just couldn't take it... the pressure. You know how it is."

"Yes, of course I do and you didn't need me adding to it. I'm sorry..." I could feel my chest heave with the explosion of unreleased sobs.

"Look, Tanya, let's meet tonight. We need to talk about what's going to happen next."

"If you just want to meet up to dump me, Nathan, please don't, just tell me now and get it over with." I said, holding back the tears.

"No. No Tanya, God, I don't want us to be over. I want to see you, we need to... sort out our future." Relief swept over me, my eyes swelled with tears of happiness.

"Ok... yes, that would be good. Let's meet this evening then shall we? I'll book somewhere and text you." I said, feeling hope rise in my chest, he agreed and I hung up the phone.

I immediately called Cloud 23, the bar on the 23rd floor of The Hilton in Manchester City Centre and reserved a table. I knew Nathan would like it there, it was contemporary but not too trendy for an early-evening drink, the views were jaw-dropping and I'd recalled Georgina said the soundtrack was 'stylish'. Nathan liked 'stylish.' I was optimistic about this reunion. Perhaps what had happened with *Hello!* and our separation had made him really think about where we were headed. I even imagined, in an excited little corner of my mind, that this might be the place he would finally propose, so I wanted it to be perfect in every way.

I arrived promptly at seven after agonising for 17 minutes about what to wear. I settled on a beautifully cut, casual dress from Whistles and a wrap to keep out the evening chill. It was late August, but it was the UK and I was already shivering... with excitement? Fear? Cold? I stared out of the window from the highest point in Manchester, enjoying the outline of the city painted against a dusky sky, the setting sun glinting from car windows below. I lost myself, imagining the evening ahead. *We need to talk about what's going to happen next...*, he'd said. Was he saying what I thought he was saying?

Perhaps Nathan was beginning to realise that commitment, emotional security and a 'Vintage Glamour' themed wedding was what we both needed? There'd been something exciting in his voice when he'd called. There was urgency, like he was desperate to see me.

I checked the time. Nathan was running late and I tried not to become anxious. A waiter came over and asked if I'd like a drink. "I'll wait for my- fiancé, thank you," I said, a sparkle in my tummy as I said the word 'fiancé'. I was playing a dangerous game with myself.

Despite the stunning views and fabulous décor, it wasn't long before there was the usual frisson of interest around me. A couple on the nearest table whispered to each other, desperately trying to look like they weren't staring at me. The girl slowly took her smartphone out of her bag, pretending to send a text – but I knew she was trying to take my picture. When I was first in the public eye people would smile at me, now they just brandished their phones to take pictures of me eating/drinking/being alone or as was often the case, arguing with Donna. It's hard enough to be in a public place on your own but when you're famous it's a bloody nightmare. I always tried to be accommodating – to smile and sign autographs when asked and pose for a million mobile-phone photos even at the risk of missing a flight or being late for a vital medical appointment. But there were days when, like any normal human being, I was upset, ill or just didn't feel like smiling for a stranger's camera while their friends and family clung to me like grim death, shouting 'cheese!' On those days, if I dared to refuse someone, my magic, celebrity-princess crown was ripped from my head and they beat me with it. 'Who does she think she is?' they'd mutter. 'She looks much older in the flesh, doesn't she? Miserable old bag wouldn't even let us have a quick photo... If it wasn't for us the public, she wouldn't have that show,' as if I had played no part in my own career achievements.

In an attempt to look busy I signalled to the waiter and ordered a coffee.

I would need to be careful how I greeted Nathan, if and when he finally turned up. I mustn't show my anxiety or displeasure – and I definitely couldn't burst into tears and climb up his legs begging for him to marry me, unless I wanted to be papped and headlined '*Old, Ugly and Desperate*' on the cover of *heat* that week.

I'd been sitting alone for over an hour and was just contemplating leaving, when he suddenly appeared at my side.

"Hello, gorgeous." He held my hand and kissed me full on the mouth, pulling me into his strong arms and taking me by complete surprise – along with the rest of the bar. All my hurt and worry melted into my coffee and I glowed inside and out.

"Can I get you a drink?" I asked as he sat down, still holding my hand, staring straight into my eyes with his deep blue ones.

"Yes, I'll have a vodka and Red Bull please."

The waiter came and I ordered his drink and a vodka cocktail for me. I felt a bottle of Dom Perignon was perhaps a little presumptuous at this early stage in the proceedings, but he was definitely in a better frame of mind: *so far so good*.

"Darling, I've been so worried, where have you been? You've not been answering your phone," I said gently.

"Oh Tanya," he said, annoyed. "I've only just got here, I re-arranged my whole night to see you and you start with the questions."

My heart sank. I knew he felt I could be possessive and controlling but I only wanted to point out that I'd been waiting for him, alone. I wanted to kick myself. Why did I always have to ruin everything by nagging?

The waiter returned with our drinks. "I'm sorry Nathan, I'm a bit stressed. It's just difficult being me, on my own in a bar – you know how it is with the public." I tentatively reached for his hand across the table.

"It's no picnic for me either, going out with you," he sighed pulling his hand away.

I took it back gently. "I know, and you're a saint for putting up with me and all my baggage. No-one else ever stayed this long, you're very special."

"And you are to me, Tanya. I wanted you to know how special you are – I got you something. Look, I know it's been tough between us recently and I want us to make up, get back together."

"Oh! Nathan... I never expected..." I looked into his eyes, searching for a clue, was this the moment I'd been waiting for? My hopes soared high over Manchester Cathedral and hovered with sparkly expectation over my head.

He reached into his pocket while I tried hard to suppress the grin that was threatening to fill my whole face. I looked from his eyes to his hand, searching for a clue. He was pulling out a small Tiffany box and I had to resist the urge to tear it from him, open it and shout 'yes, yes, yes!' like Meg Ryan in *When Harry met Sally*. Instead, I feigned restraint and gently took the blue box from his outstretched hand, with a carefully-composed look of surprise and intrigue on my face. I slowly lifted the lid, my eyes flitting between his and the emerging contents which were to dictate my future. I could feel everyone's eyes on me – like the world had paused to see what was in the box.

"Oh Nathan how lovely...it's...it's...so thoughtful... It's... earrings!" I willed my mouth to smile as the rest of me picked my heart up off the floor.

"You love Tiffany's, don't you?"

I nodded, unable to form words. Yes, I adored Tiffany jewellery. Yes, I loved the exquisite necklaces and the dainty silver bracelets and the gorgeous silver stud earrings, like the ones I was holding now. But here, in this lovely restaurant with spectacular views and stylish soundtrack, these particular Tiffany earrings were just a searing, painful reminder that whatever he said, Nathan still didn't want to marry me.

He lifted his drink, looking at me, uncertainty in his eyes. "You do like them, don't you? Would you have preferred gold?"

I'd have preferred a fucking ring, I thought, but I slurped my drink to stop myself saying this. As I looked at the pretty, expensive earrings, I thought about the pile of unopened bills that I had swept into a drawer whilst I was making the fragrant chicken.

"Um – did you buy these... on the credit card?" I tried to smile, gathering myself together, the more familiar, practical Tanya taking over.

"Tanya, there you go again. Does it matter how I paid for them? I left my mate Darren's early to go across town and get them... I went to a lot of trouble. I had to get a taxi. But it's not good enough is it? It's always about the money." He turned himself away from me and stared out of the window.

"No...I...it's just..."

"Look, you know the score, Tanya. I'm a bit strapped at the moment. Yes, I used your bloody precious card but don't worry, I'll make sure you're paid back in full. Perhaps you'd like a signed IOU?"

I sighed and reached for his hand. I was hurt and disappointed. I wouldn't have minded if he'd paid for an engagement ring with my card, that was worth getting in hock for, but he'd paid for earrings I didn't want, with money I didn't have. Talk about rubbing salt in the wound. I felt a lump forming in my chest; I swallowed hard and sat back, abandoning the drink. I smiled, which was hard, given that my heart was battered with deep disappointment. I wanted to cry, but people were looking.

"Nathan, please don't think I'm nagging and fretting and being a bore. It's just... I think I mentioned that things are a bit tight at the moment. I'm almost up to the limit on my cards," I said. "The music studio seems to be swallowing up quite a bit," I tried to add, gently. He looked away from me, out of the window. I looked at the little box on the table and I felt bad.

"I don't mean to put a downer on your gift, I'm sorry. The earrings really are lovely."

He glared at me. "So much for a romantic reunion! I buy you a present that most women would love, but you end up giving me another lecture about 'your' money. Thanks a lot, Tanya."

He was sulking now. I grabbed some wipes from my bag and, still smiling for the public, I cleaned between my fingers discreetly. This would suffice until I could get to some hot, running water.

"Nathan, I don't want you to think I don't appreciate you and everything..." I tried, putting my hand on his. "I was so happy to get your call. I love spending time together. We don't do this enough, do we?" I looked around the bar still smiling inanely, trying to give the impression we were happy and having a lovely time.

"Tanya, what's so funny?"

"Nothing," I hissed through gritted teeth. "I don't want them to think we're not happy. Just keep smiling."

He rolled his eyes. "You're always working, aren't you?" He sipped his drink, placed it carefully down and after a couple of seconds lifted his head and suddenly said; "I love you, Tanya."

Warmth surged back into my chest: "I love you too," I mouthed. He shifted uncomfortably in his chair and looked up at me.

"Tan... we need to talk."

I looked at him quizzically. "OK."

"I had a call from a reporter."

"Oh... About the wedding?"

"No, no nothing like that. It's just that ...there's a story about to hit the papers."

My mouth went dry and I felt sick. I stopped smiling.

"What story?" I squeaked a few decibels too loud, trying hard to contain my panic. "What are you talking about Nathan?"

"Shhhh Tanya...Jesus," he said, running his hands through his hair, looking round to see if anyone had heard.

"Is it another young blonde trying to make a name for herself? I'll call Donna, she can threaten legal action before any of this gets into the..."

"Tanya, it's difficult."

"No it's not, Donna can..."

"There are photos." He said quietly, his head down.

"What?" And I had naïvely hoped we'd be ordering champagne and talking guest lists and bridesmaids by this point.

"Photos of what, Nathan?" I asked, not wanting to know the answer, but hoping against hope it was something innocent. "Are you in a bar? Is she a friend?"

"No. No, she's not a friend. She went to the papers, she says she's got proof."

"Proof?" I repeated in a whisper. "Proof of what?"

"That I spent time with her...she's saying we had sex or something... I don't know."

"Nathan, what do you mean, had sex 'or something'? Did you...are you... having an affair with this girl?"

"No. God, no. I told you, I just chatted to her, in a bar." He reached across and grabbed both my hands with his.

"OK, so she's telling lies then." I said. "If she's after money, we'll just offer her more than the papers are offering her. What proof anyway? What is she alleging?"

"Tanya," he said, gripping me tightly, "please, try to stay calm. She's gone to the papers because– well, because she's pregnant."

"NO!" I shouted, pulling away from him. He cast a desperate glance round the room. "Shhh Tanya, please try not to freak out. It's not mine Tanya, you've got to believe me."

I took 13 seconds to breathe deeply. I daren't cry or throw up: one could only imagine the headlines accompanying those shots . A baby! Of all the things...a baby. How could this be happening to me? To us?

"Christ Nathan, I'm starting to feel like a guest on my own show," I said, feeling the world wobble beneath me.

"You know I would never hurt you, Tanya. You know what the press are like!"

"Yes, but did you sleep with her? Why would she claim the baby was yours if you haven't even slept with her?"

"There you go again! You're just like everyone else; I thought you knew what it was like to be a target? And it's all because I'm in love with someone famous."

"You are so naïve, Nathan." I said a sudden flash of anger piercing through my anguish. "Don't you realise what these young women will do for money and a bit of publicity? When will you learn that you can't chat to them or be nice to them because they will pretend that more happened!"

I took a long slug of vodka cocktail and looked at him: "Did something happen?"

Nathan leaned over and touched my face. "Tanya, how could I ever hurt you? I love you and I love our life together – I'd be a fool to jeopardise that. If I'm guilty of anything it's caring too much about you."

"Just answer me. Did you sleep with her, Nathan?" I wanted to be sick, I'd asked the same question of one of my guests that morning.

"No. I didn't sleep with her."

"Right, I'll talk to Donna and see what we can do. If there's no way the baby's yours then we will make sure everyone knows it's just lies and we'll get a DNA test to prove it."

I sipped my drink. I'd have given everything – anything – to have a baby with Nathan, I wanted it so much it was a physical pain, but I knew it could never be. Now another woman was telling the world she was carrying his child and my fragile heart smashed into shards, scattering all over the floor like tiny stars.

We left the bar in silence. I looked across at Nathan who stared resolutely out of the window all the way home, and I tried to squash the little flutter of panic beating like a bird within me, trying to escape through my mouth. *Why would this girl allege she was pregnant with Nathan's baby if they hadn't even slept together?* I screwed my eyes up tight. *Nathan's baby: Nathan was going to be a father.* A stab of pain shot through me and I fumbled for my wipes. How could this happen? I thought we were ok... I had everything neatly planned, this wasn't in the script. Then practical Tanya took over, as always. *Nathan isn't having a baby. This girl is just a gold digger trying her luck.* And like crumbs on a kitchen worktop, I wiped the thoughts away.

As soon as we arrived home, Nathan went upstairs to our room. I fished my mobile out of my Prada clutch and called Donna.

"JESUS, NO! It's the 21st century, for Christ's sake! You can buy bloody condoms in the local drug store ...public toilets... there's no excuse for it," was Donna's reaction when I broke the news. All the hurt and anger I was feeling towards Nathan for getting himself into in this situation and all the guilt I was feeling because of my nagging doubts about him exploded again in giant, gulping sobs.

"I think you're missing the point, Donna," I spluttered, once I could speak. "I'm heartbroken at the accusation. I'm not upset because he didn't use a bloody condom."

"Well you should be..."

"Look Donna, it isn't his. Nathan didn't sleep with her. The girl is just telling lies because he's my partner and I'm famous."

"It's not that Polish checkout girl from the Pound Shop is it? I heard he had the hots for her last time you were away."

"I don't know who she is and I don't want to know," I hissed down the phone, through a hundred years' worth of mucus and tissues.

"There's no smoke without fire, honey," she added, unhelpfully. "He's been caught with his hand in the cookie jar. Perhaps now you'll see him for what he is: a gold-digging womaniser."

"I don't need this now, Donna, I'm too upset, just sort it, will you? I can't wake up to any more pictures in the papers of young blondes in skimpy tops talking about how good my boyfriend is in bed."

"'Sort it,' she says. Is this blonde bimbo royal? Is she a celebrity? A European aristocrat? Wealthy supermodel? Big Brother winner? If it's yes to any of the above, then I could 'sort it' as you naively suggest and turn it into a money-spinning story to keep you on the front pages of *heat* forever and ever amen. As it is, I'm left with the proverbial silk purse and sow's ear – again. So what's his story?"

"Nathan's not the dad, he knows the girl but he never slept with her. He just chatted to her in a club one evening, she knew who he was and has taken it from there."

I was standing in the hall clutching the telephone as Donna banged on about tarts and gold diggers like it was a bloody themed party, when Nathan emerged from the landing. He padded down the stairs, his head down. I noticed he was carrying a rucksack.

"Where are you going Nathan?"

"I'm leaving. If you can't trust me I don't want to be here, after all it's your house, Tanya" he said in a quiet voice.

"Nathan, please don't leave!" I said, reaching for him. He batted my hand away.

"Wake up to yourself, Tanya," he said, and was gone, slamming the door behind him.

I moved into the downstairs toilet and sat down. Donna was still on her diatribe about 'Z-list tarts' and gold-digging nobodies' making her life a misery and I cried silently, allowing her to rant for another 14 seconds.

"He's gone, Donna." I said, finally interrupting her, wiping my face on a towel. "He said I don't trust him... and he's gone."

"Ha! Guilty as sin," she snorted down the phone.

I turned on the taps in the little sink, running the hot water until it was scalding and washed my hands with the phone under my chin. I caught sight of the 'Tanya Travis Engagement Announcement' magazine lying on the top of pile; Astrid must have put it there. We looked so happy on the cover. I knew Nathan was hurting from being wrongly accused, but no-one seemed to care how I – Miss Haversham, forever a spinster of this parish – felt about the day's developments. I had not only been denied a ring and a proposal, but was now in waiting to find out if my boyfriend had made another woman pregnant. The cruelty of it almost took my breath away and I wondered if I was somehow being punished for what I'd done, all those years ago.

I got rid of Donna and emerged from the toilet almost an hour later, my cuticles ragged, nails almost transparent. I staggered into the sitting room where Astrid was nursing a box of Maltesers and humming along to the opening bars of Countdown, she always Sky-Plussed it so we could watch it together in the evenings.

"Where's Nathan?" she asked.

"He's gone to see some friends." I lied.

I sat down next to her on the sofa and tried my best to switch off and watch, but before I knew it, tears were streaming down my face again.

"Ah Tanya, you silly old cow... You crying?"

"Oh it's nothing, Astrid," I said in a wobbly voice. She offered me a Malteser; normally chocolate was a no-no for me and I think Astrid was quite shocked when I took one. She patted my arm.

"Tanya, you are making me do the crying too." she said.

"Sorry, I'll be OK," I said, amazed that she was even aware of what had been going on. "I know what everyone thinks about him but I'm sad because he is very special." I tried to explain in a way she'd understand.

"Yes. It is shitting sad."

"Thank you for understanding."

"Well, you say he special... You English loved him much."

"Who, Nathan?"

"No, bollocks! Richard... Richard Whiteley, Countdowning man. They say it is not same without him, and now Carol the number lady, she goes too."

I just nodded and stared at the screen.

"Balls from hell, Tanya! What do they play at? Who is next to go? Gok? Dr Christian? I sometimes say I should piss on this Channel 4 and be watching the ITV instead." She handed me a tissue.

GOSSIPBITCH: *'Which Darling of Daytime is telling porkies about a white wedding and desperately hoping her boyfriend's DNA test is negative... just like the guests on her show?'*

9

Embarrassing Bodies and Morning Manoeuvres

When my crazed birds alarm went off the next morning, I reached out to the space beside me in our dark, empty bedroom and remembered. I had slept fitfully and felt tired to my very bones; the thought of my morning run made me want to weep but I couldn't miss it. I threw the covers back and went to the window. It was still dark outside and I could see the fading moon. Heavy dew lay on the grass and for the first time in my career, I wanted to just get back into bed, pull the covers over my head and shut out the world. Instead, I put my trainers on, did a few hurried stretches and went out into the morning to pound the pavement.

Run complete, I pulled off my sweaty clothes, padded to the bathroom and turned the shower on to super-hot. I was about to step in when I heard a knock on the door.

"Hello? Come in!" I said, my heart leaping, hoping it was Nathan.

Astrid's blonde head poked round the door.

"Good morning, Mrs soppy shithead. I've made some tea."

I smiled, in spite of myself.

"Thanks Astrid. It's not that Swedish tea that tastes of cat-piss, is it?"

"It never tastes of the cat's pissings!" she exclaimed, outraged at my insult. She set it down on my bedside table (without a coaster). "Now I go get ready for big studio day."

"Pardon?"

"Ah Tanya, you upset, yes? I come to the studio to help you."

This was all I needed, my crazy, confused cleaner accompanying me to work to ensure that my already difficult day turned into hell.

"Er, thanks Astrid, but I will be fine on my own" I tried.

She frowned at me then fixed me with a stare.

"No Tanya Travis. You are too much on your own, yes? I come and keep you company on the programme."

And with that, she left the room.

Once I was ready, I snuck downstairs in the hope I could leave quickly without Astrid noticing. But she was waiting by the door, in large, knee-length khaki shorts and a too skimpy T-shirt, looking like something from a deranged *Dad's Army*. I was just about to open my mouth and object to a) her outfit and b) her presence at the studio, when my phone started to ring.

It was Arthur my driver, in distress.

"Miss Travis. I've tried to get in the front but for some reason I can't get the electric gates to open. And – I don't know if you're aware, Miss, but there are at least fifty journalists and photographers out here".

"Shit."Clearly the story about Nathan and the pregnant blonde had hit, and the media pack was now outside, baying for my blood.

"The vehicle is situated down the road, Miss Travis" he continued. "We need to make a getaway plan. Perhaps employ a decoy?" Arthur loved being a celebrity chauffeur and even when we had only minor press interest, his SAS side would come out. He'd talk in a sergeant-major voice about 'heading them off at the pass,' like they were armed terrorists rather than a stringer from *The Sun* and a trainee reporter the *Wilmslow Advertiser*.

"OK listen, here's what we'll do," he said. "You get Astrid to take a tray of tea around the back of the house and keep 'em talking."

I could already see a flaw in his plan because Astrid would happily make tea but no doubt serve it while addressing the world's press as 'shitheads,' or 'toss-bandits.' However, this was a double-edged sword and if we were lucky may cause an international incident in itself, which would take the heat off my story. "OK, so what do I do?" I said.

"While she's talking to the press, I will keep an eye on the front of the house and when it's all clear I'll call you. I don't know why but my remote isn't working to open the electric gates so you will need to open them from inside as soon as I call, and make a dash for it before they realise. OK?"

"OK," I said, feeling a stab of panic.

I put the phone down, took a deep breath and turned to Astrid.

"OK. Astrid, there are a load of press out the front. It's very important that you make some tea and take it out of the back door to them. While they are drinking it, I will run out of the front gates. OK?"

Astrid's face spread into a grin, "OK Tanya. I will make important tea for the press toss-faces. Leave to me."

Astrid made several cups of vile tea and I popped upstairs and put my show suit (black Gucci) on as time would be of the essence. I returned to the kitchen where Astrid was carrying a tray of steaming mugs and opening the back door. "Don't worry Tanya – I am here," she smiled, shutting the door behind her. Within two and a half minutes, one of the press had spotted movement at the back of the house and, in the hope it might be me, had run round. It wasn't long before the others followed and I peeped from the back window on all fours, waiting for the coast to be clear. Two minutes later, Arthur called me on my mobile.

"Open sesame, then run, run, run!" he commanded. So I ran to the front of the house and leapt up to press the button that would open the gate. Nothing happened. What the hell? Then I remembered – I'd asked Astrid to turn the power box off last night, so if Nathan decided to come back in the middle of the night again he wouldn't be able to get in and would have to call me. That way he couldn't sneak into the spare room. Turning it back on required a key and I had no idea where Astrid might have put it. I ran round the house, looking in all the obvious places.

"Shit, shit, SHIT" I muttered to myself, flinging the contents of my kitchen drawers onto the floor and hating myself for the chaos I was causing. Still no key. Tearing myself away from the mess I had just made, I knew I'd never find it on my own, so I had to reach Astrid and ask her where it was. I snuck to the back of the house and ducked under the windowsill. Then I furtively peeked out of the very bottom of the window, praying there were no long lenses trained on the house. I could see Astrid a few yards away in the back garden, chatting animatedly over the fence to the press. I grabbed my phone and called her.

"Pick up, pick up, pick up," I said to myself. But it went to answer machine. "Astrid, I need the key for the power to open the electric gates. Where the hell is it? I need the front gate opening so I can get out. CALL ME or come back in!"

I looked out to see if she was picking up her phone but she had her back to me. I needed to get out of that gate; time was ticking on so I opened the window slightly and called her.

"Astrid... Astrid... over here," I hissed, but she was chatting away to the reporters, no doubt giving them her latest recipe for bloody soused herring. "Astrid... Astrid, you silly cow." I was still on all fours, my head half in and out of the window, and I was becoming very agitated. I couldn't shout in case the press heard me and I was now officially running late. I had a live show, my driver was waiting and my stress levels were on the ceiling.

"Astrid...you... you shithead," I hissed loudly thinking she might respond more to words she was familiar with. "Astrid, you toss-bandit..." Nothing. "Shithead Astrid," I tried again but it was a little louder than I had intended and the press gaggle became suspicious with flashes going off and the babble of voices becoming louder. Christ, I was really panicking now. I didn't know what to do and when my mobile rang I nearly leaped into orbit.

"What? What?" I snapped.

"Tanya we need to be on the move, we are due to RV at the front of the building, where are you?"

"Arthur I'm trapped, all the press are at the back – I think they've got shots of me on the floor shouting abuse at Astrid and I can't find the key to unlock the power for the electric gate."

"OK. Calm down... let me think. The only thing you can do is climb over the gate."

"You're kidding?"

"Tanya, I don't joke at times like this. It's the only way; the press hounds are at the back, I'm here with the getaway vehicle at the front and you need to be in it."

He was right, there was nothing else for it, so I gathered my stuff together and headed for the front of the house. Once outside, I stood and looked up at the huge gates and wanted to cry.

I took a deep breath and locking my fingers into the wrought iron, and hitching my skirt, began the ascent. The gates were over twelve feet high, Italian designed, handmade and installed to keep the nosy press out, but as I took each tricky foothold, I regretted the day I'd commissioned them. The gaps where my feet went in were wide apart and along with the physical challenge, I couldn't help but think how undignified I must have looked. I had almost reached the top and was precariously balanced on the filigreed hand-wrought iron when something very disturbing happened: the gate started to *move*. It was opening and I was astride it, high in the air, black Gucci skirt high over my thighs, the world's press within spitting distance.

"What the hell? Arthur!" I yelled, clinging on for dear life. The gate was gaining momentum as it opened backwards. There was nothing for it – I would have to jump off when it stopped. I waited until it fully opened, then just as I was starting to lower myself, the bloody thing started to shut again.

"Noooooo! What is going on?!" I shouted. By now, Arthur was out of his car, yelling at me.

"Jump, Miss Travis!! It's the only option!"

"I am NOT jumping from a twelve foot, moving gate!" I snarled back. "Make. It. STOP!"

The gates clanged shut again, but like some demented fairground ride, they started to open almost immediately.

""Help me someone, for the love of God!" I was starting to feel really dizzy now, and I screwed my eyes up tight so I wouldn't fall. And when I opened them – there, before me, with cameras flashing, were the assembled press.

"Tanya! Tanya! Over here! Are you stuck, Tanya? Show us your face! Is it true your boyfriend's a sex-addict, Tanya? Is it true you're a sex-addict Tanya? How do you feel about being stuck on a gate Tanya? How do you feel about your boyfriend's baby news Tanya? Tanya, are you gonna jump? Is it a suicide bid? Are you a cougar Tanya?" Stupid questions were hurled at me as the gates grinded slowly open and closed again and again.

I turned my face away from them towards the house, to see Arthur in a tussle with Astrid. As the press had left her to join me, it seemed that Astrid had finally listened to the message on her phone telling her I needed the gates open and she had found the key. And now she was pressing every button on the 'shit-controller.' Typical Astrid, she was standing firmly by my instructions to open the gate and refusing to hand over the remote control to Arthur.

"Astrid!" I shrieked, hysterical now. "Give him the fucking remote! Just give it to him! Fucking give it to him!"

She reluctantly handed it over, and after everyone had got their shot, Arthur finally stopped the swinging fairground ride. I was now very dizzy, my heartbeat pounding in my ears, my thighs poking through the elaborate iron scrollwork and decorative brass finials as they gripped for dear life. My eyes lost their focus and I could see Arthur running in slow motion towards me, his distorted voice shouting "Hold on!" My palms were sweaty and slippery on the wrought iron and I suddenly felt weak. Then everything went blurry and with the photographers snapping away as if their lives depended on it, I lost my grip and fell towards the ground.

I must have blacked out, because the next thing I knew, I was in the thick leather interior of the car, which was purring its way towards the studio.

"Don't worry, you silly old dick's head, I am here," came Astrid's voice, which was less than reassuring after the morning I'd had so far. She was next to me in the limo, holding my hand.

"Fucking Bruce Willis driver caught you," she said, shaking her head in awe. "And now he drives like crazy cop to get you to the studio on time. He is some shit, Tanya Travis."

I closed my eyes again. *Some shit, Tanya Travis.* The last person who'd said that to me in the back of this car was Nathan. A single tear slid down my cheek and the rest of the journey passed in silence.

TWEET: @TanyaTruth On way 2 studio with my PA 4 gr8 show after relaxing morning preparing 4 show! #DaytimeDarling #TruthWithTanya

10

Frothy Lattes and Frizzy Ends

Once at the studio, Astrid and I headed straight for my dressing room, avoiding the over-friendly faces and patronising smiles. They would all be desperately trying not to mention the latest instalment involving my disgraced boyfriend. I was keen to avoid their sympathy and Astrid's own take on the matter, which she would no doubt share in no uncertain terms with the whole production team.

For the first time ever, there was no sign of Georgina when I arrived. Instead, the first person to accost me with manic hugs and tearful sympathy was Judith. She meant well and I'm sure she really was upset, but I was still in shock from 'Gate-gate' and if ever I needed brisk efficiency, it was that morning. I was in pieces and didn't need Judith – another crumbling person – consoling me. One look at her veiny forehead and frizzy ends and I almost erupted into tears.

"Tanya, you look good. I mean... you always do, in spite of everything... and...that lipstick is... lovely on you," she said, like it was a consolation. *Your partner has made another woman pregnant, but your lipstick's lovely.*

"Thanks Judith it's by Dior, it's called 'Sex Addict,'" I snapped, swishing along the corridor towards the dressing room.

"Ha!" Astrid huffed at my side.

Judith put her head down, swallowing hard. "I'm sorry about everything, Tanya."

"Judith, I don't want to make you feel uncomfortable so I won't go on but I just want to say, Nathan denies it all. The girl is telling lies and we may end up in court if she tries to get money out of us... out of him."

"Oh Tanya, I can only imagine how awful it is for you," she said, holding open my dressing room door for me. "When I read about it this morning..."

"It's fine, Judith. Really," I lied. "The baby isn't his. As soon as we can, we will get a DNA test to prove it."

"It is big shame because Tanya is so old," added Astrid, tactfully. "Her ovaries, they all crispy dry... and this girl is very young so when she has the sex..."

"Yes, we get the point, Astrid" I snapped, feeling a sharp stab. "And anyway, it's nothing to do with my age. Once and for all I don't have dry ovaries!"

"Ah Tanya, don't be sad because we see Dr Christian and he look right up your..."

"Oooh, Tanya Travis, who's talking dry ovaries? We don't want any dried-up old ovaries on Daytime." It was Ray, right on cue.

"And you won't have any, Ray. All the onscreen ovaries will be pink, ripe and fecund," I said sharply. He blushed and Judith's skin exploded into hives.

"I'm sorry, but I was just saying to Judith that I don't want people to feel they can't talk about the car crash that is my love life. It's out there – I called Georgina and she tweeted it late last night before the papers could put their own spin on it."

"Yes, the papers have spun quite a tale as it is. Georgina's already drafted a statement for the press office, saying you're not saying anything."

"Georgina person is saying you not saying anything? That is stupid... She is a silly old toss."

"Thank you Astrid. Er... Ray this is my...PA, Astrid, and Astrid – this is my boss."

Astrid stood straighter, proffering her hand to Ray and slowly moving her head up and down. She probably thought I'd just promoted her. I could hardly tell Ray I'd brought the cleaner in with me because I'd just fallen off the twelve-foot gate I'd been straddling and needed assistance to get in and out of the car.

"Georgina's great," I said, as much for Astrid's benefit as Ray's. "She always knows exactly how to pitch it. She composed that tweet so well that when I read it I wondered what all the fuss was about," I sighed. Ray and Judith shifted uneasily. Astrid huffed again and plonked herself on the sofa.

"Oh come on, it's OK. I'm upset – devastated in fact – but the show must go on." I said with a sad smile.

"Absolutely!" Ray enthused, glad that I wasn't sobbing on his shoulder – and no doubt relieved to cling to a familiar cliché in such an awkward social situation.

"So, let's get on with it. Where's Georgina? I've checked the script and running order," I announced briskly, keen to get on with all that was familiar and comfortable amidst the uncertainty.

"I've just been informed she'll be working in the gallery this morning, so someone else will be looking after you," Judith muttered.

"What? I'm sorry, but I can't do without an assistant this morning" I said, horrified.

"I will look after Tanya. I am PA now," Astrid piped up.

"Oh no. Not today Astrid, thank you. If ever there was a time I needed Georgina it's now. Why does she have to be in the gallery?"

Judith looked at Ray and he looked blank.

"Perhaps she's thinking of changing her job?" Judith offered.

"I hope not. I couldn't cope without her – she's my own personal angel. I'm serious Ray – I need her today."

"But Tanya I am angel now... I tidy your desk, yes?" Astrid said, and began to shuffle my papers importantly.

"Ray, I hope you aren't telling me that you are taking Georgina away from me?" I said, trying to scare him and not to be distracted by the chaos Astrid was now causing in my dressing room.

"Now, let's not be selfish Tanya. Georgina has to have some career development," Ray said, in his usual, unfathomable way. "She is a lovely tree whose roots need to embed, she needs to grow and spread her branches and the delightful Hermione has stepped in. She's wearing her spurs and she'll just grab those reins and ride you into the... Well..."

"I don't think the analogy stretches that far Ray," I said shortly. "In fact it's beginning to sound vaguely indecent." I was irritated that Georgina wasn't there. Putting her in the gallery during a show meant that Ray was keen to see her in another role – producer? I didn't want to stop Georgina's career moving upwards, but it really wasn't the time to leave me in the lurch with someone I'd never met called Hermione. There was a knock on the dressing room door and without waiting for a response from me, Ray flung it open.

"Ah, speak of the devil. Meet the fragrant Hermione," he announced, putting his arm around a tall, skinny girl and ushering her into my room. "She is the middle daughter of our esteemed boss Dickie Truelove and with a degree in Art History, she's clever as well as beautiful. Hermione comes highly recommended, Tanya. Dickie will be watching the show today so it seemed like a perfect time to show her the ropes." Dickie's daughter would be treated like royalty by Ray and the message was loud and clear: I had to do the same.

"Lovely to meet you, Hermione," I went to shake her hand, but she held hers in the air.

"OMG it's *the* Tanya Travis – aaagh!" she squealed waving jazz hands in mock delight.

I smiled back, not quite sure how to take this. I think she was being amusing.

"Now Hermione, I won't need your help as I have my own PA with me today," I said sweetly, gesturing towards Astrid, who at this point had unfortunately abandoned her new role and was lying full-length on the sofa, snoring. "She is just resting her eyes and gearing up before the show," I offered, beginning to tidy up the mess she'd made on the desk. "She will make sure I have everything I need in Georgina's absence, so you will have the opportunity to observe."

"Well actually, Tanya," Hermione started with a big smile, "I've been told to look after you so I can learn the awesome job of being your assistant for a few weeks, before I help Daddy," she said, her plummy tones jumping around the room like a bloody kangaroo. "So I shall stay by your side this morning; I am your Siamese twin." She had way too much energy and confidence for someone so young. I looked over at poor, crumpled Judith who positively shrank before my eyes. Hermione's hair was long and fashionably untamed rather than Judith-frizzy and she had a definite trust-fund style, sporting an effortless look of oversized, chunky jumper with a rope of (real) pearls around her neck. I wondered if they would snap if I tried to strangle her with them.

I smiled, unsure of what to say next.

"Nice pearls."

Ten minutes later, my nerves were still frayed from the events of the morning and Hermione had stuck to me like a bloody leech, ruining my washing plans, my timing and irritating me beyond human endurance.

"Judith, are you ready to go through the script with me?" I asked.

She absently handed me a script which was stained with coffee-cup rings and well thumbed. Not like the ones Georgina handed me first thing each morning, all fresh and clean and unsullied.

"Actually Tanya, Ray asked if Hermione could go through the script with you," Judith looked at me, waiting for the explosion. I stared at her evenly then looked at the grinning, gangly Hermione. I didn't explode, I just dialled Ray's office number.

"Ray, can you please tell me what the hell is going on around here? First, you take Georgina away on a morning where I really, really need her, then you say Judith can't do the script it has to be Hermione. She's new, and – forgive me Hermione – she isn't a producer and won't have a fucking clue."

"Tanya, Tanya. Bear with me. I meant to say earlier that today we are looking at ways to refresh the brand and I need all hands on the deck of this trusty old vessel while we move the seafaring crew around.

"Oh?"

"Yes, in fact I wondered if you and I might have a chat about it after today's show."

"Chat about the show, you mean?"

"Yes, I thought it might be a good idea for you and I to have a healthy mind-mapping session over frothy lattes on my roof garden."

I agreed and put the phone down, uncertain of what to make of the conversation. By seafaring crew, Ray meant staff and I had a horrible feeling that Georgina was leaving me for pastures new and that he was going to break it to me that Hermione would be my new assistant. I was furious – but I wouldn't be able to object as she was 'Big Dickie's' daughter. I pushed the thought to the back of my head and tried to focus.

Then it struck me what Ray was trying to tell me in his crazy code. Georgina was being groomed for Judith's job, right under her bloody nose. That was why he wanted to 'mind-map' and 'frothy latte' with me on his roof garden. My assistant was becoming my producer, and Judith was history. No wonder she was stressed out – poor old Judith was about to be sacked for someone younger and brighter, with sparkly scripts and smoother hair.

Poor Judith, poor, weird forty-something, past it Judith with her ageing hair, kids at university and husband long gone. How I hated Ray for doing this to her.

"Hermione," I said, turning to my soon-to-be assistant. "Why don't you go and fetch us all a nice coffee. I'll have a double tall extra-hot skinny latte with a sugar-free caramel shot and Judith will have an organic Chai, made from spring water, no milk. Get one for yourself, too," I added sweetly, handing her a tenner.

"Er, OK" she said and skipped out of the room.

Once on our own, I sat down with poor Judith. I didn't have long before I had to go to make-up, but I could always find time for the needy and this morning I made time to hold Judith's gnarled fingers and look into her baggy old eyes. Judith looked as rough as one of my guests and it felt like a rehearsal, me sitting there all poised and caring while she looked like hell.

"Judith. I know."

"You do?" She let out a huge sigh. "Oh Tanya, it's awful, I haven't slept."

"Oh, my love," I went for a hug but changed my mind, she was too messy. "Look, it's sad but it's life Judith, we all get old, even me! And I know only too well that none of us are bulletproof. I'm going through personal hell right now but I am more worried about you. I don't want you to worry about Georgina taking over. I'm going to get Donna to speak to Ray and we'll sort it. I don't want you to worry."

"But you can't really blame them, Georgina's so bright and young and..."

"Yes I know, but Ray can't just replace people because he's found somebody younger and more attractive. He's such a sexist old pig, I won't allow it."

"You might not be able to stop it, Tanya. I was in a meeting this morning and when the fourth floor decide you're past it that's it – kaput, you know how it is."

"Well not on my watch. And if I can't stop this travesty, then Donna will, so no more furrowed brow and itchy hair. OK?" I hugged her.

She nodded, seemingly comforted. "I haven't slept worrying about it."

"Well I can't say I blame you but I don't want you to give it another thought. Trust me, everything will be fine. We'll both still be here twenty years from now, we might need walking sticks but we'll still be doing our jobs," I smiled.

"You will be two wrinkly old shit-bags in twenty years down the lines," came Astrid's dulcet tones from the sofa. She was awake.

"I would love for Astrid to meet lovely Tim, our floor manager," I nodded to Judith. "Perhaps he could show her a front row seat in the studio where she can watch my performance?"

"No I need to help you, Tanya, I am bloody fantastic P-Angel."

"I'm sure you are, Astrid, which is why I need you to take notes during my performance."

"Ok Mrs. I take the notes but I tell you if I don't like." Judith gently ushered her out of the room towards the studio, where I sincerely hoped she would strap her to a bloody seat.

Later when we were on our own, I managed a few snatched minutes with Georgina who'd popped down from the gallery to make sure I was OK. "I've been so obsessed with my own life that I forgot the little people," I told her. "Judith's getting older and has the same issues and insecurities I do – just on a bigger scale, but I managed to console her."

"In the middle of your own personal hell you made Judith feel better about hers," she smiled. "That's what being Tanya Travis is all about."

I smiled, grateful at the compliment. "But on the subject of poor old Judith, I wanted to have a word with you. Along with being paranoid about her age she's got it into her head that you might be in line for her job?"

"Tanya, nothing could be further from the truth," she gasped. "I wouldn't do it if they asked me. I'm really not interested in Judith's job, honestly."

"I'm glad to hear it but she's got herself a bit worked up and I reckon Ray's pushing her out at the behest of the dreaded fourth floor. It's not easy for her, she's a single parent and she's getting on a bit... Well, you know how it is, she needs the job."

"Of course Tanya and if it would be of any help I'll speak with her and tell her as far as I'm concerned, she's safe."

"Thanks. I'd hate her to think I'd spoken to you about it though. I already reassured her and it might make her even more paranoid if she thinks I've been talking about her."

"Of course Tanya but I hate to think she's worrying needlessly."

"She'll be fine. Now, before you whizz off can I just ask... today's Tanya blog? I was thinking... we need to address the 'Nathan stuff,' let's not avoid talking about personal difficulties. After all Oprah never shied away from discussing life with Stedman."

"Absolutely and I hope you don't mind, but after you called me last night I started a short post about going out with someone in the public eye. I thought it would show that you, as always, are considerate of Nathan's point of view and understand that it's not easy for him, especially as the press insist on hounding him and writing these awful stories. So, I've gone for empathy and a little bit of humour in today's post title, which is all about playing second fiddle to a famous person: '*You're a Celebrity, Get me out of Here!*'"

"Oh that is just perfect, spot on."

"No problem, that's what I'm here for. Oh and I've ordered extra Blue Mountain coffee – thought you might need it, given the current situation."

I nodded, closing my eyes, thinking about Nathan and the fact he might already have left me for good – and even Blue Mountain coffee couldn't make that better.

"Tanya, remember: what God takes away, he gives back... in spades."

She had a twinkle in her eye and I looked at her enquiringly.

"You might be having a tough time but I have great news. Brace yourself: Dettol No-Touch Handwash have two new ... yes, you heard me, *two* new fragrances."

"Shut up, girlfriend, you're teasing," I said with a wan smile.

"I don't tease about something as serious as handwash systems. I'm talking Citrus Squeeze and Shea Butter with, wait for it, Rose essence."

"Shea Butter and Rose?" I said, feeling my mood lift. "Please put an order in for industrial quantities of both the citrus and the rose please, Georgina. Now."

"Already done, Tan," she said with a flash of her perfect white teeth.

"Anything else I can do?"

"No, but thank you for making everything so... Well... normal. Everyone else is pussyfooting around pretending the pregnancy/sex-addict stuff never happened."

"You are welcome, Tanya," she said, perfect nail crescents touching perfect lips.

"Georgina, will you also get me some of whatever it is you put on your hair? It always looks... so... young."

"Sure."

"Oh and will you tweet that Nathan and I are still in love but our careers are getting in the way, hashtag sad or something like that."

"Already tweeted Tanya, hashtag heartbroken." She put on a mock sad face.

"Give it time and don't beat yourself up," she touched my arm. "I'm off to the gallery now, Ray thinks I should see the show from every angle," she started to walk away.

"As long as he doesn't want you to see *him* from every angle," I joked.

She smiled, blew me a kiss and wafted off, leaving the scent of fresh cotton and sweet pear drops in her wake.

* * * * *

"You really don't need to go through my script with me, Hermione," I said firmly as she hung over my shoulder, her face far too close to mine, peering at the coffee-stained pages. I was in make-up and even Sally's hands couldn't calm me. "Look, Hermione, I'm best left on my own when I'm busy."

"Oh, no Tanya babes, it's my job to make sure you are happy and I will be with you all morning. I told you, I am your Siamese twin!" she said brightly.

I glanced in horror at Sally as she calmly applied lipstick and raised an eyebrow. Hermione was extremely annoying, like a twittering bird hopping around my face and my feet, making me anxious. For all her nervous energy and irritatingly whiney voice, she didn't actually do anything useful; he'd even managed to get the coffee order wrong.

Sally continued to work on my make-up so I closed my eyes, hoping Hermione would get bored and disappear but when my Tanya Travis face was complete, she was still looming over me. "Ten minutes, Tanya honey!" she trilled. I rolled my eyes, thanked Sally and made for the door but Hermione jumped in front of me, opening the door and ushering me through it like I was an OAP.

"Thanks Hermione, I'm fine from here," I hissed through gritted teeth as I headed for my throne on set. "Tim the floor manager always gives me 90 seconds to acclimatise," I said and as she trotted off to annoy someone else relief washed over me. She'd just gone, completely disappeared. Perfect. However, after only seventeen blissful seconds she was back, commandeering two human beings – our first guests for the show. She smiled proudly, holding them before me like they were specimens for my royal approval. They looked terrified, so I smiled warmly, straightened up and became 'TV Tanya'.

"Good morning," I smiled serenely.

"Now, this is Craig and Britney and they both have a BIG problem," said Hermione, rolling her eyes and openly handing me a bottle of antibacterial gel. I took it quickly, hoping no-one had seen. Hermione then brandished an industrial-sized pack of handi-wipes from her shoulder bag, saying; "Ooh I heard you need these, apparently you get through hundreds of them." I took the pack graciously, while longing to slap her face with it. I quickly secreted the pack behind me on the chair, keeping the 'warm' smile.

"Please sit down, Britney, Craig," I said, motioning to the chairs. Craig heaved his large frame into the chair nearest me and purple-haired, pierced Britney perched on the chair next to him. I was about to start preparing them for what lay ahead when Hermione chipped in again.

"Wait until you hear what these two rascals have been up to," she flapped her hand in their direction and bit her bottom lip in anticipation, all clear lip-gloss and wide eyes like she was reading a really funny story on toddlers' TV. "It all started one wet Thursday afternoon when this lovely little lady was on her computer..." she said, smiling incredulously and gesturing to Britney. Britney glared at her, looking quite scary under all the heavy eye make-up and black lipstick. I would not have described Britney as a 'little lady', either and I was sure she thought Hermione was taking the piss.

"Thanks Hermione, I'll take it from here." I said firmly, with a fixed smile on my face. But Hermione was on a roll. Perhaps it was because her daddy would be watching on the monitor – or perhaps she just didn't know when to shut up.

"Their story is like, sooo amazing, Tan. These two lovely people actually met online and then began a full, sexual relationship. They have three kiddies now..."

"Three whole kiddies?" I heard myself gasp back, before I could stop myself, mocking her girlish tone.

"Yes, but guess what?" She paused for dramatic effect. "They have just discovered that they might be brother and sister! Omigod! Can you believe it?"

"No, I can't believe it."

"They met online you see and then started sleeping together, never thinking for one minute that they might be related..."

"Yes, I can see how that might occur. Thank you, Hermione. We're about to do a rehearsal so would you please..."

"Tanya babes, it's my job today to brief you on all..."

"No, Hermione." I said, a little too loudly then tried to recover.

"Gosh, you have done your research – well done. But I now need to chat to our guests," I smiled, "so they can tell me all about it themselves. On my own." I took a deep breath and gave her my best smile, trying not to lose it in front of the crew, her father and the studio audience, who were chatting quietly whilst they waited for the show to start.

"I like to get to know our guests by chatting to them myself – that's how it works," I said, resisting the urge to add 'you stupid dick's head.' Glancing round, I could see Astrid sitting in the front row, brandishing her notebook. She gave me a thumbs-up. Funny, but I was actually glad she was there, someone on my side, a friendly face in the audience on what was proving to be an awful day.

I liked to start rehearsals at exactly 20 minutes to the hour because that gave me exactly 50 minutes before we went on air. Hermione had now ruined my timings and I was all over the place. I hadn't adhered to my usual routine, I wasn't prepared and she'd stuck to me like glue and driven me insane. As if all that wasn't bad enough, she was now talking me through the rehearsal process, like I'd never done it before. It was one humiliation too far.

After I had chatted to Britney and Craig and been introduced to the other guests on the morning's show, I stood up and excused myself, heading quickly to the nearest bathroom. I turned the taps on full, plunging my hands under the searing-hot water. The relief was temporary though, because within seconds Hermione was banging on the toilet door.

'You've only got two minutes, Tanya," she said, like I didn't know, like I'd never done this before. "It's not long until the show starts and you shouldn't really have left the floor. ' I clung to the basin, taking long, deep breaths.

"Channelling Oprah, channelling Oprah" I whispered to myself, looking at my heavily made-up TV face in the mirror and trying not to crack.

I walked silently back to the set with nine seconds to spare. Feeling completely disorientated, the events of yesterday and this morning whirling round in my head, I sat down with a thump, as Judith counted us in.

"OK Tan. Three, two, one and live, we are live." I turned towards my audience, giving them my best, most sincere smile. "Good morning", I said, "and welcome to *The Tanya Travis Show*."

Once I was actually on air, adrenalin kicked in which exacerbated my feelings of mild panic to the mental equivalent of a high-pitched scream.

"Today, Britney and Craig are waiting for an important announcement," I said dramatically, gesturing towards my first guests. "They are very much in love and they have three children. The only problem is – there's a chance they could be related."

The audience collectively gasped as I tried to compose myself, not helped by the loud 'shitting hell!' comment from my Swedish guest on the front row.

"So, Craig, Britney, let's hear your story," I said, turning to them. When I knew the camera was off me, I discreetly took out a wipe and rubbed it over my hands, between every finger. Usually, once I was on air, Tanya Travis took over, but today it wasn't working. Today, inside I was screaming.

I said little as the sorry tale spilled out over the next few minutes, culminating with a video clip of them both taking a swab for a DNA test, filmed the day before.

"So, er... Britney," I said, trying to compose myself, turning to her and looking serious. "Is the daddy of... erm, your children also an uncle? Are you the mother and the auntie of his?" she looked at me in horror and burst into tears. I wanted to join her in her sobs, but kept going: "Before we find out whether Britney and Craig's children are also cousins, let's ...take a break."

I breathed a sigh of relief as runners came on and handed out water, then cleared cups away. Britney and Craig sat quietly, holding hands, whilst the frantic activity that always happens in ad breaks went on around them. They just wanted to know if they were related or not. I already knew the results of the DNA test that we were spinning out for maximum effect and after the endless ads for fish fingers, cheap loans and lingerie-clad models licking luxury ice-cream lids they would find out that yes – they were brother and sister. I looked at them, sitting silently waiting, hoping against hope that love could triumph over science and I felt a stab of pity. I had to stop myself from grabbing them both and shouting in their faces 'don't wait around until after the ice cream has been licked. In sleeping together, you have been committing an unlawful act for the past five years, so run like the wind before someone calls the cops.' I also wanted to tell them that as 'caring' as us telly people might seem, once the credits went up no-one would give a damn because we had another show tomorrow and I would be busy washing my hands a hundred times and barking at the moon. They had bared their souls and their secrets to millions before being handed the DNA bomb, blowing their lives apart. But it was ok, because in the aftermath they would get a 'Sex with a Sibling' 'Aftercare Fact Sheet' and a train ticket home. Back in their semi, they would be alone with the Pandora's Box we'd ripped open so publicly and carelessly. Trying desperately to rise above my own inner turmoil, I focussed on them – I was the ringmaster of this dark circus and had to milk it for all it was worth.

I checked my timings: one minute 47 seconds before we were due back on air for the results. Hermione was on set again and once more was glued to me. I was sticky with her presence and desperate to lose her.

"Tanya, you OK?" she said, with a patronising little pat. "Tanya?" Again, like I'd never done a show before. Like I couldn't function without her. Like I was losing it.

"You need to spin this one out," she whispered, well within earshot of the couple who were both shaking with fear.

"One minute before we go on air, Tan." I ignored her. I could feel the heat of rage rising up through my neck, my heart was pounding but I continued to look straight ahead. "Show you really care about this. Real emotion please, if you can cry, that would be great." she said, making her way off the set and sitting just out of camera shot,

"Aaaagh," I spat. On the one to ten scale of anxiousness I was now at twelve and we were due back on air in 32 seconds. I could feel angry red blotches rising up beneath my blouse, all over my neck. Disgusting red, nervy blotches that someone like Judith would get, not Tanya Travis. *Oh God, I'd be less than perfect live on air.* How dare Hermione tell me to 'spin this one out' and order me to use 'real emotion.' How dare she ruin my one minute and 47 seconds of timed peace while the ice-cream lid was being licked and before the red light went on.

"Tanya we need to..."

Itchy, dirty hands, red blotches. Hermione's whining, irritating voice, blood pounding in my head again and then the room lost its focus.

"I can't... no..." I whispered to myself.

Filthy palms, cables squirming along the floor like snakes...the studio audience smiling to reveal fangs.

"No. No. No!" I heard myself explode.

"Tanya. Tanya." Judith's voice in my ear, filling my head.

Hermione's eyes were turning scarlet, her tongue pointy like a lizard's, slipping out quickly, lashing me with her words. "Tanya..." she started in the voice of an old hag.

"She wants to know if she's shagging her brother and yes, I'm going to make her wait for it" I shouted at her, rising from my chair. "...like I've done every other morning for the past fifteen years. You've only been here five minutes, don't you dare tell me how to do my fucking job!"

I stopped talking. The air was thick with silence. Hermione backed away, a look of horror on her face. Her chin was trembling and a voice in my ear was whispering something very quietly. "On air, Tanya. We're live on air."

Suddenly everything snapped back into high definition. "Jesus. My mic was on!" I said, looking towards the studio audience who were all staring, open-mouthed.

"We're on air, we've been on air for 40 seconds. Apologise, *apologise*, Tanya," Judith's voice said urgently in my ear.

"Apologise Tanya," I repeated, my mind blank as I tried to gather my scrambled thoughts. What had just happened? Then slowly it revealed itself, the true horror of what had taken place – the ad break was over, it had been over for several minutes and my swearing rant at Hermione had just been broadcast to several million viewers.

TWEET: @TanyaTruth Gr8 show today! Sad 4 Britney + Craig. ☹ but we care @TruthWithTanyaTravis ☺ #Incest #Aftercare #WhenYourLoverIsYourBrother

11

Ray's Roof Garden Revelation

The shame, revulsion and self-loathing felt by those two poor incest survivors on my show that day was nothing compared to mine. I fled back to my dressing room as soon as the show was over, with Astrid hot on my heels. I dialled Nathan while sweeping along the corridors, desperate to hear his voice. The phone rang and rang, then went to voicemail.

"Nathan? It's me. Something terrible happened on the show today. I know you are angry with me but this is an emergency. Please call – I need you." I said, holding back tears.

"Nathan toss-face will not be calling you" said Astrid sadly, with a shake of her head, as we reached my dressing room. "He is selfish wanker. You need help. You need to speak to the bitchy American."

She was right so I called Donna, who had seen the show and was already on her way to the studio. She clearly couldn't wait until we were face to face, so spent much of her four-hour journey ranting over the phone.

"You Kamikaze!" she barked as I lay on the sofa while Astrid dabbed my forehead and rubbed my shoulders with something Swedish to calm me down.

"Donna, it was partly Hermione's fault." I began. "She was behaving like a spoilt brat. She shouldn't have even been there and I don't like her, she was making me worse..."

"Tanya. You are not in some US reality show – she's not Melissa to your Joan Rivers, Ozzy to your Sharon. The viewers want the entertainment from their pond-life. Not their freaking presenter and her staff!"

"Thank you Donna, I get it..."

"So tell me, Tanya. If you get it, why did you lose it, live on air?"

"Pressure, Donna. I've had a terrible time this week... I'd had the morning from hell before I even arrived at the studio."

"Yes, riding on an electric gate – I saw it on YouTube."

"Oh Christ! It's on there already? The gate thing isn't all... Nathan isn't speaking to me, Judith's losing her job and I might be losing Georgina." I said, my voice cracking.

"Whoa. First, I need you to rewind the gold-digger bit for me. Nathan's been sowing his seed round London and getting your name in the papers and it's *him* not talking to *you*? Nice. Ooh don't let HIM go HE'S a keeper."

"It hurt him that I didn't trust him." I said, ignoring her sarcasm and feeling stupid.

"Aw, poor old Nathan. Jeez, Tanya. And he didn't hurt you by getting another woman pregnant? Does he know about the problems you've had in *that* department?""

"He doesn't need to know thank you, we don't want children anyway" I said curtly.

"I don't know what I can do about this, Tanya."

"Donna, you said you'd out-snake the snakes and as long as you were my agent I was safe!"

"Tanya, the snake analogy is hardly fucking relevant now you've had a breakdown and used the F-word on air... But hey, every cloud....you've made Mama a very proud agent today, two hundred thousand hits on YouTube – and counting... and you've finally trended on Twitter, hashtag: 'TanyaTravisLosesIt'."

"So, you've got your dream, Donna," I sighed, clicking open a browser on my laptop to see what she was talking about. "Christ, I'm more than trending, I've gone bloody viral!" Every website, tweet and YouTube post was bursting with my ravaged old face caught mid-rant, either on air or on a gate, take your pick. I turned it off, unable to look at the videos, photos or vile comments. I was devastated, too distraught to cry. I just felt numb.

"So, here's the thing, my little whack-job. Fancy Pants Big New Boss Dickie Truelove isn't answering his phone and Ray the fucking job fairy has gone into hiding."

"Oh, God."

"The press are going bonkers, the phone lines are jammed, Facebook is awash and Twitter is alive. As for Instagram, well you've knocked Rihanna off the top slot... mind you she wasn't photographed straddling a gate at 6am this morning shrieking 'fucking give it to him'."

"Ohhhh." I put my head in my hands. Astrid tutted and pummelled my shoulders in what can only be described as a Swedish massage mugging.

"So. First you bring me an 'engagement special' that doesn't exist, your lover makes another woman pregnant and if that's not enough, you provide dinner and a show from astride a gate followed by a screaming meltdown, live on air. Mama has her work cut out this week, don't she?"

"I'm sorry, Donna. I don't know what to say. What would I do without you?"

"You without me would be crap. Give me lemons, I grab salt and tequila."

Even in my emotional and physical quagmire I could tell Donna was almost getting off on it all. She loved a client challenge, it gave her something to work with, get her teeth into – usually someone's 'ass.'

"Oh no, Donna," I said looking at my Blackberry to see if Nathan had called me back and discovering a reminder text from Ray. "Ray wants a frothy mind-mapping session on his refreshed roof terrace."

"I'll give him fucking frothy refreshment, the spineless little shit. Don't go anywhere near him without me, I want to do a 'mapping session' on his smug face. Sit tight, Mama's on her way."

* * * * *

When Donna arrived, we didn't have time to talk or make any kind of plan, instead we went straight up to see Ray.

"He's going to sack me isn't he? I'm over Donna, aren't I?"

"Fuck knows," she snapped as we walked from the lift.

Ray's secretary, Charles, greeted us, ushering us outside to the garden where Ray was enjoying the early Autumn sunshine and panoramic views of Manchester at a small, wrought-iron table. I spotted the tuft of his hair amid the various green fronds and as we approached he stood, holding a clipboard in one hand, a frothy latte in the other and wearing a pair of ridiculous sunglasses on his head.

"Tanya and the fragrant Donna! I wasn't expecting you too" he said, eyeing her apprehensively. "Welcome to my little Eden." He put down his latte and waited expectantly for air kisses. Neither of us obliged.

"No bullshit, Ray – we need to know where we stand." Donna's tone was clipped and business-like, but it didn't mean that she wouldn't punch him if he said something she didn't like.

Ray gestured for us to sit and Donna promptly opened up her leather folder, laying her Blackberry carefully on the table. She was about to hold a War Cabinet on Ray's fancy garden furniture and there was no time for small talk.

Charles delivered my latte and I grimaced, taking tiny, scalding sips so I could enjoy the pain, which took away the searing numbness I was feeling. "Ray, I'm sorry about what happened on the programme today," I started. "I've been under quite a lot of strain."

"Oh Tanya, you haven't had a day off in fifteen years. It's only to be expected that things will... pile up."

"Yes, thank you for being so understanding." Donna shot me a look.

"So what's the story, Ray?" she was, as always, to the point.

"Erm... what can I say? I know Tanya's under pressure from her personal life, a daily show etc. But today's 'performance', if I may call it that, was extraordinary and gives Dickie no option but to reconsider her future with *The Tanya Travis Show*."

"Yada, yada, Ray... Are you saying she can't continue to present the show named after her, the one she created, developed and gave her life and child-bearing years to?"

"Well, I wouldn't put it quite in those terms..."

"I don't suppose you would," snapped Donna, taking out her Gitanes and allowing Ray to light one for her.

"Look Ray, is there anything I can do to keep my show?" I said, my heart hammering in my chest.

He shook his head slowly. "Ladies, it's a sad fact, there were exciting plans in the pipeline for our Daytime Diva, but after today..."

"I could make an on-air apology, Ray. Let's not hide our flaws, that's what Oprah would say. I could take out an ad in every tabloid if it would help, a *Tanya Anger Management Special*? " I said, trying not to sound desperate. I had sacrificed so much for this show, and I felt sick at the thought of losing it.

"I don't know, Tanya. I am under pressure from the fourth floor. It didn't help that your meltdown was aimed at Dickie's daughter, my love."

I cringed. "I know, Ray. But I was the 'Darling of Daytime' until today. I guarantee your ratings, every single morning. Surely you can fight my corner with the fourth floor?"

"I'm not sure I can, my dear. I'd have to go head to head with Dickie and that's a round in the ring I don't want to have. After all, how can I convince him that you won't once again 'lose it live', as they are calling it on Twitter?"

I could feel myself getting angry now.

"One mistake, Ray, just one, in all the time we have worked together. Surely that's worth a 'round in the ring' with Dickie?"

I was facing Ray, eyeballing him, my anger rising at his weakness but Donna touched my arm. "Tanya, stay calm, this is business... So let your agent handle this in a dignified, calm and business-like way please." Standing up, she slowly leaned forward, grabbed Ray by the lapels and shook him, hard. "Listen, you little shit," she spat, "fifteen flawless fucking years she's given you. Fifteen years of early nights and early mornings knee-deep in pond-life and sexual deviants. Then one fucking morning, Tanya Travis has 'a moment' and you dump her like... like a ... like a filthy nappy... a used syringe..."

I didn't like the analogy but I was more worried about Ray. Donna was in his face, nose to nose – and given that she was a foot taller, his feet must have been off the ground.

"She's spent her youth turning your grotty little Daytime slot into pure gold," she hissed into his face, "and now you've taken everything, you aren't going to fight for her? Well, let me tell you mister, if you take out your tiny dick and piss all over her, guess who's gonna be pissing right back at ya?"

I kept quiet. I wasn't quite sure whose piss she was threatening him with but now wasn't the time to ask.

"Oh dear... No, no, no-one will be pissing on anyone ...not here on the designer roof terrace, it's Astro Turf you know, and any kind of bodily fluid would just..."

"I could kill you on the spot, you weak little tosser," Donna snapped, plonking back down onto her seat and letting Ray go. "Tanya Travis is flesh and blood. She's not perfect, she's not young and gorgeous, her love life's pretty shit... Hell who am I kidding? It's a fucking plane wreck. Consequently, amoeba-brain, the audience can *relate* to her. She has all the pressures our viewers struggle with. Any TV company worth its salt would use it to their advantage – it's fucking *publicity* Ray. Let's do this. Let's make it work *for* us..."

"Sorry... No can do." He moved his chair back, lest she be tempted to lunge for him again; one of his eyes was twitching and his arms were ready to defend his face at any moment. "There'll always be room for a taste of Tanya somewhere on the channel, Donna. After all, a spicy, sizzling dish can be too rich and we'll always want a good old reliable baked-potato on the side."

"For Christ's sake!" Donna glared at Ray. "I can see what's really going on here. You aren't kidding anyone Ray. The fourth floor don't want anyone on screen over forty, including the presenter."

Ray shifted awkwardly. "Look Donna, Tanya just needs to take a holiday. Some resuscitation here, a little defibrillation there; it's not a job for Intensive Care ... just a patch up in A & E."

"Ray, I'm tired and I don't want to have to shake you again. What the fuck are you talking about? What's the bottom line – does she keep her show, or not?"

"Er... as a result of today's little problem, a decision has been made to 'refresh' the Daytime brand," he said, cringing, waiting for the blow. "Though no-one's saying anyone's too old or past-it or whatever the phrase is, if you know where I'm coming from?"

"Yes, I know exactly where you're coming from, Ray" said Donna, stubbing her fag out in his empty latte glass, "and I know where we are going, too... To the papers. We will hang you out to dry, you little worm. See ya there." Donna grabbed her file and nodded at me to get up.

Devastated, I stood on wobbly legs intending to walk away but had to hold on to Donna so I wouldn't fall. Ray stared intently down at his drained latte in silence as we started to walk towards the door. Everything was hazy; I just propelled myself forward and gripped Donna very tightly. As we reached the door, I could see Ray's assistant Charles answering the phone in his office, probably booking him some expensive lunch with bloody Dickie. And then I saw something that stopped me in my tracks. Realisation snaked down my throat and entered my bloodstream along with the hot skinny latte. In Charles's office, stacked neatly against the floor-to-ceiling window were thousands of white mugs and Frisbees. As I looked closer through the glass, I saw that there was a face printed on each mug: a caring, beautiful face, smiling out in empathy. Under the face, the caption '*Time for Truth*" was emblazoned in red. It was the branding I had been so resistant to, that I had argued with Ray about. And there was another problem – the face on the mug wasn't mine. The beautiful, caring face smiling out at me was – *Georgina's*.

"Do you see what I see?" I almost whispered in shock to Donna, who was open-mouthed.

"Assholes. They were planning to dump you all along. What happened today gave them an excuse to terminate your contract, but honey, those mugs weren't made this morning. You were already on the way out."

I turned back towards Ray but he couldn't meet my eyes. Donna spun on her killer heels and stepped towards him. "I'll make him wish he was never born, the little tosser!" she snarled.

I put my hand on her arm. "Don't, Donna." I said quietly. "It's done now. It's over." My eyes were wet and despite wobbly legs and blurred vision, I walked away from Ray, away from the show and away from everything I'd spent my life trying to build. And at exactly 4.17pm, for the last time, Tanya Travis left the building.

GOSSIPBITCH: *Which Daytime Diva is joining her former guests in the benefits office after being sacked by both her boyfriend and her show? How will she pay for all those expensive facials and Botox now she can't even pay her mortgage?*

12

Viral Cellulite and a Promise of Prime-Time

"I did this to myself," I said to Donna as she, Astrid and I stepped into the waiting car, reliable Arthur as quiet as ever in the driving seat.

"No, it's not completely your fault. You know me, sweet-cheeks, I'm nothing if not honest and if this was all your doing, I would have had you strung up. The truth is the fucking fourth floor probably started looking for a younger presenter on your fortieth birthday and whatever you say, THAT was quite a few years ago, honey. Georgina fits the package and it was a matter of time before you were dead meat. She's young, beautiful, blonde, intelligent..."

"Thanks" I said tartly, cutting her off. "And I'm only 41."

"You crazy fool, you lie to yourself." Astrid was sat between us, handbag on her podgy knees.

"She's right," Donna nodded. "Moving on is part of life and you have to face it."

"I can't believe that Georgina would go along with this." I said, shaking my head sadly.

"Georgina-schmina," Donna lisped (it didn't really work but she let it hang). "It's life honey. As my mama always said, what goes around comes around and it does. You screwed another forty-something just like you once upon a time."

She was right. All those years ago, when *Good Mornings with Jenny Randle* became *The Tanya Travis Show* poor Jenny must have felt just like I did now.

Donna was now checking her Blackberry for emails, texts, trends and tweets and suddenly sat bolt upright, staring at the screen.

"Tanya, my little nut-job, please can you tell Mama why the hell you've just tweeted the whole world a picture of your big old fanny?"

My mouth went dry. "What?"

Astrid looked over at the phone in Donna's hand and shook her head.

"You shit-face Americans, you don't speak the English properly. This is not her fanny, it's her ass. With the orange peel.

I snatched the Blackberry and stared at the screen. There was no dialogue, just a big old picture of me baring my big old cellulite-covered, English arse.

"How the hell...where's this come from?" I started, but then I remembered. The night Nathan and I rowed about the issue of *Hello!* I'd emailed that picture to Georgina and asked her to make me a lipo appointment. As I watched, it was followed quickly by another tweet.

TWEET: @TanyaTruth Oops! Meant for my surgeon. #Embarrased #NeedAtkins.

"That bitch!" I exploded. "She's got access to my Twitter account and she's tweeted a picture of my cellulite to the world then tried to make it look like a mistake! I'll kill her, I'll...I'll..." But what would I do? What could I do? I dropped the Blackberry into Donna's bag and stared out of the window.

"Tanya, why did you do the mooning with your ass?" Astrid asked, genuinely.

"I'll explain later, Astrid. Right now I need a very hot shower." I said miserably

"You need more than that, now you've dropped your pants in the Twittersphere," Donna said, lighting a cigarette and opening the window. She stuck her head out and took a deep drag.

"Tell me what to do, Donna." I coughed through a lungful of smoke.

Astrid and I both looked at her, waiting in anticipation for the answer that would solve all the problems.

"OK. OK." She smoked in silence for six minutes, then flicked her ciggie and closed the window, hair everywhere. "So, here's Donna's five star, bulletproof, SAS-style rescue plan."

"Thank God the American knows what to do," said Astrid, resting her chin on her hand in anticipation, "even if her hair now looks like cat's arse."

"Go on, what's your plan?" I asked, leaning sideways so I could see Donna behind Astrid's head.

"How would you like to get away from it all, be on prime-time TV, change the viewers' perception of you, turn your career around and be paid a fortune?"

"Fucking hell yes, do big birds fly?" Astrid yelped.

"That sounds great." I said cautiously. "Is it the Beeb job you mean?"

"Oh no, my little psycho, I think it's safe to say that ship has sailed. I called them seconds after your meltdown, hoping to get a contract signed, sealed and delivered before it was everywhere in the known universe. I hate to tell you this but it was online so quickly I smell a rat... Someone from the production team must have posted the whole thing. Anyone who missed the live version can catch up on YouTube, along with 'Gate-gate' and probably now, a lovely shot of your cellulite-riddled ass. Ain't technology grand?"

I banged my head repeatedly on the window.

"This offer sweet-cheeks is all you've got, and it's a good one. I think you know what it is."

"Oh, is it The *Countdown*? Is Tanya new number-lady Carol?"

"No Astrid, it's not as good as that," I sighed. "It's 'I'm a Celebrity get me out of the fucking Spa'. No way."

"Hello? Earth calling Tanya?" Donna said, "a) this is exactly what you need: fresh air, a change of scene and b) you have no money, so no other option."

I stopped banging my head and gazed out of the window; we were nearly home, thank God.

"Someone tweeted that I was a barren, diva bitch this morning."

"Ah the magic of Twitter," Donna smiled, taking another cigarette from her bag and winding down the window.

"I do hundreds of great shows, help people and say stuff I'm really proud of and no-one notices. Then a couple of things happen and the world is talking about me... but not in a good way."

"Yep, and now you only have to google 'Menopause Meltdown' or 'Tanya Travis cellulite' and you have all the material you need at your fingertips, my little global phenomenon."

I felt sick thinking about how fast everything had changed, how exposed I'd become. Two weeks before, I'd been riding high, winning awards with a vintage-glamour themed wedding on the horizon. I was turning down reality programmes with C-listers up mountains thinking I didn't need it – I had a great show and a great life. Meanwhile, as I happily surfed the Prada website and endured loud lunches with Donna, the fourth floor had been grooming Georgina and Nathan was impregnating some blonde. Now I was single, with no money, no career and no hope of getting another job. I would have to sell the house, let Astrid go and say goodbye to my bespoke orangery with its views of parterre gardens and undulating lawns.

We pulled up outside the house and got out. Donna played with her Blackberry as I opened the door, making little muttering sounds and no doubt hoping I'd ask what she was looking at.

"You're my agent Donna. What's your advice? Isn't there something in my contract that says they can't get rid of me?" I said, throwing my keys onto the hall table and taking off my jacket.

She walked through and sat down at the kitchen oasis. "Yes, there probably is something in your contract about giving notice, but I guess there's also something in the small print stating you won't shout 'fucking give it to him' atop a moving twelve-foot gate in front of the world's press, or scream and swear at the production team while live on air."

"Ok, leave it. Just don't mention it again... or anything else, Donna."

I ground coffee and she shut up for a whole 54 seconds. I think she got the message.

"I know this might hurt but my guess is that all the stuff going to the press about your private life came straight from Georgina," said Donna thoughtfully, as the coffee machine whirred.

"What?"

"Well, it adds up. She knew every detail about you, every day, and it certainly helped her cause to get bad stuff out there."

My heart skipped: "So it was Georgina behind all the Nathan stories?"

"Not necessarily. I ain't sayin he's innocent honey, so don't go all dewy-eyed but the 'nine-times-a-night-Nathan' stories didn't do her any harm. I suppose we'll never know."

I started to cry. I couldn't help it. I'd pushed Nathan away by not trusting him and believing some 'kiss and tell' story from a stupid young blonde and now it looked like Georgina might have been out to get me; I'd been the stupid one. There was no-one except Donna in the world that I could trust and she wasn't exactly the warmest, cuddliest person on the planet.

"Tanya, you are so sad, I get out the box of *Kardashians* and we watch later, yeah?" Astrid's head appeared round the door. Yes and I also had Astrid, and her TV box sets.

"Look. There's nothing I can say to make it better or make it go away. If I could, believe me I would." Donna said, putting her arm awkwardly around me. She was trying for gentle and caring, but as it was so unusual for her to behave like this it came over as vaguely sinister.

"My advice is to ride the waves, accept *Celebrity Spa Trek*, make sure everyone loves you – and come back to prime-time applause."

She moved her arm from my shoulder and picked at her nails. She did that when she was nervous – which wasn't often.

"So? Whaddya say? Shall I call the *Spa* people and get you on that first plane outta dodge?"

"I can't leave now, what about Nathan?"

"What about him? He's a creep."

"I know you think I'm crazy but I believe there's still a chance for us and I know he still cares about me. I love him."

"That's up to you. Personally I wouldn't trust him as far as I could throw him. He's a cheater and whether or not it was Georgina telling the press, I told you there's no smoke without fire. Give it some space... if it's meant to be... and all that crap. Anyway, who knows, if you're up some mountain thousands of miles away, he might actually miss you? Let's face it, he loves the limelight, he'll miss that at least."

It was indeed starting to look like a rescue package. I couldn't think of anything in the world I wanted to do less – but Nathan wasn't offering to meet up any time soon and I wasn't exactly overwhelmed with job offers, so why stick around? Perhaps Donna was right, perhaps I needed space. And there was plenty of that halfway up a mountain, with no mobile signal.

"OK, so do we have a deal?" She rubbed her hands together and I nodded, discreetly turning on the kitchen tap. My hands had never felt so dirty in my life.

TWEET: @TanyaTruth: Sooo excited:) Off 2 beautiful Nepal 4 Celebrity Spa Trek. Can't wait! #CelebritySpaTrek #Nepal #LuckyMe

Part 2

13

We Have Lift Off...and Appelkaka

There were three screaming children in the business class lounge. The youngest, a little boy, was throwing a tantrum that an A-list diva could only aspire to. I shuddered and looked away. My head was throbbing, the plane was delayed and I just knew the flight to Nepal would be hellish. I had been swept up in Donna's enthusiasm and had agreed to this out of sheer panic. I wasn't totally convinced that leaving the remnants of my life and career to try and regain it in another country was the answer. I'd lost my job, my fiancé and even my beautiful home was now hanging in the balance. I'd extended the mortgage repayments to cover the cost of Nathan's sound studio – a stupid thing to do at the best of times but now, with no income, I couldn't actually meet the monthly payments. Donna was looking after everything while I was away and warned me things would be tough. It didn't look like I'd be able to enjoy my Marston and Langinger bespoke orangery for much longer. Just thinking of the way the fading gold light of evening played upon the toffee rattan and Oka cushions in washed linen brought a tear to my eye. I stood up and stretched, checking the board to see if there was any progress on the flight. From the corner of my eye I could see Astrid, tucking into the 'complimentary' business class food and I noted that she was already on her second glass of wine. "Tanya!" she beamed at me from across the room. "They have the appelkaka," she waved a wedge of cake at me. "I am loving this free shit!"

I sipped my drink and buried my head in my copy of *Vogue* to avoid the glares of the businessmen and the outraged expression on the face of the toddler terror's mum; perhaps bringing Astrid hadn't been such a good idea after all. I leafed through the mag, hoping it would have a calming effect but even 'Catwalk Ready Cruise Wear' and the herbal aroma of my favourite gin couldn't take my mind off my troubles – and we were only at the airport. There was a whole ten days of *Celebrity Spa Trek* horror to get through yet. Astrid came over with a laden plate and threw herself down beside me.

"I am loving being your PA, Tanya Travis!" she beamed. "Thank you for having me... Would you like a bite of my knackerbrod?"

I waved away the laden crisp-bread she held at my face. "Yes, well you're only my PA until I leave for the base camp," I said. "Times may be hard but I refuse to look like a total Z-lister and everyone else will have an assistant. I need some sort of entourage – even if it's only you, Astrid," I said, with images of the Beckhams and their travel posse swirling round in my head.

"This knackerbrod is gooood," she said, smiling, a face full of cream cheese and dill. Donna had insisted to the production company that I flew business class and when I invited her along to assist, Astrid couldn't have said yes more quickly. Finally after what seemed like an age, our flight was called. As we swept past all the economy class passengers, Astrid strode ahead of me. "Excuse me, toss-faces, Tanya Travis coming through!" she yelled as we made our way to the gate.

"Astrid!" I hissed, "Stop it! When I said I needed a PA, I didn't mean the type that actually made announcements."

She looked at me, puzzled. "You are the celebrity, Tanya. I am just making sure that the paps know for the photo, yes? Like that man he does it on the Kardashians' show."

I put my head down and hoped no-one would recognise me but I could already see mobile phones being taken out of pockets to take clandestine pictures of the fallen talk-show host. We got to the gate and boarded quickly. "I have never turned left on a plane before!" said Astrid, her eyes shining. "Always before, I turn to the right." At first I thought something was lost in translation and then I realised: Astrid had always flown economy. The thought that one day soon I too might be forced to 'turn right' made my blood run cold but I tried to banish such thoughts from my head. There was only so much I could take and I put on my Tanya-Travis-smile mask to greet the stewardesses as I made my plane entrance.

Once we were settled we soon took off. As we soared through thick, chalky white clouds, my chest thudded and my fingers itched to be scrubbed.

"Wow they have mother-shit TV, Tanya!" Astrid exclaimed, as the plane climbed up over the sea and away from everything I knew. She was flicking through the in-flight entertainment. "Look. So many good shows! Big Fat Losers and seasons of America's Next Hot Model. Oooh and Sexy in the City with Jessica Sarah Parkerson is here also. I will be a busy PA, Tanya," she sighed, like she'd died and gone to heaven.

I looked out of the window at the silent, soft clouds below and reflected on how, in a matter of days, my life had been transformed. All the invites to premieres, product launches and fashion shows had dried up overnight and when I Googled myself, the highest ranked results were YouTube clips of 'Gate-gate', my outburst at Hermione, pictures of my naked buttocks and lurid articles in the tabloids about *'Tanya's Toy-boy Lover's Baby'* or how my career was in ruins, along with my backside. And to add insult to injury someone was making a killing as all this was usually accompanied by ads for cellulite or wrinkle cream. I had tried to resist reading about myself but it was addictive. That morning before I left, the awful showbiz news website GOSSIPBITCH was leading with:

Which former Daytime Darling is off to the spa today to cleanse her sins and win back her fans? It will take more than a mudmask to save her!

I closed my eyes and pressed my head against the window. I missed Nathan; I missed him with an ache that sat on my chest like a big rock and never went away.

I turned to Astrid, who was engrossed in an underwater modelling assignment with Tyra Banks and 12 wannabe-top-models. I ordered another gin and popped a Valium from the emergency section of my handbag. Within minutes, the whirring of the engines and the calming alcohol anaesthetised the pain and I slept.

TWEET: @TanyaTruth So excited 2 see Himalayas + make lovely new friends on @CelebritySpaTrek #NewChapter #HimalayanAdventure.

* * * * *

After an 18-hour journey with one stop over in Abu Dhabi, Astrid and I found ourselves standing in Tribhuvan Airport, Kathmandu, amid chaos and confusion. After what felt like a lifetime waiting at the poorly-ventilated passport controls, we were spewed out from the airport, into a cacophony of clatter and noise. Porters dressed in long robes shouted and gesticulated at us, while an alarmed Astrid repeatedly told them to 'shit off,' referring to them loudly as 'tit bags'.

Suddenly, through a sea of saris and colour, I spotted a board being held aloft with '*Tanya Travis*' on it. "This way, Astrid!" I barked, needing to take control of the situation. I was propelled towards the board by the crowds and almost forced into the arms of the young man holding it.

"Hey... Tanya Travis!" he yelled above the noise.

"Hello, I'm sorry, it's just so crazy here, I didn't mean to lunge," I said.

"Hey that's OK with me, Tanya Travis. I like older women throwing themselves at me. I'm Paul," he said, shaking my hand with one hand while still waving the board aloft with the other.

"This is my clean... I mean my PA, Astrid." I said, with an imperious wave of my hand.

He repeated her name and winked at her. "This way," he smiled, setting off through the chaos. I tutted to myself as I ran after him; I wished the TV companies wouldn't send runners to collect the talent – it would have been nice to be greeted by the producer.

Paul seemed pleasant enough but his hair had been sprayed or waxed into a shape that suggested he'd been standing in a wind-tunnel. I wouldn't allow a member of staff on my show to have so sloppy an appearance, I thought – then felt a stab of pain as I remembered for the millionth time, *I didn't have a show any more*.

"You can put the board down now," I said gently, not wanting to draw attention to myself at the airport; autograph- hunters and photographers popped up everywhere. Paul was looking at me quizzically.

"You *are* with *Celebrity Spa Trek*?" I confirmed, firmly grabbing the board and taking it from him.

"Yeah, I am. Hey, wait till I tell my mum you're on the show, she's your biggest fan, Tanya." My heart sank and I set my rictus TV-grin. So much for all that tweeting and rapping and getting down with the kids. I was still the favourite with Mums everywhere.

"This show's gonna be amazin'," he yawned as I handed him my cases.

"I hope you're right, Paul, I need a bit of 'amazin'' in my life just now." I could see he was going to be one of those kids who needed guidance. I rolled my eyes at Astrid and she smiled brightly, as usual missing the point. She had a twinkle in her eye as she looked at Paul. That was the last thing I needed – my mad-cleaner-pretend-PA fancying the runner.

"Are you sure you've got enough luggage?" he asked, trying to be funny as he struggled under the weight of my Louis Vuitton.

Making sarcastic remarks to me about my luggage didn't put him in my good books from the get-go. I was irritated by his attitude but Hermione had told *The Sun* how bossy I was with young employees, so I figured Paul might be an opportunity for me to look less bossy and more caring. It was my chance to be seen guiding him through the production maze and helping him to become a better runner – and a better person.

As we headed towards the door, I linked arms with him so he could manoeuvre me through the maelstrom. The airport was a mouth, spitting out fresh tourists to the beggars who were waiting outside for money, like kids at the penny falls machines but I couldn't look. I climbed into the waiting car, averting my eyes from the dirty little children with deformed limbs and outstretched hands. "Who else will be on the show?" I asked Paul, once we were both inside the cracked leather back-seat of what the driver proudly referred to as, 'the limo'.

The names of celebrities who would be on the show had so far been kept a secret from the press and I was eager to know who I'd be sharing a tent – or God forbid – a hammock with.

"No-one's tellin' who's on the show – they think it's cool if the celebs meet on camera. It's just so – *random*."

"Great!" I snapped. As a member of the production team I guessed Paul would know and was just refusing to say. "I've only ever seen one episode of the programme before so I don't really know what to expect." I said. "So I will need you to keep me abreast of events, ideally before they happen."

"Ha! I'm not fucking *psychic*!"

"I'm not suggesting you are. But I think the least you can do is let me know what's happening and when, so I can be prepared."

"Hey, I'll do what I can but it's always a ride. Last year a sex-change footballer turned up in drag; I thought I'd dropped acid. They was all well surprised. I pissed myself laughin'!"

"Oh, I imagine that was nice, you laughing and pissing at him!" I said crossly, holding my ostrich-leather Prada tote (with detachable shoulder-strap) tight to my chest as we bumped along the appalling roads. "Well, you're going to be very disappointed this year if you think I'm going to drag up, piss myself or drop acid," I said, grandly.

"You won't be disappointin', Tan," said Paul with a grin. "You are one hilarious chick. No shit. I saw that video you tweeted of your arse. Bloody funny...and it's not a bad arse for an old lady, if you know what I mean," he nudged me. I clenched my buttocks and clutched my Prada.

Astrid giggled. I held my breath, waiting for her unadulterated thoughts on the condition of my arse but she seemed quite dumbstruck by Paul. I'd never known her so quiet – I just wished she would aim a little higher than the bloody runner.

"But the gate? Tanya, when you got up on that gate...there's nothing you won't do to get yer picture in *The Sun*..." he continued, shaking his head at what he considered to be my sheer desperation for publicity.

"I didn't climb the gate to get my picture in the papers, for God's sake!" I spat. "I couldn't find the key to the power box and...I... Oh, what's the use in explaining?"

"'Gate-gate got you LOADS of followers on Twitter... then you lost it on your show. Jeez." He started pressing buttons on his phone to find it. "What a laugh, the funniest I've ever eyeballed...have you eyeballed it on You Tube?"

"I don't need to. I was there."

"It went fucking viral, didn't it?"

"Did it?" I said, feigning indifference. "I don't really do social networking. My assistant Georgina used to do it for me. I still don't know how to put anything on to the YouTube," I sighed, picking at a bit of errant fluff on my white linen cruise trousers.

"Yeah? No shit. And now she's got your show, she's the star? I reckon you was unlucky...whoa, here you go..." he giggled, and passed his phone to Astrid in the front seat so she might once more enjoy the spectacle of me straddling a gate and yelling abuse at the top of my voice .. When they'd passed the phone back and forth and both watched it a couple of times and had a good old laugh we all sat in silence. The car continued to bump along and the journey was beginning to feel like a fairground ride. I gripped Paul's arm as our brakes screeched in front of a cow wandering in the middle of the road. Taxi drivers were bleeping their horns and people were hanging out of their fume-sputtering rickshaws.

"When I saw you was on the list, I thought you might bring your fella," Paul said, looking across for my reaction.

"Nathan? Well it may have escaped your notice, but it's called *CELEBRITY Spa Trek* – and he's not a celebrity, is he?" I snapped.

"Yeah, he is. Nathan Wells is a legend... Ten women in one night? He'll be on *Celebrity Big Brother* next year."

"It was nine actually," I hissed, like one less made a difference. "Don't believe what the papers say. Nathan isn't a sex addict, whatever *The Daily Star* are saying... I want you to make that clear to everyone, the rest of the celebrities and the viewers. Is that clear?"

He looked vacant, which was nothing new.

"Have you been making notes Paul?"

"No."

"Then find a notepad and pen please."

"OK."

I took a sly, sideways glimpse. He was pierced in places I didn't know he could be and covered in tattoos. TV had certainly gone downhill since I first started in the early 90's. This young man had been employed to look after celebrities, the least he could do was take out his body jewellery and comb his bloody hair! I heard my mother's voice saying just that and felt very old.

TWEET: @TanyaTruth: Just arrived in beautiful Nepal. So happy 2 be here at last. Can't wait 2 get 2 spa #CelebritySpaTrek #Kathmandu

14

Hog Plums at the Yak and Yeti

"Please don't beat me, Tanya Travis," joked Tiffany, the 'hilarious' twenty-something researcher who greeted me at the hotel's reception while holding a clipboard to her face like a shield in mock fear.

"Is there someone to carry my bags?" I asked, ignoring her comments.

"Yes, but you have just one night of luxury tonight so make the most of it, my lovely." She said, handing me my keys.

"Good. I'm tired after the flight."

"Oh, you can't go to bed yet, Tanya. As soon as you have unpacked you have to come straight back down here. There's a press launch in an hour, so we want you bright eyed and bushy tailed asap. You are meeting the rest of the celebrities tonight and it's all gonna be filmed. So no sneaking off to bed early, sweetheart."

I smiled, while resisting an almost uncontrollable desire to smack her in the face. I gripped my tote so I didn't give in to my violent urges. "Thank you, Tiffany," I said. "Come along, Astrid." And with that, we moved at a dignified pace towards the lobby lifts.

The strangely-named hotel, The Yak and Yeti, was in fact rather spectacular and five-star. I felt a deep sense of loss as I admired the palm frond and fountain-filled atrium and remembered that I only had one night there. All cool, white marble and sweeping staircases, there was a strong sense of Nepal's cultural heritage in the grand décor and paintings of old royals. Astrid was clearly captivated by the faded elegance and gilded glamour of it all.

"Ooh Tanya, I want to always be having your PA job. This is fucking hot stuff!" She twirled around as I staggered along with the cases. I clicked my fingers to attract a porter but they all seemed to have the same attitude problem as Paul, sauntering towards us lethargically, shaking their heads from side to side and smiling blandly. We eventually arrived upstairs, where Astrid and I had rooms next to each other. I was escorted into mine, the 'Shangri-La' room; it had a fresh feel and was pale in the lamplight, with big, bulky wooden furniture. I wondered if this was the best room available; I hoped none of the other celebs had a better room than me. A welcome drink tray lay on the side near the huge TV cabinet and I gratefully picked up the cool jug and poured myself some of the drink, which tasted like rhubarb smoothie but I later learned was in fact Nepalise Hog Plum Smoothie bright greenish yellow, slightly tart and quite delicious.

There was a knock on the door and when I answered it, Astrid stood there, all excited. "Shall I come and do the make-up in your room Tanya? This is big launch with celebrity, we need to look sexy hot, yes?" I had been looking forward to at least half an hour of peace, but this was all new to Astrid and I thought I should really help her.

"Yes, alright Astrid, give me ten minutes for a shower and then knock," I said, magnanimously.

Ten and a half minutes later, there was a knock at my door. I opened it to see Astrid in a very tight white dress with a huge blue flower in her hair. A matching bloom was pinned to her chest and I looked down to see that the dress barely covered her rounded knees.

"I come to do your make-up. I bring my best dress, Tanya," she smiled, so pleased with her outfit.

I couldn't let her go downstairs looking like that.

"Oh I'm sorry Astrid, I didn't tell you but I think tonight, it's long dresses only," I lied.

"Oh, what the shit? I will look like a dildo..."

Literally, I thought.

"I know, I know. I should have told you. I forgot."

"Tanya, no problem. I have very long nightie – no-one will know." She was about to turn round and go back to her room to put on her nightwear, when I grabbed her by the arm.

"No. No, Astrid. I have the perfect dress, you can borrow it."

I pulled her into the room, shut the door and began rummaging in my case. I soon found what I was looking for, a loosely-fitted, dark blue evening dress I'd brought with me for my 'fat days.' I threw it at Astrid and within seconds she had taken hers off and was squeezing her ample hips into the now-tight blue satin.

"Fuck me, Tanya, it's tight on my tits," she smiled.

"Yes it is," I said, slightly enviously; "but as long as you don't breathe, you'll be fine." I gently pulled the flower from her hair and re-arranged the long blonde mane, which – with a little TLC – was quite pretty. I stood back and admired my creation; Astrid didn't look half bad.

"Come on, let me do your make-up," I said, patting the stool by the dressing table.

"But Tanya, I am your PA. You don't do my face... I do yours."

"Yes, but I've seen what you do with blusher and it's not Halloween. I'd say it's in both our interests that I make up our faces tonight."

By the time we arrived downstairs, Astrid looked like a young, very voluptuous Britt Ekland. In contrast, I had rushed my Audrey Hepburn eye make-up and as I was also feeling a little queasy. I felt less '50's-film-star gamine glamour', more 'heroin-chic'.

I felt a flutter of nerves when we got downstairs. Tiff saw me and reached out her arms to hug me, but on seeing my face thankfully thought better of it. I wasn't in the mood to be lolloped over by an exuberant teen researcher and she knew it.

"Welcome, Tanya," she smiled, walking me towards a small room. "This is your 'holding area'. You will hang out here until it's time for you to meet the other celebrities. You'll see lights outside, in the courtyard area and that's where the introductions will happen. Go and get a drink and I'll give you a shout when it's your turn."

"Thank you, Tiffany."

"Oh and one other thing, Tanya. You need to surrender any phones, Blackberrys, smart phones et cetera to me."

"Sorry – what?" I said in horror.

"Well, this show relies on the element of surprise. So no connection with the outside world once you are there!" she said brightly.

I digested this piece of horrifying information, thanked her and turned towards the room. Anyway, there's nothing like a bit of sheer decadence to take a girl's mind off things and I soon forgot about mobile phones on entering the 'Dynasty Crystal Room', where I felt right at home. Perhaps the experience wasn't going to be so bad after all? The room was a study in old-fashioned opulence: all linen cloths, glittering chandeliers and antique mirrors. *If only I could spend the next ten days here*, I thought. I couldn't enjoy it for long, though, as I felt a sudden jolt of nausea and made a quick detour into the toilets directly to my left. I leant over the sink, breathing hard.

"Hey Tanya Travis," I heard, and turned to see a curtain of blonde hair disappearing into a cubicle with a giggle. I knew that voice, but couldn't quite place it. I counted to 40, waiting for the rustle of toilet paper, the sound of the flush and the cubicle door opening, the click of heels, then...

"I'm not a ghost, Tanya. It's me."

"Oh my God! I didn't recognise you...the hair. You're blonder... Cindi," I gasped to CC Starr, who began shushing her hair and smiling into the mirror.

Blonde, beautiful CC had once been my pink-haired assistant on *The Tanya Travis Show*. It didn't go so well as Cindi's laid-back attitude and inability to understand simple instructions combined with a total lack of IT knowledge brought with it too many problems. After a very short time, Cindi was moved to 'special projects' and Georgina stepped in as my new assistant.

I looked at CC Starr and marvelled at the transformation from flaky, unsophisticated twenty-something to Page 3 blonde. I suddenly remembered reading somewhere that CC Starr's ascent to fame was due to her 'association' with a well-known boy band. All of them. At the same time. Apparently, she was feeling energetic one evening and having met them all in a hotel bar decided to enjoy each and every one of them. The six-some had been filmed and then, as happens these days, was soon posted on the Internet. The *CC Starr Sex Tape* had been enjoyed at home, online, Facebooked, tweeted, re-tweeted and Youtubed through cyberspace. She had been on her way up, but it was only when CC bagged a Premier League footballer that her celebrity status was confirmed forever and ever amen.

Our eyes met in the bathroom mirror. Cindi was watching me, watching her.

"Didn't you know it was me?" she said, shocked.

"No. I had heard about the...erm...online, boy-band...incident? But I didn't realise you were CC Starr... You look so different."

"Yeah, management made me have a makeover and as I'm Cindi Charlotte, CC is now my stage name. Well, my sex-tape name," she giggled.

"Of course," I said, like it was the most natural thing in the world to make a sex-tape and use your initials to market it.

"I bet you're surprised to see me here, aren't you?" she went on. "Just think, this time two years ago I was your assistant and now I'm a big celebrity... Isn't it funny?"

"Hilarious."

I looked at the long hair, the tan, the high heels – the complete transformation. Funny, flaky little Cindi had reinvented herself and was riding high, while I was on my way down.

"You OK, Tan?" she asked as I leant against the sink, trying to get my breath back. I nodded.

"I hope this trip sorts out – stuff for you... after losing your show and that," she started, while washing her hands.

"Oh, it was time to move on." I smiled with gritted teeth, turning the hot tap on full.

"Yeah, sometimes the maddest stuff turns out to be the answer. I was totally lost," she said, gazing ahead, twisting her hair extensions round her fingers to give them life. "The sex-tape saved me, really. Once it was out there in the Twittersphere, an agent called me and booked all these deals with the lads' mags. Then I signed up with a management company who put me in reality shows. Then I went out with Mike, you know, Mike Chilcott, the footballer? Anyway, that didn't work out so I am now single and ready for the spa!" she said.

"Great," I said, with a big fake smile.

"How's Nathan?" she asked suddenly. "He's got his sex addiction now, hasn't he?" she said, like his 'sex addiction' was a newly acquired possession he carried under his arm at all times; his own, little toilet bag of 'sex addiction.'

"He's not... He never..." I stuttered. The soap had run out, so I moved to the next sink. "I mean, it's not true, any of it." I said, trying to make light of the situation. "If you believe everything you read, Nathan had sex with half of Manchester!"

"He did, didn't he?"

"No Cindi. According to the *papers*, he did – and you and I both know that what the papers print and what is true are two different things." I said, irritated.

"No. Honest Tanya, it's true. He's a right one. I know some of the girls who..."

"I don't mean to be rude but it's not really any of your business, Cindi," I said curtly, stopping her mid-sentence. I didn't want to hear any more. "And anyway, the papers exaggerate. I mean, how many boy-band members did they say you took in one sitting? Six? Surely that's not physically..."

"Ooh Tanya, you are funny – one sitting? Ha! Yeah, course it's true, the papers were spot on, six in one 'sitting'." She giggled to herself, shaking her head at my comedy gem, then concentrating hard on the serious stuff of applying thick, sticky lip-gloss and pouting at the mirror.

"My mate was a sex addict," she said, returning to subject and screwing the lip-gloss lid back on. I concentrated on washing my hands, hoping she'd get the hint that it wasn't a conversation I was keen to dwell on.

"Oh, my life! His girlfriend went through it. All night, every night, Tan...on all fours, over the kitchen units, up the back of..."

"Nathan's not like that. Can we please move on, Cindi?" I said in my best, regal Tanya Travis voice, trying to hold it together.

She turned and peered at me through flapping false lashes.

"Is it off then?"

"What?"

"You know, the fairytale, vintage, country-house wedding with Vera Wang dress and tiered, bridal fairy-cakes made by hand by Stella Weston at The Cake Fairy? I saw it in *Hello!*"

"I don't know," I sighed, sadness sweeping over me like a wedding veil. I stopped washing and gripped the sink.

"Aw...and the honeymoon on Richard Branson's Island...is that off too?"

I shrugged.

"Ah, that's a shame... That's really sad that is – I'd love to go there."

I looked at her in silence as she made the final titivations to her already-perfect face. I stared at my own reflection, lines, too much black eye make-up and a few stubborn greys at the roots of my honey-caramel bob. Cindi put her cosmetics away and stared at me.

"Tan."

"What?" I said curtly.

"Here." She offered me a wad of paper towels.

"My hands are dry, thanks" I snapped.

"I know, Tan. It's just... Well, it's just that they're bleeding."

I quickly looked down at my hands, red and cracked. They were indeed bleeding. "I have eczema," I said. "You worked for me, you should remember that, yes?"

She smiled kindly.

"OK, Tan. Well, let's get out there, shall we? I am dying to know who else is on the show!"

She teetered out of the ladies' on very high heels, her blonde hair swishing and her tiny hips wiggling as she walked. The door closed softly behind me and I took a deep breath. *I am Tanya Travis*, I thought to myself. *I have faced addicts, abusers, cheaters and liars. How hard could it be to hang out with celebrities like me for twelve days? I am Tanya Travis, and I can do this.* I stepped quickly into the corridor and walked purposefully towards the holding room.

GOSSIPBITCH: *Who's being tipped as talk show host of ground-breaking prime-time new Beeb format? Looks like this new Daytime Darling will be more successful than her predecessor in her bid for mega stardom.*

15

Celebrity Heaven and Hog Plum Hell

"Tanya, I believe you've just met CC", Tiffany said, clearly annoyed, as I walked back into the party area. "You aren't supposed to meet until you are on camera, sweetheart. We can't affect reality. Can you pretend you've never met?"

"Actually Tiffany," I said, eyeballing her, "it turns out I already know CC. She used to work for me and I am afraid I cannot lie to the public... But if it makes things easier, I'll not deliberately let on that I've just seen her in the toilets." I gave her a tight smile. "OK?"

"OK lovely. Listen, we are going to introduce you first. So when I give you the nod, you will go out of those doors" she motioned to the glass doors leading onto a patio, where I could see lights and cameras. "Then you walk along the red carpet until you are in front of the cameras. Then just wait there. We are going to get people in pretty quickly as we want it all to be filmed during sundown – we put you first because we thought you'd be good at introducing yourself and the others. OK, my lovely?"

"Not a problem, Tiffany" I said, pleased they had recognised my expertise but keen to smack her in the gob if this twentysomething called me 'sweetheart' or her 'lovely' ever again.

"Great. So they'll come in, one by one and then when you've all met you will find out what's happening tomorrow. Then that's it for filming, though there will be food laid on in the bar for everyone afterwards."

"Great."

The walkie-talkie Tiffany had on her hip crackled and she turned and spoke into it for a few seconds, before turning back to me.

"OK Tanya. Thunderbirds are go! Please walk through the doors now. This is all being filmed, please try not to swear."

I glared at her then swept out of the holding room, through the doors and towards the lights. It was very strange, walking on to an empty set in silence. None of the crew spoke and I was very aware of the camera right in my face, clocking my every reaction. I walked slowly from the cool, marbled hall out into the balmy late afternoon and onto the grass. I stopped in front of a beautiful lake in the hotel grounds which had been lit up for the filming. I was feeling queasy (which was probably down to the hog plum smoothie) and was glad of a moment to compose myself and take some deep breaths. The low sun was starting to set, casting a pinky-gold light over everything. It was still warm but we'd been warned the nights could be cool in Nepal in September and I wrapped my pashmina firmly around my shoulders. Standing there in the silence for a moment, I almost forgot where I was and what was happening and just stared at the amazing sight before me. Beyond the hotel's expansive pools and beautifully landscaped gardens were the Himalayas. The colossal mountains, surrounded by pink cloud, their tops sprinkled with icing sugar snow, stood in the distance as if they were welcoming me into this other place. Then I heard soft footsteps, and I knew the first celebrity had arrived; I turned around.

"Tanya! Hello!" said a tall, muscly woman, striding purposefully towards me. "Gosh, I'm glad I know who you are!" It was Kara Jackson, former Olympic athlete.

Her body was honed to perfection and she'd clearly oiled her muscular frame, adding a dose of spray-tan to accentuate the ripples. Her skin was orange and her dress was designer but she looked out of place, like she ought to be in running shorts on a track.

"Kara," I said warmly, also relieved I knew who she was. She clasped my hand in hers and shook it roughly, her bare, muscular arms like those of a man.

"I imagine you will be far more used to physical endurance than me," I smiled.

"Oh, I don't know. I haven't done any sport for a while, Tanya, I just go down the gym these days." She had a bright, quick, smile and a tough, cockney accent.

Running-track-hero-turned-sports-presenter, Kara was once a popular TV personality until she fell madly in love with married straight actress, Dina Marsh. They struck up a friendship, but her feelings were unrequited. Clinging to a hopeless dream that her love might one day be returned, Kara planned to surprise Dina one evening by breaking into her flat and spreading herself across the kitchen worktops, wearing nothing but a smile. Despite Kara's best efforts at romance, Dina was terrified to find an Olympian lesbian on her finest black granite and called the cops. Poor Kara, who had only wanted a 'girls' night in' ended up with a court injunction, a suspended sentence and a career in ruins.

After what seemed like only a few seconds, the next celebrity arrived. A small, untidy man shuffled on, with a hopeful smile and watery eyes that darted between us both. I knew his face and quickly scanned my memory. I could see Kara desperately trying to do the same.

"Erm, hello, Tanya Travis," he said. "And hello, Kara Jackson."

There was an awkward silence and I could feel Kara's face redden. Then suddenly, I remembered.

"Jonny!" I said, with a broad smile. "How wonderful to see you!" Jonny Lester shook my hand, pleased that I knew who he was. Poor Jonny was a tragic clown, a one-time comedian, all cheesy one-liners and goofy routines. He had never been quite good enough to hit the big time though and in recent years his star – and his talent – had really faded.

"I think I once interviewed your wife" I said, brightly. "Yes, I remember now, it was a *Tanya Travis Celebrity Special*," I smiled. "She was lovely, very young, you were divorcing, she cheated on you with... Oh, it was the *lesbian* celebrity special," I said, before I could stop myself. I caught the eye of Kara who was staring at Jonny in horror and I recalled with a start exactly who his wife had left him for.

We were saved from our awkward threesome by Cindi, who skipped onto set on the arm of a man in his later years.

"Hi, everyone! I'm CC and this is Marcus," Cindi said brightly.

"Darling girl," toned the man, annoyed, "you have quite spoiled my entrance."

He was small in stature but wearing a huge coat and ankle boots he had a physical presence and resonance that belied his slight frame – this one I knew straight away. Marcus Saunders was an old Shakespearian actor that no-one under 35 had probably even heard of. He'd said goodbye to BBC Drama and hello to reality shows after being caught trawling King's Cross for rent boys in the late 90's. It landed him a night in the cells and his story across the tabloids, ending with a suspended sentence and a request for three other offences to be taken into consideration.

"Ooh sorry, perish the thought anyone should spoil your entrance, Marcus!" Cindi giggled. I smiled politely and shook his hand. I was starting to feel quite hot, probably from the combination of lights, nerves and hog plums. My hands had become sweaty and my mouth was suddenly very dry.

As Cindi and Marcus said hello to the other celebrities I had to steady myself as I was feeling faint. I took a few deep breaths, and noticed it had gone silent. I turned around, and saw Cindi, Marcus and the others, gaping at a man who was striding towards us. "It can't be..." Cindi whispered. The silence could only indicate one thing – we were in the presence of a genuine A-Lister. I recognised him instantly – it was movie star Rex Cannon. I used to drool over him when I was about twelve and though he must have been quite old – and a bit of a has-been in today's movie terms – I could see he still had that 'something'.

"Howdy" he said, with his smooth Texan accent, hands in the pockets of his faded jeans. He was wearing a Stetson and his checked shirt was open at the collar, his craggy old face still deeply handsome. Everyone was stunned and I felt maybe I should take control. I stepped forward purposefully – but as I did a wave of nausea overtook me. My outstretched hand flew straight to my mouth, and he looked at me, quizzically.

"Erm... I erm..." I said, knowing now that I was imminently going to be sick. "I'm Tanya," I managed, before clamping my hand over my mouth and bolting from the set. I streaked past the startled cameraman, pushed Tiffany out of the way as she tried to accost me at the door and ran into the toilets where I was very, very sick. Judging from the bright green colour, the hog plum smoothie had been a big mistake.

I continued to retch hog plums for some time and as a result missed the rest of the filming. Tiffany kept banging on the toilet door and demanding I came out, "Tanya, sweetheart," she cried urgently, "we've only got a few minutes before the sun sets and we need to wrap this bit. We need you now, my lovely!"

"I don't care," I snarled, spitting hog plum saliva into the toilet bowl. "I've got a mouth full of hog plums I'm not coming out, *sweetheart* and that's all there is to it."

Five minutes later, there was a more urgent knock on the door; "Tanya, are you finished with the vomiting and the hog's plums yet?" It was Astrid.

"No I am not, now bugger off."

"Oh Tanya, the pixie-girl Tinkerbell... She says you sucking hogs in the toilet and I have to be a fucking sweetheart and get you out. Filming finished now, all the celebrities are here but where is Tanya? I say to her, if Tanya was here the sick would be everywhere. Is that what you want, Tinkerbell? Stupid shithole says...but sweetheart, but sweetheart..."

"Yes. I get the gist, Astrid," I sighed, wobbling towards the door to open it.

She rushed in and put her arm around me.

"Oh you look like a very big crap, Tanya."

"Thanks."

"Now you lean on the sinking here, while I put on some of the lovely lipstick."

"No... Astrid, please..." She delved in my bag, produced a lipstick and proceeded to assault me with it. My Chanel Hydracaresse in Sugar Plum was never meant to be wielded like a weapon, or wiped hard and unevenly across my lips. But Astrid managed to add a shade of 'crazy' to the heroin-chic-just-thrown-up look. Even in my post-vomit-exhausted state I knew that re-appearing at an event covered in regurgitated hog plums with strangely-painted lips would have people talking, but I was helpless as Astrid grabbed me around the waist and heaved me back towards the party.

"Tanya, I am very excited. Shitting hot star is here – I swoon on the bloody floor when I see him..."

"Yes, I know. Rex Cannon...I have been in love with him since I was twelve." I said.

"You insane bitch, you so funny!" she yelped, laughing loudly and slapping me on the back, catapulting me back into the room.

I still felt dreadful and landing somewhere near the food table, I had to use it as a way of standing up. I leaned against the huge table covered in banks of spicy pastries, tureens of warm dhal, their pungent smell wafting into my nostrils, threatening a further – and possibly more violent – hog plum recurrence. Astrid was filling her plate and chatting away to me but I couldn't really understand her, it was very excited and Swedish and full of unusually inventive expletives.

I stood for a moment, trying to calm my insides and take it all in. The huge, beautiful hall was like something from an opulent past dotted with artwork and glitzy statues. Waiters wandered languorously through the crowd, carrying trays of champagne and smiling. For a moment I found it hard to believe this was the same city that had beggars on its streets.

The rest of the guests and press were mingling and I spotted a couple of reporters I'd encountered in the past. It wasn't long before one of them headed straight for me and, knowing the questions would be all about Nathan, I hid behind Astrid and shouted for Paul. He should have been nearby, it was his job to protect celebrities from the press asking any questions other than *Spa Trek* ones.

"Paul," I called from behind Astrid, clutching her for ballast.

"What the buggering bollocks are you up to now, you crazy old-?" she turned round, still munching.

"Astrid, call Paul."

I could see him hanging out at the other end of the food table, drinking and chatting with Tiffany the researcher. I wouldn't have had that on my show. It was the first time I'd seen him for hours and I'd just been ill – the least he could do was check whether I needed anything.

I gathered myself together and, still using Astrid as a crutch, staggered over to him. I was feeling rough but my irritation at his lack of attention had caused an adrenalin rush. "Paul," I said pointedly, tapping him on the shoulder. "Would you be kind enough to keep the press away from me and get me a drink?" He turned around, surprised at first, then he smiled.

"Of course, Tan, no probs." He took champagne from an ice bucket and holding the bottle, stood back a little from me with his eyes screwed up. "You trying out a new way with lipstick? 'Cos it's looking pretty...fly." he said, uncertainly.

I glared at Astrid, while he poured my champagne carefully into an empty flute.

"Thank you. Beautifully done," I smiled, always happy to give credit and encouragement. "He needs to get his arse into gear," I murmured to Astrid as I wiped my lips with the back of my hand then sipped my drink.

Astrid held out her empty glass: "You will be needing to gear it up your arse, Paul?" she said flirtatiously as he poured champagne into her glass.

"My arse is none of your business, Astrid," he flirted back. She giggled, went scarlet and muttered something under her breath about 'dick's-head but cute.'

I felt like a gooseberry. Christ, I knew she was bonkers but she was part of the Tanya Travis entourage and it was wholly inappropriate for her to be flirting with a runner. *I bet Posh and Becks don't have this with their staff*, I thought, enviously.

"Now Paul, you may have heard, I've been a little off colour and haven't had chance to talk to everyone," I said. I swigged a large mouthful of cool fizz. I was still feeling ropey from the hog plums and wasn't sure champagne was the answer but I needed something to do with my hands.

"Will you take Astrid and me over to the others please?" I said.

He nodded and then the cheeky little sod poured himself a big flute of champagne. He took a huge glug then linked me which made me feel like a granny, whose grandson was helping her across the road.

"Paul," I snapped, "I don't need your *physical* help to get across the room. I just ask that you please bring everyone together for the formal introductions. It's embarrassing. I just met them briefly on camera, I don't know any of these people, yet I'll have to sleep with them."

He smirked.

"You really aren't across this, are you?" I snapped.

He had the cheek to giggle, then put his head down and roll his arm forward in a 'come this way, madam' gesture. I couldn't believe it. "Astrid, come along!" I commanded. "Come and meet the others." She followed me, wide-eyed, towards the celebrities.

I wobbled alongside Paul; my heels were unusually high but as I'd be spending the following two weeks in mountaineering gear, I wanted to make the most of it. We arrived at a little celebrity huddle and Paul casually said hello in that irritating, laid-back way of his. Marcus the Shakespearian actor was deep in conversation with Rex the old movie star.

"...and my *Lear* – oh my dear, how the critics loved it!" he was saying.

Rex had an amused half-smirk on his face. "Really, big guy? You ever made a movie?"

Marcus puffed up his chest. "Movies aren't really my thing, dear boy," he said, buffing his nails against his neatly creased shirt. "I am more of a thespian, myself."

"Is that so?" Rex said, chewing gum, nodding slowly, his eyes twinkling in amusement. "Well good for you, Marko. Of course, movies make all the money, but I guess you don't get the same atmosphere, right?"

Marcus blinked.

"Do excuse me, Rex, dear boy," he smiled, too sweetly. "I must get another drink." And with that he moved off. Rex shook his head, laughing to himself. Jonny had been standing on the outside of the group witnessing the exchange and I moved next to him, remembering our earlier encounter.

"Hello again, Tanya" he said with a small smile. "I do hope you are feeling better and not 'sick' of us already."

I pretended to laugh at his joke.

"Something I drank disagreed with me, I think." Then, before he could come up with another lame joke I said: "Jonny, about earlier, when I mentioned your wife... Ex-wife. I'm sorry. I have interviewed so many people with so many stories they sort of jumble a bit and sometimes it all comes out... Unravels, you know?"

"Don't worry about it, Tanya."

"It must be awkward for you – with Kara here, I mean?"

"No, it was a long time ago and Kara's had her own troubles since. Anyway the past is the past and we are all in here for one thing, to have fun!" He said this with the drooping brows and heavy jowls of a man who hadn't had much fun recently.

I smiled and looked round for Astrid who was now deep in conversation with Paul. He was resting his arm lightly round her waist and she was bending her head in to talk to him. Annoyance flared though me.

I marched over to them. Their heads were together and for a moment I was stunned as I thought they were kissing. On closer inspection I could see they were listening to something on his iPod.

"Hi guys," I tried to be gentle, as I didn't want to embarrass them. "Paul, I think the producer needs you to clear away some of the cables," I started.

"Oh?"

"Yes... over there. Anyone could trip over them, we have to be aware of Health and Safety at all times, don't we?"

"Yeah, s'pose so..." With that, he wandered aimlessly into a throng of people where he was then completely distracted and high-fiving everyone.

"Jesus, where do they get them?" I hissed in Astrid's direction. "And you have to remember, Astrid, you represent me when we're here and you can't be flirting with Paul. It just isn't professional."

"Fucking hell, Tanya! I was listening to his music, not doing the flirting... He's bloody delicious boy though, no?"

"Mmmm, just keep yourself to yourself, Astrid. We don't want any problems with the press on this trip."

"None of the worries, Tanya. Paul is hot and delicious, even cuter than perfect Gok Wan, but I only see Paul at night... He tells me I can listen to music later, in his room."

"No, Astrid..." Oh, what was the point? And who was I to tell Astrid who she could and couldn't sleep with. She couldn't make any mistakes worse than I had. After all, it wasn't like she didn't know what she was doing, I still hadn't discovered who she'd been secretly entertaining in her bedroom that afternoon. I decided to mingle and as Astrid was embarking on another lap of the buffet table, I approached Kara the celebrity lesbian.

"Please don't mention kangaroo penises," was her opening gambit, palm in my face like a stop sign.

"I wouldn't dream of it," I said. I assumed she was referring to her time in the Australian Outback on *I'm a Celebrity*...which clearly still haunted her.

"Isn't the plural of penis, peni, anyway?" I said.

"Why can't anyone let me forget?" she shovelled a large chapatti into her mouth.

"I'm sure it all will be forgotten, eventually," I lied, recalling the photos and forums hinting at bestiality – that would stay online for eternity. "Anyway, I watched it and thought you looked great."

"Thanks, do you really think so?"

I nodded and she smiled – probably thinking I fancied her. I couldn't decide whether she'd had dodgy Botox or was raising her eyebrows in a 'come and get me' way. My heart sank. I didn't want her splayed across my Mark Wilkinson, in an attempt to surprise me when I got home. I continued to try and make small-talk and tried not to let my eyes wander, lest she thought I was admiring her Olympian bodywork.

It may have been the thought of chewing on testicles or the remains of the hog plums still swirling around my guts but I decided to call it a night. I didn't want a fuss and I didn't need Astrid's foul-mouthed farewells or observations from the buffet table, so I slipped off to my room. Once in bed my mind turned, as always, to Nathan. I'd promised myself I wouldn't keep trying to contact him; he'd said he needed his space and I had to respect that. Nevertheless, I found my fingers dialling the international code and punching in his number. My heart was somewhere in my throat, lowering slightly as each ringtone continued until I had to face it: he wasn't answering. Perhaps he was busy... Or asleep... Or something else?

GOSSIPBITCH: *A little bird tells me the air was thick with the smell of vomit at a recent celebrity bash in Nepal. Mmmm, so the rumours about a disgraced Daytime Diva being an alcoholic anorexic are all true?*

16

Prime-time Pretty in Pokhara

I woke the next morning with the sun streaming in through the window. Tiffany had told us to assemble in the lobby and I got ready quickly, though it took me a while to make a final decision on what to take. I had to be methodical and brutal in the packing process, as my lime and ivory leather quilted Moschino backpack was exquisite, but small.

Arriving in the atrium I was early and enjoyed a few peaceful moments listening to the fountains and the low hubbub of the hotel coming to life.

"Oh, darling. Darling! I am bereft of my baggage – some gorgeous boy offered to hump it for me…"

"Here it is," Cindi appeared. "That 'gorgeous boy' was about to run off with your stuff, Marcus. You should be more careful."

"Oh dear, you can't trust anyone these days. Did we all sleep well?" Cindi and I nodded, as we were joined by Paul and Rex who both looked the worse for wear and clearly hadn't slept at all.

Jonny and Kara soon appeared and were chatting quite happily which was a relief to me: I'd worried that my mediating skills may have been required for those two. Once the whole cast was assembled, Tiffany eventually appeared with a piece of toast in one hand and a clipboard in the other, barking orders at us to get on the bus outside.

We all trooped out and I was just boarding the bus when I heard Astrid's dulcet tones. "Tanya you crazy cow… You nearly go without me saying the goodbyes!" She leaped on me, hugging me hard, only releasing me when I began flailing my arms in alarm to indicate difficulty breathing. I extricated myself from her bosom and she held me by the shoulders, looking at me and smiling. "I very proud to be your PA… You go and give them crap-balls, Tanya Travis."

For a moment I stood and looked at her beaming face and her genuine pride and thought I might cry. In all the horror of the past couple of weeks, Astrid had stood by me. She'd been there each morning with a cup of toxic tea, an expletive and a smile and each evening she'd be waiting, her box set of *Doc Martin* on standby; 'because it gives you smiles and you such a miserable old bitch at the moments.'

I hugged her back gratefully. "You're not just my cleaner, or my PA, Astrid. You're a good friend." I smiled.

"Oh shut up, you sloppy old tit-bag," she giggled, fobbing me off, though she was clearly pleased at my affection. I kissed her on the cheek and climbed onto the bus. I looked through the window once I'd taken my seat and saw her wipe her eyes as she stood waiting to wave us off.

Celebrity Spa Trek: a place, according to the promos, 'where bad celebrities go good' was taking place in Pokhara, a very beautiful area near the mountains, about 90 miles from Kathmandu. Known as the jewel of the Himalayas, Pokhara was a haven of snowy peaks, serene lakes and lush greenery but the perilous, mountain-top journey to reach it by bus would take some time. I had anticipated the duration of such a journey but once seated I realised to my horror that Paul was getting into the driving seat. I wasn't ready for that.

"Marcus!" I hissed. He lowered his sunglasses.

"Problem, dearie?"

"Yes there's a problem! They are only letting bloody Paul drive!" I said, appalled.

"Yes, rather him than me... Quite a challenge, getting up these hills," he smiled and went back to looking out of the window.

"Too right it will be a challenge," I said, incensed that the production crew were recklessly risking our lives like this.

"Don't worry, dear. I think there's some kind of dual-control thing," he said, and motioned towards the front, where a Nepali driver sat next to Paul. A cameraman was recording us all getting on and climbed in next to Paul at the front.

"At least there will be video evidence for the courts," I grumbled, mostly to myself. "I can see the headlines now: *Death By Bus – TV Company Drives Celebrities off a Mountain*."

"Better than driving us round the bend!" Jonny piped up with a hopeful smile as he climbed on board.

Rex, who was sitting on a seat parallel to mine snorted and looked out of the window, stroking his bristly square jaw to hide a smirk. Jonny lowered himself into the seat next to Rex and started fussing with his seatbelt.

"Hey, clown guy," said Rex, turning to face Jonny. "I kinda like my space, you know?"

Jonny looked at him, blankly. Rex unwrapped some gum and popped it into his mouth, staring at Jonny.

"What I mean is: there are other seats, right?"

"Oh! Yes of course," said Jonny, embarrassed. He jumped up, but was pulled back into his seat by the seatbelt and he fumbled for what seemed like an age to unclip it. He got up and walked further down the bus, taking a seat on his own. I noticed when he tried to do up his belt again, his hands were shaking. Everyone else was either looking out of the window or down at the floor – anywhere but at Rex or Jonny.

"Was that really necessary?" I found myself saying.

Rex turned his stare onto me. "Sorry, who are you again?" He said.

Flames of anger licked my chest and I was on the verge of a Tanya Travis style confrontation, when I remembered where I was. I had to control myself on this occasion, as there was a camera on board the bus. I could only imagine what it would look like if following on from my studio meltdown I accosted an international film-star. I felt like I'd been on that bus an hour already and we hadn't even set off. I pressed my head against the window, then I remembered the germs and moved it away.

Astrid's little face was still there, all shiny and smiley and I gave her a final wave as we pulled slowly away.

"Bye, Astrid, you gorgeous little Scandinavian," Paul blew her kisses and she blew them back. "You are one HOT! Chiquita banana," he was shouting through the open window.

"Paul, keep both hands on the wheel!" I yelled from my seat. "And please don't shout about bananas to my PA, it's indecent – have some respect and concentrate on what you are doing. If you have to drive, I would appreciate it if you didn't kill us."

Once on the open road it soon became clear there were no luxuries like air-con or vehicle suspension. So as we bounced along, I tried to take my mind off the heat and my imminent death by gazing at the spectacular mountains. This was a mistake, though, because looking downwards I was met with a sheer drop at the side of the mountain road and the unnerving sight of fallen buses, hundreds of feet below. When Paul took both hands off the wheel and shouted 'look no hands' I thought I might pass out. When we finally shuddered to a halt some hours later and everyone cheered, I sent up a little prayer to God, Buddha and Allah – just in case it was one of them that had delivered me safely.

In other circumstances, I would have appreciated how the serenity of the lakes against the magnificent backdrop of the rising Himalayas created an ambience of peace and ethereal magic, but being on that bouncing bus had made me feel very sick. I hadn't felt myself since the hog plum incident, plus the champagne and dhal at the party last night hadn't helped.

I tried to think of Citrus Squeeze cleaning products, cool water and clean worktops as we clambered off the bus and carried our backpacks into a clearing that would now be known as 'celebrity base camp.' Situated at the base of a mountain, the area was nestled among trees and shrubbery quite close to the lake. I walked away from the other celebrities, taking deep lungfuls of the deliciously clean air while admiring the spectacular, snow-topped mountains, dramatic against a navy blue sky. Dotted through the blue and white were tiny prayer flags, strung like bunting through the skies and valleys, *like confetti of the gods*, I thought to myself.

"Beautiful...yes?" said a voice at the side of me.

"Yes." I turned to the voice next to me and did a double-take. Standing at my side was what Astrid would describe as a 'delicious, hot' man.

"The sky is so blue and the air...it's so...fresh, I said quickly, to stop myself from saying anything else.

He smiled, taking it all in like it was the first time he'd seen it.

"Oh... I should introduce myself. I'm Tanya Travis," I smiled, then added; "one of the celebrities." Being from Nepal he may not have heard of me. My natural instinct was to shake his hand and as he seemed reticent, I took the lead, reached out and gave him a firm hand shake. I later discovered that in Nepal it was considered deeply offensive for the opposite sex to touch. So in effect, I had greeted the trekking guide by doing the cultural equivalent of rubbing his crotch.

"Namaste, Tanya. My name is Ardash, I'm the trekking guide and first-aid officer on *Celebrity Spa Trek*," he said proudly, tearing his eyes away from the view to look at me. I smiled back and we stood for a few minutes in silence watching the glittering lake fed by tiny streams, like fairy-lights running through the earth's cracks.

"Ah, the sun, she paints a beautiful picture," he whispered. "And there... Over there is Sagarmatha, you know her as Everest."

"Sagarmatha," I turned to him, thinking absently how his eyes were like dark chocolate flecked with milk chocolate. "In Nepali, Sagarmatha means 'Mother of the Universe'."

He looked at me again with those big brown eyes. They were soft, kind eyes; I couldn't imagine those eyes ever showing hate or contempt, just warmth.

I listened in silence, loving the way his Nepali accent danced on familiar words, making them sound new to my ears. Then someone called for him and he put his hands together in a prayer-like gesture and left.

I watched him walk away. Firm, slim thighs in tight jeans, jet-black hair, confident and strong negotiating treacherous terrain. I was torn for a moment between the beautiful lake and mountains and the rear of this delicious man.

Returning my eyes to the beautiful landscape I was suddenly hit by a viscous wave of dizziness and nausea. Before I could move, I doubled over and heaved, retching up bright yellow vomit. Everyone turned from the majestic mountains to see where the racket was coming from. Seeing Tanya Travis, Queen of Daytime, projectile vomiting neon-yellow like the child in *The Exorcist* was some competition for those ancient mountains.

Everything was still and silent. Then Cindi rushed forward in an attempt to dab me, but by now I was beyond 'dabbing.'

"Ooh Tan, that's not going to look pretty on prime time," she understated, continuing the futile dabbing in the I-never-cleaned-anything-in-my-life way one would expect from a sex-tape-glamour model.

"I'm sorry... I am so embarrassed," I said, on all fours, holding on to Cindi and trying to get to my feet, which was proving impossible given the slippery quality of regurgitated dhal. "I need a hot shower," I hissed to perky Tiff the researcher, who'd turned up to see the spectacle and was looking at me with a curled lip like I was a mutant zoo exhibit.

"Erm... Sorry Tanya, no showers here... Sweetheart, there's a stream a few hundred yards down there," she said apologetically, before adding an unnecessary "ew."

"You are kidding, Tiffany? No-one told me there'd be no showers. I expected a shared one, at least!"

"Sorry lovely – no mirrors, no showers and no beds" said Tiff, brightly. "It was all in your contract." I looked at her in disbelief. My hair was matted and covered my face, I was soaked in vomit, my Moschino was wrecked and she was talking to me about my *bloody contract*.

"OK. OK..." I tried to calm down. After all, there was history here and I must not be seen yelling at researchers. "So Tiffany, tell me...where is the clean water for washing?"

She didn't take her eyes off me as her arm came out and her finger flopped downwards towards some crags with water trickling through between them.

"This is an emergency. I need help. Where's Paul?" I bellowed into the mountains.

Silence.

"Paul!" I yelled again.

"Here babe," Paul eventually appeared from behind a crevice, as unfazed as ever, rucksack hanging from his shoulder, fag dangling from his gob.

"Put that cigarette out and get here now," I snapped. He ambled over like he had all the time in the world.

"Cover me," I hissed, handing him my congealed rucksack. I couldn't bear my sticky, sweaty vomit-covered clothes a second longer. I had to take everything off and was starting to shake with the whole revolting, dirty mess I was in. Grabbing him round the waist I manoeuvred Paul to stand in front of me so I could quickly whip off my T-shirt and my shorts.

"Quick nurse, the screens!" Marcus screamed, holding up his hands in camp, feigned horror as Paul stood limply in front of me in a half-hearted attempt to protect my modesty.

Cindi handed me a tissue, over Paul's head. "Tanya, girlfriend, you kill me. We've only just got here and you've got your tits out," she giggled.

"I haven't got my...anything...out." This was my worst nightmare. Paul was a waste of space and kept moving so everyone saw every bit of my ageing flesh and cellulite. Mind you, who was I kidding? My cellulite was old news to anyone in the western world who'd read a paper or been online in the past week. I hated Donna for sending me here and vowed that the first thing I would do when I escaped from there was murder her, then sack her as my agent.

Paul stood with his back to me, his arms limply held out in a futile attempt to cover me. It wasn't working and to make it worse I knew he was sniggering because his shoulders were going up and down. He was still smoking like a bloody chimney and I was desperately trying to waft the dirty clouds of smoke away.

"Paul!" I shouted. He jumped; that's how I liked it. "Will you please put that cigarette out and find something other than yourself to hide me. I'm worried this might look rather...inappropriate."

"Yeah. I'd say it's well dodge, Tan," he nodded, "you standing there in your pants clutchin' at me." He was playing to his audience now who were all chuckling, which encouraged him to elaborate. "There's me thinkin' you was a nice old lady just like me ma, but you is one cougar, Tanya Travis."

He made a vile thrusting gesture with his hips, everyone collapsed in fits of laughter and Cindi shouted; "Go girl!"

I'm glad the runner is so bloody popular, I thought, trying not to acknowledge the dry vomit now gathering between my breasts. Just as I was considering a mercy dash to the mountains never to return, Cindi turned up again, giggling and carrying a large bath towel.

"Here you go, Tan," she said kindly, handing it to me.

"Thank you" I said gratefully. Then I demanded Paul hold it round me while I took off my bra and pants.

"I need to get into the water, Paul. Come on." I snapped. Obviously I needed to get clean, but I also wanted to get away from the crowd of has-beens and crew that was gathering round for a good laugh. He started to walk with me, still holding my towel. He had to keep holding the towel while I rubbed Sanihand cream into my screaming palms, but I didn't want anyone to see what I was doing. I didn't need OCD adding to the list of Tanya Travis Tragedies mounting up in the minds of my fellow celebrities. I squeezed out the last few blobs under the towel and rubbed discreetly but vigorously, trying not to panic that I had none left.

I was trying hard to be subtle but Paul suddenly became aware that my hand was moving briskly under the towel.

"Whoa, Tanya! What are you doin', girl?" He yelped, leaping back. Everyone turned to look at my jerky, under-towel hand movements.

"Nothing," I hissed. He was still holding the towel but standing a little distance away in staged mock-surprise and horror.

"Show some control, laydee!" Paul joked and everyone erupted with laughter.

"It's only...hand-cream..." I tried. I'd been so desperate to put some anti-bac cream on my hands and in secret that I hadn't considered what it might look like to onlookers.

"Oh, don't mind us dear...you just keep lubing yourself up," came haughty Shakespearian tones from behind some rhododendrons, where Marcus was having a cigarette.

"Paul. Will you keep the towel still?" I was cross now. "I need you to keep it round me while we walk. Stop laughing, you're making it go up and down."

"Ooh, Matron!" came Marcus's voice again, from behind the bush.

"I have to get clean," I hissed. "Get a bloody move on, Paul."

"You got it Tan," he said, still smiling, fag dangling from his mouth but at least he was now holding the towel more firmly as instructed.

"Nothing to see here," I shouted, feeling like the back end of a pantomime horse. "Please go about your business," and to my relief everyone slowly wandered off while Paul and I walked on to the stream.

"Well Paul, we've got our work cut out. Vomit is hell to get out of clothes...and I ate all that dhal," I said, as we galloped downhill together. "I don't know if you've ever fought a washday battle with turmeric, but let me tell you, it's one we are in danger of losing if we don't step to it. Speed is of the essence." I said, a little breathless now from the steep incline.

"If only I had my box of Stain Devils with me. I have one for every stain," I added. I clutched at Paul as we tripped over rocks, me now holding the towel while he carried my designer backpack. On reaching the stream he was still holding my dirty clothes. "I'll keep that towel round me and wash my underwear," I smiled. I wouldn't expect a young man to wash my pants, whatever his job. "But it's up to you to get the sick stains off my top and shorts. And do it properly Paul, don't just scrape the dried, crusty bits off," I added, dunking my fabulous new Rigby & Peller bra in misty rose into the running stream. I squeezed and scrubbed at it, then splashed water all over my hands, arms and legs, still trying to keep the towel in place.

After about an hour (it was torture without a watch to know timings) I eventually managed to get me and my underwear as clean as possible, given the conditions I was working in. I sighed as I squeezed out the last of the antibacterial gel. We weren't allowed luxuries but this was a necessity and I'd made sure Donna negotiated it into my contract. I slapped on the final droplets and left Paul to finish scrubbing at my vomit-stained top. He'd tried to get away with a little rub here and there but I told him I wouldn't allow him to leave until my garments were absolutely spotless.

I decided to have another go at my hair and no sooner was I submerged than the lazy sod was quietly sloping off back to base camp.

"Paul, have you definitely got all those stains out?" I shouted from under a wet mass of hair and soap foam.

"Yes. I think so..."

"You *think* so? Let me see," I beckoned him crossly.

He offered me the sodden ball of T shirt and I snatched it off him, giving it a vigorous squeeze before checking it. "SQUEEZE, Paul, you need to squeeze it hard."

"I thought you might want some privacy while you washed yourself," he tried, but I wasn't buying it.

"No, you can wait for me. Not too much to ask is it? Or are you too busy doing other stuff?" I said sarcastically, but it was lost on him.

He grunted then reluctantly staggered over to retrieve my backpack while I finished dressing.

"Look, you should make the most of this opportunity, Paul. Most youngsters would kill for a chance like this – it's better than being unemployed."

"Yeah. I suppose it is," he said, shrugging as I joined him to stagger uphill back to the camp. He carried my bag and wet towel while I burned calories with a vigorous power-walk, leaving him in my wake.

"Christ Paul! Get a move on!" I shouted back down to him, shaking my head in despair as he huffed and puffed his way up. He stopped to catch his breath and was now bending over, wheezing. He only had a couple of bags and a towel but he was so out of condition for a young man.

"That's what smoking does to you," I said.

He shrugged. So rude.

"Tanya, have you left Paul down there, struggling with all your stuff?" giggled Cindi, who still seemed to find me hilarious: "You're even worse now than you were when I worked for you."

"No I'm not. I believe in tough love as you know, Cindi. Young people need guidance and strict discipline."

"Yeah, so you said, Miss Whiplash." She smiled, unfurling her sleeping bag onto the cold, hard ground.

"Are you sleeping there?" I asked, surprised.

"Yeah. We all are," she replied. I looked at her, horrified. It was getting dark and the altitude meant it was quite cool, despite the warmth of the setting sun. Marcus was huddled in his large coat and Rex was asleep on top of his sleeping bag nearby. Kara and Jonny were chatting by the camp fire, apparently cooking dinner and sending welcome wafts of warm, spicy scent across the camp. Despite my terrible reflux I felt quite peckish but had to deal with the problem of sleeping arrangements first.

"This can't be right!" I announced, and stomped off to find Tiffany who took great delight in informing me it was in my contract to sleep under the stars.

"My agent wouldn't agree to that."

"She would, sweetheart. She did."

"Well she'll be doing more than sleeping under the stars when I get back to the UK. She'll be sleeping with the fucking fishes!" I hissed. This was the final straw. I couldn't sleep in a bag on the ground. I had no toiletries, no hot water and now no bed. A tent with a small bed inside would have been bad enough but this? This was uncivilized, unspeakable. I would call Donna to spring me, first thing in the morning.

"I'm not sleeping here, it's filthy!" I called over to Marcus, who was sitting on his Cath Kidston sleeping bag, with a cup of tea in hand.

"Oh don't be such a drama queen, dear. Wouldn't we all rather be at the Kathmandu Hilton tonight? But that's what the show's about: roughing it."

"I'm not 'roughing it' for anyone," I snapped. I was disappointed that the old thespian wasn't getting his codpiece in a twist over the sleeping arrangements. I was sure he'd have a problem with dusty old sleeping bags on rocky ground and join me in my crusade for humane treatment. It looked like I was on my own.

"Join me for a cuppa and I'll tell you all about my time with Kenny Branagh at the RSC," he offered. I didn't have much choice and I needed to think about what to do next. I mustn't do anything rash – especially as the cameras would soon be whirring, I needed to be on my best behaviour to be seen as fun, young and happening. I decided that a theatrical gossip queen and a squeeze of Earl Grey teabag in those Spartan surroundings might be quite pleasant. I staggered over and was soon enjoying delicately-perfumed tea with a delicately-perfumed homosexual. It was all very acceptable and Marcus was just settling down to recount 'my Lear at Stratford', when everyone else began heading towards the campfire on the other side of base camp.

"What's happening?" I called from behind Earl-Grey steam and mid-way through 'Kenny's Edmund'.

"Team meeting, Tanya," Tiffany shouted back. "You need to meet the producer, she's going to explain how it's all going to work over the next few days."

"But we're not starting until tomorrow, are we?"

"Already started sweetheart," she chirped.

"Yes but the actual filming?"

"We've been filming you all for hours."

"But you need our permission, surely?"

"Got it. All in the contract, now come on, you two old lovelies."

My mouth dropped open in horror. "It's not possible! They can't film us secretly without our knowledge?" I hissed to Marcus, who had just poured himself another tea and was settling down for Lear's descent into madness.

"O let me not be mad, not mad, sweet heaven! I would not be mad," he spat everywhere, in full Shakespearian throttle.

I could see I wasn't going to get any support from Marcus, so made my way to the campfire, determined to have it out with the producer. Railroaded by yet another effervescent, nubile researcher we all took our places for the meeting. I sat next to Marcus and as we watched, two young women walked through the clearing towards us. The first was carrying a clipboard, her dark hair pulled into a simple ponytail. She was super slim, wore combats and a white T-shirt and was talking earnestly to the other woman, who I knew was Carol-Ann Langham, our presenter. Carol-Ann had been absent from the welcome party in Kathmandu as she'd had to fly in late from another job and here she was, fresh and buoyant and tiny. Carol-Ann was in her twenties and had only recently given birth to a perfect baby girl. According to Donna, nothing ever got in the way of Carol-Ann's career; "She was back doing a piece to camera while birthing the placenta," Donna had announced with deep admiration. I tried not to think about Carol-Ann's placenta as we shook hands.

"Tanya Travis," she smiled. "I grew up watching you, from a little girl."

I smiled stiffly. Why did people always feel it necessary to remind me how old I was and how long I'd been around?

"You're my idol, Tanya, I'd love to do a show like yours... Like the one...you had."

"Oh, I'm sure you'll get there," I smiled, attempting to help her over the embarrassment of my loss.

The other woman cleared her throat and motioned for us all to be silent.

"Hello everyone, I'm Flinty, the producer on the show" she started with a megawatt smile. "I'm going to explain how it's going to work over the next few days, so you know what to expect."

"*Celebrity Spa Trek* is aired every day at 8pm UK time and as Pokhara is 5 hours 45 minutes ahead, all our celebrities need to go to bed early each night and get a brief sleep, in which time the crew will be editing the highlights from your day. No, stay with me... Then you will be woken up, at 1.45am Nepal time, which is when the live show airs in the UK," she smiled, holding her clipboard to her chest like a shield.

"Any questions so far?" We all shook our heads, everyone equally horrified at the prospect of little sleep and extremely early morning calls.

"So for the live show, everyone will gather around our campfire. The first half of the show is catching up with the highlights of the action, the trials and the challenges leading up to the vote. Now, most of the time, the public will be voting for who they want to do a trial or who to send home, depending on what is planned for that show. The format at the moment is that we will alternate nightly between a trial and an eviction. Of course, we like to keep you on your toes, keep it fresh, so this isn't set in stone."

When Flinty had finished, she looked around with a smile. "Is everyone OK with all that? Any questions?"

"So when does it start, exactly?" I asked.

"Tonight!" she said. "We've been very busy editing the highlights of your meeting last night and your journey here today. It would be advisable for you all to go to bed shortly, because we'll wake you at 1.45am, when you will gather here so everyone back home can watch what you've been up to!"

I was horrified. I'd been at *Spa Trek* base camp for about 7 hours and had already vomited, stripped, then had appeared to be pleasuring myself under a towel...and it was all on film.

"Flinty, I need to speak to you about the edit for tonight." I said desperately.

"Later, Tanya" she looked at her clipboard. "Now, I need to just film a few quick words from you all, about how you are feeling."

How I was feeling? About what – the fact I'd come all that way, left the remains of my wannabe wedding at home and the love of my life in pieces to rebuild my career? Or how I felt about doing all of that, then being filmed for seven hours without my knowledge, my lunatic behaviour then broadcast to the nation?

Then the cameramen appeared. I was glad, I needed a distraction as I was worried I might lose it again. As soon as he saw the camera, Rex started banging on about shooting from his left as it was his 'best side' and how he couldn't face the light. Cindi wanted shadow for her curves and Kara was demanding full, warm lighting to show off her 'light-hearted and fun side.' I sympathised with the director, who had his work cut out to capture 'light-hearted' and 'fun', given Kara's manly muscles and stalking convictions.

I stood waiting anxiously while my campmates bid for seats and 'baggsied' lines to say. I was so used to being star of the show and having people fawning around me that I was finding it surprisingly difficult to fight my corner.

I suddenly spotted the camera light on. Perhaps I needed to give some 'performance' for the camera, as everyone else seemed to be doing? Let's face it, I had a lot of damage limitation to do regarding my treatment of young researcher types and this was a perfect opportunity, so I thought on my feet and reached out to gently pull Paul towards me. Touching his face tenderly, I began my Tanya Travis Show speech: "Paul, I will guide you in your journey through TV. But remember, I can only take you so far down that long and winding road... (pause for dramatic effect, close up on camera five). It's up to you to be the best you that you can be." this was said in my best Oprah voice, while nodding gently and never taking my eyes from his.

Smiling serenely, I did big-hearted and sincere with just a little sprinkling of Mother Earth...nothing too ageing. Oh yes, I could still give Oprah a run for her money. Everyone was looking at me – I hoped in awe, but they were all so stupid the prevalent feeling appeared to be confusion.

"Now, I think I'll sit over there, if that's OK with everyone?" I said, daring them with my eyes to object. Paul looked bemused, but I felt I'd made my point.

Marcus was peering at me – no doubt worried I'd be in his shot, but softer now we'd almost bonded over tea and Shakespeare.

"What are you up to now, Gloria Swanson?" he lisped.

"I'm getting ready for my close-up, Mr DeMille," I joked, clicking my fingers for Paul to help me as I lowered myself to sit down on the rocky ground.

"Put him down, dear," Marcus giggled. "You're like a rampant cougar."

"I need him to help me," I protested. "I am a slave to my back as it is; God only knows what lying on hard ground will do to it while I'm here. I'll be begging for bloody eviction after the first night." I said preparing the ground for when I was the first one voted out.

Suddenly, poor old Jonny saw his chance to be on camera. "Six big celebrities sitting on a wall, if one big celebrity should accidentally fall, there'll be five big celebrities sitting on the wall!" he sang as we all perched awkwardly round the fire, embarrassed at his outburst but smiling stiffly in case the camera caught us. Rex rolled his eyes and uncrossed his long, cowboy legs. Not only was Jonny embarrassing, he was making us all nervous. Tomorrow night the first eviction would take place: no-one wanted to be first and we all had something to prove.

"Right, let's get a wide shot of everyone sitting round the camera talking," barked producer Flinty. "Then we will speak to everyone individually."

All the celebrities sat up straighter, their smiles wider as the camera began to pan between us. I noticed Paul was still sitting next to Rex and this made me uncomfortable. The viewers didn't want to see Paul, the spotty teenage unknown, contaminating their pure-celebrity line-up. Was nobody going to say anything? I knew that once Lance the director realised that the runner was right in the middle of the shot, he would have to film the scene all over again and none of us wanted to do extra filming, we were all tired. *So, it's up to Tanya to sort them out again,* I thought, leaning forward. "Paul!" I hissed at him. I guessed he must be slightly deaf because he never seemed to respond when I called him.

"Paul," I said more loudly, willing him to turn round.

He stopped speaking to Rex and looked at me.

"Paul you're in the middle of the shot," I said, shaking my head and waving my arm vigorously in a 'get out of the way' gesture.

"You are outrageous, Tanya," Cindi giggled in my ear.

"Don't take this the wrong way, Cindi, he's a nice enough lad and one day he might even be good at what he does," I said quietly to her. "But we need to get him to move or we will have to shoot this bit all over again."

Paul shuffled a little, aware he was causing controversy but typically ignoring it. Suddenly I was fed up of it all. Someone needed to get a grip – all I wanted was to get this done and try and get some sleep as I'd just been informed we would be woken in the middle of the bloody night. There were no tents, no showers and now Paul the sodding runner was ensuring that we would have to reshoot this bit and I'd never get to bed.

"Well I'm damned if I'm sitting through this with the runner sat right in the middle of a celebrity line-up," I said loudly, trying to get to my feet. Cindi grabbed my arm and pulled me back down.

"What?" I snapped.

"The *runner*?" she mouthed, confused. She was looking straight at me with that annoying face she made when she worked for me, when I asked her something simple that she didn't understand.

"Yess," I hissed, "runner."

"Tanya, what are you going on about?"

"OK, I know everyone wants to be a celebrity," I said, "but this is just silly. It's bad enough having my former assistant sipping champagne next to me but at least you had the decency to do a sex tape and get famous first. There's a limit, Cindi and Paul the runner is not famous, nor to my knowledge has he done a sex tape – therefore he needs to move, so we can all just get on with it."

"*The Hissy Fits*, Tanya?"

"It's not a hissy fit. I'm just fed up with this."

"No, Tanya, I mean Paul. You do know that he's the lead singer – with, *The Hissy Fits*?"

"What... Who?"

It took a few seconds while I processed what she'd said, and then my stomach lurched down the mountain. At speed.

"Hissy... Fits?" I whispered.

"Yeah. Ten number ones? Platinum albums?" She was still whispering, but I heard her loud and clear.

"Even I've heard of *The Hissy Fits* and I'm an old Mozart-queen," grumbled Marcus, unhelpfully at my other side.

No. No. No. I remembered Astrid playing their music, which would explain her reaction when she met him – she was obviously star struck. The truth was, all males under twenty five with that windblown hairstyle looked the same to me, he could have been anyone. And now it was all coming back to me, *The Hissy Fits* were one of the biggest-selling bands of the last few years. They filled stadiums. *No. No. No.*

My mind slowly whirred back over the last few hours, during which time I'd made Paul carry my bag, take notes, make tea and cover my naked body in a towel. I'd then demanded he scrub vomit from my Tshirt, and informed him that if he played his cards right, I would pull strings and get him a runner's job on a daytime talk show – that I'd been sacked from. And every manic, obscene second of it had been caught on camera, to be aired tonight.

I wanted to die and be buried right there in the Himalayas, never to return to Western civilization ever again.

I got through the rest of the filming in a haze, managing to stutter a few coherent words when it was my turn to be interviewed and as soon as I could escape, I found the production truck. I was breathless on arrival but tried a casual, "Hi," to the editor as I stepped into the tiny suite. He half turned and smiled from his cramped little work space and I began to work one of my irresistible charm offensives on him. "I just wondered if you know what's going to be on the programme tonight...Dave?" I said, spotting his name badge and going for the personal approach.

"Don't worry Tanya, it's all about you tonight," he smiled, like that's what I wanted to hear.

"Now Dave, listen to me very carefully. That stuff...when I thought Paul was the runner, it can't go out. My agent would have a fit."

"Sorry Tan, it's good...already been signed off."

"Dave, if this footage goes on air tonight, I will look to the viewing public like a crazed, nymphomaniac, control-freak cougar."

"You've seen it, then," he mono-toned, without looking up from his controls.

"Funny, that's very funny Dave. But it's my career we're talking about...this is my life." Oh God, I was right, it was. This was all I had.

I was waiting for him to give in. That's what people usually did to Tanya Travis – they gave in. But not anymore: I was invisible now. Dave continued to be engrossed in his knobs.

"Tanya, what are you up to?" Flinty appeared at my shoulder, making me jump and addressing me like I was a four-year old. "You're not trying to influence reality are you? You cheeky minx!"

"I wouldn't dream of it," I snapped, trying to sound assertive, not desperate.

"There is a problem," I was trying to gain some semblance of control, but wanting to cry. She cocked her head at me and gave me a big smile.

"Are you OK?"

"No, I'm not."

"But we have such fabulous footage, Tanya!"

"Well, you might call it fabulous footage, Flissy, but I would call it my death-knell. Look, the Paul stuff... It was a case of mistaken identity." I was very anxious now. I'd hoped Dave would be a pushover and that we could just press delete on the last 24 hours but it wasn't going to be that easy and now she'd turned up it was looking impossible.

"It's Flinty. Come on, Tanya. The public will love it...though I wonder how much you were playing to the cameras – I mean everyone knows Paul from *The Hissy Fits*, even someone from your generation!"

"I'm only forty, I'm not from the bloody Stone Age," I protested. "And I honestly didn't know who he was. He collected me from the airport, for God's sake..."

"Not exactly. He agreed to share a taxi with you and we left a sign at the airport for him to hold so you wouldn't miss each other. He thought it would be funny."

"It was your fault then that I thought he was the runner. Therefore you shouldn't show any of it..."

"Tanya, whether you knew or not, in the contract you signed it says we can film what we like, when we like, from the minute you arrive here and that's what the viewing public want to see." She said, her smile disappearing.

"'I took off my bra and pants, for Christ's sake!' I snapped.

"Yeah, that was a bonus... We didn't ask for that in the contract," she sniggered.

"I was covered in vomit, I had no choice. Oh God, I made him scrub the crispy bits off..."

"Yeah, that wasn't in his contract either." Dave the editor snorted.

"Look Flossy, I don't bother with the small print in contracts – I leave all that stuff to my agent, I just sign it."

"It's Flinty." She was now standing in front of me, arms folded, barring the way to Dave and his knobs, like I might leap-frog over her and try to sabotage the footage.

I decided to try a different tack. "Please, er, Flinty. Please don't air the bits with me and Paul." I touched her arm in an awkward attempt at intimacy. By now I was close to tears.

"Sorry, Tanya. The show goes on. " She smiled at me, patting me patronisingly on the arm and turned her attention back to Dave and the monitor. I was dismissed. I stomped back to camp and attempted to get some sleep in my flimsy nightie, in a sleeping bag on the cold, damp grass.

TWEET: @AstridLun I laff till the crying @TanyaTruth being shouty filthy with hot @PaulHissyFits #TanyaTravis4Queen #DocMartin4Ever #GokWan4Me

17

A Scary Night and a Dirty Massage

Before I knew it, I was being shaken awake by Tiffany and told to go to the campfire for the first live show. I couldn't believe it was time to get up. I'd barely slept and the last thing I needed was Tiffany's twenty-something face, shouting, 'wake up lovely'.

"I am NOT lovely," I hissed.

"You can say that again, dear. Ill met by moonlight!" Marcus could be bitchy, day or night.

Cindi was rising from her sleeping bag and apart from a few tangles in the hair extensions, she looked stunning. "Come on, Tan, let's be girlie and put our make-up on," she offered, rummaging around in her bag. She held up mascara, a lip-gloss and some foundation – all part of her allowance – I'd used mine up on anti-bac creams and wipes.

"How can we put make-up on? It's pitch black and we don't have mirrors," I said, feeling lost, alone, exhausted.

"Oh come on, Mrs Grumpy-Drawers, there's a bit of light from the cameras over there and we can help each other."

The last thing I wanted was a girlie make-up session with Cindi but if I looked as rough as Marcus implied and we were about to go out live in front of millions, I needed it.

"Now, close your eyes," she commanded, coming towards me with the mascara. I put my hands to my face instinctively, remembering Astrid's insane lipstick application.

"I'll be fine. I don't need make-up, Cindi."

"Oh, yes you do," she giggled, slapping foundation on my cheeks and following with a little lip-gloss."

Marcus said it was a definite improvement and Jonny whistled, which was both embarrassing and, I felt – patronising – but I didn't say so. He had enough on his plate with 'Rottweiler Rex'.

As Cindi, Marcus and I approached the campfire, Rex and Paul were settled by the firelight, chatting.

"Ooh, you dirty stop-outs – you two haven't been to bed, have you?" Cindi said, plonking herself between them.

"Hey, us cowboys don't need any sleep. But if you fancy sharing a sleeping bag, I could be convinced?" Rex offered.

Cindi giggled and slapped him playfully on the arm. "Cheeky!" she said, but I could tell by her face she was pleased.

"Hey Marcus," Jonny tried as he took his place at the fire, "Rex is looking for someone to share his sleeping bag." Rex didn't even respond to this, just curled his lip. We all took this as a visual cue to ignore what Jonny said; we'd all seen *Brokeback Mountain*, but no-one was going to call *this* cowboy gay.

Marcus suddenly began making strange, guttural noises and I couldn't decide if it was a heart-attack or a distraction technique.

"I'm doing my voice warm-up," he said, dramatically. "No actor can go before his public without warming up the old vocals." He continued to make strange noises and followed these with 'la la la la', at which point Kara seemed to be really wound up.

"Will you bloody SHUT UP!" she yelled. "It's not the Marcus show." For a moment, everyone went quiet and Marcus sulked.

"Oh Kara, come on, don't be a spoilsport," Cindi soothed. "Let's all do voice exercises together."

Cindi convinced Marcus to continue with the strange sounds, and copied him, followed by the rest of us. In the end, Kara reluctantly joined in and we took it in turns to make the most ridiculous sounds we could. And so it was that as I made loud, mewling, animalistic sounds in the darkness, Carol-Ann appeared, led by the gorgeous Ardash through the bush towards us, cameras following her.

"Great, I'm now captured on film forever, mewling like a depraved cat," I hissed to Cindi. "I can see the headlines now."

"So, you've seen what's happened in the last 24 hours, now let's say hello to our celebrities!" Carol-Ann said enthusiastically to the camera. I grimaced and tried hard not to dwell on how I might have looked, or sounded. Everyone sat up straight and smiled. "Well, today is our first challenge," announced Carol-Ann, with a flick of her strawberry-blonde bob. "You, the public, have been voting since the beginning of the show and one of these lovely celebrities is going to be enjoying some time in a spa!"

I didn't see that as a hardship and if the public wanted to see me relaxing in a face mask, having exotic massages and healthy vegetable purées I could live with that. But I wasn't daft; I knew there'd be a sting in the 'spa' tail. I just prayed I'd slipped under the radar and that the delightful 'voting public' had gone for Cindi (hoping she'd get her bikini on), Paul (hoping he'd put tiny trunks on), or Marcus (hoping he wouldn't).

"'Scary Sparry Night' is the name of our very first challenge here in the beautiful Himalayas and it's a good'un!" She teased. "In a special twist, our sleep starved celeb will be enjoying this treat – tonight!" I looked round, horrified; I had assumed all the challenges would take place the following day. I could see from everyone else's expressions that they were shocked too, as Carol-Ann taunted and flounced, revealing slowly but agonisingly what tonight's 'pampering session' would entail for 'one lucky celeb.'

"Our celeb will spend the rest of tonight enjoying the delights of the 'Celebrity Spa Trek Hillside Spa', including a rat-infested hut, a filthy, exfoliating mud massage and bespoke facials using, among other ingredients, the finest and stickiest snake mucus."

"Ridiculous!" I heard myself say, shuddering as something walked over my grave.

"And of course, the whole night will be spent alone, without electricity so that means no light-bulbs, just a torch... After all, this is about finding yourself...even in the dark!" she quipped.

"So... who's it gonna be? Is it gonna be..." she pointed her perfect finger in our general direction, waggling it up and down and making us wait.

"...you Cindi? Pretty Cindi with the beautiful blue eyes? Or are you in for a bit of a rough night on the massage table, Marcus?"

He rolled his eyes and pursed his lips, but I had the feeling it was right up his street, especially if the masseur were male.

"Mmmm... Who's the lucky celebrity going to be? I think it's gonna be... it's gonna be... Time for a commercial break!" she said with a giggle and a flourish.

"Let me at her," spat Marcus.

"She's only doing her job," Cindi said, rubbing Marcus's knee in a calming gesture.

"I'm scared of the dark," he said. "There's no way I'm doing it – even for a very, very rough massage."

"I agree," I hissed into his ear, "let's stick together on this and if either of us are chosen we must stand strong and support the other one. It's me and you against the world, Marcus." He nodded in agreement and squeezed my hand.

I knew the show would entail some horrors, that there'd be a few tough nights under the stars too – but a dirty mud massage? A whole night spent in filth on the side of a mountain?

"I wouldn't have set foot on the programme if I'd known we'd be expected to get so... dirty," I said, to no-one. Staying alone in the dark with rats was bad enough but it was the sticky mucus and the dirty massage that upset me the most. I hadn't had a hot shower since I left the hotel and I was beginning to feel extremely anxious.

"I had no idea of the extent of their depravity," spat Marcus, crossing his legs tightly as we returned from the commercial break.

"So, here we have six celebrities. Ten days, tough challenges and lots of gooey stuff in between... Just so, at the end of it all, you guys out there..." she said, gesturing at the camera, "...can choose your very own Himalayan God – or Goddess?"

She waltzed up and down the camp, making sweeping gestures with her hands and smiling – always smiling – for the camera.

"So...tonight, the viewing public have decided. The person the Great British Public want to enjoy the sheer, unadulterated 'luxury' of 'Scary Sparry Night' is...the very fragrant...and ooh, just a little bit of a bossy boots... Tanya Travis!"

She did a strange little victory stomp (something she'd picked up working on satellite, no doubt) while the other celebrities sighed with relief and tried to look sympathetically in my direction.

"So Tanya, if you would kindly step this way..."

"No."

"Ha..." she was about to giggle, thinking I was playing it up for the camera but saw the look on my face and knew I meant it.

"I am not doing it," I snapped.

"But Tanya, the viewing public, they voted..."

"And if they voted to have me put in the electric chair, I suppose the programme would insist on that too, would they?" For me, dirt was the equivalent to a thousand volts of electricity, not to mention a rough, dirty massage so I felt death by electrocution was a fair comparison.

"But Tanya, if you don't spend the night at the Spa the whole camp will suffer... There will be no breakfast tomorrow. They can't trek on empty stomachs..." Carol-Ann tried for the emotional-blackmail approach.

"Oh come on, dearie, you've been sleeping with a rat for the last four years, why stop now?" Marcus piped up and everyone sniggered; so much for the solidarity.

I could feel the swell of emotion from my campmates, willing me to do this and earn them some decent food. Carol-Ann was now leading me through the trees and to a clearing where the hut of filth stood waiting for me.

"Jesus, no..." I heard myself say, as a man appeared from inside the ramshackle old building looking like a dirty old tramp. He was holding the filthiest towel I'd ever seen in one hand and a bowl of what must have been the 'mud face mask' in the other.

"There are two parts to this challenge, Tanya," she was saying as much to camera as to me. "Firstly, you will be given a lovely face pack. You have to lie with the face pack on for 60 seconds before it can be removed. Then a 'luxury' massage after which you will enter the hut where you will spend the night with the inhabitants!"

My skin was crawling and my hands were shaking. Then Ardash appeared and gently took over from Carol-Ann.

Holding me firmly by the arm, he helped me to lie down on the makeshift massage table made from bits of rotten wood. Even in the midst of all this horror, his touch sent a thrill through me. The 'masseur' was smiling; he was filthy with no teeth and very little hair, like something from a horror film...or a guest on my show.

"Don't you dare come near me!" I hissed.

"If you close your eyes, you won't have to see," Ardash whispered in my ear, as he covered me in a towel. His soothing voice placated me slightly as I reluctantly lay down, closing my eyes tight like when I was a child and scared of the bogeyman.

I never used a towel twice to dry my hands at home – it was one wipe and straight in the laundry bin. So the dirty towel lying across me and the one the masseur was carrying worried me far more than he did. I tried not to think about it, but I opened my eyes and had a peek. I was covered with a cloth that was stained with foul colours, including what looked like blood. Screwing my eyes shut again, I couldn't see anything approach but as soon as I felt a waft of something near my face, I shot up with a strangled scream. My arms jerked out instinctively in self-protection and I inadvertently swiped the bowl from Mr Massage's hands.

"Do not worry, Tanya." It was Ardash again, speaking quietly. "These towels are not what they seem. The dirt is not real dirt."

I gave him a small, grateful smile and took a deep breath. The masseur had picked up the bowl and he gestured for me to lie back down. I felt sick and I could feel the rising panic as my heart-rate increased and my palms started to sweat.

The masseur approached me. I could hear the squelch as he dipped his fingers into the bowl of mud. I breathed deeply and thought about the last facial I had before I left, trying to imagine this filthy, horrible mud mask was just the same.

I felt a small, wet blob on my face. I could hear the blood roaring in my ears. I desperately tried to think happy thoughts but as soon as the masseur began smoothing the filthy mud onto my skin, I lost it.

"Get it off me! Get it OFF!" I cried, clawing at my face. I was feeling genuine panic and Ardash quickly wiped the mud off.

"It's OK" he said in a low, calm voice. "The mud is gone. Don't worry." He patted me on the shoulder and I tried to stop shaking.

"Oh dear! You've failed part one of the challenge, Tanya!" said Carol-Ann brightly. She had a smirk on her face, and I could see members of the crew trying to stifle their laughter.

"Never mind – let's try part two!"

"I'm sorry but I refuse to do any more of this...this ridiculous stuff." I huffed, gathering myself together. I was furious at being made to face the thing I feared the most – filth – and then being laughed at for having a go.

"Just have a try, Tanya" she said encouragingly. "At least come and have a look." Ardash took my hand and, despite my deep reservations about the whole thing, it calmed me. He led me over to the 'shack'.

"For the second part of the challenge, Tanya will spend the rest of the night in our scary spa building!" said Carol-Ann, like it was the Hilton. Ardash put his arm around me and I lent into him. For a moment I felt warm and safe but the feeling was soon gone when I stepped inside. I had to crouch to get through the rickety, rotten door and the hut itself was tiny. Ardash switched on a torch, and shone it on a woven mat on the floor.

"Here's your bed, Tanya!" said Carol-Ann brightly.

"What's that?" I said sharply, as something ran over my foot. Ardash shone the torch down, and I could see cockroaches – dozens of them. "Arghhh!" I yelled, hopping up and down. Then, as I was trying to shake the insects off my foot I noticed something else. The torch picked up two yellow eyes, staring right at me.

"What...what the hell is that?" I whispered, frozen to the spot.

"This is a rat" said Ardash, calmly.

"No, no, NO!" I said. The hammering in my head returned with vigour and I broke into a sweat. "I can't do this, I am sorry, I have to leave," I shouted, pushing my way past Ardash and running outside. I was feeling light-headed so I leant over and put my hands on my knees. Ardash was beside me again.

"You must breathe slowly, Tanya, yes?" he said, handing me a paper bag. I put it over my nose and soon, the stars swimming in front of my eyes disappeared.

Carol-Ann swanned over. "Oh dear, Tanya!" she said cheerfully. "The celebrities will be going hungry tomorrow!" I glared at her, unable to trust myself to speak.

"Never mind! Tune in tomorrow to see how the other celebrities react to starting their day with no food!"

As Carol-Ann wound up the show, Ardash escorted me back through the trees. He didn't say much.

"I'm not mad, you know." I said, for some reason worried about what he thought of me. After all, he'd witnessed me vomiting, mewling like a cat and now this – I couldn't blame him for assuming I was bonkers.

"I think you might be just a little bit crazy, Tanya Travis," he smiled and his eyes twinkled; he was teasing me. I liked the way he said my name.

Leaving me near base camp, Ardash wasn't allowed to go any further. I guessed the twisted psycho TV bastards wanted to get a good old close-up of me returning on my own, empty handed – for the twisted psycho bastards at home to hate me just a little bit more.

I decided to brazen it out and just before I came into view, I put on my best Tanya Travis face and smiled widely, showing my teeth (or baring them, depending on how you looked at it).

Murmurs of 'Tanya' echoed through the trees as I arrived. They were all pottering around stoking the fire, washing pots – no doubt discussing my trial and waiting for news of their next meal. "Hey I thought you were supposed to stay in that place all night?" was Rex's first comment as I came into the camp. *Trust him to have a go*, I thought.

"Oh Tanya, was it awful?" Cindi asked. The others looked at me open-mouthed, waiting to hear what had happened and whether or not I'd passed their test.

"I'm sorry everyone," I said. "I couldn't do it... I tried, but I couldn't, it was absolutely vile."

"Oh honey, never mind. At least you had a go," Cindi came up and put her arm round me. The others nodded, making agreeable noises but you could have cut the atmosphere with a knife. From the vibe I was getting, I wasn't sure it was safe to sleep near any of them that night.

GOSSIPBITCH: *Which bright, blonde, beautiful new presenter has just been paid six-figure sum for her misery memoir 'No, Tanya No!' The book, to be published next autumn, will dish the dirt on the cruel, bullying ex show host who made the rising star's life a misery.*

18

Smelly Old Goats and Stroppy Old Cowboys

At what felt like about 4am I lay awake under the stars, feeling the dust in every pore. I was so uncomfortable I seriously wondered if I might have been better off in the filthy spa with rampant rats and a weirdo holding a towel. What could be worse than sleeping on the ground outside in the cold? Marcus was snoring at one side of me, Cindi tossed and turned at the other. I was beyond desperate for a hot shower; I hated the way my perfectly-highlighted and expensively-cut hair was dusty from the rocks and ruining the style aesthetic. And my armpits whiffed...something I'd never allowed to happen in my life before. It was torture and even if I could forget about the dirt and the smell of my pits, I was scared to fall asleep because I knew there were infra-red cameras just waiting for me to drop off with my mouth open. Finally, as dawn broke and I was just falling into an exhausted coma, everyone around me began waking up. Alarms were sounding from the diary cave because apparently we now all had to go and do a piece to camera about how we were feeling. We'd spent the night outdoors in the cold with no supper – how did they think we were feeling? I looked around, Rex was still snuggled up, Cindi was brushing her teeth vigorously in tiny pants – no doubt a directive from her 'management' to make sure her pert, cellulite-free bottom stayed famous.

"Morning Tan!" she said cheerfully, waving at me after rinsing her mouth. "Did you sleep well?"

"No" I replied curtly. "And before you ask, I am not going into the bloody diary cave to tell them all about it."

Cindi rolled her eyes. "Alright, grumpy-gills!" she said. "Let's go and get some breakfast."

We made our way to the clearing, where I was faced with the result of last night's failed challenge. No hot breakfast of sizzling bacon here – just one piece of dry toast and one orange-flavoured energy tablet each.

"Yum," I said, trying to make a joke of it. No-one laughed.

"I can't bear these damned tablets. I took them every day doing my Hamlet in Peru... they turned my pee neon." Marcus grumbled through dry toast crumbs.

"Eat up, guys!" said Tiffany, who was marching round the camp like a Nazi foot-soldier and looking much too bright and perky for that time in the morning. "We start the trek in half an hour!"

"This is totally unreal." Rex was looking at our 'breakfast' in disgust. "Man. How am I supposed to trek up a mountain on this?"

"I agree," I said, jumping on the bandwagon. "I'm going to..."

"...Call my agent?" said Kara, sarcastically. I looked around at the others. They clearly hadn't forgotten whose fault breakfast was.

"Tanya, I need you in the diary cave," said Flinty, appearing suddenly at my side, clipboard in hand.

"No thank you, Flinty," I said firmly, trying to regain my composure. Who cared if they all hated me I'd be voted out soon anyway and I could get away from this hell.

"It's not a request, Tanya," she said with a little smile. "I don't want to keep saying it, but it's in your contract."

I closed my eyes for a second and counted to ten.

"OK fine" I snapped. "But don't expect me to say anything."

With that, Flinty led me to the diary cave, where I was given a clip mic and settled onto a bench. I felt like I was in one of those old fashioned photo booths they used to have in Woolworths. As kids, me and my sister would go into town on a Saturday and sometimes spent our pocket money in the photo booth. It was always so funny to see who could pull the most ridiculous, ugly face each time the machine flashed. I had to resist the urge to stick my tongue out at the static camera...but even in my stressed state I knew it wouldn't help my cause with the Great British Public.

The voice started and it was clearly Tiffany putting on a weird accent, to try and camouflage her voice.

I felt stupid and very vulnerable. I wanted to cry. This was the last place on earth I should be while in this state, but in my mind's eye I saw Donna bearing down on me, her voice in my ear; "Go for it sweetcakes, you can do it, tits and teeth, tits and teeth."

"Hi." I smiled to the camera, or tried to, but I could see my unmade-up, wrinkled face in the monitor and it was more a horrified grimace. And my hair... oh god my hair... the obscene image shall forever be imprinted on my mind... It was positively feral.

"Tanya, the public voted for you do the task last night but you didn't – what do you have to say?" Tiffany's weird voice echoed through the mountains and back into the cave.

"I couldn't do the challenge." I snapped then I suddenly remembered this was my opportunity to turn things around, appeal to the public and stop them from voting for me.

"What I mean is..." I said, attempting an endearing smile, "it wasn't a case of 'wouldn't'. It was 'couldn't'. I physically could not do it."

"But Tanya, all you had to do was lie there," said the disembodied voice.

"Look, I gave it my best shot" I tried, "But I just couldn't bear it. I won't frolic in mud, fish guts or live insects nor will I put my tongue or my hands near anything that may harbour bacteria. So please don't waste your texts and your calls and please stop voting for me."

"Tanya, are you trying to influence the public vote?"

"No! I just don't want the viewers to waste their money." I said, desperately.

"Do you think the public can be influenced that easily?" came the voice sternly.

"Look... Just vote for Paul or Rex instead." I hissed, attempting a smile, which probably looked more like an evil grimace. There was silence from the voice. It seemed my attempt to gain sympathy had backfired. *Nice going Tanya*, I thought, a solitary tear falling down one cheek.

"Thank you, Tanya... you are now free to leave The Diary Cave," came Tiff's strange, over-wrung vowels.

I left the diary cave with a heavy heart and went back to join the others.

"Ooh, who needs kedgeree! *That* would make a delicious breakfast," cooed Marcus, looking past me. I turned to see a shadow heading towards us in the sunlight: it was Ardash.

"Come over here sweetie," Marcus was smiling and patting the spot on the ground next to him for Ardash to join us. "Ardash, are you taking us trekking today? Are you going to move me to the core at the side of a mountain, dear?"

"Ah Marcus, you love the mountains, yes?"

Marcus pulled a disgruntled face. "I'd rather be in a hotel room dear... I'm not one for sleeping under the stars. Not alone anyway." He fluttered his eyelashes, winked at me and mouthed 'gorgeous,' as he shuffled his bottom to make space for Ardash to sit with him. At least Marcus was including me, perhaps the others would eventually forgive me too, I thought.

Ardash was smiling and gently teasing Marcus. "Wait until the sun arrives fully... Marcus you will fall in the love. Ah, the way she shines on the lake..."

"Oh, she sounds bloody wonderful. I think I've already fallen in love. Take me to that girlish sun and warm these old bones," he giggled coquettishly.

Ardash was sitting opposite me, smiling at Marcus's comments but every now and then looking over in my direction. I smiled back under my eyelashes, hoping the misty dawn light was flattering the encroaching crows' feet and that the flush on my face was the campfire, not the menopause. Then I realised: it wasn't just me he was looking at so appreciatively. He'd moved his eyes to Cindi – 15 years younger, blonder and with a body to die for. And her eyes were locked on his.

* * * * *

After most of us had done a stint in the diary cave, Flinty arrived.

"Here is everyone's lunch," she announced, handing out small rucksacks with Tiffany, her henchwoman.

"Where are we going, dear and who'll be carrying our stuff?" asked Marcus.

"I'm coming to that... In each of your rucksacks is lunch and some water, which by the way you will carry yourselves. Ardash will, as always, be your guide."

Ardash was over by the trees packing a rucksack with extra water and first-aid stuff – he smiled and waved at us.

"Oh, man!" Rex swore and kicked at the ground, like he'd been told he was going to his death.

"When is the bus collecting us, love?" Marcus asked hopefully.

"The clue is in the title of the show you're in, Marcus... it's a trek." Flinty snapped sarcastically. Obviously, she'd also had little sleep and was as grumpy as everyone else. "We'll be with you all the way," she said, "don't look at the camera...forget it's there and think reality. Oh and do try and stick together. We don't want to lose anyone!" she yelled over her shoulder as she went off to bark at the cameramen and take a nap. Marcus was furious, it could take him ten minutes and much assistance just to get up from his seated position, and God knows how long the trek would take him. I doubted Cindi and Jonny were strong hikers and despite all the plastic surgery Rex was well past it.

Within minutes, we were stumbling around in our still unfamiliar trekking boots, trying to keep up with Ardash's strong, confident stride. It was going to be a long morning.

* * * * *

The trek to Phewa Tal lakeside was tiring, downhill, and quite beautiful. We trailed through dense forests, catching glimpses of the lake and the Annapurna Mountains through the trees now and then. We were all of varying stamina, fitness and willpower and it wasn't long before some of the group began to slow down. Everyone was tired and grumpy but we all kept going and I tried to stay positive, despite Rex's constant digs that he was having more difficulty because he hadn't had breakfast. Ardash was our pace-setter; I certainly wasn't as strong as him but my regular morning runs at home had kept me fit and my breathing was good. It made sense for me to stick with him because he knew the land and he'd keep me going. Ardash and I began chatting early on and he was knowledgeable and interesting. Despite the hellish midnight wake-up call, the early night and the fact that everyone hated me, I was starting to enjoy myself.

After about two hours' solid trekking, we arrived by the lakeside where a pile of bicycles awaited us. Apart from the spin-bike at the gym I hadn't been on one in years and Ardash held the bike still for me as I gingerly placed one leg over the contraption. "Tanya you keep steady yes?" he said gently, holding the back of my saddle like my dad did when I was a little girl and learning to ride. He ran alongside and despite the bike veering all over the place, I felt secure just having him there with me. Once I was more comfortable I got in line behind Ardash and turned to hear Cindi screaming with joy and a little fear as she trundled along at quite a pace. Rex, Paul and Kara cycled together, Jonny was alone and I could see in the distance Marcus was walking his bike, assisted by another hunky trekking guide.

Once we'd ridden round the lake I saw 20 or 30 brightly coloured canoes laid out by the shore: a boat rainbow, framed by the snow-topped mountains.

"So beautiful," I said to Ardash as we waited by the boats for the others.

"Ah, Yes. In summer during Monsoon, Annapurna disappears, now in early autumn the sky is clear. Annapurna is Goddess of the Harvests... Without her there is hunger."

"Oh, let's not talk about hunger. No-one's speaking to me after I lost breakfast and they're all cross and hungry," I sighed.

"People from your country don't know hunger, Tanya," he said, gazing across the lake.

"I suppose you're right," I said, feeling a bit silly.

I suddenly heard a strange chanting and distant drumming reverberating through the trees and mountains. It was exotic and trance-like. "What's that?" I asked.

"Buddhist monks at prayer... You will see soon." He looked up to where the sound was coming from and high up through miles of forests I saw a small pagoda shape.

"What is it? I asked.

"Wait and see. You need patience, Tanya... Not 'now now, now'," he smiled, teasing me again.

"I'm not that bad," I giggled, "I have patience. I can wait."

"Ah, we shall see," his eyes twinkled.

When everyone had arrived we all clambered into the boats and were taken across the lake, which felt surreal. Here we were, gliding across a lake in Nepal, the water lapping gently at our boats, all quiet as we took in the sheer beauty and tranquillity. The sky was navy blue and cloudless: I'd never known such peace. Nothing seemed to matter here – tabloid stories, lack of money, cellulite shame, they all melted into the water.

Approaching the land on the other side, I now saw the gleaming white pagoda high up the hill.

"We are here, at the World Peace Pagoda. Climb to the top and you have won today's trial," announced Ardash, helping us off the boat.

"We'd better start climbing then, campers," Jonny piped up as Ardash led the way, heading the group uphill. It took about half an hour to reach the pagoda temple and sometimes Ardash had to touch my back to guide me. When he did, I felt a strange tingle in my spine. I smiled at him but suddenly felt a pang for Nathan. Being in the close company of another man had made me think of him, I could almost feel his presence. Was there still a chance for us? My hopes fluttered up through the prayer flags, rising higher into the sky. The chanting was louder now and with the drumming thumping at my heart I knew I had to keep hope alive in my heart. It was all I had left.

Ardash nodded for us to walk on and on completing the 375 step hike to the temple I couldn't enjoy it straight away. I just wanted to lie down... forever.

"Come Tanya, look at spectacular view." Ardash was as fresh as he'd been at the start, fit and keen to keep going. I looked up at the small but stunning Japanese-style temple, white and gleaming, strung with bright red and yellow flags, dancing in the sunshine. He could see I was exhausted and held his hand out to me. I reached for him and felt a fizzing in my chest; was it the altitude, thoughts of Nathan or the fact I'd had no breakfast?

Rex was holding on to Kara, who seemed to have taken on a mothering role towards him. Marcus had turned precious and I could see him sitting down on one of the steps demanding 'a cable car, dear,' as Paul and Jonny trudged along together. Another trekking guide arrived and Marcus told him he was 'an angel,' asking if he could hold on to him. I smiled to myself and carried on to the top of the temple with Ardash.

Cindi caught up and I linked her arm as we walked into the temple. It was cool and dark and covered in dead and dying flowers. "Ooh, it stinks in here," she said, holding her nose and spoiling the moment of serenity.

"You really would be happier in a nightclub, wouldn't you?" I teased.

"Oh Tan, this isn't for me. I just saw someone carrying a dead goat up those steps. I mean, seriously?"

"Yes, people bringing sacrifices," Ardash appeared at Cindi's side, a twinkle in his eye as he looked at her.

"I hope you've not brought us as sacrifices, Ardash," she tittered. He smiled. He obviously thought she was amusing, not to mention young and very pretty.

Cindi chatted easily with men, like you do when you're in your twenties and know you look good. She talked to Ardash, giggling and flirting, making him laugh and I felt my own light fading next to hers.

The two of them clearly had chemistry, so I left them to wander up to the roof of the temple on my own.

Once outside, I leaned over the white brick balcony which ran round the temple roof. I gazed down onto the landscape's green, arable past of patchwork fields and crops, slowly tracing the brickwork with my hand I moved round. The view changed again into its concrete future of Coca-Cola tourism dressed in vibrant billboards holding up the ramshackle buildings of Pokhara. The past causing ripples in the future and the future taking from the past... from greenery to billboards, it all felt so fragile and unreal.

A little later I joined the others for lunch in the nearby temple courtyard. We were now all sweaty and grimy and despite being hungry, no-one enjoyed their cold chapattis with greasy dhal and bottled water.

"I'm so bored of this shit," Rex complained, spitting dhal everywhere, while the rest of us ate in silence, not responding, not wanting to provoke him in any way. "Hey, Tanya, Kara tells me you were the 'Darling of Daytime' before you 'lost it live'?" I smiled and continued to eat. The guides and the cameramen were all setting up the next shots and working out the walk and some stuff with Cindi and Kara so it was just me, Marcus, Rex and Jonny. Paul was leaning over the edge having a cigarette, clearly the fresh air was far too clean for him.

"So, what happened to breakfast? Let's hope the 'Daytime Darling' doesn't get voted for a challenge again, or we'll all go hungry. Again." he snapped.

"You don't know the meaning of hunger," I said, remembering Ardash's words.

"What? What did you say, DARLING of DAYTIME?" he sniggered.

I ignored him and the three of us ate in embarrassed silence.

"Would you like a sweetie, dear? Marcus was smiling at me and fumbling around in his shorts pocket until he found and produced a rather sticky pink sweet. Normally I would have refused this outright on various grounds, diet and hygiene being uppermost. But I was grateful for his kind gesture in the face of Rex's aggression. I took the sweet, unwrapped it and put it in my mouth. It made my jaw ache with sugariness and I sucked and smiled while trying hard not to contemplate whereabouts on his person he had been hiding his secret confectionery stash.

The sun was high in the sky by the time we left the lunch area and on reaching the lake I saw Ardash, sitting by the boats.

"Where's Cindi?" I asked, sitting down next to him, surprised to see him on his own.

"Ah, she and Kara they were tired, they go back," he smiled. "I waited for the rest of you. A bus will take us back, it should be here soon."

The cool mountain breeze was like a fresh, tingly wipe across my face, taking turns with the melting sun that gently warmed my flesh. The ground was firm beneath me and I stretched out on it, feeling every part of it on my legs, my back, my head. I stared at the clouds now melting into ice-cream pink and gold. I sighed. "This really is the most beautiful place on earth."

"Yes," he nodded.

"Every day must be different, just as beautiful, but different. The light, the seasons..."

"Yes, that's true. Winter is white and it sparkles in the mountains. England is beautiful too, no?"

"Yeah, I suppose so. Not like this."

"Big Ben, red buses, I see them on TV?"

I smiled. "Mmmm, trust me, it's not worth leaving these mountains for red buses and Big Ben. You just can't compare this to rainy old Britain."

He smiled. "I could never leave. They are part of me, the mountains. I know them so well, like...like..."

"Like the back of your hand?" I said and he lifted his palm to his face, looking sideways at me with querying eyes and an uncertain smile.

I giggled. "It's an English saying, it means you know something very well – as well as you know this." I touched the back of my hand to show him.

I ignored the tingling feeling in my stomach. Ardash was nice, but talking to him made me even more aware I needed my own man back in my life. I longed to see Nathan, I ached for him and I was determined we would try and make a go of it once I was home.

GOSSIPBITCH: *Which blonde Page 3 girl has the hots for a handsome hunk in the Himalayas? Early reports suggest he feels just as hot for her...*

19

Bacterial Hand Wipes and Prolonged Agony

Later that day we gathered around the campfire for yet more rice and dhal. Everyone was more relaxed after the trek and the mood was lighter, now we knew each other better.

It was nice to see Jonny and Kara had bonded; clearly their meeting hadn't been the bloodbath the producers had hoped for. They were chatting about a model who Kara knew from her time in *I'm a Celebrity*...

"She was gorgeous, Jonny and such a lovely person. Sadly she's straight, but we've stayed great friends... Hey, perhaps I could organise a blind date for you? She loves funny men." Jonny was smiling enthusiastically, delighted to be put forward for a blind date with a model and equally pleased to be called a 'funny man' again.

"Kara, quit humouring him." Rex suddenly butted in. "You said this model likes guys who are funny, so why would she hook up with Jonny boy?" His face was humourless, almost angry.

Jonny deflated like a balloon and Kara looked embarrassed but said nothing, clearly keen to align herself with Rex, the Alpha Male of the pack.

"Why don't you just leave him alone", I said angrily before I could stop myself. He looked across at me.

"Tanya Travis..." he said slowly, leaning back onto the rocky ground and using his rucksack as a pillow. Everyone turned to look at him. "Tell me, Tanya Travis, Queen of Daytime. Why are you here?" His eyes were cold, his jaw clenched, he wanted a fight.

"For the same reason as the rest of us, Rex: money and profile." I said tightly, with a smile.

"So how exactly do you expect to survive in the mountains, if you can't even sit on the floor without brushing the dust off your fanny?"

"He means your arse, not your vagina, Tanya... In American fanny means..." Cindi offered.

"Thanks Cindi, I realise that." I said. "You're right Rex. I probably shouldn't have come on the show but I stupidly listened to my agent, who implied it was like a bloody health farm."

Cindi and Jonny giggled. Rex didn't.

"Go home then."

"I don't want to. I want to stay here." I spoke slowly and calmly, surprised at what I'd said. I clearly still had a lot to learn about myself.

* * * * *

"So, everyone, are you prepared for the first eviction?" Flinty and Tiffany bounced around enthusiastically like bloody cheerleaders. We all stared at them, bleary eyed, hating them for being so perky at 1.45 in the morning.

We'd only been to sleep for a few hours and with the hard ground and after-effects of the trek destroying my back, those hours hadn't involved much sleep on my part. They led us to the campfire and left us to chat, whilst the pre-recorded part of the show was screened to the nation.

"The public will never forgive me, for the way I treated Paul when we first arrived," I sighed, leaning back against a rock and staring into the fire. "Despite the trek today, which went OK, the programme's probably been completely re-edited to make me look bossy and controlling."

"I doubt they'd have to do any editing to make *you* look bossy and controlling, dear," Marcus sniggered. Then Cindi joined in.

"Yeah, they don't need to edit 'get here now and clean this sick off me you chart-topping bloody rock star'." He and Cindi giggled to each other at that and I just rolled my eyes.

"Whatever I do the press will crucify me," I said, "whether they edit or not."

"Look. There's nothing we can do – what will be, will be," Marcus said.

"And the press do exaggerate stuff but in my experience there's always some truth in it," Cindi added.

"Yes but it's cruel and unnecessary. I'm fed up of reading that my boyfriend's a sex addict," I said.

"That's my point exactly," she nodded slowly, like she was talking to a five-year old.

"I told you, he's not a sex addict, Cindi. The press make up lies."

"They don't. When are you going to get it, Tan? He's a sex addict and you're a control freak. Nothing's good enough for you and you spent your time just ordering everyone around on your show." The others stopped what they were doing and looked over at Cindi, who was twisting an extension round her finger and looking at me sincerely.

"Thank you Cindi...your compliments are making me blush," I said, using sarcasm to hide my surprise.

We sat in silence for a couple of minutes, but I couldn't leave it. I turned to her: "Really, Cindi? I thought I was quite nice to work with...a good boss. I cared..."

"Yeah, I know you cared Tan, but you were a bit of a stressyBessie, everything and everyone had to be just so. You worked too hard, everyone said so – you just completely lived it, and expected everyone else to do the same – but they had other stuff, other lives, they weren't obsessed like you."

"I was just doing my job," I said, sad and a bit surprised that what I'd thought was assertiveness and perfectionism had been perceived as fussy and obsessed.

"Oh, to see ourselves as others see us, dear," Marcus added unnecessarily.

The fire crackled and popped and for a while we all just gazed into it, looking for answers or killing time until the inevitable. It was OK for the rest of them, they knew they were safe – but I was going to the gallows. Not only was there my treatment of Paul, but also my failed challenge to consider. I must have looked so weak and pathetic and spoiled. As we counted down the minutes until Carol-Ann appeared, it seemed we were all reflecting and all hoping not to be the first one out.

I was confused at the contradictions in my head. I didn't think I wanted to be here, but I didn't want to be the first celebrity evicted. And what's more, I had almost used up my limited ration of super strength bacterial hand wipes.

"I hope my mum's remembered to Sky Plus this," Cindi sighed.

"Not sure I'd want to watch it all over again. I'm so nervous," I whispered back.

"When I'm scared Tan, I always think of this famous quote; 'It's okay to be afraid as long as you show up'."

"Mmm that's philosophical. Who said that?

"Sharon Stone. What an actress."

"Yes, she's great," I agreed.

"Tan, she's amazing...the woman was over forty when she crossed her legs and showed her fanny in Basic Instinct. In my book that's courage. A fanny over forty on film? Respect."

"Respect." I agreed, hoping the conversation wasn't audible on air.

Carol-Ann walked confidently across the rocky ground towards us, in scarlet patent Jimmy Choos, her skirt barely covering her bottom. *I bet she can get up off the ground seamlessly, without having to get on all fours and lever herself upright,* I thought enviously. As she approached, Carol-Ann prattled on to camera and I contemplated strategies for coping with another rejection, this time not just from one person (Nathan) or one company (ITV) but from the British Public.

"Is there medication I can take?" I whispered to Marcus.

He giggled. "I think both Rex and Paul are taking enough for all of us, dearie," he patted my knee.

"Carol-Ann's very good," I murmured, trying to dissipate the ball of dread accumulating in my stomach.

Marcus wrinkled his nose: "Too young, too straight, too obvious. She's from the homogenised, post-Eighties school of presenter," was his verdict. "It's all about youth and looks and not about talent." I'm ashamed to admit his comment made me feel a little bit better.

"We've now reached that part of the night, the live eviction when one of our celebrity spa trekkers will be trekking home," Carol-Ann rubbed her perfect hands together before turning to us with her 'sad face' on.

"Seven very special celebrities sit before me," she started, "we've enjoyed their antics for the past few days... But who do you, the viewers want to send home tonight?"

Turning on cue, she walked confidently forward to stand facing us, hands on hips, smiling, safe in the knowledge that her career was going up and time was on her side.

"The voting results are here," she teased, waving her *Celebrity Spa Trek* cards. Each one of us longed to snatch those bloody cards from her perfectly-manicured hands and see whose name was written there. The air was tingling, everyone was tense, desperate not to be the least liked, the most hated...the one so boring, so past it that no-one could even be bothered to vote for them.

Carol-Ann paused as she'd been instructed, prolonging the agony and accelerating our collective blood pressure.

"...The person voted out by the great British Public and the celebrity trekking home tonight is...going to be... Announced after this commercial break!"

The mountains seemed to groan around us as we flopped in disappointment and temporary relief around the campfire.

"Tell us, you little witch," commanded Marcus, clutching Carol-Ann's arm.

"Nah, you cheeky fucker!" she snapped, in an accent that was pure cockney. It was good natured, but I don't know what surprised us the most – the accent or the language.

Marcus and I looked at each other: two judgemental old dears over a garden fence. "Oh, I never expected that, thank God the ads were on and we were off air," I said, raising an eyebrow.

"Yes, amazing what elocution lessons and designer clothes can do... Let's hear some more of those 'cor blimey' tones, it will inspire my next performance in *Oliver Twist*."

"Carol-Ann, pray tell who's departing, I can feel 'Madame Angina' coming on. My death will be on your conscience forever dear," he said to her dramatically. But Carol-Ann just smiled, she was busy practising her words, raring to go: a beautiful, perfectly groomed storm. All cockney inflections were eradicated along with skin imperfections as the make-up lady applied powder and the cameras started rolling. Carol-Ann was nothing until that camera light clicked on. I knew how that felt.

"And welcome back..." she did another two minute and 34 second intro, by which time I'd convinced myself (not for the first time) I would die, live on air. Even if I survived to live another day, there was every chance my eviction would be punctuated by the same explosion of vomit as my arrival. I tried to think of cool, calm waters and gathered myself together for my inevitable departure, from the show or this world, whichever came first.

"So, voted for by you the public... The first celebrity to leave *Celebrity Spa Trek* is...is...the lovely...the headline-making..."

This eviction was making the scary spa challenge look like a day in the park.

"...Kara! So sorry, Kara!" Sad presenter face.

I was stunned. I'd convinced myself it would be me – mind you, I'd also convinced myself I would die or vomit live on air and that hadn't happened either. *Yet.* I was relieved not to be the first but my mind was still a dark, tortured place. OK, this meant people were voting for me to stay, but it didn't mean they liked me – did it? What twisted reasons could they have for keeping me here? I glanced over at Cindi, who raised an eyebrow and a tentative, congratulatory smile. Kara hugged us all, waved goodbye then tripped off through the mountains to a cold glass of champagne and a decent bed.

"Ah Kara, how we shall miss her." Marcus said for the cameras, but giggled in my ear: "No actress is safe...she will stalk again..."

* * * * *

Despite the late (or should I say early) hour, we were all too hyped to go to bed so we gathered by the fire for a post-eviction beer and marvelled at the fact it hadn't been me. "I hate to say it but I don't know how you stayed in," sighed Cindi. "I just held my breath thinking, Tanya's a goner."

"Well, they just wanna see her suffer, don't they?" Paul added, confirming my fears.

I nodded; "Yep. I'm on borrowed time. They hate me because I failed the trial and you guys haven't eaten a decent meal because of me... I am genuinely sorry."

"Man, that Kara, what a swell camp-mate," Rex said, kicking out his legs and leaning back on his elbows. "She sure would go the extra mile for any one of us. I mean, there was nothing that *she* wouldn't do, right? Shame she never got a challenge," he said, looking directly at me. "It shouldn't have been Kara gone tonight."

I didn't know what to say. I could feel my face redden. There was an awkward silence and everybody looked at the floor or into the fire. Rex was a popular guy and it was clear that they all shared his opinion. He was always laughing with Paul or flirting with Cindi and he even found time for Marcus, who he referred to as 'my fellow actor,' and Marcus was flattered by the A-list attention. I managed to stop myself from pointing out to him that an SS guy with a Texan accent in a Nazi mini-series was not comparable to Marcus's Lear at the RSC – but Rex had them all eating out of his hand. Jonny was watching me with his watery eyes and I think he felt sorry for me, because he tried to change the subject.

"Hey Rex, I bet you'll miss Kara's massages. She gave you a good shoulder-rub today didn't she?" Jonny said with a smile.

"What you tryin' to say, Jonny boy?" said Rex slowly, turning to face him.

"I didn't mean nothing Rex...it's just... You two got on well, and she was good at sports massage...that's all I meant."

Silence. You could hear a pin drop.

"I hope you ain't tryin to imply that me and Kara were anything other than buddies?" He said, threat twitching in his voice, anger simmering just under the surface.

"No, no Rex, me old mate... I just ..."

"Don't you say that, Jonny boy. I have a reputation, a good one. Don't even think it."

"I wouldn't – I didn't. Oh I'm sorry mate, I don't want to..."

"I am not your mate, Jonny." Rex said slowly. "A guy like me and a guy like you – I don't think so." He stared at Jonny for a few seconds, before Jonny averted his eyes and looked at the ground. "That's better" Rex said quietly, too low for the cameras to pick up, but loud enough to give Jonny a clear message. I looked over at Jonny who twitched his mouth slightly at me in a 'that was awkward' face and I smiled back. I wanted to shout at Rex, to tell him he couldn't speak to someone like that – but I couldn't, I was in enough trouble without seeking it out. I knew I was as bad as the rest of them, keeping quiet not wanting to get involved and find Rex's heat on me. What was happening to the Tanya Travis who told the truth, who was never scared of anyone, from gangsters, to drug dealers to wife-beaters? Since when did Tanya Travis keep quiet, just because someone was a big celebrity and no-one else dared say anything? I'd hoped this place would give me strength but so far I'd just discovered weaknesses I never knew I had.

TWEET: @AgentDonna Tanya T denies sex with toyboy, sex with Sharon Stone, sex with Cindi Starr + all booze/sex binge claims #Don'tBelieveThePress

20

I Scream and a Thespian Queen

The next day, we were woken early once more and taken on a trek that was more arduous than the one the day before. It also involved swimming in the lake, much to Marcus's horror.

"I don't do water, dear" he said, shivering. "I'll wait here."

"Ah, come on Marko!" barked Rex. "We can't all be jessies, can we?" he shot a look in my direction. "C'mon, I'll wade in with you."

"Well, seeing as you are offering" said Marcus, dipping his toe in the water with a squeal.

The day passed quickly and we returned very tired to the camp and went to bed. It seemed like I had only been asleep five minutes before Tiffany was shaking me awake, ready for the live show.

"Now, Carol-Ann's just in make-up, she'll be with us shortly. Same as before, you all sit round, Carol-Ann sets up the VTs of the past 24 hours then about 48 minutes in she will announce who's been voted to do the next challenge. Is everyone OK with that?"

"Yeah, as long as it's not Tanya," Paul winked kindly at me. I nodded in agreement. "I hope it isn't me, because if it is no-one will eat tomorrow."

Cindi shot me a look and once Tiffany had flounced off she crawled over to where I was sitting. "Tan, you aren't going to refuse again, are you?"

"I didn't exactly refuse, but if it's anything like the first one I can't do it, Cindi." She looked disappointed. "I'm not saying I won't Cindi, I'm saying I can't."

She nodded and went back to her seat without saying a word, but everyone could see by her face what we'd just spoken about, and looks passed between them.

Carol-Ann eventually appeared. Her freshness and vitality seemed to be increasing in direct contrast to our ingrained dirt and exhaustion. Her shiny, clean bob swung around as she spoke and I envied the flowery scent of lathering soap and the stinging heat of a shower – something I'd always taken for granted until now.

Carol-Ann went through the same routine as before, seducing the viewers and teasing us with who it may or may not be. "Who have our viewers chosen to do tonight's challenge?" she giggled to the camera. "Ooh, you naughty people at home are determined to make our celebrities suffer. And tonight's challenge is called 'I Scream' – geddit?"

"She'll 'geddit' in a minute," hissed Marcus, whose colour indicated his blood pressure was rising by the second.

"If it's me, I will vomit," I whispered under my breath.

"I don't doubt it, dear," Marcus responded and Cindi smiled sympathetically.

"'I Scream' is an ingenious little challenge from our spa think-tank, involving a bucket of ice and a vat of yak's cheese." Carol-Ann said brightly to camera. "Yak's cheese is a big part of life here in Nepal and in a nod to this national cheese our celebrity will sit, fully clothed, in a huge dirty great vat of it. Now, that's all very well, you might say...but where's the scream in that?"

Where indeed? From my perspective, total immersion in a container of putrid cheese would definitely provide me with endless possibilities for 'screaming'.

"Well, the chosen celeb will be asked three questions, but with a bucket of sloppy yak's-milk ice cream hanging precariously over them. Yummy!" Carol-Ann continued lightly, (like she was talking about Häagen Dazs). "Now, for each question the chosen celebrity answers correctly they will win a meal course for everyone in the camp, which, if they get all the questions right means a slap-up breakfast, fabulous lunch and lavish dinner tomorrow night! If they get the questions wrong, they get an icy, cheesy shock over their head...and they lose a course."

"Sounds darling," Marcus whispered, "up to my neck in cheese on prime-time, it's what my career has been leading up to all these years." I closed my eyes, unable to speak.

"So, the question tonight is, who is going to have the chance to sit in a vat of smelly yak's cheese that's been sitting in the sun all day, with the delicious threat of frozen yak's-milk ice cream landing all over them?"

"I can't wait," I whispered. Everyone was tense. Paul and Rex were gagging to do it, wanting to prove their masculinity and prowess and – in their defence – they were also keen to eat a decent meal. Cindi caressed her hair extensions protectively, clearly distraught at the prospect of a wrecked fake golden mane. Who knew the effects yak's milk ice cream would have on hair extensions? I doubt the manufacturers ever considered this a possibility and had therefore not included this in their product testing. Marcus was playing up the revulsion but I reckoned he and Jonny would probably both do it for the air time. I, on the other hand, would have willingly poked my own eyes out with knitting needles rather than immerse any part of my body in greasy, foul-smelling cheesy goo that had been sitting in the sun all day. Apart from the obvious physical horror of it all, what on earth would such an act achieve – apart from public humiliation followed by another on-air meltdown? I had had enough of that before I even got to Nepal.

I tried not to let the thoughts of warm, sour cheese hit my stomach as Carol-Ann continued with the taunting dance in her cute little Havaiana flip flops. Her toenails were clean and shaped, perfectly painted in sugar-pink, while mine were dirty, snagged and unpolished. In the middle of all this I had been stung with deep toenail envy, something I'd never had before. I wanted to cry.

"So you, the Great British Public have had your wicked way again!"

My hands itched, my head tingled with anxiety and the thought of ripe yak's cheese all over me made my stomach lurch and my now infamous reflux twitch.

"And...the celebrity Britain wants to see up to their neck in warm yak's cheese is... Tanya!"

I put my hand over my mouth in an attempt to prevent an instant projectile event.

"No. I can't...no...no way. I can't..." my head was shaking fiercely, my heart was pumping and my stomach was turning over and over.

"She'll do it dear, she's been up to her neck in worse than yak's cheese, darling," Marcus announced, like I wasn't there.

"I'm not... I won't...I..."

"Come on Tanya, let's take a stroll through base camp," Carol-Ann cajoled, all fake smiles and sugary lip-gloss. "Come on, cameras too... We'll walk together to see just what this entails and then you can make your decision," she said, assertively. The producer was obviously telling her to make me do it.

"Carol-Ann... Don't you understand? If I had to jump off a mountain, even swing across a rope bridge – with the correct harness and all Health and Safety procedures applied – I would. But this... The stickiness, the smell..." I began to retch just thinking about it.

"We have to go to a commercial break now but join us in four minutes to find out if Tanya Travis has the courage to sit up to her neck in warm, smelly, yak's cheese and win a meal for her hungry fellow celebrities. See you very soon!" she beamed to camera.

We went off air and relieved, she gently took my arm. "Look Tanya, this is silly. Our challenge project team have been working all week on this one and you owe it to them and the rest of the camp to do it..."

This had me straight back on my high horse. "If it's taken a week for the so-called 'challenge team' to come up with the idea of filling a fucking tank with yak's cheese for someone to sit in – then might I suggest you find a new 'challenge team'?" I spat.

"Tanya, Tanya, calm down. You're an old pro, you know the score," she pleaded, like a nursery teacher to a four-year old. "The more you refuse to do it, the more the public will vote you in. They don't like cowards, Tanya. You only have to prove yourself once."

"I'm not a coward, but the idea of sitting in something disgusting horrifies me deeply. More than you can imagine. I can do icy water – well, if it's clean... I can do snakes even, but I just can't do slime and smell and dirt. And please don't tell me yak's cheese is in my contract – because it isn't." I said, starting to feel desperate.

Carol-Ann sighed. "OK, OK. Look, just do me a favour and pretend you're undecided when we get back after the commercial break. Make it last, too. Lots of 'will she, won't she' – if you flat out refuse, I'm left with 12 minutes of air to fill and I'm not that good," she smiled.

"OK, I've been there myself. I won't do that to you... I'll pretend to think about it."

So we came back after the commercial break and I ummed and ahhed and made like I was actually contemplating a vile bath of sour cheese. Then Carol-Ann said "Come on Tanya. I'll take you over to the challenge – we know you can do it!"

I walked on shaky legs with her through the camp until we came to a large wooden tub with a lid on top. I could see three buckets suspended above a cauldron and the whole scene was lit up, like some kind of hellish fairground attraction.

I took deep breaths as we approached.

"So Tanya," said Carol-Ann, looking into my eyes. "We all believe in you. The British Public believe in you. Now is the moment of truth!" and at her signal, two crew members pulled the heavy wooden lid off the sweating vat of putrefying cheese. The smell nearly knocked me off my feet. My hand was clamped firmly over my mouth and I could no longer hear what Carol-Ann was saying. Dimly, I saw the crew members put some steps up to the tub. Carol-Ann, still talking to the camera, took my hand and tried to pull me forward, but my feet refused to move. "Tanya? Tanya?" she was saying.

I was shaking my head, eyes watering. Carol-Ann had her hand to her ear and was listening to instructions from the producer.

"Tanya, the show has decided you can pick one camp-mate to help you with your challenge." she said then turned to the camera. "Who will Tanya pick? Who can help her face 'the cauldron of courage'?"

I was still staring at the bloody cauldron in horror.

"I'm going to have to press you on this, Tanya... Who would you like to come and help you with this challenge?"

"Marcus," I whispered, not taking my eyes from the vat, still trying hard not to vomit from the foul smell. I felt he'd be firm but kind and didn't – to my knowledge – have hair extensions that might perish in yak's cheese.

"Marcus it is!" said Carol-Ann. A member of the production team ran off to get him.

I took deep breaths and looked around. I was aware of Ardash, standing just off-camera with the first-aid equipment; he was looking at me. I smiled despite myself and he smiled back.

"Once more unto the breach, dear friends, once more!" came Marcus's voice, as he was led through the trees towards us and on entering the area he almost collapsed from the smell.

"Oh my Lord, dear...God..." he breathed at the sight of the cauldron. Which didn't help. One bit.

I hoped Marcus would be strong, support me and cause a scene if they tried to make me do anything I didn't want to. However within moments, he began screaming for smelling salts.

"How could you do this to Tanya, the poor wretch?" he wailed, throwing his arms around my waist. I moved up a step to get away from him, which was horrific as it took me closer to the yellow mucus-like contents of the vat. I was trying to contain my overwhelming nausea, but of course Marcus viewed this as a prime-time audition; I should have known.

"Hell is empty and all the devils are here!" he spat at the crew, now in full Shakespearean throttle.

"You can hold Marcus's hand, if it helps," offered a desperate Carol-Ann, ignoring his drama, more worried about the ratings if yet another challenge failed to take place. I didn't think Marcus's hand would be much help but I had to at least pretend and I tried my hardest to imagine getting in. I stood on the top step, and leant over the steaming, putrid muck.

"I can't... I can't... I'm sorry" I said, the fumes making me sway.

At this point, Marcus seemed to remember why he was here. "You can do it, dear Tanya!" he said, and went to hug me hard in an effort to provide visible on-screen consolation. In doing so, he inadvertently missed his step, fell into me and before I knew it, I was suddenly face deep in the viscous cheese. It took a couple of seconds for me to realise what had happened.

"Arghhh!!! No! Get me out!" I screamed.

"Give me your hand, dear!" said Marcus, leaning over the side and reaching in. But my hands were covered in a cheesy slime, and so slippery that the more I grabbed, the more I was sucked down into the fetid depths and the more we both shrieked. Like yellow sinking sand, it pulled me into warm, vile slime and as I retched and heaved it occurred to me that my life couldn't get any worse. But I was wrong, because above me were three tubs of yak's milk ice cream and Carol-Ann leaning in with a camera, to ask me the first question.

"What is the Nepali name for Everest?" she asked, like it was a simple maths question.

"What? I haven't a clue..." desperate to avoid another dunking and only too aware of the icky stickiness in every crevice of my body I looked at Marcus questioningly.

His head was to one side; "Oh darling, I have not the slightest. I'm so very, very sorry Tanya..."

"Oh dear, Tanya, this means ice 'scream' for you!" Carol-Ann said gleefully.

"No, no wait!" I said, before an exuberant Tiffany could pull the chain and send freezing gunk all over me.

"It's Sagarmatha."

"Correct! Well done, Tanya! You've won the celebrities a delicious breakfast!" said Carol-Ann, amazed.

"Oh bravo darling, well done – how on Earth did you know?" said Marcus admiringly.

"Ardash," I said, "he told me on the first day we were here."

"Well Tanya, next question!"

I tried to shift position and felt a wave of nausea. I could feel the yak's cheese seeping in everywhere and I was desperate to get clean.

"I don't think I can do another one, I need to get out," I gasped.

"Oh no, the show must go on!" announced Marcus theatrically.

"And you're doing very well, dear." he whispered.

"So, Tanya, what is the national dish of Nepal?" Asked Carol Ann.

"Dhal Bhat," I said quickly, before any ice cream could land on me. I'd seen enough rice and lentils already in my time here to know that one.

"Correct! And finally, why is the Nepali flag so unusual?"

At this one, I was stumped. "Marcus?" I said hopefully.

"Alack! I know not!" he said, throwing his hands to the heavens.

"I'm going to have to press you on this one, Tanya" said Carol-Ann seriously, as if the fate of the world depended on it.

"No, I'm not sure!" I said, panic rising. "I don't know...wait! Yes, it's the shape! It's a funny shape, not a square or a rectangle!"

I turned triumphantly to Marcus – just in time to receive freezing, thick, foul-smelling gloop, right in my face. Tiffany had been a bit trigger-happy when she thought I was going to get it wrong. My triumph fled, to be replaced once more by revulsion as I wailed and flailed in hot and cold cheese and ice cream hell.

"Out, out, OUT!" I screamed and was heaved inelegantly from the sticky mass by two burly crew members. I retched as soon as I was on dry land, but Carol-Ann was clapping and congratulating me.

"Well done, Tanya!" she said. "Amazing! You've won three lovely meals for the camp tomorrow. Now, off you go and get washed!"

I needed to get the smelly, sticky clothes off me pronto and I didn't want another stream episode live on air, so I bid farewell to Carol-Ann while she wrapped up the show and hurried off-camera to find a bucket of water.

"That was marvellous dear!" said Marcus, going to give me a hug then thinking better of it. "How on Earth did you know the flag question?"

"Just something I picked up," I said airily. What I didn't tell him was that Ardash had the flag of Nepal embroidered on his jeans. On his back pocket, to be precise. Some things were better left unsaid.

Tiffany let me strip off in one of the production tents (she was feeling guilty about the ice cream) and I doused myself in a bucket of freezing water. Then with a towel wrapped around me like a sarong, I made my way back to camp.

"Does anyone fancy three lovely meals tomorrow?" I called as I wandered into the clearing, where the others were still up, waiting to hear what happened.

"Yeah, but till someone does a trial it ain't gonna happen," drawled Rex. I ignored him.

"I believe the chef here is excellent," I said.

"You did it?" Cindi screeched.

I nodded.

"Shut the front door, Tanya!" she did a little dance and everyone else gave me a hug or a thumbs-up.

"That's amazin' Tanya, thanks" said Paul with a smile.

I smiled back and the hell of the cheese and my desperate desire to get some Sanihand on was momentarily forgotten. It was so nice to be in favour with everyone – I just hoped it would last.

TWEET: @AgentDonna Tanya Travis NOT engaged 2 Marcus. NO plans 2 make sex tape in bath of cheese with yak! #Don't BelieveWhatURead #PressBS

21

Tabloid Trauma in the Cave from Hell

The next day I woke feeling happy. I had finally passed a challenge – albeit thanks to Marcus – and we were roused from sleep by the smell of bacon frying.

"Mmm, Tan, this is amazing, thanks!" said Cindi with a smile, as she took a big bite of her bacon sandwich and glugged her orange juice.

"Yeah, nice one, old lady" said Paul with a cheeky wink. Even Rex gave me a half-smile and I was pleased to have their approval for the first time since I had arrived. Apart from the odd comment or smile I had avoided Paul since 'vomit-gate.' I knew he was matey with Rex and not only had I behaved abominably but my refusal to do the challenges had put me on a sticky wicket with everyone, so I hadn't felt able to face him properly. The mood in the camp was cheerful, so I felt the time had come to address this.

"I'm sorry Paul, about us getting off on the wrong foot...my misunderstanding..." I said, "...thinking you were a runner."

"Ah... It's cool, Tanya. I'd heard you were a bit of a diva," he smiled. "From the stuff I'd read about you in the papers, it was no surprise to be hauling your luggage and washing your stuff..."

"Paul," he announced in a posh 'Tanya' voice; "please can you tell me when we're filming? Paul, please would you do your job? Paul, please wipe my arse..."

"I liked it when she said 'Paul. you. can. be. the. best. you. that. you. can. be.'" said Rex slowly, hamming it up, on the edge of fake tears with a fake New York accent.

I'd thought I was being Oprah, but Rex's portrayal made me sound more like something from *The Sopranos*. I sensed he was enjoying my humiliation a little too much but I smiled and resisted saying anything. I wasn't going to start a row with the lion just as I'd been accepted into the celebrity jungle.

Paul was still giggling about my unreasonable but admittedly hilarious demands: "I didn't mind carrying your rucksack. But the sick? And what is it with you and the hand gel, girl?" I laughed lightly and steered the conversation in another direction.

"Thank God Cindi told me who you were when she did, I could have become even worse."

"Jeez, how much worse could it get? You made him clean up your spew," added Rex.

"OK, so he's a hotel-room-trashing, millionaire rock-star, but you're never too famous to wipe up celebrity sick," I joked. Everyone laughed.

"Hell, who do you think you are, Tanya bloody Travis?" More laughter as the international rock-star clinked his cup of tea with mine.

However, the happiness was short lived. Tiffany was soon approaching me and told me to go into the Diary Cave, at producer Flinty's insistence. I reluctantly left the group and headed for the cave, once there I sat myself down, and waited for the disembodied voice.

"So, well done for your trial yesterday Tanya. How are you feeling about it today?" Flinty's badly disguised voice filled the room.

"Good" I said with a smile. "I was pleased I could win everyone some nice food."

"That's great. Now, it's fair to say that you suffered at the hands of the press before you came to Nepal, Tanya. Would you like to know what they've been saying about you since you have been here?"

My stomach lurched. "I... I don't know," suddenly the calm, self-assured persona began to crumble slightly.

"Look to your left, Tanya and you will see a pile of newspapers. You have 60 seconds to look at them... If you want to."

Oh God. Oh God – the temptation. I wanted to grab and devour every page, every headline, I was hungry for news of Nathan, Georgina's success and even lies about me. I sat there for eight seconds, nine, ten...and at 14 seconds like a drug addict, I couldn't resist and grabbed the first paper, desperately scanning it for my name. Of course they'd made it easy for me and provided every headline about Tanya Travis that had appeared in the press since I'd gone into *Spa Trek,* three days before. There would be no frantic searching for stuff about me and my life, it was all there under the headlines: I could inject straight into the vein.

'*Bossy Tanya Makes Rock-Star Rub her Breasts*' was the first one, with an accompanying photo of me washing myself in a very unflattering light as Paul from *The Hissy Fits* looked on in horror. '*Tanya Travis in Mountain Meltdown*', another timely piece about my apparent 'mental health issues.' I picked up another to read in big, bold letters about my 'vitriolic outburst against Georgina,' my 'hate, lust, anorexia, menopause madness, weight gain, weight loss, break-down' and that old favourite '*Tanya's Addiction to Plastic Surgery*.' This segued into a gossip mag mud-fight with; '*Georgina Ronson Hits out at Tanya Travis*', '*Tanya's Travis Hits out at Georgina Ronson*'; '*Tanya Brands Georgina a Talentless Tart!*' and '*Georgina Brands Tanya 'an Ageing Diva!*' I hadn't said a word to or about her nor her to me since I left that day, yet '*Tanya and Georgina's Bitter Feud*' seemed to be everywhere.

Then it came, thick and fast: a photo of Nathan falling out of a club, a new blonde clinging to his arm; '*Nine-Times-a-Night Nathan Tries for a Ten*', another pap shot of him leaving a strange house apparently at dawn: '*Tanya's Toyboy Flees Britain*', '*Nathan Wells and New All Night Love*':

'*Shamed talk-show host Tanya Travis's toy-boy lover has hit out at claims he bedded a pole dancer at the couple's £2m Cheshire home. Tanya, 46, is currently in Nepal...Love Rat Nathan, who recently claimed to have slept with 100 women in two weeks said...insatiable...*'

'*...was caught in clinch with willing blonde... nameless blonde... Blonde Candy 22, said Nathan 'is the best lover I've ever had.*'

And so it went on...

In the short time I had, I skimmed the lines, touching on the words over and over again. How he'd held her hand, 'bedded' another, told yet another he 'wanted to make love to her in Tanya's bed.' Perhaps in my panic and hurt and stress I thought that reading it again and again would desensitise me in the way kids are supposed to be desensitised by violent computer games. But each word – each phrase – each quote – was agony every time and rereading revealed a previously overlooked nugget of fresh, searing pain.

I wanted to scream but if I gave in to the slightest emotion it would be a matter of time before I was thrashing around the Diary Cave in grief and stress and... Well, God only knows what the press would have headlined that shot.

"So, have you enjoyed seeing news from home?"

No, you sick, twisted bitch was on the tip of my tongue, but I resisted. "Yes thank you," I smiled, my chin now trembling, my eyes brimming with tears. I wiped at my face, pretending it had dust or a fly in it. The voice waited, clearly hoping for me to break down. I bit my lip, stared at the ceiling and counted to ten.

"Now Tanya," came the voice, finally. "All the other celebrities will have to wait till tonight for their video postcards from home but we want you to be the first to have yours."

I'd have given anything to hear from Nathan, a video of him saying 'don't believe anything you read, Tanya.' Or even better 'Tanya I love you – that girl was my sister's friend...' like he always did when horrible lies like this turned up in the press. Anything to suggest he'd been thinking about me would be a cooling poultice on my raw, wounded heart.

"Is it Nathan?" I asked. "Is it from him... Is it...?"

"No, it's from your PA, Astrid Nordlestrom," Flinty announced and suddenly Astrid's flushed face appeared on the screen in front of me. Her face was shiny and she had on her best dress, which made her look like something from *Little House on the Prairie*. She sat up straight, peering into the camera, her hands clasped on her knees, taking this very seriously indeed. I couldn't help but smile back, through my tears.

"Dear Tanya," she started. (Being Astrid, she would take the 'postcard' bit literally.)

"You are the shit. I have been doing laughing and crying as I'm watching you on the ITV – but not on Wednesday because Gok is looking good naked and I NEVER fucking miss him. I laugh to see you asking Paul Johnson from Hissy Fits to clean you up... Piss me, you are so funny. He is so hot! I looking forward to you coming back but have terrible, terrible news that is very urgent and very, very shit..."

I held my breath...was it the baby? Was it Nathan's after all? *Oh please don't tell me here, live on air in what is ludicrously referred to as 'The Diary Cave,'* I thought.

"I heard news yesterday that makes me cry and you will too. Tanya I hate it to say, but there is rumouring that no more *Doc Martin* programmes. No more lovely comedy drama with cute doc Martin Clunes and taking place in Cornish. I cannot live without that little doctor and his funny, cross face so me and Freda are going to see him in Cornish and beg, beg, beg him to make more of the fucking television series. Bloody hell Tanya, lots of sick people for him to be making better! A doctor scared of blood is so fucking crazy we LOVE him," at this she chuckled, like she hadn't laughed about it a million times before. "So I take my box set and he will sign with a pen and Freda says he's not being so grumpy in real life.

"And before I will forget it. Embarrassing the Bodies last night... oh my fucking hell Tanya! Dr Christian he was telling man in clinic not to put the foreign objects up in his man parts! You can't believe what he had in there, so I recorded for you.

"Anyway I need to go now, Come and Dine with Us is on and it says in Televisions Times' that it's a 'hell of a week with food fight, big pole dancing, black puddings and sex worker from Scarborough'. Yours sincerely Astrid Nordlestrom your best PA."

I sat for a few seconds to let it all sink in... Not the *Come Dine with Me* menu, the end of *Doc Martin* or Dr Christian's experimental patient. It was the fact that I hadn't realised until then how much I missed Astrid. She was such an odd girl with a foul mouth and surreal thoughts but under it all, she was kind and always happy. A visit to the set of *Doc Martin* to accost 'that funny little man,' Martin Clunes, would be the highlight of her adult life and no doubt provide bizarre stories over herring dinners for years to come. Though it did occur to me that should they ever come across him, Martin Clunes might view Astrid and Freda's affections in a more worrying light. I couldn't help it: a few more homesick, Nathan-sick tears appeared and I tried to stay calm and collected.

"Thank you – it was lovely to see Astrid...my PA," I smiled.

I left the diary room with the bubble of my new-found happiness well and truly burst. Who was I kidding? I had managed to complete one challenge, with the help of Marcus, and I thought that everything was alright again. Clearly the public still hated me, and the papers had been a horrible reminder that I was still in the public eye for all the wrong reasons. And worse still, if only a few of those stories were true, it seemed that Nathan and I had no hope of reconciliation.

I went and sat by the fire. Everyone had finished breakfast, and was preparing for the day's trek. I put my head in my hands and stared glumly at the embers.

"You OK, Tan?" Cindi plonked herself next to me.

I didn't answer her, and we both sat in silence for a few moments.

"You look sad," she said, touching my arm.

"Oh, they showed me some headlines, in the Diary Cave. Stuff about Nathan..." I felt my chin tremble again.

"Tan, you don't have to hold onto the pain, to hold on to the memory..."

I smiled at her. "I didn't realise you were a philosopher," I said.

"Not me Tan... That's Janet Jackson. I know lots of quotes... you name 'em; Cameron Diaz, Angelina Jolie, Kerry Katona..."

"I suppose they're all philosophers in their way," I said, mystified.

"Were you upset about that Georgina taking over your show?" she asked, suddenly.

I blinked, surprised at the directness of her question.

"She didn't take..." I started

"Well, I think it's outrageous, them ousting you and giving your job to someone just 'cos she's younger and prettier. She's a piece of work." She said, shaking her head.

"Did you know her?" I asked, surprised.

"Yeah, you know what telly's like, everyone knows everyone else. Before she got my job as your assistant, she used to be a secretary in Sport. We'd bump into each other in the coffee shop, she was always so friendly, she'd buy me a latte and always wanted to know stuff about you. Now I know why. Then, when she got my job, I heard she was sleeping with Ray. I wouldn't sleep with someone just so I could be on telly," she said, like a six-some sex-tape with a boy band didn't have 'Reality Show' written all over it.

So, Georgina's rise was far more strategic than I'd realised. I should have known, she always worked so efficiently, so cleanly – nothing was left to chance. But Ray? That part of the plan must have been the hardest.

"You know that Hermione is her best friend, right?" said Cindi, looking up at me.

My mouth went dry. "Really?"

"Yeah. I wouldn't be surprised if she got her to wind you up during the show. She didn't have to work too hard to get what she wanted. When I worked there, Ray was always banging on about needing a 'new, fresh face for Daytime' so her turning up at the right time was good for both of them," she pulled a face.

"I was so naïve, Cindi." I said, shocked. "I trusted Georgina and I thought I was different. I believed I had the talent and the viewing figures to overcome the fact I'm not blonde and no longer in my twenties."

"Oh don't get all paranoid, hon'. You're not past it yet!"

"Apparently I am," I suddenly heard my own voice. "And I'm scared. The public clearly hate me."

"Don't be daft, Tan. Yes they do hate you and you're quite old for a show like this but I've told you before, you remind me of my mum...and she can do anything."

To my surprise, I found my eyes were wet. The last few days had been such a roller-coaster of emotions and I was beginning to realise that the invincible Tanya Travis, who demanded her own way and got whatever she wanted, wasn't really me at all. I reached for my anti-bac wipes and started cleaning each finger, one by one.

"Don't," said Cindi softly and gently took the packet away. A tear slid down my face, and I put my head in my hands, and I sat for a little while just staring into the flames. When I looked up, Cindi was gone and Ardash was sitting in her place.

"Where's Cindi?" I asked looking up, my face wet with tears.

"Tanya, you don't need to keep cleaning the hands," he said, taking one of my hands in his and looking at it. It was dry and cracked and disgusting: I felt totally exposed.

"I... I know, but I just find it helps me to stay calm. I'm very homesick, you see..."

"Ah, I understand. But wherever you are, home is always here," he touched his heart. Mine did a little somersault. He was so gentle and seemed to really want to talk, something I found hard to do with Nathan, who never had the time. Being with Ardash made me think even more about Nathan and how much I missed him but also about all of our problems – which made me very confused

"I'll be getting off now..." I said, attempting to leave the fireside like a will-o'-the-wisp. But as I got up, I felt a sharp sting in my toe. The pain was horrendous and I made an awful, unattractive, 'umph' sound as I landed heavily, face-down.

"Tanya, what is it?" Ardash said, concerned, leaping to his feet and helping me up. The pain was subsiding but I lifted my foot up and pointed at it.

He sat me down, pulled off my flip flop and examined my foot more closely. "Ah, maybe a bite... A spider."

I was horrified... Jesus, I hadn't washed my feet for hours!

"Yes, you've been bitten," he confirmed, his hands gently caressing where the pain was. "You should not wear the flip flops here, Tanya. There are many insects, you must always wear the trekking boots."

"I know" I said, feeling foolish. "It's just my feet were hot and sweaty and I wanted to get some air to them."

I could feel his breath on my toes as he scrutinised the wound. A little shiver ran through me and my mouth broke into a smile. It was totally involuntary and I just smiled away to myself, hoping my feet didn't smell too bad. As a trekking guide, Ardash was medically trained for such emergencies so I was in safe hands – and they were good, firm hands too. As he continued to examine my foot, I half-opened my mouth in near-ecstasy and tried not to gasp. Having not had human contact for some time, the delicious sensation of Ardash's long, probing fingers squeezing each of my toes was unbelievably fabulous and felt very...intimate.

"Can you see anything? I asked, my stomach fizzing.

"Keep still, Tanya," he said, still caressing. Then just as I was drifting off he made a sudden movement and lunged at my foot. I felt a searing pain and looking down saw to my horror that his mouth was on my toe.

"Christ...!" I yelled, jerking my foot away. "What the bloody hell are you doing?" Toe-sucking headlines had done little for Sarah Ferguson's marriage or reputation and I certainly didn't want it on my CV or in *The Sun*.

"Get off!" I yelled.

"Tanya, I am sorry."

"That's disgusting. You taking advantage... you make me sick..."

"The bite is poison."

"Yes, poison to my relationship and my career, you disgusting... Ah...poison...disgusting poison? It's poison? In my toe?"

"Yes Tanya, I'm sorry, spider venom. It must come out."

"Oh... Oh I see, yes it must," I said, feeling foolish at my outburst of which he seemed quite unaware. He picked up my leg again and holding my foot in those gentle hands, put his soft, warm lips around my big toe. I giggled nervously. I was enjoying his medical treatment far too much and tried not to groan with pleasure, as he once more bore down hard on the soft, fleshy pad.

After a few moments of unadulterated bliss, he pulled away from my foot with a mouth full of poison, spitting it behind him. Which I have to say was gross and the only thing that stopped another projectile vomiting incident was the distraction of his soft hands on the soul of my foot.

"What can I say?" I was embarrassed, "Thank you, Ardash," he nodded, still trying to get rid of the poison from his mouth. I looked away just in case my reflux let me down, the poor man had been through enough already.

I was about to delve for my wipes and remembered Cindi had taken them. I'd been so distracted by Ardash's toe-sucking I'd completely forgotten.

"Spiders here can be poisonous," he said. "But I think you're safe now. You must come to the first-aid tent and take the anti-venom now, just in case. Then if you feel any pain, or nausea, please let me know."

I nodded, and he helped me to limp over to the first-aid tent.

After I had taken some antihistamine and the anti-venom, I went back and joined the others, who had gathered together in anticipation of the day's trek. I could see Ardash talking earnestly with Flinty, who was frowning.

"Tanya, I hear you have been bitten" said Flinty, a little crossly.

"Ardash doesn't think it's wise for you to trek today. He thinks you should stay here."

"Ha!" snorted Rex, looking disdainfully at me. "Sure, Tanya, you rest your ass while the rest of us work ours."

I glared at him.

"Never mind, dear" said Marcus, smiling at me. "You could have a nice little sleep."

I looked at Flinty hopefully. A 'nice little sleep' sounded just what I needed.

"Fine, Tanya stays here" she decided. "Rest your foot. Ardash says it will only need a few hours, which is good. Everyone else, let's go! Don't forget, it's an eviction tonight, so best foot forward!"

The others moved off and congregated with Ardash and I went back to my sleeping bag and laid on top of it. I could hear their voices, a murmur in the background and before I knew it, I had drifted off.

I must have slept for a long time because before I knew it, the others were traipsing wearily back for tea.

"Ooh, Tan, that was a tough trek" said Cindi, flopping down next to me. "You were lucky to miss that one! How's your foot?"

I squeezed my toe experimentally. "It's OK thanks" I said with a smile.

"Well, that sure is good to hear" said Rex sarcastically. I ignored him.

"Hey old lady, I'm gonna make some dinner. Wanna help?" said Paul, coming over.

I clambered to my feet with as much dignity as I could muster, and went to help Paul make our specially delivered lunch – my 'winnings from the day before. millionth dish of rice and lentils.

We were just finishing eating and I was thinking about an early night, when Carol-Ann appeared.

"What's she doing here at this time?" I said. "I thought we wouldn't see her until tonight's eviction?"

As we watched, she hurried through the trees towards us, followed by the camera, and Flinty.

"Hello, celebrities!" She greeted us. We looked at each other uncertainly.

"It's a twisty, turny thing, this spa experience," she went on, turning to the camera. "And today is bittersweet. We will be saying goodbye to one of our lovely celebrities before the live show tonight and they won't even get the chance to pack."

There were murmurs and gasps from all of us. Why was there an eviction happening in the afternoon? Had something happened?

"I'll get me coat," chirruped Jonny, making a desperate grasp at prime-time comedy. He had nothing to worry about. Jonny was the underdog and everyone loved an underdog.

"So, my celebrities," she smiled, cocking her head in fake sympathy, catching my eye.

Even though I'd been expecting it, I was still surprised, a shock-wave went through me at the thought of going back home and I wasn't sure I wanted to. Of course I wanted to see Nathan and I needed to get my life back, but it all felt like too much of a challenge – almost as bad as a bath of yak's cheese.

"The person leaving us today is... Wait for it... Tanya Travis."

Everyone was suddenly hugging me and saying how sorry they were (but secretly glad it wasn't them) and Carol-Ann wasn't letting me hang around for goodbyes. "No time to pack, Tanya, let's go!" she said chirpily, leading me away from the camp clearing to a narrow wooden bridge that went over a mountain stream. "I'll see you in a few minutes with a glass of champers, Tanya," she called after me while discreetly pushing me in the back, to get me off-camera.

"Thank you Carol-Ann, there's no need to push," I yelped. She at least had the decency to look embarrassed, I thought, waving behind me as I crossed the rickety bridge to the waiting press.

I was in total shock. One minute I was sitting round the campfire with my newfound friends, the next I was on my way home. I walked gingerly, the bridge creaking under me as I tried not to look down, holding tight to both sides of the flaking wood that would take me across the mountain stream and ultimately, home. Then it hit me: *I had no home.* By now I was sure my house would have been repossessed and my career had done the equivalent of falling off this bridge and being swept downstream, away, never to be seen again. I sighed and pressed on. I eventually reached the other side, expecting the flash of cameras, the 'over 'ere, Tan,' that we'd been told would happen after each eviction. But after a few seconds I realised there was no-one there; no press, no Carol-Ann joining me for the eviction interview with that glass of champagne and a list of probing questions. The silence was deafening and all I could think was: *what the hell have I done now?*

I stood on the other side of the bridge and gazed around me. In my shocked state I took comfort from the bluest sky, fluttering prayer flags and snow-topped mountains and despite my anxiety, I allowed myself a moment to take in the sheer beauty. I gulped lungfuls of air, taking slow, deep breaths in an attempt at calm, while desperately searching my head to work out why I might be alone. What had I said or done on the programme that meant there had to be a press blackout? Hang on...had I simply come over the wrong bridge? But looking back there was only one. Then my heart lurched down hundreds of feet into the mountains. What if something had happened at home? Was it Nathan? My sister? Had they got me out of there away from the cameras and was a professional on their way to break terrible news? What the hell was going on?

Within about four minutes, I heard a rustling and Tiff appeared with her clipboard from behind a tree. She was still wearing her talkback which meant we were probably being filmed.

"What is it? What's happened? Have I said something terrible? Does everyone in Britain hate me?" I blurted at her as she skipped towards me, all made up for the cameras.

"Tanya... Say nothing...come with me," she whispered, with more drama than even Marcus could have mustered. I felt my knees give way and clutched at her, hoping to God she'd be able to keep me upright.

"It's OK Tanya, this way," she almost dragged me forwards and stumbling, I clung to her arm like my life depended on it. All I could think was: *please no more shocks, no hurt, no rejection, no more blondes or betrayal waiting in the wings.*

We soon arrived in a clearing where several of the crew were standing with cameras and sound pointing straight at me. I must have looked like a rabbit in the headlights.

Then a voice: "Tanya Travis, you have not been evicted. I repeat: you have not been evicted. This is a trial."

I looked around, amazed. "But... I don't understand. Why?"

"The producers like to mix things up a bit, Tanya. It keeps you celebs on your toes and gives the viewers a few surprises," Tiff whispered.

Suddenly the disembodied voice again: "*Celebrity Spa Trek* pampers your body and plays with your mind, Tanya Travis. In this trial you will learn what the other side of life is like and if you pass, you will be richly rewarded. Good luck."

"But am I coming back here? Why me? Am I staying in Nepal? I don't understand..."

"Walls have ears, sweetheart," said Tiff, still playing her low budget MI5 role.

"But you have to tell me what's going on!" I called, my voice echoing through the mountains.

Again the melodramatic Wizard-of-Oz voice: "You will find out in due course. You are now going on your own special journey Tanya."

Shivers went through me. My anxiety levels were now at twelve out of ten and rising.

Within minutes a taxi screeched to a halt in front of me and the door was flung open. I peered inside to see Ardash: "Get in, Tanya. I take you to the next destination."

Still unsure, I climbed into the taxi and it sputtered and lurched off.

"Where are we going?" I asked, feeling like I'd been kidnapped.

"We are going to Kathmandu."

"Why?"

"You are going to see how the other half live Tanya. This show is supposed to change your life. I think that perhaps this time it will."

I sat back, trying not to think of the passengers and their animals that might have inhabited the seat before me.

Dusk was falling as we left and I tried not to look down as we bumped over the perilous mountain roads with their sheer drops on each side. I looked across at Ardash, who had his eyes closed. He had guided the others on a long trek and was clearly in need of a sleep himself. Despite the danger, the view was stunning. It was a long journey, six hours. I nodded off myself towards the end of it and I awoke as we entered Kathmandu, desperately hoping my lolling head hadn't landed on Ardash and that I hadn't snored or dribbled in my sleep.

It was around 11pm when we sped into the city, a rollercoaster ride through Kathmandu by night. The driver chatted animatedly on his phone, sped through red lights and took both hands off the wheel to exclaim at a traffic violation ahead. It was clear there were no road rules to break, amid the screeching and beeping and yelling. My nerves began to feel very frayed when we drove through a village and our car screeched to a halt, just inches from a cow's hooves. This caused a rickshaw to halt too sharply, spilling several surprised passengers onto the road.

"The cow is sacred, here in Nepal," Ardash explained when he saw my horror. "She is like Lakshmi, Goddess of wealth and prosperity. We allow the cow to wander freely, even invite her into our homes."

Not on my watch, I thought, imagining the horror and filth of a big old Friesian tramping across my luxury hand-tufted, pure wool taupe. But watching the startled passengers stagger about in the dark before they clambered back into the rickshaw, I marvelled at the way these people valued spiritual life over human ones.

"I suppose a grazed human knee is a small price to pay, to save the animal that will one day guide your soul to heaven," I smiled.

* * * * *

The taxi eventually dropped us off and we met with the cameraman and Tiffany, who looked very perky.

"How did you get here before us?" I asked, a bit snippy.

She shrugged. "We flew. We needed to get set-up shots".

I counted to ten and tried not to scream. We then filmed my short and perilous jaywalk through Kathmandu's steaming streets, jigsawed with shop signs, taxis and mad macaque monkeys. It looked like I was alone but Ardash was just off-camera, guiding me. It was midnight by then, and despite my daytime nap, I was very tired.

"Where are we going?" I snapped at Tiffany. "I'm tired, why do all these challenges have to happen in the middle of the night?"

"We are nearly there, lovely," she said with an irritating grin.

The lanes shimmered in the night's dusty heat as Ardash pointed out an old palace, a strangely shaped temple and the mountains, always there in the distance, watching over everything. He gave me a secret glimpse of a city caught in its nightclothes, not yet ready for callers. We stopped at one of the open-fronted shops. "There is little food where we're going, so let's eat here," he suggested. The cameraman finally put his camera down and Ardash ordered us all a thick, warming dish of rice and lentils.

After we had eaten, we set off again. "Nearly there, Tanya," said Tiffany, mysteriously. "It's just round this corner."

She and Ardash melted into the background as the camera filmed me walking round a corner and stopping in front of a ramshackle old building, a stark contrast to the pagoda-shaped palaces and brightly-coloured buildings nearby. The next monsoon season would probably finish it off, I thought, looking up through the darkness at the half-shuttered broken windows and the water bouncing down from the roof. I felt a sudden heaviness within.

"Where are we?" I said quietly. No-one answered me.

"Knock on the door, Tanya" hissed Tiffany, off-camera. I gently tapped on the door and within seconds, an elderly woman opened it and held her hands in prayer as a greeting.

"Hello, I'm Tanya Travis. I'm with the TV show." I said, unsure of what to say.

"Namaste." She nodded and gestured for me to enter. "Welcome to the orphanage."

Orphanage? Was this some kind of joke? My heart sank as I thought of all the grimy street children I had seen when I first arrived in Nepal. The last thing I wanted was to be confronted with a house full of them. Oh how I needed to wash my hands.

"This is a mistake" I started. "I am no good with children."

"All part of the challenge, Tanya," Tiffany smiled. I glared at her, and followed the woman inside.

Once inside, I could just make out the open brick walls and the darkness was filled with the stench of unwashed bodies and re-boiled rice. My heart sank further as in the dim light I spotted the filthy floor, the stained walls.

"I speak English, my name's Sunita," the woman smiled. "You stay for a few hours here and sleep, then you work for one day here. Let me show you to your room."

She led me through to the back of the building, into a bare room and pointed at a very small, worn-out wooden bed.

No way would I be sleeping under those covers, I decided. I would be sleeping fully clothed, on top of the bed. I shuddered.

"I wonder, is there a bathroom?" I asked, wondering if this was all a big set-up and if behind the peeling wall my fellow campmates were drinking champagne and watching me through two-way mirrors.

"Of course, come with me," She led me into what could only be described as a large cupboard with a tap. Nearby, several huge canisters of water stood like soldiers in a row. Gesturing towards the water, Sunita left. I was devastated and had never in my life needed a boiling hot shower like I needed it now.

"Shit," I said to the cameraman. "Someone call my agent, I want to go home."

TWEET: @DonnaAgent Tanya Travis NOT returning 2 UK 2 marry Gok Wan. Tanya in Kathmandu 2 help poor orphans #Don'tBelievePress #MotherTheresaTanya

22

Lost Children and Luxury Face Cream

I didn't really sleep; I was waiting for someone to wake me and worried about what I might be expected to do in the orphanage. The place was filthy, the room was disgusting and as dawn broke, beetles seemed to be emerging from the walls. It was almost a relief to see Sunita in the doorway at 6am. She was followed by a large camera which was quickly in my face.

After a very unsatisfying 'scrub' in the 'bathroom,' I went to the kitchens where my first task of the day was to help serve breakfast. Arriving in the 1960's kitchen I was informed that there was no electricity – apparently, power cuts happened all the time in Kathmandu. They were also running low on cooking gas, so breakfast would have to be cold.

"There is usually rice soup for breakfast" said Sunita. "But today, we have little cooking gas, so we cannot prepare."

"Can't you get some more?" I asked. She shook her head.

"Here in Nepal, gas for cooking is very expensive. We used to cook in traditional oven, which is using wood. But this is bad for the health. Our fingers were black from soot and American volunteer programme said we have to use gas instead. So we change, but we can't always afford."

"Where are the volunteers now, then? Can't they get you some more?" I asked. She shrugged her shoulders.

"Gone." She said, simply.

Soon the kids were up and about and came into the main hall where some rickety tables and chairs wobbled under their minuscule weight. "Namaste, Miss," they all said in unison, at Sunita's request. Ardash appeared and helped the cameraman to set up his shot nearby, while Sunita explained to the children in Nepali (Ardash loosely translated for me) that this lady was a big star in England and the camera would be filming us all day.

At first, the children were quiet but as Sunita and I handed them out-of-date cereal bars for their breakfast they were soon shouting, laughing and fighting.

As they ate, Sunita told me what had brought the children to this place. "Domestic violence, parental death, poverty and natural disasters all orphan our children," she explained.

"It is imperative that we keep the orphanage open, but I am so worried we will have to close soon as there is no money. The alternative is child slavery, trafficking...drugs. We keep them safe from the streets: without us they will have no protection, and no love."

"Where is your funding from?" I asked her as we sat down.

"We have some government grant, but this is very small." She said. "We also have some charities from other countries, but it is not enough." She sighed and shook her head.

The orphanage was old and dilapidated, with no amenities and due to lack of money, few trained staff and equipment. To me, the hygiene was a serious problem, but none of that really mattered to the children – it was their sanctuary from a cruel world. I watched them eat and chatter, unaware of the possibility that their safety net, their home – their future – was in danger.

After breakfast, we cleared up and Sunita and a couple of assistants helped the children wash their hands in the tiny sink in the hallway. Then everyone, including me, sat on the floor in a circle for prayers. These tiny pre-school children in clothes that were too big and noses that dripped were of many different religions, with different abilities and different problems. I watched them all lisp their prayers – baby faces, big brown eyes, some with cleft palates, others with deformed or missing limbs – but all of them smiling.

And then Sunita said "Tanya, teach us an English song."

"Oh... Er, I don't know..." I said, backing away. At this point, the children reached out to me. The little hands that had been up noses and on filthy floors as they'd played patted my arm and touched my face. I had an overwhelming sense of panic.

My reluctance to sing caused several of them to try and clamber onto my knee, saying "Tanya sing". I laughed awkwardly and smiled, while gently pushing them away. I was very uncomfortable; children had no sense of personal space and these ones hadn't seen a bath for days. I was struggling with this situation in my head, when suddenly everyone turned towards the entrance; Ardash appeared and was walking slowly into the room, clapping in rhythm and smiling.

"Buddy you're a boy, make a big noise, Playin' in the street gonna be a big man someday..."

He was singing the opening lines to *We Will Rock You*.

The children erupted, abandoning me to rush over to him, hugging and climbing up him, swinging from his belt like baby monkeys. "Ardash" they yelled, "Rock You!" while some of the slightly older kids joined him in the rhythmic clapping, singing the words.

"They know this song?" I said to Sunita.

She nodded: "Yes, Ardash teaches them the English songs, he's been helping me for years. He used to live here, his own parents died when he was a baby."

"So, Ardash was an orphan too?"

"Yes, he's now like a son to me. He came with his sisters, who were very young."

Ardash and the kids were singing and clapping and he looked over and smiled at me as I clapped along, joining in the chorus. It was odd for me to see him in this new light and in such a different environment away from the camp and the mountains and there was something quite lovely about the way the kids reacted to him. I felt a little tug of my heart as he gently bent down to lift up one of the smaller kids. *He'd make a lovely dad* I thought, feeling a wave of regret for what might have been in my own life.

Almost all of the children were involved in the impromptu singing session but I was suddenly aware of a little girl of about three, who wasn't taking part, she just watched me. She was sitting on the floor quite close, yet she looked away when I smiled or tried to make eye contact. She had a dirty face and damp eyes.

"Hello," I said, leaning towards her. I didn't want to get too close, she clearly hadn't washed her hands, but she had a sweet face. "Namaste" I tried. She didn't speak, just stared then looked away again. The singing and laughter continued, but I couldn't stop looking at her. Then just as *We Will Rock You* was reaching a crescendo and everyone was singing and clapping in rhythm, she moved. Slowly, like a little cat, she came towards me, cautiously climbing up onto my knee like I wouldn't notice. She was as light as a loaf of bread and I barely felt her thin little arms slowly winding round my waist where she held on tight and after a few minutes, buried her head in my chest. My heart was in my throat. Such intense and immediate trust both touched and scared me at the same time. I was a stranger, yet this little one's need for affection was so present, so deep, that she would take it from anyone.

"Her name's Maya and sadly her parents both died," Sunita explained, getting up and coming over to me. "They died from AIDS and Maya is HIV-positive."

"Oh..." I looked down and – I'm ashamed to say – for a split second I almost took my arms away from her, wondering at the wisdom of holding a child with HIV so close.

"She's fine – and so are you," Sunita nodded kindly. I knew the facts, we'd done HIV enough times on my programme for me to despise the ignorance involved and, surprised and ashamed at my initial instinct, I embraced her back, rocking her to the music. After a little while, I felt the need to pull her closer, I didn't care that she smelt of old clothes and her hands weren't clean. For the rest of the morning, little Maya stayed by my side or on my knee, clinging to me – never smiling, never speaking but nevertheless communicating in her own way. If I moved across the room to tidy up toys or help another child, her tiny, cool little hand found a place in mine.

The few 'toys' at the orphanage were very old and were kept in a locked cupboard. "The older children sometimes take them," Ardash explained. "Orphans have nothing to call their own, you see."

Later, as Maya and the other children had their nap, I considered popping up to my room to put on some make-up and brush my hair. I'd been filming all morning 'sans make-up' and was desperate to cover up the wrinkles but Sunita had other plans for me. "Come to the baby room while the children sleep – there's lots to be done," she said. I froze in horror.

"No, Sunita. I can't go to the baby room, I am sorry, I just can't." She smiled at me and took my hand.

"Come," she said. I followed her, protesting, through the courtyard into another building, all the time being followed by the camera, where I heard the sound of babies crying. We went up the stone steps and into a large, relatively airy room with rows of mismatched, shabby old cots made from cheap plywood. The hot, acidic stink of urine-soaked nappies made me gag but ignoring my retching, Sunita asked me to start changing nappies.

"Sunita, this is... This is too hard for me. I'm sorry..." I said, with my heart hammering.

"Yes, you can, Tanya." she said calmly. "These babies need you. Please, let's start."

I took several deep breaths and counted to ten in my head.

"Which baby shall I change," I asked slowly.

"As many as you can," she said. There must have been 25 babies in the room and only one other carer at the far side who was white and sounded American so was probably a volunteer.

"I'm not quite sure what to do." I said. "I don't have children of my own." My sister had had her babies in Australia and when you only saw your niece and nephew every five years you tended to miss whole stages in their development. I'd assumed that one day I'd change my own baby's nappy, but that wasn't meant to be.

"Nappies are here, cream for nappy rash is there – use sparingly as we have very little, thank you," Sunita said, and disappeared. The cameraman was present, as always. As I looked down into a large cot where four pairs of huge, brown eyes looked back at me, I felt totally helpless, a rising panic building up through my chest. They were all so vulnerable, so completely at the mercy of strangers and I wanted so much to do something to help them. But I couldn't.

I saw Ardash carrying some boxes of baby stuff through the room and called him over. "Ardash, Sunita asked me to change nappies... I'm not sure I can." I said.

"Why?" he looked at me without smiling.

"Well, I might catch something... I might be sick... I can't stand anything dirty... Lots of reasons,"

"Lots of reasons not to change the nappies, Tanya... and all beginning with 'I'," he smiled sadly and walked away.

"No... no... I..." Calling after him was pointless, oh God, I'd disappointed him. He'd obviously thought I was a better person than I really was. I thought about what he'd said and what he must think and even though it was the last thing I wanted to do I reached in and lifted the first baby out of the cot. It was a little boy (I only discovered this when I changed his nappy – no pink and blue gender ID here in clothes and blankets) and he clung to me as I tried to lie him on the floor. I began to undo the pins. There were no disposables, all the nappies were cloth and I staunched the urge to vomit as I placed the warm, dripping nappy away from the child on the floor. I began dabbing and cleaning his red-raw bottom with cool water and an old towel, trying not to breathe in, then I applied a tiny amount of cream. I thought about all the creams and lotions and potions and wipes I got through daily – not to mention the extortionately priced products I used on my face. The money I spent on one pot of youth elixir would probably have kept every bottom in this room soft and pain-free for a year. I made a mental note to arrange a shipment of supplies when I got back to Britain...though where I'd get the money from, God only knew.

I used the dripping, foul-smelling threadbare cloth as a guide and taking a clean one, carefully copied, folding it into the triangle shape. I gently placed the struggling baby onto the cloth then fastened the well-worn material around him. I held him, gave him a little, awkward cuddle but feeling his tiny body close, an unexpected rush of love swept over me. His trusting eyes locked onto mine and I realised how vulnerable these tiny babies were. In this moment, I was all he had. Making this baby comfortable and clean was almost like the sensation I experienced when washing my own hands or after a thorough shower. I had a feeling of pure contented clean, but this time on someone else's behalf.

The next baby was bigger and a little feistier, making the whole process even more of a struggle. But the clean, creamed bottom, the big, trusting eyes, the cuddle and the tickle that caused the baby to giggle at the end was worth the acrid smell and dripping cloths.

Ten baby bottoms (including a couple with gag-inducing diarrhoea) and an hour later, Sunita arrived. "Thank you Tanya, they all look happy and content," she smiled.

"Yes, but wouldn't it be so much easier with disposable nappies?" I offered.

"Money, Tanya. It's cheaper to have the cloth nappies."

"Yes, but your laundry bills must be high?"

"Ah...." she smiled and nodded. "Please, I will show you."

I followed her out of the room and down the stone steps into the courtyard, where at the far end was a large tub containing water. A tiny, well-worn piece of soap sat on the rim.

"This is where you will wash the nappies," she smiled.

"Oh, you wash by hand?" She nodded. "But isn't the water cold?"

"It's freezing," she smiled. "And if you don't hurry, night will come and you will be washing in the dark."

I retched. "Sunita, this is too much, I have to leave now." I said, feeling tears pricking behind my eyes. "I found it so hard to change the babies and now this...it's more than I can do. I am sorry." And I turned away from the camera and sobbed. I saw Ardash crossing the courtyard towards me. *Great,* I thought, *I've disappointed him again.*

"Tanya" he said softly.

"I know you think I am spoiled, Ardash and I suppose you are right. But you don't understand – I can't do this." I whispered.

"Yes you can, Tanya. Look, I have these for you."

And with a smile, he gave me a pair of industrial strength rubber gloves, and a bottle of disinfectant. I could have kissed him. "Please try" he said.

I wiped my eyes. "OK, Ardash. No promises, but I will try." I said.

So for the next two hours I gagged and scrubbed and retched and heaved. The water was cold and my back was breaking but I just kept on scrubbing those filthy nappies until they were clean.

* * * * *

Once I'd washed what felt like a hundred nappies I headed into the main hall, where Ardash was playing with the kids, a child on his shoulders and several little hands in his. The staple (and only) meal of rice and lentils wafted through the orphanage and I guessed it was time for tea. On spotting me, Maya ran to me, wordlessly, her little hand pushed its way into mine and my tummy did a somersault. This day was turning into an emotional minefield with motherless babies everywhere and now Ardash with the kids and Maya with her desperate need for human contact made me want to cry again. Something like love and adrenalin filled me with a feeling I'd never had before.

After I'd helped serve their evening meal, Ardash stood by me and watched the children.

"In my world, what people pay for dinner would feed these children for weeks," I sighed. "I know people who tweet pictures of their pets' breakfasts, yet here...it really is another world. I had no idea children still struggled like this. I've read about global poverty, child hunger, I've seen it on the news but I just assumed someone was dealing with it."

"Yes, it is sad when the world forgets. Here, there is very little food, no medical supplies, no money for toys – the simple things that keep children alive, keep them safe and happy."

"Keep them children," I added. "I promise I won't forget. I will send stuff. I'll get toys and medicine... Whatever they need."

"Like many people, you are not as you first appear to be, Tanya," he smiled, watching the children but looking sideways at me. "Your heart, she is not selfish."

After tea, the cameraman worked on some shots of me playing with the children. I went into the courtyard and they held my hands, hugged me, thirsty for affection, desperate to be loved, touched. The filming stopped and Tiffany asked if I wanted to go for dinner with her and the rest of the crew. "No thanks, I'd like to help put the children to bed," I said, as three of them swung from my hips.

"We're not filming it my lovely, you don't have to, you can come with us, we're off now." she said.

"I want to stay," I answered.

Ardash stayed behind with me and agreed with Tiff to escort me to the next destination and we sat around talking with the kids. They taught me some Nepali songs and Ardash told us all a Nepalese folk story about a parrot. He pretended to be the brightly-plumed bird, making parrot noises throughout, which made them all giggle hysterically. Watching them and hearing their laughter made me giggle too.

At 6pm the children all trouped up to bed.

We left the orphanage and I promised to return soon. It had been a wonderful experience but as we walked out into the evening, I realised it had left me with an overwhelming sense of grief.

"I can't believe the lives those kids have had to endure already," I said. "Who knows what will happen if the orphanage has to close? And there's me worrying about my life and whether or not my boyfriend will come back to me." I shook my head.

"Everyone has different problems and if it hurts your heart, you are right to worry. Do you love him, yes?"

"Yes, I do, no-one knows what he's really like. When we're alone he's different, and he does love me whatever anyone else says. Other people have always caused problems in our relationship, so it's just not worked out for us. But seeing those children today made me realise that a family, even if it's only a family of two people, is worth fighting for.

"Ah, so true," he smiled, guiding me down the path and out onto the street.

"I've always believed that people are responsible for their own destinies. I thought that if you wanted something badly enough you just had to work for it. But that's not the case here, is it? Some people are victims of circumstance, accidents of birth..."

"We have droughts, political unrest – which leads to violence – and we have poverty," Ardash said. "It is often beyond an individual's control. So yes, you are right, it doesn't matter how much a child needs food or security, they are at the mercy of society, the climate, God, if you like. It's easy for a child or woman to find herself alone here in Kathmandu," he sighed. "Children are orphaned because their mothers are widowed or divorced – perhaps for failing to bear a son or because of a dowry dispute. Often the poor are forced to sell their children or put them in orphanages; there are no unemployment benefits here, like in your country."

"God, we take so much for granted in my world!" I looked at the fire in his eyes.

"It is true, life here is hard and there is much sadness. But I tell you Tanya, Nepal – she gets inside your blood – she will draw you in."

We both stood together outside the orphanage in silence.

"I think we have some time until your reward," said Ardash suddenly. "Would you like me to show you my city?"

"Yes," I said, slowly. "Yes I would."

"Come, Tanya, this way," he said. He gestured for me go first as we walked out into the dusk together, into the bright lights, the shouting and the car horns.

Ardash took me to a cafe where he ordered deep-fried chilli chicken momo (dumplings) and cold beers. We sat on cheap plastic seats and as I bit into the squidgy dumpling filled with spicy chicken, my jaw tingled. I realised I hadn't eaten for hours.

"You like, Tanya Travis?" Ardash said, biting into his dumpling after dipping it into the bright red, garlicky sauce.

I smiled at him, my heart lifting. "Yes" I said. "I like."

The Kathmandu night was thick with the heavy smell of diesel, it filled my nostrils: I tasted metal on my tongue as we started down the main streets teeming with people and traffic and panic. Then suddenly, no lights or bustle just a blanket of quiet darkness around us, as Ardash guided me down a labyrinthine lane shimmering in splashes of moonlight, dogs barking in the distance. Then we turned a corner and were back in brightly-lit streets, the air sweet and smoky with aromas of incense and hot, buttery ghee. Sleepy goats staggered along, too slow for the coloured rickshaws that whipped past them through the streets selling everything from pastries to pashminas. For a few moments, I was enchanted, until we came upon the city's lost children, reaching out from pavements, crying in the streets, dirty, unloved and vulnerable to everything and everyone. I felt torn between wonder and horror – that's what life is like in Nepal.

Ardash checked his watch. "We go back to join Tiffany now. She will meet us outside the orphanage. Come." And we walked back to where our tour had started.

Seconds later, a taxi screeched to a halt on the kerb and Tiff leaned out; "Get in Tanya, you passed the trial. I'm taking you for your reward!"

"I feel like I'm in Narnia," I said, waving to Ardash and stumbling into my chariot.

The taxi came to a halt outside The Radisson, Kathmandu. I could hardly believe the contrast. Within minutes I was whisked from the glossy, palm-lined atrium to the Spa where I enjoyed a relaxing sauna. After all the hard work and heartache of the day it was good to just switch off for an hour – but my mind was whirring. The sauna was followed by a deep, penetrating massage and an all-over body-conditioning rub. After all this, I felt so different and wafted from the Spa to my bedroom on angel's wings. At my insistence (coupled with my threats to 'walk off the show'), Tiff supplied me with a large pack of Sanihand and I wiped whilst I gazed at the wonderfully big bed, clad in beautiful cotton sheets. I'd dreamed of a real bed every night in the mountains and it was so good to be back where I belonged; in luxury, sanity, hot water and fresh, high-count cotton. The mountains were lovely and the sunsets spectacular but the lack of scented candles and hairdryers at base camp was just appalling. The only thing that was denied to me, apparently, was the TV – there was no remote and the plug was missing. I guessed the producers hadn't wanted to risk me catching up on the outside world.

The phone rang; it was Tiffany.

"Hi Tanya, as a special treat you can order anything you want from Room Service! She announced brightly. "Unless you would rather eat in the restaurant?"

"No thanks, Room Service would be wonderful" I said, marvelling to myself at how two words could sound so utterly beautiful.

"OK, I will send the cameraman up to film you when it arrives, then we will leave you in peace my lovely!" she said.

I went into the bathroom and sitting by the bath was a gift basket containing a Crème De La Mer 'Return to Youth' travel set. I held my breath as I picked up the card; could it be from Nathan?

Darling, I am so proud! Such fabulous ratings, my little Drama Queen. Use some of this – you look like you need it, crows' feet all over the screen, HD is a bitch! See you back in Blighty xxxx

Great, a gift from Donna. I was hoping that the treat at the end of an arduous, traumatic day might have been a gift from the man I loved – but the production crew thoughtfully arranged for me to receive something from my loud-mouthed agent instead. I sighed and turned on the shower. Standing under the burning hot spray, I rubbed and scrubbed and boiled my skin until it felt better – not great – just better.

Climbing out, I dabbed my face with the towel and reached for the Crème De La Mer, warming it in my palms as directed. This apparently activated the 'Miracle Broth' and released its youth-replenishing elixir. I patted it onto my skin, waiting for the hit. At home I'd used this cream regularly for years and it never failed to make me feel fabulous in front of the cameras. I continued to gently pat the deliciously floral-scented cream all over my face, breathing in for the pleasure rush. I took in deep, flowery lungfuls while sweeping the 'Regenerating Serum' with its ultra-light elixir gently over my face and neck. I stood in front of the mirror in the shiny hotel bathroom waiting for the face-cream moment, the thrill of the 'beauty-product orgasm,' but after almost three minutes, nothing had happened and I was left un-sated. I slapped more on, then more, I patted harder and softer but it didn't matter how many applications I made or how I applied them, the skinny kids from the orphanage and the streets with their beautiful, grubby faces and tiny outstretched hands made me feel ashamed. I put the two containers back into their lovely, pale-green silk bag and wrapping my towel around me, wandered back into the bedroom and picked up the Room Service menu. There was a knock on the door and the cameraman came in, along with Tiff, to film me choosing my dinner. After I had picked a light salad and fish dish (no rice or dhal in sight) the camera crew left. I felt somehow deflated as I ate alone in peace, then as it was quite late I decided to go to bed as it would be back to basics the next day.

I laid my heavy, sleep-deprived head on the cool Egyptian cotton (600 thread – count 'em) pillowcase. I fully expected to sink into deep heaven, but no matter how long I lay there I couldn't sleep properly. The minute I tried to close my eyes I saw Maya's face, damp eyes, a lost little soul reaching out her tiny hand to touch someone.

I endured fitful dreams of Nathan lying in a bath of yak's cheese and Ardash kissing a blonde in a bikini, all to the tune of *We Will Rock You*.

A bed was all I'd thought of during those awful nights in a sleeping bag, listening to Marcus's snoring while trying to find a dip to put my head into on the rocky ground of the Himalayas. However, after two hours and 36 minutes, I abandoned the Egyptian cotton and the Indian silk throw, got out of bed and threw back the curtains, starting into the inky night. Thoughts of Maya and the orphans were whirring around in my head, as were thoughts of Nathan; was he about to become a father himself? I couldn't bear it. The baby ought to have been mine and Nathan's, not someone else's. Why was life so cruel? I finally fell asleep in the upright chair in my room, in a very uncomfortable position with my head lolling onto my shoulders.

I didn't sleep as well as I'd hoped in my luxury bedroom that night and when I woke up and looked at the beautiful bed, adorned in rich cotton sheets, I smiled to myself. *So much for luxury!* Who would have thought Tanya Travis would reject high-count cotton for a chair because it made her feel bad to sleep in it? Being in this show was making me crazier by the day.

TWEET: @DonnaAgent Tanya Travis did NOT swig champagne + order 3 toyboy hookers + crack cocaine @Radisson Hotel Nepal #Don'tBelieveWhatURead

23

Guess Who's Coming to Dinner?

The next morning I was woken by loud knocking on my bedroom door and sighed with relief, remembering where I was and the breakfast of muesli and fresh fruit I'd ordered the night before. I padded over to the door, fully expecting to see my laden trolley but instead, a camera was pushed in my face.

"Tanya, get dressed, we're taking you back to camp," Tiff said, emerging from behind the cameraman and talking like the bloody villain in a James Bond film.

"But I've not had breakfast."

"No time. Breakfast is a luxury now... We'll meet in reception." With that, she swept off down the corridor while the cameraman did a close-up on my horrified early-morning face.

I was put on a bus with a cameraman and after five hours' driving perilously through the mountains and seriously risking all our lives, the driver suddenly announced "We are here," and stopped the bus.

The cameraman filmed me getting off – and my heart did a swoop through the valleys, to see Ardash standing nearby. I was pleased to see him, very pleased. After the previous day at the orphanage together, I felt like we'd shared something and he understood what I was feeling – and what's more, he actually listened.

"What's happening?" I said, approaching him with the camera following me.

"Ah Tanya, now we trek back to camp," he said.

"OK," I smiled. "Where do you want us to start?"

Ardash knew the ground well and said we had a couple of hours trekking ahead of us, so we set off with Lance wandering slowly behind us, the other cameraman ahead, shooting back.

"How was your night in the hotel, Tanya?" was the first thing Ardash said as we walked through the trees in the first part of our journey back.

"It was OK. Yesterday made me rethink a lot of stuff... About me and my life. And Nathan." I stopped to take in the mountains. "They look different from here," I added.

"Everything changes when you look at it from a different place," he smiled, gazing out at the view.

"Why do you always sound like you're speaking in riddles?" I smiled. There often seemed to be a subtext to Ardash's comments, like he was trying to impart ancient human wisdom.

"What will you do when you go back to England?" he said, signalling with his hand for us to walk on.

"Well, that's the million dollar question. I was a celebrity in England, I lived a different life. I don't know any more if I want to go back to that life, even if it's still there. I think it might have been bad for me."

"Perhaps it wasn't your life that was bad? Perhaps it was the way you lived it?"

"There you go again, it's like you're giving me a clue and I have to solve the riddle. I hope it isn't a Celebrity Spa Trek test" I smiled, feeling vaguely paranoid. He didn't answer, just smiled enigmatically, he was either on a mission or didn't understand a word I was saying.

"Oh, who knows what I'll do," I sighed as we trekked on. "What do you think I should do?" I didn't know what I wanted him to say but I was beginning to trust him and wanted his advice.

"Only you have the answers to your own life," he said with a smile.

We walked on and the cameraman continued to shoot as Ardash pointed out trees and shrubs. We talked about the mountains and the connections with religion, the gods and goddesses.

"There are more deities here than there are humans," I smiled.

"Ah yes, but your country no longer has a spirit. You only worship the God of Gap every Sunday at the mall." He said with a smile. And I suppose he was right.

"I thought I'd miss the shopping," I said, "but I don't. I get homesick, but not for the shops."

"I would be homesick if I ever left, for the mountains and my bahinis..."

"Bahinis?"

"How you say... Ladies...girls?"

"Oh, girls... Bahini means girlfriend?"

"Yes... I have four."

I closed my eyes and smiled at his arrogance.

"Gosh," I said, unable to add anything but feeling rather surprised. It didn't matter where you were in the world – all men were the same. Did these four women know about each other? Perhaps that's how they did things here? Like Mormons... Astrid and I had watched a series about a man with four wives once. We couldn't get our heads round the fact they were all so cool about their husband sleeping with other women. We concluded that we would rather be alone than share our husband with several wives. In fact Astrid expressed a preference for monogamy with some passion and her usual profanity.

When I arrived back at camp it was late. Tiff made me wait before I entered, to build the drama.

"Right Tanya, the others have just made dinner. You need to walk into camp and demand some, OK?" she said, grinning. I gritted my teeth. She clearly wanted me to play the celeb diva for her. The cameraman got ready and I held my breath. I actually felt nervous about returning to my camp mates, I hoped that they wouldn't be disappointed to see me. Apart from the embarrassment of such a public rejection, I'd be genuinely hurt if they were indifferent or disappointed at my return. The camera followed me as I walked back into camp. I could see them all, gathered around the fire, eating yet more rice and dhal. Marcus was the first to spot me.

"Oh my dear, I don't believe it!" he squealed.

"Is there any left for me? I'm quite hungry," I smiled.

To my relief I was welcomed with such warmth by my fellow camp mates it brought tears to my eyes. "I don't believe it – Tanya

Travis, we thought you were back in Britain!" Jonny hailed my arrival.

I wasn't under any illusions for long though, as Cindi was quick to point out; "We're so bored of each other we're even excited to see you, Tanya!" But nevertheless their hugs and 'we've missed you's were lovely to hear.

"So what about your eviction, man?" asked Paul. "Did you call your agent?" he joked. I smiled at him. "It was a trial" I said. "I had to work at an orphanage. I was rewarded by a night in a luxury hotel."

"Luxury hotel? I remember those," Cindi chuckled. "You lucky thing!"

"We were all sad to see you go," Rex said sarcastically, without making eye contact. Cindi ignored him and carried on.

"Guess what, I did a trial last night Tanya, on the live show!"

I smiled. So whilst I'd been trying to get comfortable in a hotel chair, Cindi had taken on a *Spa Trek* challenge.

"Ooh Tan, it was called 'Mountain Milkshakes' and it was THE most disgusting stuff in long glasses with straws! I had to eat liquid fish guts and this disgusting smoothie made from insects."

"We are all very proud of you, Cindi but let's face it dear, you've had much worse in your mouth," Marcus added, giving her a wink.

"I don't think so, Marcus. It was horrible but I just kept my eyes forward and thought to myself: what would Katie Price do?"

"She'd swallow," Paul smirked.

"Exactly. That woman is a trouper," Cindi said seriously, "the way she bit down on that kangaroo anus on *I'm a Celeb...* was legendary." I smiled weakly, trying not to retch and hoping the production team didn't have similar plans afoot for me.

"So what did you win, after you'd ... swallowed?" I asked, hoping for a nice salad again.

"Tents for everyone," she smiled, clasping her hands together with joy.

I heard a rustle in the rhododendron bushes and turned to see that Tiffany was still hovering with a little smile on her face. Then Carol-Ann appeared again.

"Hello, camp mates!" she said, cheerily. "We've gathered you here, ahead of tonight's show, for an important arrival. The viewers have been voting in droves!"

Marcus started pinching his own cheeks for what he called, 'that just kissed the blusher' look. "Who can it be?" he asked no-one.

"Oh, you can always find a 'celebrity' for these programmes," Jonny smiled.

"Yeah...or someone who's shagged a celebrity and therefore the infection of fame has been passed on," I laughed.

"Yes, it's a sort of celebrity Munchausen's by proxy," Marcus added and we all laughed as we tripped between the crags to see which celebrity specimen had dropped in.

"Is everyone sitting comfortably? Then I'll begin," started Carol-Ann, once we were all ensconced in front of the fire.

"We have a new arrival in camp today and one of you guys is going to be *very* pleased to see this VIP."

Jonny smiled and Rex did another of his nonchalant, long leg-crossing actions, when he was pretending not to care. Marcus, being single, was in the realms of fantasy. "Ooh, it might be a blind celebrity date for me? He might be an impostor, hoping to rough-arm his way into my affections and sleeping bag... Oh, be still my beating heart, I do hope so."

"Marcus, it's not some knocking shop for old poofs," Paul said, nudging him affectionately.

"A queen can dream, dear."

"...and the celebrity that's joining us tonight is VERY close to someone's heart! And he's here until you decide to vote him out...or make him your Himalayan King."

"It's singer-songwriter, playboy heartbreaker..."

"Oh no," sighed Cindi, "I don't have the energy to do another boy band."

My heart stopped. I held my breath...it couldn't be?

"...he also happens to be camp mate Tanya Travis's toyboy. Welcome, Mr Nathan Wells!"

Everyone clapped to the beat of my hammering heart. *Oh God. He was here, now, with me in the mountains*. I clapped along with everyone else and smiled calmly, aware the camera was doing a close-up reaction shot of my face. I was stunned, not knowing where to look and wondering if this was a trick, one of their twisted TV mind-games. And he was only two years younger, so why did everyone insist on referring to him as my bloody toyboy?

Carol-Ann turned around, held out her hand and there he was, emerging from the trees, smiling confidently. He looked every inch the seasoned celeb, taking Carol-Ann's hand and waving, strolling into base camp like he'd been doing it all his life. He looked so handsome, so assured in his army combats and aviator glasses, like Tom Cruise in *Top Gun*. My knees almost let me down just watching him. My lust for Nathan flooded back and despite a few niggling little doubts, I had no choice but to let it take me over. Again. I smiled uncertainly in his direction; as his eyes were hidden behind designer shades I wasn't sure about his reaction to seeing me. Everyone watched, open-mouthed (including me), as he walked slowly towards me, every footstep tramping on my heart... I counted each step: *one, two, three, four.* Then he was grabbing my hand and pulling me up from my cross-legged sitting position to wrap me in his arms and kiss me full on the lips. I fell into him; and in that one wonderful moment, my heart told me this wasn't just for the cameras, and whatever Donna might say, Nathan hadn't come here for fame or money. I'd doubted him before I left, my time in the mountains had blunted my feelings and the day with the orphans had confused me so much I hadn't been thinking straight. But now I knew I still loved him passionately and I couldn't deny it, even to myself. Our time apart had obviously changed Nathan, I knew from his kiss that he was here just for me.

Carol-Ann clapped while everyone smiled awkwardly, obviously pleased for me but there was definitely a 'what the...?' hanging in the air. I doubt anyone there knew who he was and the viewers at home would only know him as 'Tanya's Toyboy' and – 'nine-times-a-night-Nathan'.

"Well camp mates, I'll leave you all to get to know each other. I will see you later for the live show. As we've just had a celebrity joining us, there won't be another eviction tonight...although one of you will face another trial! Ha! See you later!"

Once Carol-Ann had signed off and skipped off through the trees and we'd stopped kissing, I wondered what to do or say. *What would happen with Nathan and me now?*

Rex lifted his hand to merely acknowledge Nathan for the camera and Jonny did his usual fawning. "Oh, you're Tanya's toyboy?" he smiled, shaking his hand.

"He's only two years younger." I snapped.

"Yeah, but he looks ten years younger," I heard Tiff mutter under her breath as she cleared up the running orders scattered on the ground – God forbid this should look staged in any way.

"Hey, my man," said Paul, slapping Nathan on the arm, probably hoping to get some tips later on how to seduce women. "I just knew they'd bring you in, mate," he was beaming.

"How did you know?" I snapped.

"Tan, I told you – he's a legend and... Well, I ain't bein' funny but you two are a car crash...and everyone loves a car crash... It's dirty, man."

Nathan laughed. But I was hurt at this. *Is that really what people thought of us as a couple? Is that how we looked to the world, like a car crash?*

Nathan was now looking at Cindi. "Hey blondie," he smiled, his arm still around me. My heart sank a little; did he fancy Cindi – like everyone else? "I remember *you*," he said, giving her a wink.

"Yeah. And I remember *you*, Nathan," she snapped and walked away.

He turned immediately to me, pretending it hadn't happened.

"Well, I guess we should get some sleep before tonight's live show" said Jonny brightly. "Cindi has won us all tents but we have to share." I had been allocated a tent with Marcus but he thoughtfully offered Nathan and me the two-man tent so we could be together.

"I'll bunk up with Paul or Rex," he said hopefully.

"No. Come in with me," called Cindi, much to his disappointment. "We don't want you trying to get jiggy with Paul in the middle of the night, it'll be bad enough hearing Tanya and Nathan," she giggled.

Though this was slightly embarrassing, my heart skipped a little at the thought of holding Nathan in the night again after so long.

"Tanya, look, when they called me up and asked me to come out here, I dropped everything to be with you," Nathan said, as the others disappeared off to their tents.

"Did you? Have you heard anything about...the baby?"

"Oh I forgot, you don't get any news here. Yeah, the results came just as I left...the baby isn't mine. I told you, but you wouldn't believe me.

I was relieved, but it didn't mean he hadn't slept with 'Titillating Tracey, it just meant she'd had several other 'suitors'.

"I've missed you, Tan. I'd like us to start again... I'm ready now." I was holding his hand tightly in mine.

"Oh Nathan, I've missed you too," I couldn't believe he was here. There were a thousand thoughts scrambling round in my head but I shut them all out, just pleased that he was here, now, with me.

I touched his arm, he turned to me and despite the constantly-whirring cameras and the fact we were probably in full shot he took me in his arms and kissed me.

"Shall we go to your tent?" He said, after much kissing – his hair all ruffled from my hands, his voice husky with desire.

"We can't, we're being filmed..." But as we kissed my resistance began to melt slowly like wax in the camp fire flames. "I think we need to talk first," I tried.

"We can talk for the rest of our lives," his hand brushed my back tantalisingly.

I wanted to hold back but I was already lost. I had to have him and when he stood up and held out his hand for me to go too, I took it.

"I want you so much, Tanya." he mouthed in my ear as we walked arm in arm to our tent.

Giggling, we fumbled with the zip at the doorway and once it was open we fell into the tent kissing. His hands were all over me in the pitch black, his tongue in my mouth, his hot, excited breath in my face. He caressed my skin, erasing the hurt and the longing and the pain I'd felt after we'd parted. Drunk with lust, he pushed me down onto the ground tugging at my T-shirt and pulling it up over my breasts, kissing and caressing.

"Nathan, we can't. Not here..." I whispered.

"But I want you. I want you here..." He pulled down my jeans and was soon on top easing his way into me, gasping with pleasure, moving quickly and easily. I couldn't get enough of him, my heart and my body were soaring into space and I never wanted it to end. Then suddenly in no time he exploded with relief.

"I've missed you," I said, aware that he was spent but I was still unsated, kissing him, wanting more, needing more.

"I've missed you Tanya, nothing's the same without you," he whispered and kissed my forehead chastely – a sign that told me sex was over.

I lay there in the dark feeling delirious, but still wanting him. I told myself I didn't mind, I was flattered he'd been so turned on by me he couldn't make it last. We'd make up for it later.

GOSSIPBITCH: *The new, surprise camp mate on* Celebrity Spa Trek *once made a pass at one of his fellow celebrity trekkers... under his girlfriend's nose.*

24

Brad Pitt's Chopper and the
Downward Dog

The next morning we were all assembled early in a clearing overlooking the lake. Everyone was groggy from lack of sleep the night before, but at least I hadn't had to do the trial. Paul had been voted to eat a variety of Newari cuisine – the most exotic in Nepal – and had feasted on, amongst other things; steamed buffalo blood, castrated goat meat, fried brains and boiled tongue. Boy, was I glad the viewers let me off that one.

"We have a treat for you today, boys and girls!" said a chirpy Tiffany. "Yogic Guru Rainbow Stone is here, to lead you in a motivation and meditation workshop. Enjoy!" she said, with a wicked glint in her eye. I was holding on tight to Nathan's hand, enjoying the familiar closeness I'd missed. Tiff was instructing everyone to gather round, look amazed and clap at Rainbow's entrance. We heard the sound of a helicopter getting closer and closer and finally hovering over base camp. The wind it created was ferocious, whipping our hair and nearly knocking little Cindi off her feet.

"That chopper's small, it's nothing like Clooney's!" I heard Rex yell nonchalantly over the noise. I was watching him gazing up at the hovering helicopter. "Brad's chopper's even bigger though," he said loudly to Nathan. "I've ridden on Brad's chopper."

"Lucky, lucky boy," sighed Marcus, with genuine longing.

As we watched, yoga guru Rainbow Stone emerged from the helicopter, hung in the doorway for a few seconds then hurled herself out, screaming like a banshee. Tiff needn't have worried, our surprise was genuine. We all held our breath as she ripped her parachute chord and came at speed towards us. She landed with a yelp, rolled and leapt to her feet.

"Who are you?" she barked at me.

I jumped. "Tanya Travis."

"No. Who are you *really*?"

"Tanya...Travis?" I said uncertainly, adding the high inflection at the end because that's what everyone does these days – well, people under 30.

"You are a hollow shell, a husk!" she said, shouting in my face as the chopper moved away overhead.

"Excuse me?" Nathan hid a smirk behind his hand and took a step away from me, eyes dancing.

I turned to look at Marcus; he was staring at her with barely concealed venom and when I turned back she was crouching at my side, twitching, causing me to jump with surprise. Close up, Rainbow's tanned face was covered in perspiration and her hair was matted with God only knows what.

"Tanya, you will 'find yourself' here."

Her nose was now touching mine. And she wasn't moving.

"We all have dark, secret selves, Tanya and you're gonna find yours."

"I'm not sure I want to."

"Then why are you here?"

"Money?" Which was the honest answer.

"Forget superficial chattels, that's not the real reason you're here is it, Tanya Travis?" her eyes were desperately searching mine, begging me to lie.

"I'm here because I want to be a better person," I said, trotting out the line I knew she wanted to hear – but also surprising myself with the ring of truth in it. Her mouth twitched in approval.

"In order to be that better person, you need to let go. Open your heart and set yourself free."

"OK."

"It isn't a one-night stand," she continued. "This is a lifelong commitment – and Tanya, remember this: there's no such thing as a free glass of milk, it's time to buy the cow."

I nodded, like I knew this and it made perfect sense to me. I looked round at the others. They were staring, open-mouthed at Rainbow – all apart from Marcus, who had retreated behind the rhododendrons for a cigarette.

"And you! Who are you?" she barked at Rex. He sneered at her.

"Rex Cannon. And I don't need to find myself, lady. I sure am happy with the me I am." She paced round him, staring at his face.

"The more we think we know about ourselves, the more we have to learn" she said. "We will all learn together. Come. We must each find a song to sing on our journey. But the song must be silent, within."

This made no sense to me, but I wasn't going to question her, leaping around on her haunches and talking in riddles like bloody Gollum. She then demanded we meditate for three hours, before we 'seek the sun' in an 'enlightening' yoga session. She sat herself in the lotus position right in the middle of base camp, her hands upturned her eyes closed. "Ohm," she said, every few seconds.

"I'm not downward-dogging for anyone, dear," Marcus announced from behind the rhododendrons, lips pursed, cigarette held high.

I looked around and apart from him, everyone else was meditating but there was a space where Nathan had been sitting. I smiled to myself, he hated anything like this and I guessed he had snuck back to the tents; Rainbow seemed deep in a trance and probably wouldn't notice. I was longing for us to spend some more time together, so I decided to go and find him. I stood up quietly and left.

When I got back to the tent, I was shocked to find it empty. I gazed around, panic beginning its familiar curl in my stomach until I spotted him by the production tent. He was talking to Tiffany and laughing in that easy, handsome way he had. She was laughing too and tapped his arm in a reprimand at something he'd said. *What had he said? What could he possibly say to Tiffany?* I saw the way her head went on one side and her lips pouted as he looked into her eyes, smiling, one arm leaning on the tree, the other on one hip. Was he telling her how much better she would be in bed than me? How her thighs were firmer, her face smoother, younger? I shook my head to dismiss these thoughts and walked over to them.

"Hello Tiffany," I said with a big smile.

"Oh – Tanya. Hi," She said, and smiled back. "Nathan was just helping me...get some water."

"Really?" I said, feeling the heat rise to my face. "That's nice." I turned to Nathan.

"You only got here yesterday. I'm amazed you know where the water is." I said, trying to stay calm, but knowing I couldn't. Tiffany's eyes widened and she shot Nathan a look then quickly walked away.

He stood awkwardly, angrily shaking his head: "So, here we go again. Halfway up a mountain in the Himalayas and now you're jealous 'cos I'm helping a researcher do her job."

"Exactly. *Her* job. So leave *her* to do *her* fucking job," I spat. I looked at him and his face was like thunder. I backpedalled slightly: "Look, you are supposed to be here for me, Nathan. Please, can't we just enjoy this time together?" I fished a Saniwipe from my pocket.

"I am not here 'for you' as you put it, Tanya. I was asked to star in this because of my music, or had you forgotten I'm a musician?"

"Of course it's about your music," I lied, "but it's also your connection with me that gets you publicity and people recognise you as my partner."

"I don't see anyone else's partner here." he said, taking off his sunglasses and looking into my face. He stood back and looked me up and down. "I can't put up with this. No-one could. Look at you, standing there with a wet rag, scrubbing at your hands. You're ridiculous, stop being so possessive and controlling. Have some class, Tanya." And with that he'd swept off downhill and joined Tiffany, who'd clearly been observing the whole spectacle. She looked worried and I was hurt to see him reassuring her with a pat on the back as they walked off together on a mission for water.

'Have some class, Tanya,' he'd said. His words echoed in and around my head, bouncing off the mountains and returning to me on a loop. I watched him disappear into the darkness and then heard Tiffany's tinkling laugh and my heart turned to crushed ice.

Maybe he was right, I thought as I sat down heavily and put my head in my hands. I did become paranoid and imagine all kinds of things and it wasn't his fault, it was because the press made up so much about him that I was beginning to find it hard to tell the truth from the lies.

"Tanya, why you look so sad?" Ardash's gentle voice penetrated the gunk of hurt in my head.

"I'm... I'm just tired," I smiled.

"Your boyfriend, is it Nathan, the new guy?"

"Yes, he's my boyfriend."

Ardash whistled, almost imperceptibly.

"You are not happy he's here?"

"Yes. Of course," I almost snapped, wanting to add that if he was right here, by my side, I would be very happy.

"Then why are you being sad?"

I looked down without replying, moving a stick around the craggy earth in the shape of an N. Ardash had a way of looking at me that made me feel open, exposed. I wanted him to go. The stuff with Nathan had made me feel very vulnerable. I grabbed another wipe and tried to discreetly scrub at my palms.

"Tanya, Buddha says that three things cannot be hidden: the Sun, the Moon and the Truth." he said, gently.

There he went again handing me cryptic crossword clues to life.

"What's that supposed to mean?" I asked.

"It's not rocket surgery, Tanya." He said.

I smiled in spite of myself and looked up. He was staring at me with such seriousness like he'd said something profound and I had to giggle.

"Well that's all very nice Ardash but in my world, love is sometimes stupid and complicated...and the truth *can* be hidden, or at least hard to find."

"Ah forgive me. It's just that in my world, love is really a simple thing. I do not mean to upset you."

"I don't want to talk about it, Ardash." I said, annoyed. "I come from a different culture to you and we do things differently". *And we don't talk in riddles*, I thought.

"Anyway, it's not right in my culture to be shagging four women at the same time," I said, referring to his earlier disclosure that he had four girlfriends, "...but have I said anything to you about it?"

"No," he said, bemused.

"No, I haven't provided you with a psalm or a list of the Ten Commandments, so just keep your own counsel and, well, just leave me alone." I raised my voice and stood up, grabbing my shawl and staggering over to my tent. First Nathan and now this; I was furious at the way Ardash thought he could criticise my lifestyle, my culture, my relationship in a way I wouldn't dream of doing with him. I tore at the zip to open the tent, cursing and leaning hard into it to get it open and realised to late it was open already. I lay face down inside the tent with my legs out, stunned.

"Pissed again, dear?" came Marcus's voice from the camp fire.

"Oh, fuck off!" I shouted through canvas.

I didn't know what was happening any more. The foundations of my life had been rocked in the last few days and I just didn't know what to believe. I unclipped the microphone pack that we were supposed to wear all the time and pushed it outside the tent, then I zipped up the front, shutting out the cameras, the public, the world. I lay on my sleeping bag and finally followed one of Rainbow's instructions: I let it all out, curled up in a ball, and cried.

GOSSIPBITCH: *Which shamed talk-show host is on the verge of another on-air breakdown? And who's been making secret plans to meet in the mountains for hot celebrity sex?*

25

Celebrity Sex and a Mountain Meltdown

I must have fallen asleep because when I woke up it was dark. With no watch, I had no idea what the time was but I knew it couldn't be past midnight as we hadn't been summoned for the live section of the show yet. I looked over at where Nathan should have been sleeping and my heart plummeted – there was no-one there.

I started to unzip my tent when I heard noises from outside, low voices and giggles, carried in the still night air. A man's voice...and a girl's. My blood started to pulse in my head. *Nathan and Tiffany?* I lay back down on my sleeping bag, trying to push the thoughts out of my mind. It could easily be someone else – couldn't it? It was no good: I sat up, straining to hear the voices, which were now peppered by moaning. My head was rushing with blood, and the noise was deafening. I had to know. I slowly unzipped the tent and clutching my heart in my hand, dared to follow the sounds, away from the sleeping area, away from the camp fire, which was now silent and dark. I followed the sounds quite a distance from the camp into a small clearing which the production crew sometimes met in, which wasn't usually covered by the cameras. *Which Tiffany would know.*

As I drew nearer, each step was agony as I heard more moaning and now giggles and kisses. I held my breath and slowly dropped on all fours, crawling slowly towards the noises. As I came nearer, I could make out their two bodies, *in flagrante*. Naked, writhing limbs shone in the moonlight as they moved together panting, my heart was in pieces and my mind too as I stumbled to my feet, wordlessly watching. His muscular back was as broad as ever as his buttocks thrust up and down. *No class, eh?* I thought to myself as I walked with ninja-like stealth towards the fire. I was enraged. My head was filled with the sound of a crashing sea. *How dare he come here on my ticket and have sex with a young researcher? How dare he break my heart again?* I saw the bucket of water nearby that had apparently taken them all day to 'collect.' I was ready to face this, finally. I'd put my head in the sand for too long where Nathan was concerned. I'd been so desperate to keep him that I'd put up with anything and along the way, I'd lost my heart and my self-esteem some time ago – it was time to face the truth and reclaim what was left of myself.

I don't recall in detail what happened next, but I do remember picking up the bucket and shouting; "I'll help you get the fucking water... Here's water for you... You bastard! How about that for class?" I hurled the bucket of water over them, screaming something unsavoury about 'rutting dogs'. I was only doing what any red-blooded woman would do when she caught her lover having sexual congress with a young woman in a moonlit clearing. I dropped the empty bucket, waiting for their shocked faces to emerge into the moonlight.

Two angry faces emerged from the tangle of sweaty limbs and to my earth-shaking horror, they weren't who was expecting. It wasn't Nathan and Tiff – it was Cindi and Rex Cannon!

Rex roared like a beast and climbed off an exhausted-but-furious Cindi. "You are one crazy, mixed-up bitch," he spat.

"Oh God... I'm so, so sorry... Cindi... Rex."

"What the fuck, Tanya? That was dirty water you stupid cow, you've ruined my extensions." Cindi was lying on the bare ground, naked, writhing around trying to squeeze and cajole at her mane of fake hair.

"Christ, no! I'm so, so sorry. I thought you were...someone else."

By now, everyone was out of their tents and grouping around Cindi and Rex, passing them bits of blanket or towel to dry off with. The production team were quick off the mark and when I looked round, I saw a cameraman. I wondered how long he had been there and how much he had caught on film. Then out of nowhere, Nathan appeared – alone. "What's all the racket?" he asked, walking towards me. "I thought someone had been stabbed, you could hear the commotion down by the stream."

"That stupid old broad you sleep with, she's finally losing it, kid. I'd trade her in if I were you." Rex snarled, as charming as ever. I didn't respond, despite a deep urge to grab another bucket and put it over him again.

Nathan looked slightly bewildered. "You OK Tan? I was worried about you. I knew it was you shouting, I came straight away."

"I'm just tired and emotional," I said. The phrase always worked for other celebrities when they were drugged, drunk or compromised.

"Tanya, don't be upset. It's all fine," he said, his arm around me while I clutched the other one. I was relieved at his sympathy, his caring and when I looked up into his eyes he kissed me gently on the forehead.

I stood on my tiptoes and whispered in his ear so no-one else could hear: "I... I thought, I thought Rex and Cindi... I thought it was you, Nathan," I was holding onto his arm, my eyes were full and about to spill any second.

"*Me*? You thought it was me?"

"Yes... I thought you and Tiff had been off somewhere. You've been hours and I was so worried I thought you and she were..."

"Tanya, please give me a break. Why do you always have to be so jealous?" he said in a raised voice.

"Sssh Nathan please, not here, you're forgetting, the cameras are on all the time. Everyone can hear – they'll think I'm mad."

"You *are* mad, Tanya. You make my life hell with your constant accusations!"

"Nathan, please keep your voice down." Christ, this was all I needed on top of everything else, a big row with Nathan where he tells me I'm a mad, stalking bitch who never leaves him alone.

"Look, I'm sorry," I said desperately, realising that everyone had gathered around now to see what all the fuss was. "You going off with Tiff like that made me stupid. But I just don't understand why, if it isn't a sexual attraction, you would want to spend time with someone almost twenty years younger than you?"

"For the hundredth time Tanya, I was helping her!" He shouted. "This is your problem, and the sooner you get help, the better."

I could feel the heat rising to my face, and the dull whooshing sound in my ears was becoming louder again.

"This is why you are impossible to live with," he said, stepping away from me. "Yeah, she's young and pretty but that doesn't mean I'm sleeping with her. I'm sorry, but I don't know how much longer I can do this Tanya... You're destroying us." With that, he turned to go. I could feel everyone staring at me, and the air crackled with tension.

"Nathan. Nathan, please," I whispered. "I'm sorry. I really am." I turned to the others. "Cindi, Rex, please forgive me. I didn't mean to..." Their faces glared up at me in the moonlight; Cindi's matted, foul-smelling extensions said it all as they danced around, her face distorting and twisting. The sneer curling on Rex's lips grew wider and wider and Cindi's blue eyes bored into me balefully. I began to feel short of breath. Images from the day swam in front of my eyes, Rex and Cindi, Tiffany and Nathan. The babies at the orphanage, Nathan holding a baby. I felt faint.

"Nathan... Help me" I whispered, almost imperceptibly, reaching out to him. He brushed my hand away, and his touch seemed to burn. I heard him stamp away into the trees, each footfall cracking loudly in my head. My breathing quickened.

"Tan, you alright?" It was Paul, reaching towards me. The others drew closer, trapping me in, reaching for me with claw-like hands. I screamed: an animal sound that didn't even seem to come from me. Then I was sick. And then I blacked out.

I awoke some time later to find myself surrounded by medical staff and crew all with walkie-talkies and all in my face. I wanted to scream, I wanted to say, 'I'm OK, just everyone GET OFF ME' but nothing would come out of my mouth. Ardash was leaning over me. "It's alright, Tanya." He said quietly. "We move you to the diary cave, OK?" Then I heard him stand up. "You will turn the cameras off now" he said in a very authoritative voice.

"Ardash my lovely, everything is filmed, that's the point" I could hear Tiffany pipe up.

"You will turn them off, now." He said again.

Then I could hear Flinty say, "Alright, boys. Stop rolling. Let's get her to the diary cave."

My head floated away again as they carried me to the diary cave and when things came back into focus, it became clear the production team were in a panic.

"Jesus, we need to chopper her out ASAP," Flinty was shouting. "I mean, she's seriously lost it... She's cuckoo, did we do any psych tests on her before she left Britain?" Silence. "Shit, they'll throw the book at us. We are all gonna carry the can for this."

My eyes were closed, they'd assumed I was asleep. It was scary lying there, hearing all that stuff about me. 'To see ourselves as others see us,' Marcus had said. I was doing that now and it was terrifying. Tiff said nothing. There were no 'sweethearts' or 'lovelies' – presumably she was cowering in a corner and wondering whose head would roll as a result of 'Tanya's Meltdown: Part Two'.

ONLINE ONTIME NEWS HEADLINES:
Travis Meltdown on Mountain

Today, Celebrity Spa Trek *producers were in crisis talks regarding the mental health of 47-year old former talk-show host Tanya Travis. Tanya, 44, who once hosted popular daytime talk show* The Truth with Tanya Travis *was said to have remained in camp and was 'comfortable' last night, after collapsing during a showdown with three other celebs. "All precautions are being taken as always to ensure the health and safety of our participants," said series producer Flinty Adams. "Unfortunately, on this occasion our celebrity contributor was suffering from previously undisclosed health problems affecting her stability."*

Tanya, 49, whose toyboy lover Nathan Wells, 40, recently joined her on the show has suffered serious setbacks in both her personal and professional life. Once known as the Darling of Daytime, Tanya lost her role as host of The Truth with Tanya Travis *to blonde Georgina Ronson 24, earlier this year. Since taking over the programme, now renamed* The Georgina Ronson Show *the series has enjoyed record-breaking ratings and 'Rear of the Year' Ronson is bookies' favourite to win this year's Darling of Daytime award.*

Tanya 48, was sacked from the show after a live on-air rant at a young researcher. This was followed by claims from an underwear model that Tanya's lover Wells was the father of her unborn child.

A source today said: It's been an industry secret for some time that Tanya is heading for a breakdown." Miss Travis's behaviour since starring in Spa Trek *has done little to quell the media rumours that she's suffering a serious mental breakdown. On arrival at the camp in Pokhara, Nepal, she screamed and shouted at Paul Roscoe, the 21-yearold former drug-addict and boy-band star of* The Hissy Fits. *Miss Travis demanded the millionaire singer 'wipe' her down and 'step up to the plate' before making it clear she wanted a sexual relationship with the much younger rock star. This was followed by an hysterical rant at production staff on location, climaxing in a tirade against fellow celebrity campers, Cindi Starr and Rex Cannon. Throwing a bucket of water over Cindi, 23, and Rex, 56, Travis screamed that they were 'rutting dogs.'*

"It was completely out of the blue, she is one crazy broad," said Cannon, famous for his roles in 80's action movies and more recently the Nazi miniseries Desperately Seeking Hitler.

A spokesman for the TV company said today: "We believe the kindest and safest action we can take regarding Tanya Travis would be to send her home where she can receive the care and help she needs."

Tanya's spokesperson made a statement in response to our enquiries, saying; "My ass she's coming home. Tanya will stay and win, I don't give a f*** what they are saying about her mental health – there's nothing wrong with her, she's always doing that kind of crazy shit. And you can quote me on that!"

26

Camp Parties and Indecent Proposals

After a couple of hours' rest, a visit from a medic and a hot cup of tea, I felt slightly better. Suddenly, Nathan appeared in the doorway of the diary cave.

"Tanya, oh thank God you're OK, we need to talk," he said, gently now he'd had time to calm down. Tiff was standing next to me, her face white with fear, she was clutching a towel like I might suddenly explode and it would get messy.

"Thanks Tiff, I'll be OK for now. I'm feeling a bit better... Do you mind leaving us alone? Nathan we do need to talk... Come in here – but whisper, please?"

He stood in the doorway: "I don't want to talk in here, it's stuffy. Do you feel well enough to come out here, into the fresh air?"

"No Nathan, I don't want to fall apart in front of everyone again – I'd rather stay here." I said, my voice cracking.

"The fresh air will do you good. Please Tanya. I want to ask you something." He took my hand, and led me gently outside.

"Tanya... We've been together for four years now." The camera was whirring and he was speaking very loudly.

"Shit," I said under my breath. *So be it*. If he wanted his fifteen minutes of fame by dumping me on air then who was I to deny him that? I'd put him through enough.

"Tanya... I want to say is...Will you marry me, Tanya Travis?"

"Marry?" My ragged heart transformed instantly into white satin with scalloped edges.

"Yeah, I think it's time we got hitched, don't you?"

"Nathan please, don't joke...is this a joke? Some kind of twisted trial?"

"No," he shook his head, horrified I should say such a thing.

"So this is real... It's nothing to do with the show?" I asked, watching the camera-light, hearing the buzz, knowing we were being filmed.

"Stop playing hard to get Tanya, or I might change my mind," he teased, now openly playing to the camera.

"Yes. Oh yes... Yes!" I stammered, feeling disorientated, exhausted but relieved he wasn't dumping me live on air. I hugged him tight, thinking *we can do this* and in my cotton-wool head I was writing the guest list and ordering the canapés.

Right at that moment, Carol-Ann appeared with the camera. It was later than I thought and we were clearly live. Apparently, Flinty had made the decision to keep 'the crazy bitch' in the programme... After all, everyone loves a wedding.

"So what's the news, guys?" she skipped over to where Nathan and I were sitting.

"I just asked Tanya to marry me," Nathan announced proudly. "And I am a very lucky man because she said yes," he put his arm around me and squeezed gently as if to say, I'll do the talking.

"Hurrah!" Carol-Ann yelled with some enthusiasm. Of course she was pleased; an on-air proposal was a dream for the viewing figures and would take her to places other shows couldn't reach.

"So happy for you both," she smiled from ear to ear. "And to celebrate, tomorrow you will all enjoy a very special lunch – we will be throwing you a camp party!"

"I LOVE camp parties," squealed Marcus. "Congratulations Tanya love, I hope you'll be very happy. And you've certainly earned yourself another night in camp, dear," he whispered to Nathan.

"So! Back to tonight's challenge!" said Carol-Ann brightly. "Let's see who the public have voted to take on 'Snake Slalem'!"

I watched, almost detached, as Carol-Ann went through the process of teasing out who would be taking on the challenge. And then, finally, it was revealed. "The person taking on 'Snake Slalem' is....Rex!" I looked across at him, wearing his shades even though it was the middle of the night. He didn't move. "Rex!" said Carol-Ann again. "Let's go, Rex!"

Rex slowly got up, and walked over to her. He took off his shades as he swaggered past me and if looks could kill, I would be six feet under. "OK, Carol-Ann" he said in his best Texan drawl. "Bring it."

Rex was led off to do the challenge, which apparently would win us some booze for our camp party tomorrow. Then the rest of the live show passed in a blur and I fell into my sleeping bag gratefully at the end of it. My head resting on Nathan's shoulder, I finally fell into a deep sleep.

TWEET: @AstridLun Tanya 2 marry Nathan but he is sex addict + needs @DrChristian 2 help his man parts + @GokWan 2 make Tanya look good naked x

27

Kim Kardashian's Philosophy for Life

The following morning we were woken by trundling trucks bringing a lavish party to camp. The day before had been quite a day, with a steamy sex scene plus a live, on-air wedding proposal and they were determined to keep up the momentum. With an eviction scheduled for tonight the air was fizzing and we were all wondering which one of us would be voted out.

Before I could enjoy the celebrations planned in my honour, I knew I had to at least try and make peace with Cindi and Rex. I found Cindi's tent and asked if I could go in.

"Cindi, I am so sorry about throwing water at you yesterday" I opened. "I thought you were Nathan and Tiffany...I don't know what came over me."

She looked at me for a minute then smiled. "Don't worry about it, Tan. I think your meltdown took the heat off me and Rex. Besides," she went on, "my management team will be pleased. They told me to try and shag someone while I was here!"

I didn't quite know what to say to that.

"Anyway, when things get tough, I try not to stress about it and remember some of my inspirational quotes." she said, looking at me earnestly. "You should do the same, Tan."

"Well, that sounds like a good idea...What's the quote for this situation?" I asked.

Cindi looked at me seriously, and putting on a very grave voice, said: "I learn... from everything I do."

"It's lovely, Cindi." I smiled." Are those your words? Is that your philosophy?"

"No, it's Kim's, but I know what she means."

"Kim?"

"Kardashian."

The penny dropped. Bless her. We sat for a bit longer and as it was a party we were waiting for, she decided to share a 'party' quote with me. She sat up straight and pulled her extensions off her face to give the quote more ...depth? Emphasis?

"Tan...listen to this: 'You haven't partied until you've partied at dawn in complete silence with Buddhist monks'" she shook her head in wonder.

"Buddha?"

"No you daft sod, it's not Buddha's – it's Cameron Diaz's..."

Fortunately, I didn't have time to respond as we were called outside by the production crew where a magnificent champagne buffet was delivered. Strains of music started up from a PA system somewhere in camp and as we hadn't heard music since we arrived it sounded beautiful and intense, like a long, cool drink on a hot, dry day. Mesmerised by the sound I was whirled around the craggy 'dance floor' by Marcus then by Paul, followed by Ardash who was soon moved on by Nathan. I leaned into him, embracing my soon-to-be-husband while dancing to *I Don't Want to Miss a Thing* and resting my head on his shoulder. The music was playing, my head was full of wine and wedding vows and I looked up, about to say something to him, but he was looking at someone behind me. I turned to see Tiff, smiling, her hand mid-wave and as I turned back, to settle my head on his shoulder I saw Ardash. Just watching.

Rejoining the group, I swallowed hard. "Nathan...how soon would you want to get married?"

I held my breath, waiting for the ums and ahs, the delaying tactics followed by the humiliation of everyone asking 'when's the big day', followed by pitying looks and whispers behind my back.

"Well, I was thinking..."

"There's no rush," I said, suddenly feeling like everything was going very fast. My head had been messed around so much since I got here, I wasn't sure what was real and what was *Spa Trek* any more.

"Tanya, I want to marry you as soon as we get back to the UK," he said with a smile. I hugged him. I could stop doubting him now. This time would be different: I had changed and it seemed he had too.

"So, shall I call Vera Wang... and...and the Cake Fairy?" I asked, almost testing him, still not believing this was really happening.

"Yeah, sure, if the producer will let you," he smiled, indulgently.

Flinty seemed only too happy to let me make some 'wedding-y calls' as she called them, on condition that I let the cameras film me talking on the phone about the dress and the cake.

I talked for 47 minutes to Vera's assistant about final fittings for the dress I'd had hanging in my wardrobe for so long. Then I called Stella Weston at The Cake Fairy. She said edible pearls and ivory lace cakes were currently *de rigeur* in Hollywood and this would work well with a vintage wedding theme. I booked 250 fairy wedding cakes, there and then.

"Oh Tanya, you're soooo lucky," Cindi said when I told her. She clasped my arm with her impossibly long and perfect nails: "You've got the dress, the cakes and the man of your dreams."

"Yes. It all worked out in the end, didn't it?" I smiled.

* * * * *

The camp 'engagement' party was amazing; champagne and chocolate fountains and a huge, snow-frosted, Himalayan-shaped cake adorned the table. I was among friends, the show apparently had great viewing figures, the venue was booked, the cakes ordered and – the most important part – the groom was keen. *Yet...* I couldn't shift the niggling feeling in my stomach. But all soon-to-be brides felt like this, surely? After all, getting married was a life-changing event.

"You must be very happy, Tanya?" was Ardash's opening line as we all gathered together late in the night, ahead of the live show and eviction. Though everyone was joking and appeared to be happy, there was an undercurrent of nerves. No-one wanted to be the next one to go. I didn't want to leave yet, not now Nathan was here. I'd already faced a barrage of mixed emotions when I thought I'd been evicted last time, to find out it was all just a trial.

"I'm ecstatic," I said, smiling quickly.

He smiled back and looked as if he wanted to say something, but instead put his hands together in a prayer salute and moved away.

Then Carol-Ann appeared. She wasn't skipping and flouncing, in fact she looked like she had just come from a funeral. The cameras were with her and in her 'serious' voice she asked us all to gather round now to record 'something very important'. For a moment, I wondered if the production team had choppered in a vicar and were planning to marry Nathan and I on the spot. I couldn't bear that – the best part of getting married was the planning and I wanted a few more delicious weeks pondering venues, menus and floral displays.

"So, we're filming this segment in advance of tonight's show," she said, with no flirtatious giggle or flip of the skirt. "We've had one eviction, one fake eviction and with Nathan's entrance, we've had an 'in-viction'. However, it has come to the attention of the production team that someone has been behaving 'inappropriately' on this, a family show."

We all gasped and looked at each other – hadn't most of us behaved 'inappropriately' at some point? "I'll get my coat," I whispered to Marcus, who raised an eyebrow and muttered something about Cindi and Rex 'in flagrante, dear'. I noticed Rex stir slightly and look uncomfortable, so perhaps Marcus was right.

"So it leaves us no option," Carol-Ann continued "but to cancel tonight's public eviction and ask one of you to leave. I'm sorry Paul, but we have been informed by an impeccable source that whilst here, you have been in possession of an illegal substance."

There was a stunned silence. The camera whirred as we stood there like goldfish, mouths agape. Carol-Ann looked sternly at Paul, and signalled two burly security guards.

However, oddly, Paul didn't seem too bothered.

"OK. I'm off then..." he said, standing awkwardly between the two guards. "Sorry guys and everyone at home – I let you all down."

We all hugged him, saying how sorry we were to see him go and within minutes, Paul was escorted off the mountains.

"Right everyone, I will see you later for tonight's show." said Carol-Ann. "As yet, I don't know the format, as the eviction has been cancelled. See you all later."

And with that, she trouped back through the trees. We all watched her go.

"Ah, I'll really miss Paul," said Cindi.

"Me too," I smiled. "I wonder what he was caught taking? I always thought he would win – funny how things work out."

"Yeah...but that's life Tan, and these things happen, you can't ask why. As Angelina Jolie once said: 'You're young, you're drunk, you're in bed, you have knives; shit happens...'"

GOSSIPBITCH: Question: *Which international rock star pretended to be in possession of class A drugs on a mountain reality show?*

Here's a clue – the lead singer had a big (and more lucrative) gig in the US and his management were having hissy fits. Once his 'stash' was discovered, they choppered him out to Madison Square Gardens ASAP.

28

The Show Must Go On

We were all a bit depressed the next day, after Paul's eviction. The show had been an anti-climax for us, though no doubt brilliant for ratings as the viewers at home learned about Paul's departure. We gathered round the campfire at breakfast, a sombre little group, wondering what the day ahead held for us.

"I do hope it's not more walking, dear." said Marcus, crossly.

"These boots were made for walking!" said Jonny brightly. We all glared at him.

Flinty appeared through the trees. She was followed by a camera, so we all sat up to attention.

"Hello everyone!" she said brightly. "Well, I am sure you are all waiting for your task for today. You will be pleased to hear it's not more trekking, Marcus!"

"Thank the gods for that, dear" he muttered to himself.

"Today's task is a result of a Twitter explosion!" Flinty declared. We all looked at her blankly. "The episode where Tanya visited the orphanage caused an outpouring on social media," she went on to explain. "So, as a result, we would like you all to go back there, and do something for the children. You have a few minutes to think about what you as celebrities can do for these poor kids who have nothing."

I was delighted. So people at home had been as moved as I was by the orphans? Hopefully this would mean more publicity, more support and ultimately more volunteers and money for the children. We all sat and thought, racking our brains as to what we could do. Then an idea came to me. "Could we do a show?" I said. "What about if we all went in and gave a performance of something? I bet the kids would love that."

"Oh Tanya, can I do the hair and make-up for the show?" said Cindi, clasping her hands together in excitement. I nodded.

"Yesss... Oh...oh... I just thought, I used to do kids' face-painting in between jobs, let me paint their faces too, they'd love it!"

"Great idea," I said.

Nathan settled down next to me, his arm around my shoulder; "I have to sing for the kids," he said.

I melted: "Ah...Of course you do, Nathan." It was true what Ardash said, anyone with a heart had to do something for these kids. "What about doing a musical show of some kind?" I suggested. "The kids love music and Ardash has taught them lots of western songs so they are familiar with some popular rock and pop."

"Kids love slapstick... I can do slapstick. I used to be a children's entertainer," said Jonny, his face lighting up.

"You still are, man," Rex snapped.

"Fabulous," I smiled at Jonny.

"This is all great stuff!" Flinty said, listening to something on the talkback in her ear. "You've got the rest of this morning to think of some ideas then we will bus you to the orphanage this afternoon. You'll stay the night in a room there, then rehearse and perform tomorrow! Tanya, as it was your idea, you are in charge." She said.

"One more thing, Flinty" I said. "Could we please arrange for each child to have a toy? They don't have much at the orphanage and it would be nice for them all to have something they can call their own."

She nodded. "That should be OK. I'll look into it. Good luck!" Then she disappeared off through the trees, to arrange it all.

"I'm definitely singing," Nathan said, once Flinty had left. "I have an idea, why doesn't everyone do their own thing and do a public vote – like *X Factor*?"

"Nathan my sweet, that *is X Factor*... Why do *X Factor* on another show? And well, it's not quite the point is it?" Marcus said slowly, looking Nathan up and down. "Apart from the fact that the *X Factor* would probably be lost on these children, it's not about us auditioning on prime-time is it, dear?"

"Well, you come up with something better," Nathan snapped.

"I've just had a fab idea," Cindi announced. "What about a panto?"

"Oh, I like that idea. What does everyone else think?" I had to be careful, with all the egos around. "We could use a simple fairy story that the kids would understand; lots of Jonny's slapstick, Marcus and Rex's acting, Nathan's singing..." I started. Marcus and Jonny nodded enthusiastically.

"OK, shall we say it's a panto?"

"I'd want a solo... If it's a panto," Nathan said, tersely.

"Ooh, listen to *her*," Marcus hissed. "Will you want a Winnebago too, dear?"

Nathan ignored him.

"Can we avoid any artistic differences please?" I attempted to joke but only Jonny and Cindi laughed.

"So what panto shall we do?"

"What about *Cinderella*?" Cindi suggested.

"OK," I said, making notes. "So *Cinderella* it is and I think we all agree: Cindi will make the perfect Cinders. Now, Rex... Would you like to..?"

"I'll come along."

"Oh. And?"

"And *what*?"

"Well, what part will you take?"

"I said I'll be there."

"Oh that's more than enough," Marcus lisped sarcastically. "Let's not ask for the moon, we already have the stars... Ooh *listen* to me. The mere whiff of greasepaint and I've come over all Bette Davis. God, how I've missed the life!"

And so it was that the dysfunctional family of Z-listers washed up on the shores of celebrity and found themselves on the side of a mountain in one of the poorest countries in the world, planning a pantomime.

I was the self-appointed director, Marcus and Jonny were the Ugly Sisters and Nathan was Prince Charming. Rex refused to even entertain the idea of Baron Hardup (*Marlon who?*) and being American, the whole British panto thing was lost on him anyway. I left that one hanging for now, hoping I could persuade him when we got there. With casting finalised we headed off in the micro-bus to Kathmandu and the orphanage.

"Oh, how I long to tread those boards again... Like a sailor misses the sound of the ocean I've missed the roar of that crowd," Marcus proclaimed loudly as we all clambered off the bus after the six-hour drive. I'd been sitting with Nathan who had spent the whole journey writing his music for the panto. I squeezed his arm as we walked up to the entrance; I was grateful for his enthusiasm and so happy to be sharing this with him.

It was late when we arrived and we were shown to the shabby room where I'd slept last time. "Oh, I feel like I'm in a concert party," said Marcus, unfurling his sleeping bag next to Jonny's.

"As long as you don't party near me," Jonny quipped as the rest of us bedded down for the night next to them.

"Wow, this place is stinky," said Cindi, wrinkling her nose.

My heart sank a bit. "You don't regret coming do you, Cindi?"

She shook her head. "Course not, Tan. Anyway, there are no regrets in life, just lessons."

"Germaine Greer?"

"Jennifer Aniston."

We settled down for the night, and before we knew it, fingers of sunlight were creeping over the window sill. It was morning and there was lots to do if we were to get this show on tonight.

I sat up, feeling excited and nervous. I couldn't wait to see the children – one particular little girl especially.

I introduced everyone to Sunita who said the children would play outside in the courtyard after breakfast, while we rehearsed in the dining hall.

"I can't begin to tell you what this means to us all," she began. "We told the children last night that the nice English film-star lady was returning with her friends and their excitement and happiness was heard throughout Kathmandu," she smiled.

Sunita showed us into the dining hall where 63 beaming little faces sat waiting for us. The children had probably been told to sit still and not chatter when we arrived as just beneath the calm surface, their excitement simmered. The thrill was tangible and the air was filled with last night's dhal, unwashed bodies and anticipation.

"I know now what is meant by the roar of the greasepaint and the smell of the crowd," Marcus said, pulling a face.

"Oh, you'll soon get used to it," I smiled.

We all stood in front of the children and Sunita asked them to welcome us to their home.

"Namaste, Meess Travees. Namaste friends," they chanted in unison, holding the prayer-like gesture with their hands.

Then typical child chaos took over as they skipped over to us, to investigate these aliens from another culture. Cindi was soon holding a child on each hip, Marcus was tweaking noses and Jonny had a huge group of kids in thrall by blowing massive raspberries. As I watched them all, a little hand pushed gently and silently into mine.

My heart melted as I looked down to see two huge brown eyes looking up at me. I smiled down and her little face lit up – for a moment I swear the world stopped turning. After a few seconds I composed myself and squeezing Maya's tiny hand I tried to shout over the madness to tell the children about the show. "Does anyone have a favourite song they know that they'd like us to sing? We want you all to sing along with us during the show tonight!" I yelled.

"I get Ardash, he will know," Sunita said, walking through the hall and calling him. Within minutes of Sunita going to fetch him, Ardash walked into the room. I glanced over at Nathan who was stood against the wall talking to Rex. I was a little disappointed he wasn't playing with the kids, but perhaps he would bond with them later through his music.

Ardash wandered over to me, smiling. "The children cannot believe that you come back here. Sunita, she is so happy, and the children are essatic!"

"I'm glad we can help," I smiled. All the time, Maya was clutching my hand tightly.

Eventually, Sunita and the helpers managed to move the children outside so we could rehearse the panto. Cindi and I 'co-directed', creating a scene-by-scene story and suggesting visual ways of explaining the narrative and moving it forward. Cindi kept inviting Ardash over, asking him questions from a cultural perspective and which songs children would recognise. We realised quite soon that even with people doubling up, we were short of actors so I asked Ardash to play Buttons.

"What is the 'Buttons'?" he asked, amused.

"He's Cinderella's friend. He loves her, but guides her and helps her to meet her dream prince," I explained. "Ah, this love you have in your country," he said, shaking his head. "It truly is a hinji minji state of affairs!"

Cindi and Ardash began rehearsing their scenes together, Cindi planning what they'd say and Ardash teasing her by pretending to be confused. They were both laughing and clearly enjoying each other's company and I felt a sting of jealousy that surprised me. I liked Cindi but perhaps I envied her a little too; she had such an effortless way with men. I spotted Nathan and thought it might be an idea to help him with his lines and actions. He seemed to be taking up all his time on the songs – which was great – but it was vital we made the storyline clear for the kids who spoke little English and didn't know the story.

"What are you singing, darling?" I asked gently, inadvertently stopping him mid-chorus.

"It's a new one...about new lovers, old ties," he smiled.

"Oh, I thought you were doing *We Will Rock You*?" I said, trying to hide my disappointment.

"Nah, I'm not doing some old *Queen* number when I can do my own."

"But the kids need to sing along, that's part of the fun for them."

"Tan, this is my big chance, if I sing my own stuff on prime-time I could get a record deal out of it... The kids will love it, babe."

I didn't want to antagonise him or come over as too bossy, but perhaps he didn't understand what we were really doing here.

"I can see what you're saying darling, but the kids don't know the story, so we need to think about your lines..."

"Tanya, you are a bossy boots," he smiled, ruffling my hair good-naturedly.

"Thing is sweetie, the kids haven't heard your music, so they can't sing along."

"No. But then they're not after a record deal, are they?" he said, trying to soften it with a smile when he saw my face. "Look Tan, these kids don't care what songs we sing, we're doing them a favour. It's amazing what we're doing here – they're lucky to be having this show."

"I don't think they're lucky," I said.

"Oh, don't go all funny on me. You know what I mean... I just don't want to miss this chance. You don't get many like this... it's golden."

"Yeah, golden," I repeated, and walked away to deal with Marcus's boned corset and Jonny's three-foot wig.

The production team had provided a packed lunch for us all and mid-afternoon we stopped work to eat chapattis and drink bottled water.

We all sat round cross-legged on the floor and Rex deigned to join us. "Here's the thing" he said. "I'm not interested in this panto, and I sure don't understand it. But I guess you are desperate, so I will 'step in'." This was all for the benefit of the camera and as we were being filmed throughout the day he'd obviously realised he wouldn't be on air if he didn't take part. He conceded to play the Baron and as there was no-one to play the wicked stepmother or the fairy godmother, I had offered to play these parts as well as directing. This meant that at the beginning, I'd have to be married to Rex. To say this was awkward was an understatement.

We ate our chapattis and were going through our lines when Jonny decided to try and build bridges with Rex.

"You've made quite an impression on the kids," he said, desperately trying to ingratiate himself. I groaned inwardly. Why did he feel the need to do this?

"What are you saying, boy, are you being sarcastic?" Rex said, putting down his chapatti. Everyone concentrated on their lunch or their lines. I almost choked on mine.

"No, no...I'm just saying... The kids...seem to like you. Have they seen your films?" He tried.

"*No they fucking haven't seen my films,* Jonny." He let it sink in, but as Jonny didn't react, he went in for more mauling.

"I make films for grown-ups. I'm not a kid's entertainer, like you."

I desperately wanted to defend Jonny and tell Rex just what I thought of his bullying but now wasn't the time.

All I could do was move the conversation along in an attempt to stop the intimidation. "So, is everyone happy with rehearsal so far? I tried.

"Oh it's wonderful darling. Kenny Branagh would die of jealousy at my Drusella and Jonny's Anastasia is an inspiration, my love."

Jonny smiled, pleased with the compliment.

"I can understand what you were trying to tell us now Tanya – about this place and the kids..." Cindi said. "Bless 'em, all they are looking for is love."

"You're very profound today," Jonny said.

"I am a very profound woman Jonny. I'm not just a pretty face you know."

Rex and Nathan sniggered.

"Pretty, maybe, but I wouldn't say profound." Rex sniped.

"Yeah, well the only rule in life is: 'don't be boring and dress cute'," said Cindi, eyeballing Rex. "So I think I'm ok."

"Who said that, the Dalai Lama?" Rex sneered.

"No, he never dressed cute – it's a quote from Paris!" she said, glaring at him like it should be obvious.

"Where in Paris?"

"Paris *Hilton*, silly." she said, and flounced off to rehearse her lines.

After lunch, we continued with rehearsal. There was much activity and noise as the camera crew filmed everyone being busy. Cindi and a couple of helpers were transforming all the children in the courtyard into tigers with face-paints. Little Maya never left my side and though she didn't speak, she made it clear she wanted to help me wrap the toys that had been delivered for the children. She was mesmerised by the brightly-coloured gift paper and gently caressed each soft toy, before placing it delicately and lovingly in the crinkly wrapping. Then I noticed her very carefully rocking a small blue elephant. She did this for a while and I assumed she wanted it for herself. I was just about to say she could have it when she began wrapping it slowly and with great care and offered the 'gift' to me, her big shining eyes looking into mine, searching for a reaction. With tears in my eyes, I nodded and placed my palms together before accepting the gift.

"Namaste, Maya," I said, overwhelmed. She smiled and went back to wrapping the toys. I took a few minutes to compose myself, and continued to wrap.

I was aware we were running out of time and there was still lots to do but everyone was busy. Rex was napping on the floor and Jonny was rehearsing his scenes with Marcus and Cindi; the only person who appeared to be hanging around was Tiff, so I asked if she could help me wrap – but she said no as she was helping Nathan.

"I'm printing off 63 copies of his song lyrics, so every kid can sing along," she said, rather smugly.

"It's kind of you, to spend all that time doing lyric-sheets for the children," I said as she shuffled them with care into a pile, a job she clearly thought more important than gift-wrapping all the orphan's toys. "Thing is, Tiff, the kids don't all read and if they do, they don't usually read English. Shame you've wasted time doing that when we're all so busy. But I'm sure Nathan will be very grateful."

I looked straight at her, but she didn't meet my eyes.

I left quietly and went to find the others. Curtain-up was in less than half an hour and I was starting to feel really nervous.

As *Spa Trek* went live at 1.45am it would be too late for the children, so the show was going to be filmed in the afternoon and we could watch it back later at camp. We all finally assembled in the hall, behind our makeshift 'stage' and it was clear I wasn't the only one with the jitters. Everyone looked great in their costumes, but I think we were all somehow more worried about this show than the reality one we had been starring in since we got to Nepal. Then Flinty was in our faces, trying to make sure the cameras caught our nerves.

"Ten minutes to go!" she said, dramatically. "Are you all ready?"

We shuffled nervously. She grinned at us then went off with the cameraman into the hall to get some establishing shots.

As the minutes ticked by to curtain-up, the tension mounted.

Jonny looked across at Rex and tried to lighten the atmosphere with a corny joke.

"Hey Rex, why are film stars cool? Go on, ask me?"

Rex rolled his eyes at Nathan, who responded with a grimace. "So, why are film stars cool?" Jonny repeated, like he needed to because no-one had heard him. And when no-one responded to his stupid joke, he answered it himself.

"Film stars are cool because they have fans... Geddit?"

I noticed Rex's jaw tighten, but it was too late to throw Jonny a lifeline.

"Here's a joke for ya," Rex said slowly, staring at Jonny. "Why did the clown lose his career?" Jonny smiled nervously and we all held our breath.

"Because he was a dick. Geddit? Stop with the fucking audition. It's over."

"What's over?" Jonny laughed nervously, looking around questioningly at us all, an embarrassed smile on his face. We all looked at the floor.

"You don't get it do you? *You* are over."

Jonny opened his mouth to reply but nothing came out. He shut it and opened it again, like a goldfish. "No-one here will tell you you're not funny. None of them have the balls... And you know what Jonny? You know what? These 'friends' you've made, they're glad you are such a loser. That way you're no competition. You've no chance of winning this – because nobody backs a loser, Jonny. You are pathetic," he spat.

"I was... Only trying to make you laugh," Jonny almost whispered, his head sinking into his chest.

"Yeah well, that's never gonna happen, Jonny Boy, because you are an old, talentless, waste of space!" Rex spat.

"Just *who the fuck* do you think you are?" I heard myself say. Everyone's heads snapped up in my direction, mouths agape.

"Leave it Tanya..." Nathan started, like he was already my husband, like he had some influence over my actions, my feelings.

"Don't you DARE tell me what to do, Nathan. You're no better than he is, just standing by. I won't leave it." I said, turning to Rex. I'd stood by and watched as Rex bullied Jonny ever since we had arrived and enough was enough.

"Do as your boyfriend tells you and keep out!" Rex snarled. He was leaning forward now, in my face, trying to intimidate me, but I wasn't scared of him. I'd prodded vicious gang leaders in the chest and told them to run home to mummy. I'd slapped errant husbands and chastised druggie sons and the more I saw of this guy, the more I saw the similarities.

"Who the fuck *are* you anyway, Tanya Travis, with your Jerry-Springer circus and your tight little tits?" he snarled.

"You get your kicks crucifying people," I said calmly. "But you are a coward, Rex Cannon. I've met more courageous, more honest people on my 'tight-titted circus' than you will ever be."

"Ha! You losers make me laugh," he snorted, gearing up for combat.

"Hey, Rex, easy," Cindi tried.

But Rex was on a roll. "Last night you showed me a photo of your ex," he said, looking at Jonny. "Do you really think a woman like that ever loved you? Yeah, at the time there were a few hundred thousand reasons why she 'loved' you and when she'd spent them all she hit the road..."

Rex's cruelty took my breath away and made me think about my own life, my own success and how I'd ended up here.

"That's enough!" I heard myself bark, in a voice that used to make everyone stop in their tracks on my show. *Wow, so it still works*, I thought as everyone turned to look at me.

"We've all hit a rocky patch," I said. "That's why we're here, desperately trying to get our celebrity back. We've not given up, we're not hurting anyone, we're just trying to make the best of what we've got before the 'the end of the pier show' beckons. No-one's kidding themselves that they are still at the top of their game; if we were, we'd be too busy to take weeks off, a million miles from home. We know this won't win us Oscars and Baftas, we'll be happy with an ad for *Iceland* and a few fête openings. It's better than nothing...it'll pay the rent and at least we're not lying to ourselves, Rex." I said, loudly and clearly.

"Yeah? Well, I'm still someone in Hollywood" he spat, "and I got paid more than anyone else to be on this show. I'm the pull, the real star. This is just something I'm doing in between films."

"In between films, she says... Methinks the lady doth protest too much!" Marcus hissed.

"Like I said... WE aren't lying to ourselves," I said, calmly. "Not any more, anyway."

"Until I came here, I Botoxed, spent a fortune on face-cream and believed cosmetic surgery could hold off the inevitable. But we all die in the end and all the facelifts and lies in the world can't hold back time. The world is moving on."

He huffed.

"Your attitude stinks, Rex," I couldn't stop now, "...and what's more, your forehead's so flat and eyes are so wide apart from surgery you look like an... An extraterrestrial."

The last bit sort of spilled out, (I'd been thinking it, but until now had fought to keep it to myself) but it was the thing that finally wiped the smirk off his face. Rex was scarlet with rage, Marcus's cheeks were sucked right in and Cindi's mouth was wide open.

He didn't care about the personality assassination; it was the 'alien' attack that hurt him. His shallowness ran deep.

"You bitch," he said, stepping towards me.

"You don't scare me, Rex."

"Well you scare *me*, Tanya Travis, with your cleaning and puking. Seems to me that the lady who runs the freak circus is the one who really needs a shrink. "

"Look, Rex" I said, taking a breath and trying to calm everything down. "Some human beings are stronger than others, physically and emotionally. Isn't it up to the strong ones to help the weaker ones – not push them further into the ground? Hurting each other isn't going to help any one of us."

Rex stared at me. I looked calmly back at him, refusing to break eye contact. All I could think was 'Christ, I've done it now'.

Then I heard a slow, solitary clap and turned to see Ardash; calm, strong, standing in the wings serious-faced, hands clapping.

I flushed.

Then Cindi took the cue and started clapping, followed by Marcus and Jonny. Nathan saw how many were clapping and he joined them.

"Oh, screw you all!" said a furious Rex, and he stormed off. Cindi looked at me with confused admiration and Jonny smiled in gratitude, but Nathan couldn't look at me.

"Bravo, exquisite performance dear," said Marcus.

"Yeah, thanks Tanya," added Jonny, weakly.

I took a deep breath. I was shaking. But this reminded me why I got into this whole business in the first place. My ambition hadn't always been about bespoke kitchens and designer suits, I'd wanted to help people. My sole aim when I started all those years ago was to be the voice for those who were too weak or too broken to speak for themselves.

"Tanya, we now have a big problem." Flinty was saying, looking at me. I looked up at her with a start. I hadn't noticed her and the cameraman come back in but judging by her expression, they'd caught the whole argument.

"You and Rex open the show. He's just stormed off, with five minutes to go. What shall I do?"

They all turned to me, expectantly. I took a deep breath.

"Go and find him. Tell him it's in his contract to participate – and tell him that it won't look good for him on prime-time to ruin the show for the kids. He'll come back." I said, confidently.

We all stood anxiously behind the makeshift curtain as the kids trooped in, squealing and skipping and singing. Rex still hadn't appeared. My mouth went dry as I heard Sunita and the other staff quieten the children down. Cindi, Marcus and Jonny looked at me with concerned faces, afraid that Rex wouldn't come back. Then suddenly, just as I prepared to announce that the show would have to be postponed, I spotted Rex storming back in. He arrived behind the curtain, angry (but I have to say still handsome) in his Baron's costume.

"Alright, you losers" he spat. "I don't wanna see any of you ever again, but I won't be the bad guy. Let's get this over with." Which would have been tough and intimidating, had he not been wearing a hat with a huge purple feather which waggled around every time he spoke.

"Well done, Rex" whispered Cindi, giving him a pat on the back. He shrugged her off. And his feather waggled some more.

I bit my lip nervously as the curtain was raised, then stepped forward onto the makeshift stage. There were cheers from the children as soon as they saw me. Rex also strode forward. "I am Baron Hardon!" he exclaimed. My mouth went dry.

"HardUP" I hissed at him. I could hear Marcus sniggering behind in the wings.

Rex glared at me. "I am Baron HardUP," he tried again. "And this is my lovely new wife!"

That bit must have killed him.

"Now, where are my beautiful daughters?"

Then Marcus and Jonny skipped onto the stage, dressed up like two deranged drag queens, Cindi's make-up all over their faces. "Ooh Mummy!" Marcus exclaimed, batting comedy eyelashes. "The Princey-wincey is having a ball!"

I don't know how much the children understood but they were soon laughing and cheering along. Even Rex was pulling a performance out of the bag now he was in front of everyone and the cameras were on. When my part had finished, I stood in the wings for a few moments and listened, delighted at the reaction.

The panto was basic, patched together in an afternoon by a well-meaning group of people. It wasn't award-winning, the costumes were rubbish and the set kept collapsing, but watching the kids scream laughing at Jonny's antics and their hilarity at Marcus's camp glamour was pure magic. Jonny's slapstick falls and funny facial expressions went down a storm and an old queen in a corset with a bowl of fruit for a hat was funny in any language. He fell over, camped it up and when his mangoes accidentally fell out of his bra I thought the kids would never stop laughing. I had to make another cameo as the Fairy Godmother and the children cheered loudly again as I stepped on and transformed Cinderella's fortunes. Then Nathan came on as Prince Charming, singing his latest song and looking incredibly handsome. I'd secretly hoped he would keep it short, but the longer it went on the more anxious I became and had to do a quick wipe of the hands to try and calm myself. Our audience sat quietly, politely listening but I spotted Sunita doling out a few gentle warnings as the kids began to lose interest, get bored and chatter. I hated myself for not feeling supportive and proud, but it was tortuous watching the audience fidget and gaze around. We were losing them and I just wanted Nathan to finish so we could get back to what the kids could enjoy. Fortunately, Cindi was on next and they loved 'beautiful princess' as they called her and clapped loudly and whistled when she went to the ball.

At Marcus's insistence, we had an interval after Cinderella fled from the ball and her coach turned into a pumpkin. "We have to do everything properly dear, no short-cuts – this is a performance after all." He said, readjusting his mangoes.

During the interval, (where orange cordial was served in paper cups courtesy of the production company) I bumped into Ardash.

"So Tanya, you came back, you brought friends... And lots of happiness."

"Yes and it's not just about the TV show; when I'm home in England I won't forget the orphanage, Ardash. I promise." I smiled.

"I can't believe how brilliant it all is," Flinty said, rushing over and congratulating me. "I'm going to start editing now and I will be spoilt for choice, there's so much great stuff here. I have to tell you Tanya, I didn't think you'd still be on *Spa Trek* by now, let alone bringing everyone together and putting on a show like this... I mean – hell, we thought you were off your rocker a few days ago!"

"I think I probably was," I said, sipping the sugary orange. Ardash and I exchanged smiles as Flinty skipped off to her edit.

"I was in a bad place. I just felt so lost, but I'm feeling better now," I said, smiling at him.

"I hope you have found peace, Tanya, but as we say in here in Nepal, we look for light while carrying a lamp...sometimes we don't see what is already there."

I smiled at him and heard Marcus's imitation buzzer for the second act. Everyone was back in their seats and it wasn't long before the audience were roaring again. When Prince Charming brought the slipper round for the Ugly Sisters to try, Marcus had us all in stitches with his wayward mangoes and over-the-top acting.

"This is my shoe, it's mine, all mine," Marcus screeched, squeezing his size tens into one of Cindi's size three stilettos. "Oh, look how pretty I am," he exclaimed, getting up and staggering around the stage with half his foot hanging out. The kids loved it, he was such an outrageous ham it didn't matter that he didn't speak the same language. They understood it all from his exaggerated actions and facial expressions.

For the grand finale – Cinderella's wedding to Prince Charming – Nathan was in his best suit, brought from home for the programme final. He walked on stage and I caught my breath at the sight of him: tall and handsome, smiling just like a fairy-tale prince. I imagined how he'd look at our wedding but couldn't help but think what a good-looking couple he and Cindi made. The kids liked the handsome prince but it was the beautiful princess that drew the yells and applause. I smiled to myself in the darkness; young beautiful women are admired at any age, in any language.

Nathan as Prince Charming sung the song he had written again, as a wedding present to Cinderella. Even though I was glad he was able to sing it twice, it felt like a bit of an anti-climax because it was the last bit of the show and the kids didn't know it. As he finished the final chords and the kids clapped politely, I knew what we needed to do next. "Ardash!" I said. "We need an encore."

His face broke out into a grin and together we stepped forward to join Cinderella and Prince Charming, starting to clap out the beat to *We Will Rock You*. As soon as the kids heard it, they went wild. The noise was deafening and they joined in loudly and joyfully. Nathan looked a bit surprised but picked up his guitar and started strumming the chords and the room was filled with a cacophony of children's voices, clapping and music.

I glanced over at Ardash; the pride and love on his face caused a lump in my throat. Like a father, he'd taught the children the words to songs like this since they were babies, and now he conducted from centre-stage as his 'pupils' sang loudly and confidently, to be heard by millions of people, thousands of miles away.

I glanced at Maya sitting in the front row and thought I saw her mouth move. I leaned forward. Looking into her face, I almost wept to see her lips moving slowly and awkwardly over each word.

Ardash had been right. It had always been about me until now, but this was something different – a feeling I'd never felt before. Expensive French face creams and high end splash backs had never given me a rush like this.

As I sang along with Maya and the others, I put my arm around her tiny shoulder, my heart swelled with the sound of the voices. It was music so loud and beautiful I swear it could be heard throughout the Kathmandu night.

TWEET: @AstridLun I bloody love Tanya + all the kids she should have made @GokWan Prince Charming not sex addict @NathanWells #BringBackDocMartin

29

Twinkling Porn Stars and Big Dark Clouds

Arriving back at camp, there was much excitement as the live show was about to begin and we would be watching the panto on a monitor live on air. We were all on a high – apart from Rex, who spent the long journey with his eyes shut, though I doubt he was asleep.

We gathered around the camp fire and waited for Carol-Ann to come over and the show to start. I snuggled up next to Nathan and we giggled to each other privately as Marcus held forth on his 'Summer of '91, playing opposite 'La Mirren' in *No Sex Please, We're Italian* at The Young Vic. He was still wearing his corset outside his clothes, smoking a cigarette and reminiscing as everyone listened, the afterglow of the panto still shimmering upon us.

"The critics loathed the play, of course," he sighed. "Such snobbery. All because the storyline covered illegitimate children, incest and small willies."

"Sounds like one of my shows," I smiled.

Everyone laughed and Nathan squeezed me around the shoulder with pride.

Things were finally coming together for me. I felt very happy sitting in a huddle waiting for the film with my friends and soon-to-be husband; I had plans for the future which didn't involve me and TV and – for the first time in a long time – I actually liked myself. I was reflecting on this when Flinty came over to tell us the panto bit would be on last and to make sure we were ready when Carol-Ann came to the campfire to introduce it.

"Darling, did you capture the essence of my Drusella on film?" Marcus asked. Flinty laughed.

"I can assure you, everyone was 'captured' beautifully!" she said. "I've also used some of the footage from Tanya's visit to the orphanage the other day," she said. "I almost cried editing it – moving stuff. Anyway, just three minutes before we go live, so lots of energy tonight please, guys, see you on the other side."

Carol-Ann arrived, did the usual long-winded hello and after some live interviews with us and several VTs finally introduced the panto footage. There was great anticipation waiting for the panto VT to roll. We all crowded round the monitor with cameras in our faces, filming us as we watched, which was surreal. The film began with rehearsals, lots of shots of Cindi's perfect body getting dressed and undressed, Marcus smoking from his cigarette-holder outside in a corset with lipstick on. In one shot Rex was asleep and the kids were tying his trainer laces together. Then there was a shot from a distance of Rex shouting at me and storming off. Then the show itself came on and there were lots of slow motion close-ups of kids' smiling faces, mad slapstick from Jonny and camp, corseted outrage from Marcus. Cindi looked stunning in her gown at the end and Nathan looked pretty damn hot. Then Nathan looked into Cindi's eyes at their wedding celebration and told her he was going to sing a song just for her. He got his guitar and strummed the first line. Then the VT cut to the kids jumping up and down in their seats and clapping the rhythm to *We Will Rock You* and Ardash, me and the whole cast singing along in one triumphant, happy finale.

Then suddenly, the action returned to the day I'd been at the orphanage alone. Music had been edited on and as the whole orphanage sang along with Ardash, I thought, *this is as it should be – it's their show – not ours.* I could feel a cool, wet tear slip from one eye, it was so moving, so unstaged. Then as the strains of *We Will Rock You* died out, the music became softer. And there was footage of me, playing with the kids, changing the babies and having a little cry when faced with the pail full of dirty nappies. Then me again, this time with my industrial gloves on, scrubbing. The VT ended with a slow motion shot of Maya running into my arms on the day I returned, then the children's happy faces at the end of our panto. I was stunned. It was such a short section, only a few minutes – but it made me realise how far I'd come since I had been here.

As it came to an end, Carol-Ann rushed towards us on camera, her hands held high, clapping. "What a show you lot – what an amazing show!" she was clearly moved by what she'd seen and before going to the next VT said: "This show is about entertainment, it's about showing celebrities in their true light, it's about taking someone out of a life of luxury and attention and offering them... nothing. After ten days the celebs will go home – these kids won't. Please go to our website and give."

I was delighted. They had used the footage to show the viewers what life in the orphanage was like and how just a little could make a big difference. And they'd clearly set up a donation site too. The tears fell easily now, and I was unashamed.

"Well, what a night!" Carol-Ann was saying. "But despite theatrical success, it's still eviction night, people! We will be back after the break to see whose acting didn't impress and who will be leaving the mountains tonight!"

I had almost forgotten it was an eviction but I was beyond caring whether I was voted out. I sat with Cindi and we squeezed each other's hands as Carol-Ann's make-up was touched up in the break. Then we all sat together as she went through the torturous eviction process, taunting and teasing until she came to the final announcement.

"So, the celebrity that the public has voted out tonight is..." she said, pausing for dramatic effect "...Big, bad Rex Cannon!"

Rex was genuinely surprised, but after what the viewers had seen today, I wasn't.

"Oh My God," said Cindi, squeezing my arm. "I'm still here! I don't believe it!"

"Neither do I, honey... You Brits have no taste," said Rex and without smiles or hugs he marched away from the campfire and was gone.

"So many failed comics to taunt, so little time," said Marcus, right on cue.

The show ended and we looked in wonder at each other, most of us close to tears but proud of what we'd achieved that day. I went to find Nathan, who was sitting very quietly on his own. He had liked Rex, so I wondered if he was sad about him leaving.

"You OK, darling?" I whispered. He put his head down: he was upset.

"It's what happened at the orphanage," he said.

"Aw, I know I felt the same when I went there first time. It's a shock isn't it? But I think we can do something... Babe I have plans. We can help them as soon as we get back. I want to start a charity, do a documentary about the orphanage... We have to make people aware..."

He pulled away sharply, turning from everyone. "Shut up about the bloody kids, Tanya," he said under his breath. "Christ, you're obsessed. What about me? I had the chance for some serious exposure tonight and that bitch Flinty cut my singing." With that he got up and walked quickly into the darkness.

I was about to follow him when I noticed Cindi twinkling over a glass of wine and Marcus hugging Jonny. They were giggling, drinking, allowed to stay happy and still on a high, relive the madness and fun of the day. But I had been brought down with a bump by Nathan. Like a big dark cloud he'd descended on me, taking away the glitter and the stars with what seemed to be his constant refrain; *'What about me, Tanya?'*

Not once had he said, 'well done', or 'how do you feel Tanya?' It was always about him. Is that how I seemed to Ardash? Selfish, self-obsessed: the 'what about me' westerners.

For a moment I almost gave in and went after him but I was actually a bit ashamed and annoyed by his behaviour. So I walked towards the light and laughter to join the others and was overwhelmed by the warmth of their welcome as they congratulated and hugged me. OK, it was all a bit over the top and 'luvvie-ish' but that was the way celebrities did things, with hugs and air-kisses and lavish compliments. There was nothing else to do but smile and hold out my beaker for someone to fill it with wine.

"Come here, girl," Cindi was slightly tipsy already and leaning on me.

I smiled as we clinked beakers.

"I know I'm pissed, but I have to say this before it's too late Tan... are you really, really, really sure you want to marry Nathan?"

"Oh Cindi, I don't want to get into all that now."

"I mean, when there are men like Ardash around?" she started.

"Mmmm. Has it occurred to you I might actually love Nathan?"

She sniggered; "I reckon it's more like lust. You're not that daft – I mean Nathan's a cute guy, but love...seriously?"

"What about you and Rex..? Seriously." I mimicked her voice.

"Oh he's rich, and a film star...what's not to like? Anyway, he's gone now... there was never anything in it. I just did it to please my management. But Ardash... Now *that's* a man."

"Oh no, you've been taken in, Cindi. He's got lots of girlfriends, he's quite a player. I've noticed you both whispering...catching each other's eye, secret smiles...the odd wink?"

"Is it that obvious?"

So I was right, there was some chemistry between Cindi and Ardash.

"I've never been known for my subtlety but I didn't realise our little chats were quite so noticeable," she chuckled, putting her hand over her mouth, horrified to be discovered.

"Well, they were," I smiled. I felt a chink of light go out in my heart. I didn't even know it was there. *But why?* I was in love with Nathan, my future husband, I shouldn't feel a twinge of sadness because Ardash had fallen for Cindi. It was bound to happen, she was gorgeous... and so was he.

"Tan, you just don't get it, do you?" Cindi was slurring in my face: "The reason me and Ardash have been whispering and winking is because he told me he luurves you."

I looked at her blankly. The chink of light returned.

"Yeah, Ardash had really got it bad for *you* Tanya and when Nathan turned up he was a bit down. I was someone for him to talk to. We both feel that Nathan is... Oh god I'm drunk, I shouldn't be saying this... He's no good for you."

"Oh Cindi, Nathan isn't perfect, but who is?"

"Well it's up to you, Tan," she said, grabbing a bottle and pouring us both some more wine. But all I could think was: did she mean it about Ardash liking me? Or was she just drunk and feeling a bit sorry for me? And where the fuck had Nathan got to?

It wasn't long before one of those questions was answered. Nathan returned and sat in the dark under a tree, probably waiting for me to go and placate him. Within seconds, Tiffany joined him and even in the firelight from a few yards away I could see the desperate eagerness to please him dancing in her eyes.

I watched them, waiting for the sting of jealousy to hit: that familiar salty taste of resentment and hurt I'd feel as he talked intimately with another woman. I thought about the children we'd never have and felt incredibly sad for what might have been. And all the time I saw Maya's pleading eyes, her tiny hand.

Nathan looked up and I caught his eye; he smiled sulkily, like he was suffering and it was all my fault. I looked away – he was only using Tiff as a shoulder to cry on because I wasn't there for him. I felt guilty: if he needed to chat with her as a result of my treatment of him, I had only myself to blame. I looked over again, unable to keep my eyes from him, willing him to come back to me, to make it alright again. I didn't want to lose that but I knew from now I had to be stronger and not give in to him so easily. He stood up, left Tiff alone by the tree and wandered over to where I was, with the other celebrities. He'd done the maths: he was beautiful and selfish and he had to stay with me on this show if he wanted any kind of stardust.

"Hey guys" he said with a weak smile.

"We were just talking about what we are going to do after the show, Nathan" Cindi said. "It's nearly over, after all!"

His jaw clenched. "Well, hopefully I'll be singing my songs to an audience bigger than the orphanage!" he quipped. I turned away from him, towards Jonny. I had to make him realise that he was the one in the wrong this time.

"What about you, Jonny?"

"I don't know" he said with a sad smile. "What if Rex was right? What if I am over and I can't get my wife back?"

"Jonny. Take my advice and face the truth, she might never come back. And you can waste your life wishing for something that may never happen, being something you're not and looking over your shoulder to see if anyone's guessed. We all grow old and we have to stop kidding ourselves that we can be the person we once were. That young, talented person who thought anything was possible doesn't exist anymore. Once you realise that, you can get on with the rest of your life," I said, realising that I had only just realised that.

He nodded.

"Anyway, what about being a children's entertainer? You were great with the kids."

His face brightened. "I could do. But would I get work? I just don't know anymore."

"The truth is you don't know what is going to happen tomorrow. Life is a crazy ride, and nothing is guaranteed," pronounced Cindi.

"Ernest Hemingway?" I asked hopefully.

"No! Not some old geezer called Ernest, what do you think I am, Tan? Can't you guess who said that?"

"Strindberg?" offered Marcus, getting into the swing with a wicked grin.

"Eminem," she said, like it was obvious.

Marcus unfurled himself and held out his arms in full Shakespearian mode. "Ah, Eminem! That profound social commentator – the Plato of our times – the great man otherwise known as, 'Slim Shady'."

TWEET: @AstridLun Can't shitting wait 4 @TanyaTruth 2 come back. She will piss with happiness @KimKardashian new baby #TanyaMountainQueen

30

Sad Goodbyes and a Time for Truth

The following night we were back in the public firing line for another live eviction. We'd all been allowed to sleep for the morning after the panto and though we still hadn't spoken, Nathan had tried to cuddle up to me in the night. For the first time, I didn't feel relief or gratitude that he still wanted me. I didn't know what was going to happen with us, though I did know things would have to change. In the afternoon, Ardash led us on a very tough trek and Nathan gave up and went back to camp about half way through, claiming that he'd hurt his ankle. The rest of us finished it and were rewarded with a delicious curry.

"With just five celebrities left, tonight's eviction is a double... and it's gonna be a good'un!" said Carol-Ann joyfully. "Vote to save your favourite, and join us after the break when all will be revealed...Who's leaving *Celebrity Spa Trek* tonight?" She did a cute little skip and winked at the camera. Her skirt flitted upwards, rewarding the viewers with the promise of another glimpse of young thigh if they returned after the commercial break.

She skipped off, returning within seconds in a tight little evening dress, which seemed wholly inappropriate for a mountain in Nepal but she looked lovely. Twenty-four hours of our lives were condensed into 47 minutes and we waited in taut silence for our fate.

"So yesterday we said goodbye to big, bad Rex Cannon" she started. "And tonight, we say goodbye to two more spa-trekking celebrities." I was so nervous. It was too soon for me to go; I still had questions to be answered. I wanted to learn more about myself and didn't want to leave my friends – or Nathan. I had to work out what was going to happen between us.

Of course, there was also the horrific prospect that if I was voted out tonight my lovely agent would be waiting at the end of the rope bridge screaming about 'deals.' She'd currently be doing her darnedest to get me into as many fake magazine stories as she could, while I was still in the public's consciousness.

"So, the celebrities going tonight are..."

"Just tell us, you silly cow," Cindi murmured, her leg waggling constantly despite her toothy smile for the camera.

Marcus clutched his chest. "I am having a heart-attack," he whimpered and collapsed in front of the campfire. I stood up, thinking he was dying but just as I reached him he sprang back to sit cross-legged, his floral, rhododendron headdress slightly askew.

"You are wicked Marcus, I almost believed you," I said, ripping out a wipe.

"That's because I am an actorrrrr darling," he purred, pleased he could still do it.

"So tonight, the first celebrity to be sent home, voted out by you the public is...drum-roll please..."

"Fuck the drum-roll dear, pray tell who... Who...?" pleaded Marcus, wiping his eyes.

"...The marvellous, the talented, the ever-theatrical Marcus Brightman!"

"Oh, no!" I heard myself say.

"Oh My God," shouted Cindi. "I don't believe it!"

Marcus was smiling graciously and stood up to take centre-stage.

"It's been...emotional" he said, breaking into tears. "I don't want to do a Gwyneth but I do want to say it's been the most amazing experience of my life. I have trodden the boards with the greatest thespians the world has ever known; I've dined with Dench, I've danced with Mirren and I've shared a codpiece with Kenny Branagh (on different nights you understand). But my time here in Nepal..." he broke down again and at the risk of this speech continuing through the ads for tampons and tea bags, Carol-Ann stepped in, gently pushing his back with her hand.

"And thank YOU for being a wonderful camper," she said. "I'll see you for lashings of champagne later," almost pushing him into the bushes to get him off.

The remaining four of us looked at each other warily. We weren't friends now, but competitors. Even Nathan had a determined look on his face and it crossed my mind (uncharitably) that he'd become so obsessed with winning that if he had to choose between me and him, he'd throw me under the bus.

"And the second celebrity to leave tonight is..."

We all held our breath.

"It's that lovely old comedy genius and all-round good egg... Jonny!"

I gasped with relief, shock and gratitude to the Great British Public. What was going on outside in the real world that was causing me to have a modicum of popularity? Obviously I'd be next, but at least I had another night.

We all hugged Jonny, who seemed so used to defeat he took it well, like it was almost inevitable. "I told you..." he kept saying, over and over again. "I knew it would be me... I want to go...it's time..." – all the stuff we say when we don't really mean it but are just trying to save face.

This may have started as a shot in the arm for our careers and bank balances but somewhere along the way it had changed. Being there seemed to bring out a genuine human need to be liked, approved of – loved, even. We wanted this from the voting public and also from our peers. So Cindi, Nathan and I sat in front of the camera, all flawed, all fragile, all deeply grateful to be given a reward, an acknowledgement, a sign that we were liked.

The show closed and though I was pleased at the outcome, I was exhausted – being up every day in the middle of the night was taking its toll. None of us really felt like drinking around the fire to celebrate being in the final three, especially not now Marcus had left. So we all went back to our tents.

"I don't want to sound mean, but I'm glad the others have gone, well – apart from Cindi." I said to Nathan as we got ready for sleep. He was snuggling down in his sleeping bag but I wanted to try and get him to talk. We had a lot to sort out... like our future.

"It will be good to spend these last two days together – just you and me and Cindi," I said.

"Yeah," he said, gazing at the tent roof. "It's a lovely place."

"Romantic," I added, with a smile.

He nodded.

"Nathan. I know it's been stressful here. You and I haven't really communicated the last couple of days, have we?"

"I was upset. Frustrated, Tanya – I had an amazing opportunity to sing on prime-time and it was taken from me."

"Nathan, I don't mean to make your problems seem unimportant, because they're not... But being here has made me see things differently," I touched his knee and leaned into him to soften what I was about to say. "You not having prime-time exposure isn't the same as a child without a home, a mother, a limb."

He didn't look up. OK, so I would avoid that subject for now.

"Are you happy, Nathan?"

"Yeah."

"I mean, about the wedding. About us?"

"Of course, I can't wait to be married. And Tanya, I'm not being selfish... I get what you mean, about the orphans."

"Oh Nathan, I knew you just needed to get your head round it. We'll really get involved in the orphanage when we get back home, it's a vision we can share. I just want to put everything bad behind us. We need to start with a clean slate now...and I hate to bring it up, but if we're being honest...that includes your friendships with women. I know I've been jealous and I was wrong but you must respect me and see things from my point of view."

"Yes I know, but those girls... I keep telling you, nothing happened. They were just out for what they could get," he said, turning to face me. "I knew that baby wasn't mine, but you never believed me."

"Nathan, I didn't know who to believe. She seemed to have proof ... She described our house, our...bedroom in detail, she mentioned your birthmark – how did she know all that?"

"Oh Christ, here we go."

"I don't want to upset you. I believe you, but you have to see it from my perspective. I still don't know what happened, how she came to know all about my wardrobe, my cleaning fluids, the face creams I use..."

"She'd seen them in the glossy mags."

"Nathan, I never let the magazines in my bedroom. I always got Astrid to dress up the spare room and make it look like it was mine."

"Stop with the interrogation. I'm marrying you, isn't that proof enough that I want to be with you and no-one else?"

"Just tell me the truth. I can put up with anything – and it doesn't matter anymore whether you did sleep with her or not. But if we're going to make this marriage work, we have to be honest with each other from the beginning."

"How honest do I have to be? I'm telling you the fucking *truth*, Tanya," he said, turning away from me. "And if we're gonna make this marriage work – as you say – how about less jealousy and paranoia from you?"

I looked at him steadily. I didn't want to beg for his forgiveness as I had always done after these sorts of conversations. If we had a future, I had to be strong. It was up to me to make this work, to help Nathan to become a good partner, because no-one was perfect and he was the right one for me. I was too old to start looking again, but too young to commit to a life alone, so the answer was Nathan. I knew if I was there for him and supported him, he would make a good husband. "Are you looking forward to going home?" I asked.

"Yes I can't wait to go home and work on my album. I should get some interest after being on this show."

"I need to tell you something Nathan. I think I've lost the house." I said quickly.

"What do you mean? You can't have – my recording studio's there."

"I'm so sorry, but it will have been repossessed by now," I started to cry. The plan had been for Donna to deal with it all in my absence, which was easier for me but it meant I hadn't really had the time or the opportunity to take it in properly myself. Everything in England felt like something on another planet, in a different time-zone.

He looked at me like I'd slapped him. "I can't believe you'd let it go! Has someone bought it? Can we rescue it?"

I shook my head. "I don't think so. Oh, I know it's a shock and we were happy there, but it was only a house... We still have each other..."

"I'm not talking about the fucking *house* – I'm talking about my recording studio!" he shouted. "You earned loads of money, where's it all gone, Tanya?"

"I earned enough, but we lived beyond my means if I'm honest. I never owned the house, just had a huge mortgage that realistically

I'd never have paid off – then I took out a second mortgage to pay for the studio."

"Fucking hell, have you any idea how much that studio meant to me? It was my life."

"We can always get another home, another studio. It might be smaller and not quite as good but..."

"You lied to me. I finally got my recording studio and you just gave it away..."

"Well, I didn't actually lie. You never asked me. And if I talked about money you said I was being tight. You wanted the recording studio so much that I couldn't refuse you. And it would have been OK, but...then I lost my job and...everything else..."

I leaned on his shoulder, sobbing. His arms hung loosely around me but I didn't feel warmth.

"Look Tanya, I need time to think about all this. I don't know what I'm going to do if my studio's gone, it's my livelihood."

"I know, I know," I didn't have the heart to point out that he hadn't actually earned anything from the studio yet.

"So we'll just have to get somewhere when we get back that's big enough for another recording studio," he said.

"We won't be able to afford it, Nathan."

"You'll get a huge fee from this show, won't you? I bet it's a damn sight bigger than mine, they're paying me peanuts," he snapped.

"Yes they are paying me well but I need to pay off my debts back home and...I'm going to give the remainder to the orphanage."

"*What*? We're pot-less and you're giving it away? Are you *mad*?"

"No... I thought you understood, about the children?"

"The children? What about me? I can't listen to any more of this, I'm going for a walk," he snapped, unravelling my arm from his.

"Let me come with you..."

"No. I need to be on my own. I am so upset about everything Tanya, I can't believe you'd do this to me."

He set off into the night, away from me. I didn't follow him or plead with him, I just let him grow smaller and smaller until he disappeared.

I couldn't sleep, so I got up to sit by the campfire. I felt lonely, especially now Marcus had been evicted and Nathan hadn't returned. I wondered if he was OK and when I heard a rustle behind me, I thought he was back. For a moment my heart lifted, perhaps we could talk things through, make it all better?

"Nathan?" I said. I clambered up and ran towards the sound, landing slap-bang into Ardash. He was surprised and so was I. "I'm sorry, I thought you were..."

"Nathan?" he asked, guiding me slowly back to the campfire.

"Well, yes. We had...an argument, he's upset. I don't know what to do. I should just forget about stupid reality shows and go home...I have so many problems that need to be sorted." I said, and started to cry. I felt a soft hand on my back.

"Tanya please, why are you crying?"

"It's Nathan, I sold his recording studio – well it was taken actually. I have no money, my home is gone. And he can't write music without a studio...and..."

"Stop the talking, Tanya, see what is in the front of you. " he said, sitting down by the campfire and gesturing for me to join him, "why are you looking for light while carrying a lamp? You have your health? You have food to eat?"

"Yes I'm healthy but there's no recording studio, no house, all my shoes will have been sold..."

"So you have nothing to put on your feet?"

"Well, yes, I do...but...my Jimmy Choos have gone..."

"So this Jimmy Choos has left you, but you have shoes. Tanya, many people in Nepal have no shoes. They have no home – they don't know what a recording studio is. They will be lucky if they have a meal tonight so don't tell me you are crying about your shoes, Tanya."

"Oh God, Ardash... I'm not...it's just everything I worked for has gone and I mourn it."

"I know, but when we say we have nothing, we have nothing. When Tanya Travis says she has nothing she means she has food, clothes, somewhere safe to sleep...which to us is everything. Tanya, you are rich."

I smiled at the irony and the contrast between my conversation with Nathan and Ardash's simple reaction to my whingeing, which translated to 'shut up and count your blessings'.

"You always seem to give me perspective at just the right time", I smiled. As I looked at him, his hand reached up and gently touched my face, his hand now softly cupping my cheek. In his eyes I saw something I'd never seen before, I didn't know what it was but it made me feel giddy and guilty at the same time.

"Tanya, you are wise, but you don't see...I think you are lovely."

"And I... I think you're teasing me again," I tried. I had to lighten the atmosphere, it was all so intense and I was so vulnerable and mixed up I didn't know what was going to happen or if I'd be able to stop it if it did.

"Ardash, I have to say before I leave tomorrow that spending time with you, particularly at the orphanage and on the mountains, has truly changed my life. I hope you are happy in the future, but if I can, for once, offer you some advice – you need to choose between your four girlfriends."

It took a few seconds for him to digest what I'd said.

"I have the girlfriends?" he asked, looking surprised, holding his head to one side questioningly.

"You said you had four? And someone's going to get hurt."

He held out four fingers to check that's what it meant. "Four? Ah, very lucky man to be having four of the girlfriends... But no."

"But you said so. You told me, you have four bahini, four girlfriends?"

"Ah Tanya," he smiled, shaking his head. "Yes, I have four bahini, which means girlfriends, yes...or sisters. Now, I have four of the sisters. Nepali language is difficult for the English. I call you bahini as you are a female friend, but my sisters also bahini... You read the Nepali dictionary, sometimes confusing."

"Yes, very," I smiled, surprised at my own relief that he wasn't some 'love 'em and leave 'em' womaniser with four on the go at the same time. This news almost restored my faith in men...almost.

Later, I sat alone by the campfire and thought hard about everything that had happened to me in Nepal. The night turned to dawn, then to bright morning. The birds started singing and the sun rose over the stunning mountains. I felt the warmth on my face, and as nature started to stir around me, I could see Nathan return, snaking back through the trees. I didn't know where he had been or what he had been doing – and I was surprised to discover that I didn't have the energy or the inclination to find out. As he headed towards me I got up and went back to our tent. With the sun streaming through the open flap, I curled up on my sleeping bag like a cat and went to sleep.

TWEET: @AgentDonna wedding date now set for @TanyaTruth. Read the #exclusive in #OKMagazine #TheCakeFairy #VeraWang #HoneymoonOnNeckerIsland

31

Same Story, Different Blonde

I was awoken after a few hours by a runner. There were still tasks for us to do even though it was our last day in camp. We assembled by the campfire and Flinty appeared with her clipboard and three packed lunches.

"Well, it's been all about teamwork so far!" she said brightly. "But as well as teamwork, today is about reflection. It's about seeing the mountains and taking on board everything you have experienced. It's also about testing your orienteering skills!"

She handed out maps and compasses to the three of us.

"What's this for?" asked Cindi, turning her compass round and round. Flinty ignored her.

"Today, you will be planning your own trek. You need to plan a route that will take you three hours and land you back here, at camp. You will of course have a camera and a guide following you, but at a distance, so you will lead the way!"

I wasn't too enthusiastic. I felt awkward around Nathan and though we needed to clear the air, I felt I needed to sort my head out first.

Cindi was really up for it as she wanted to firm her thighs for a swimsuit shoot booked for the following week and we all set off with our trekking guide, Raj. Ardash for once wasn't leading us. Flinty had given him other tasks in camp in preparation for the show's finale.

We sat around the campfire together awkwardly and looked at the map.

"Well I think we should go this way!" said Cindi, randomly pointing to a place on the map.

"Why don't we just trek to the lake and back?" I suggested. "We should be able to remember the way, from our treks with Ardash. Remember all the times he told us which way the sun was, and where North is?"

Nathan and Cindi both looked at me uncertainly.

"OK Tan, you lead the way." said Cindi with a smile.

I sighed and got to my feet. "Let's go."

Nathan, Cindi and I walked side by side, saying nothing to each other, though I did see out of the corner of my eye Nathan looking at me. He was probably expecting me to try and make up with him and be the first to reach out as I'd always done but I wasn't sure. I needed to think clearly about everything.

Cindi fell back with Raj, who was walking behind us all and when we were alone Nathan said; "Tan... I'm sorry about everything last night – I didn't mean to upset you. I just needed to be on my own, when you told me about the recording studio...it just broke me, Tan."

"Yeah, I'm sorry too."

"I was wondering... Have you thought what you are going to do when we get back...I mean, about somewhere to live?"

"Oh Nathan, I don't know. It's been a bit like a weird holiday in here and I've put all my worries and plans on a bit of a back burner. Now I need to think...and it would probably be best if I just had some time on my own today, while we walk, just so I can fathom everything out. Do you mind?" This was the last day and as soon as we got out of there I'd have Donna breathing down my neck, along with Nathan and would have to find work of some sort and somewhere to live.

To my relief, he slowed down and fell in behind. Walking along, my mind drifted from my immediate problems at home and I thought about the experiences I'd had in Nepal. I'd spent the first half of this show wanting to leave but in the last few days I'd grown to love the place and I was surprised to realise that I didn't want to go home.

But where was home? I hadn't got a clue – one thing for sure was that life was going to be very different for me and Nathan when we returned to the UK. As I trekked for the last time through the beautiful, challenging mountains of Nepal, I realised one thing for certain: I was a stronger, wiser person than when I arrived. And that, at least, was something.

So finally, after twelve arduous days in the mountains it was the night of the last show. We had survived the day's trek with little conversation and amazingly I'd remembered the route quite well. It was a good last challenge – as Flinty said, a good opportunity to reflect. I went into Cindi's tent to get dressed.

"We're ready for your close-up, Miss Travis," Flinty joked when she came to get us.

"We're on air in a few minutes," she said. "Come on!"

I smiled and walked with Cindi over the craggy ground to the campfire setting for the grand finale. The mountains were engulfed by darkness and the cameras and lights were being set up.

"It's gone so well, Tanya," Flinty whispered, turning round as we ambled along, "...and...I shouldn't really tell you this – we don't want to affect 'reality'" (she did that annoying twitchy thing with her fingers to denote speech marks) "...but the ratings are the highest in the show's history. Everyone at home is talking about *Celebrity Spa Trek*... In fact," she stopped and turned round, "the Prime Minister joked about it on PM's Questions this week."

"Why?"

"Oh, nothing is as it seems, Tanya," she smiled enigmatically.

I was back in *The Truman Show* and feeling over-anxious, so did a few wipes to be on the safe side. *The PM? Highest viewing figures ever?* I bet Donna was delighted. Or furious. Was it something I'd done or somebody else? I had no way of knowing what the hell was going on in my own 'reality life'.

I arrived at the campfire where Nathan was waiting. He looked up anxiously.

"Tanya, where have you been? I was so worried, when we got back from the trek you disappeared. I thought you'd lost it again and gone on one of your rampages."

"I was getting dressed with Cindi," I smiled, thinking how he mustn't have been too worried as he'd managed to do his hair and take his place at the fire rather than come and find me.

Before he could say anything else, Carol-Ann turned to us, milking it for all it was worth: "Tonight we crown our Mountain King or Queen, and only one of you can be the winner of *Celebrity Spa Trek*. So welcome to the show everyone's talking about. Will she, won't she?"

"Will she, won't she what?" I hissed to Cindi, who looked puzzled.

"I don't know... Will she, won't she go bonkers again and throw water at everyone? Be sick everywhere? Scream at people? Take your pick." she said, rolling her eyes good-naturedly.

"Mmm, when you put it like that..." I shrugged. She was right, I might as well have just walked off there and then and let Cindi or Nathan have their crown.

"First," said Carol-Ann, "here are the results of the voting so far and the name of the first of our finalists to leave us." She waved a card at the camera and kept the suspense going for as long as humanly possible.

"And the next celebrity leaving Nepal tonight is... A lovely lady...who's come on quite a journey since she arrived here."

I moved in preparation for my departure.

"Goodbye, Cindi!," Carol-Ann said, as Cindi opened her mouth in shock.

"I don't believe it,! She said, anxiously titivating her hair. She had no artifice, and was unable to hide her surprise like everyone else had when they were evicted. Standing up, she leaned over to me, gave me a warm hug and whispered, "Don't let that little shit win this... You go for it, Tanya," before a half-hearted embrace with Nathan and a wave to us as she walked towards the rickety bridge and freedom.

"So before the phone lines close, we want to show you guys and the viewers just what you've both been up to during your time here in Nepal." said Carol-Ann, turning to Nathan and I.

"Now, Tanya Travis, Queen of Daytime and... Well, you're a bit of a dark horse... Take a look at this."

We both looked straight at the monitor to see a lovely mountain setting, all green and snow-topped and frilled with little prayer flags and light-hearted music. Then the camera came down the mountain to where everyone was arriving and admiring the view. Then straight in for a lovely close-up of me, covered in sick and in my underwear, giving Paul strict instructions and waving a towel in his face. This was followed by my manic under-towel fumbling, sped up, which caused the crew on set to virtually pass out in hysterics and the blood to rush to my face. This was followed by a succession of shots of me vomiting – which seemed to be on an endless loop – and of course a quick seven seconds of me hurling a bucket of water over two of my camp mates and shouting inappropriate and completely unwarranted abuse at them.

Then the music slowed with a wide shot of the lake at sunset, me touching Ardash's hand and then lying down next to where he was sitting. He was leaning over me talking and though it had all been perfectly innocent, it was made to look like he was staring into my eyes. I could see how, with a clever edit and the right music, it could be misconstrued. I smiled and looked over at Nathan, hoping he wasn't too jealous (but perhaps this might give him food for thought?)

The next shot revealed Ardash and I chatting round the campfire when everyone else had gone to bed, which moved seamlessly into a close-up of him sucking my toe. This was followed by my face thrown back in what appeared to be orgasmic pleasure. There were close-ups of our eyes meeting across the campfire, our faces flickering in the flames; giggle from me; a smile from him. All this was accompanied by Jane Birkin's oversexed French panting of *Je t'aime*.

The film ended as the camera swooped straight onto my surprised face for a reaction. I tried not to be sick.

"It looks like things were hotting up round that campfire for you, Tanya!" Carol-Ann read from her cue card.

"Not at all, no," I responded, still shocked at how they'd made it look like something was going on between me and Ardash. Nathan was sitting next to me, just staring ahead. *What was he thinking?*

I patted him on the knee, aware the cameras were on, but this was about real life, not about the bloody show. "You OK?" I asked, quietly, not wanting to make this into a feature film. Whatever happened now with Nathan and I, the truth was nothing had gone on with Ardash but the way it looked, Nathan would never believe me. I'd done nothing wrong, yet as a result I might lose my future husband and any chance of happiness I had. And they could now add unfaithful to my title of 'Britain's Most Hated Woman', I thought, worrying what the PM would have to say in Parliament about this new development.

Nathan continued to stare ahead.

"Nathan. You're not upset are you? I mean, it's the way they've edited it they can do all sorts with the edits..."

"You've humiliated me, Tanya," was all he could bring himself to say.

"It wasn't like that... There's nothing..."

"Don't insult me, please. All this time you've been accusing me of being unfaithful and look at you. Sleeping with the bloody trekking guide." I inwardly cringed.

"Nathan, I didn't sleep with him." I said. "Don't do this."

"Why?" he said, almost to the camera. "You do it to me all the time. How do you like being accused of something you haven't done?"

I wanted to cry, but I was desperately trying to hold it together. This was my nemesis – all the times I'd accused Nathan of being unfaithful when he wasn't – he was right: I deserved this injustice. At this point Carol-Ann patted me kindly and told me it would all be fine. I smiled, thanking her and just wishing she and her bloody cameras, all the crew and smirking bloody Tiff would go away.

"Now, it wouldn't be fair if we only showed Tanya's 'best bits', would it?" Carol-Ann said, walking towards the camera as it closed in on her. "...so before you decide who you want to win *Celebrity Spa Trek*, take a sneaky peek at this."

She swept off-screen and we saw on the monitor how Nathan arrived in camp, the bitchy comments from Marcus about him not being a celebrity and a quite nasty diatribe from Rex behind Nathan's back about him being 'a hanger-on,' which I could see shook Nathan. Then we saw our tent, the shadowy figure of me on top of Nathan in the semi-darkness, I was making quite a noise, thrashing and yelping with joy. I didn't realise I'd enjoyed it quite so much. I turned scarlet and glanced over at Nathan who was turning white as the blood drained from his face.

"How embarrassing" I mouthed to him, trying to bond, but he kept on staring ahead, his jaw flexing. Then the tent action subsided and there was a close-up on the slow unzipping of canvas as Nathan clambered out smiling...followed by me...but I looked so much younger, thinner, blonder? I looked up from inside the tent...but...it wasn't me. It was Tiff, her tousled blonde hair all over the place, her clothes rumpled, shirt buttons fastened in the wrong places and her skinny young legs bare and firm. I gasped, but before I could take in what I'd just seen, we were treated to more shots of them together, at the side of the mountain, behind a tree. I wasn't even spared the intimate whispers between them of what they might like to do to each other at some point in the near future when the show was over. The VT eventually came to an end and the camera honed straight in on my face. I put my hand up to the camera. "No more. Please – I've seen enough."

I stared ahead, as if made of stone, images of what I had just seen whirring in my head. But in the pit of my stomach, the deepest recesses of my heart, I wasn't really surprised. I was angry that Nathan had lied and had made me feel like everything was my fault. I was upset that my humiliation had been beamed to millions of viewers, live on air. But surprised? No. For the first time I felt in control, almost liberated and I realised that throughout the shocking on-air revelations, I had yet to shed a single tear.

"Here are the numbers to vote for your favourite King or Queen of the Mountains... So get calling and texting. You can also vote online via Facebook. Join us after the break, when we will be announcing your winner."

"Tanya, oh my God! Can you believe what they did with that edit?" Was Nathan's hilarious opening line as he leaned over to me and touched my knee.

"It's amazing what editors can do these days," I said, stony-faced.

Then I heard the familiar whirring of the camera.

"I know being with me has been tough on you," I started. "And I have given you the benefit of the doubt for the four years we've been together..." Nathan began to protest, but I put my fingers gently to his lips.

"Please don't try to insult me with an explanation because at this stage it's irrelevant. I believed that I needed you so much I couldn't live without you. I would have stayed with you, whatever the truth was. As it is, I now know the truth...and it is the truth that has given me the strength to say goodbye to you. I am not frightened of being alone anymore. It's over, Nathan."

He was visibly shocked and had it not been such a sad moment I might have giggled at him, his hair standing on end and his mouth open.

"It was the edit... They made it look like..."

"I'm not stupid. Though I think I have been until now. Even the most skilled film editor can't make someone look naked and like they are having sex when they aren't," I snapped. "No more lies...just goodbye."

"But... Tanya, I can't live without you..."

"I don't have any money, Nathan. And I don't have a career in TV anymore... oh and I lost your recording studio. And that's what you can't live without."

"But it's not – and it doesn't matter you haven't any money. You're Tanya Travis... You can make money, you'll always be famous."

"And you will always be unfaithful."

But he wasn't listening. "You can make loads of money after this, Tanya. Dump Donna and I'll be your husband and manager. There are other reality shows, commercials, corporates, you can do them for the rest of your life if nothing else comes up, you'll never be stuck for work. I still want to marry you."

"I don't want to marry you."

"Tanya, look, we're both grown-ups, so I might have played the field a little... Tiff was chasing me for days before I gave in. She means nothing – wouldn't take no for an answer. It's you I really want and I won't ever sleep with anyone when we're married. Besides, we'd be stupid not to get married, we can make big money from the magazines with the wedding." he joked.

"Gosh, and they say romance is dead."

"You can't just push me out of your life like that, Tanya. I'm your fiancé, we're meant to be together. I can't live without you... We're a team."

"We aren't, Nathan. We aren't a team. You don't have a job and you rely on me for everything."

"It's all about money with you, isn't it Tanya?" he said angrily, trying a different tack. "You think you own me then dump me and you won't see me anymore. Do you think I'll just conveniently walk out of your life – that I won't go to the papers and tell them what a sad, paranoid bitch you are?"

I looked at him steadily.

"Through all that, not once did you say you wanted to marry me because you loved me, Nathan."

I'd spent the past four years worrying about blondes in their twenties who'd apparently hounded him in bars and taxis and now Tiffany. But at that moment, it dawned on me that they weren't the reason Nathan didn't love me. He didn't love me, because he could never love anyone but himself.

There was nothing left to say.

"Tonight it's *your* final," Carol-Ann walked slowly, carefully back into shot while talking to the camera. "So... you heard it here first, the 'romance' everyone's been talking about is over. Tanya Travis dumps Nathan Wells, live on air. Now, you the public will decide the fate of this year's hottest love affair."

I sat quietly, looking straight ahead. The result no longer mattered to me – I had to think about the things in my life that were actually important.

I sat by Nathan, not really caring about the outcome, just wanting to get away as Carol-Ann made the most of her last few minutes on prime-time. Would she still be young and beautiful enough next year, or would someone else take her place? *Make hay while the sun shines, Carol-Ann*, I said to myself, *it's later than you think*.

"Well, it seems the British Public have decided who they want to be this year's winner of *Celebrity Spa Trek*..." again the pausing, the waiting, but by now I didn't care. All I could think about was how sad and tawdry my life had become and how ridiculous I must look in the eyes of the world.

"And now what the whole country has been waiting for... The winner of this year's *Celebrity Spa Trek*...the King or Queen of the mountains by a landslide is... Wait for it... it's... Congratulations Tanya Travis! You are the *Celebrity Spa Trek* winner! And Queen of the Mountains!"

I was amazed. What had the viewers seen? They'd obviously enjoyed my madness, my ageing cry for help and my incessant need to vomit. I was dumbstruck as a makeshift crown was plonked on my head and Carol-Ann helped me up to guide me to my 'throne.' The celebrities from camp trouped back (even disgraced Paul, who looked a little the worse for wear) hugging me, clapping and shouting 'Go Tanya!' as fireworks went off and streamers exploded over me.

I'd spent twelve days on another planet, during which time I had endured discomfort, bitchiness, filth, anxiety rates in double figures, gallons of sick and a public breakdown. I had just watched my fiancé have great sex with another woman and my beautiful wedding was now cancelled. I would never be a bride, but hey, I was Queen of the Mountains and I had my very own plastic crown and ridiculous throne. You couldn't make it up.

TWEET: @AgentDonna Gr8 show tonight as @TanyaTruth was crowned #QueenOfMountains. Hurrah! #BestAgentEver #AlwaysListen2Agent #Don'tBelieveWhatURead

Part 3

32

The Moon on a Stick and a Plastic Crown

The wrap party was loud, exuberant, full of press and hangers-on and I wanted to leave after four seconds. The only reason I made it there at all was Donna. As soon as the show had wrapped, she had swept onto the set and accosted me on my throne. "Honey bee!" she shrieked, rushing towards me on stilt-like Louboutins. "You have made Mama Bear SUCH a proud agent!" and she threw her arms round me, enveloping me in the familiar and comforting aroma of Shalimar and tobacco fumes. I smiled sadly. I was pleased to see her, but everyone else on the show had been met afterwards by friends, family or partners. It was clear from the kisses and the tears that there had been lots of love and lots of missing. The irony was that Tanya Travis, 'Queen of the Mountains', had won the title but was the saddest contestant at the party. Since arriving there I'd lost my home, my fiancé and any chance of walking down the aisle in this life. I wasn't ungrateful, but a plastic tiara and a double page in *heat* could hardly compensate for a lost life, no veil and no future.

"We have been offered the moon on a freaking stick," Donna screeched, waving a wad of papers in my face. "Where shall I begin? New York? The way of Piers Morgan with your own talk show, working title: 'Trailer-Trash Talks Back'?"

She was talking ten decibels louder than everyone else and was beside herself with excitement.

"Donna. Please keep your voice down, they might still be filming."

"All the more reason to shout from the rooftops how fabulous you've become... I was right. Oh boy, was I right. This little sojourn up the mountains has done for your career what Viagra does for Hugh Hefner every Friday night!"

"Yes, that's great" I monotoned, looking around to see where the others had gone.

"'Bitch Stole My Job?'"

"*What*?"

"A new documentary series, about people who've had their careers stolen by younger, prettier women," shrieked Donna, leafing through her papers. "Oh and...hold your breath... *Oprah's* people... Yeah, you heard it right girl... *Oprah's* people are talking 'Public Person Private Breakdown'..."

"Oh, really... I'm not sure that would be..."

"Oh and before I forget, Dr Oz is LOVING your menopause and that guy is desperate to share it with the Western World. He wants your hot flashes and low libido all over his 'Menopause Mayhem' special."

"I don't."

"And FYI, *the Guardian* are talking up a piece about the orphans of Nepal starving while rich westerners drink champagne and celebrate the price of gold... You know *the Guardian*, it's something along the lines of: 'how can celebs drink disgusting Dom Perignon in a country where water is scarce and orphans are starving and trafficked.' But I think you should go with the 'Hot Celebrity Magazine' perspective. It's along the same lines, but with a more refreshing angle: they want you in Nepal drinking Dom Perignon and partying WITH those orphans – obviously only the very cute, photogenic ones. "

"You *are* kidding me?" I said, swivelling in my throne to stare at her.

"OK, I take your point. Not easy to find photogenic orphans...don't sweat it babycakes, I'll get pretty ones shipped in."

I looked at her face. She wasn't joking. I'd heard enough.

"Can we go, Donna?" I asked quietly, looking round to see if anyone was still watching me. Although I was still on my 'throne', the cameras had stopped rolling and the crew were striking the set. Flinty came up to me.

"Tanya, there are a lot of journalists that want to speak to you. The show has been a ratings success, so they are very interested to hear from the Queen of the Mountains!"

"Do I have to?" I sighed.

"Hell yes, you have to!" screeched Donna, and pushed me towards the waiting press.

After what seemed an eternity, but was really only about an hour, the interviews were over. All I wanted was to have a boiling shower and find somewhere to curl up and sleep but Donna had other ideas.

"What's wrong with you, Little Miss Celebrity Royalty? Donna rasped, too excited to be grumpy. "There's a wrap party with your name on and don't say I don't think of my Queen's needs – I have brought supplies!" Along with my wipes of choice, she brandished a large box of Clé de Peau make-up. It was very expensive and hard to get hold of but she'd had it flown over specially. I smiled at her and opened the box, unable to contain a little yelp of pleasure on spotting the beautiful container of Luminizing Face Enhancer. The illuminating beads promised to capture 'the ever changing radiance of the Mediterranean' in my skin and if ever I needed some of that, it was now.

I applied my make-up while leaning against a tree as Donna held up a mirror. She barked instructions at me like a sergeant major about where to put the blusher and once I'd finished with a slick of the lip-gloss that 'dazzled with diamond clarity,' she took me by the hand and guided me towards a large tent. As we drew nearer the door, she pushed me ahead and lifted the canvas flap. I stepped inside and suddenly party poppers were going off, phones were flashing and everyone was cheering. A sea of smiling, friendly faces greeted me and I almost burst into tears.

"Well done, Tanya!" cried Cindi, rushing over to us, Marcus in tow.

"Ooh Tan, you dark horse. The viewers loved you all along. Bossy old Tanya Travis, the nation's sweetheart. Who'd have guessed it?"

"Yes," I smiled weakly, taking it as the compliment it was meant.

"Darling, you were fabulous but don't get any ideas – I'm the only queen around here," Marcus giggled, emptying a glass of bubbly and reaching for another.

"You OK, Tan?" Cindi held her head to one side, a concerned look on her face.

"Oh yes I'm fine. I...just...I don't know what I want anymore. After all that has happened and all the stuff with Nathan, I feel very wobbly. I'm angry and I'm upset and... Well I can't believe that I was so taken in by him."

"Well, I didn't want to have to tell you this, but Nathan... he once tried it on with me you know, when I was working with you." She looked straight at me, ready to give me the details, but I couldn't listen. I was too fragile to take any more, wrapping my arms around myself I put my head down, shaking it slowly, willing her to understand and change the subject.

"Tan...don't let Nathan put you off men forever. I mean none of them are perfect, some are just a bit better than others," she placed her arm around my waist and leaned in:

"We come to love not by finding the perfect person, but by learning to see an imperfect person perfectly."

"Yes... I suppose you have a point...but I reckon Nathan's imperfections are so numerous, that the perfect bit would be hard to find. Is that one of your quotes?"

"Yeah... Well, actually it's another one of Angelina Jolie's, she's fab."

"What a crock of shit," screamed Donna, who'd obviously been earwigging. "Didn't Angelina Jolie also say: 'I am so in love with my brother right now'?" At this, Donna staggered around laughing, giving Marcus the opportunity to take her aside to discuss his Lear.

Cindi smiled at me and shaking her extensions in amazement at Donna, wandered over to her mum who clamped her arm around her with pride. She smiled lovingly at the porn-star daughter whose tits would pay for the conservatory she'd no doubt longed for all her adult life. Marcus was now quaffing his second glass of champagne, eulogising on something thespian and introducing Donna loudly to his 'dear, dear, friend' Harriet who'd apparently played a 'feisty' Ophelia to his Hamlet in a 1974 production at the Old Vic and had flown over to be with him at the end of the show. Jonny joked alongside, unaware he was now being an unfunny gooseberry – but Nathan, and Rex for that matter, where nowhere to be seen.

I realised I needed to clear my head, and there was someone I had to find and talk to.

"Hello, I wondered where you were," I said, spotting him at the makeshift bar. He was standing with his hand in his pocket, sipping from a bottle of beer. He was wearing a sky-blue cotton shirt buttoned loosely, open at the collar and his eyes were smiling as they took me in. Gazing at him I noticed, not for the first time, how muscular his forearms were as they emerged from the blue cotton to lift his beer bottle. He drank slowly, never taking his eyes from mine.

"So... Tanya, the winner, eh?" he said with a smile, placing his bottle on the bar. I smiled back at him.

"Yes. It's great," I sipped my drink and leaned on the bar. "I should be happy but I'm not."

"Tanya, happiness isn't a gift that's given to you... Happiness is a flower, a friend, a beautiful day. It happens; you can't order it up like one of your takes aways."

"I guess you're right Ardash. You are a good friend and I'll miss our chats. I know I just sound like a spoiled westerner to you but you've helped me to see things a bit differently."

"We all make mistakes in life, Tanya, don't feel bad. You are a good person."

I sighed. "I try to be but I always seem to fail. Like now, everyone else has families and lovers here and... Well, you heard about Nathan and I?"

"Ah yes, very sad," he looked down, playing the grieving friend for a second but when he looked up I saw the twinkle in his eyes.

"Oh, you don't have to pretend. Everyone else seemed to realise it was wrong except me."

"You thought you were in the love..?"

"Yes, I thought I was in love with him. But then, I thought I was happy in my crazy talk-show life and naïvely thought I was making a difference. But none of it was real."

"Ah, Tanya, love and life is very confusing, yes?"

"It certainly is. I'm not sure now that I ever really loved Nathan – maybe I just needed him, which is a different thing."

We were both silent for a few moments. I looked round at the party which was in full swing. It was to celebrate my victory – and I was the only one who wasn't having a good time.

"Anyway, I've had enough here... If I don't go now, I'm just going to be boring everyone, going on about Nathan. I'll get off now, I just wanted to say goodbye," I sighed, finishing my drink and moving to go.

"No Tanya. You can't go – it's too early for the 'Queen of the Mountains'. I come with you. You like to spend the time away from here but with me instead?" he asked.

"Oh...well... I don't know." And I saw a flicker of disappointment across his face and in that moment thought *why not?* "Yes, that would be nice," I nodded, surprised at this sudden focus on the two of us.

"I was going to say... Are you liking the moonlight?" he smiled.

"Yes, I love the moonlight."

"Tonight is a full-moon party at Pokhara Lake, very beautiful. You like to see the moon over her water?"

"That sounds lovely... Yes I'd love to go with you...to the party." I heard myself say. I was going home tomorrow and maybe I'd never see him again. But just for tonight, I could pretend I really was someone else. He smiled and sipped some more drink but he didn't move.

"Shall we go...to the party then?" I blurted.

"You British, always rushing, rushing. Tanya says, 'I want now, I want now'," he teased.

"No. It's just that if we're going, I'll need my handbag... I have to wash, if I'm going to a party."

"Tanya, you don't need the bags and the washing." The smile on his face made me feel 18 again and despite feeling desperate for wash or a wipe, I resisted and concentrated on what was happening. We left the tent and walked out into the night without a word.

He guided me across a little scrap of grass and I liked the way he seemed to take care of me – I felt safe again. Then we stopped in front of an old motorbike.

"This is the ride, Tanya Travis," he said with a smile. I froze for a moment. There were two shiny helmets hanging on the handlebars and he handed me one of them.

He could see by my face I wasn't keen. "I am very good rider" he said. "And it's not far."

I stared at him, and at the bike. I breathed in the night air and calm swept over me. "Alright" I said, taking one of the helmets and swallowing hard. "Let's go."

The ride was a short, breathtaking one, through the dark countryside. I had no choice but to wrap my legs around him and cling with both my arms around his waist. The wind breathed new life into my face under the silent stars above and I felt truly happy for the first time in years. When we finally shuddered to a halt and he climbed off at our destination I was reluctant to let go. And I realised then that this might be more for me than just friendship – I could have held on to him through the darkness all night.

We walked towards the lake side by side. My heart soared above the dark water. It hovered there for a while, mingling with the tingly aroma of Indian spices; expectation seemed to pepper the night breeze. Arriving at the lake we stood together and I felt like I was standing on the edge of the world. My whole body was suddenly alive with anticipation. Ardash opened his arms, gesturing silently to the lake, like it was his gift to me. The moon was huge and luminous, reflecting in the black water. The lake was still and quiet save the odd shimmer as a gentle breeze stirred across its perfect surface, leaving gentle ripples. We spent a few moments just watching.

Looking across the water to the far side of the lake, where the gentle but insistent thump of trance music throbbed, Ardash suggested we take a boat across. I nodded, tired and happy and feeling like I was in another world. He spoke to one of the boatmen and within minutes we had climbed into a rickety wooden boat, illuminated by a small lamp, and were on the water. Despite the brilliant moon and the gentle slapping of the oars in the water, I couldn't drag my eyes away from him. In the lamplight I thought he was pretty spectacular – tousled, black hair, deep, brown eyes and a smile that seemed only for me.

Here, where no-one could see, he took my hand in his, gently, slowly, giving nothing away like it wasn't really happening. A secret between us in the darkness. Then on reaching the shore, he let go, like it had never happened.

Arriving on the other side, we found a makeshift bar for beers and clutching our bottles walked back to the water's edge, where we stood for a long time staring at the black lake, glittering in the milky moonlight.

"This is magical," I said, drinking it all in, not wanting to miss a second.

"Yes," he said. "This is what it is to be Nepali – being here, being part of this. Nepal is not about being anything or anyone, it's not about being Hindu or Buddhist, it's just 'being'... Being here."

I'll never forget the look on his face, pure love and pride for the land he was born into. As I looked into his eyes, my heart turned to liquid and slipped unnoticed into the black watery depths, lost forever, in Pokhara. I felt a million miles away from my life back home in rainy Britain, with its rules and recessions and endless pressures. Tonight I wanted only the 'being,' the 'now' of Nepal with him and the lake at Pokhara.

Later we danced and laughed, ate chilli chicken and drank more cold beer. All too soon, the thumping music succumbed to the breaking dawn and we had a short, thrilling ride back to base camp.

The party there had only just wrapped and some of the others were still up, sleepily chatting and drinking. Ardash and I strolled into camp to be met by the sight of Nathan, sitting by the campfire, staring into the flames.

I looked from Nathan to Ardash who seemed to know what I needed and leaving me alone, he wandered off to chat to the huddle of early-morning revellers. I took a deep breath and walked towards Nathan as he watched the last few flames struggling for survival.

He looked up, almost hopefully, as I approached.

"I'm sorry Nathan...about everything."

"Yeah well, *you'll* survive. You're the one with the fame and the money... I don't know what'll happen to me now."

"I don't have any money and I doubt there'll be much interest in me when I get back home." I said. "But you'll be fine. There's no point in going over it – I just don't think you and I were forever."

"Who knows?" he said, looking up at me, trying to read my face. "I mean, we could start again, Tanya... I'd give it a go..."

Those beautiful eyes, that smile, almost catching me off my guard again... It would be easy to go back to something familiar and then I wouldn't have to be on my own when I got home. And for a second I wondered, just *wondered* if...?

"I...really hoped we had something, Nathan. But I think I knew all along that you didn't really love me." I sat down next to him. "Do you know, I thought if I convinced myself I loved you enough, it might be infectious, that you'd catch it like a cold...and love me as much."

"Tanya, I did love you, in my own way... I still do...but you never let me be free."

"But 'your way' isn't mine, Nathan. I wasn't possessive; I didn't want to be your whole life – just the best part. And for you, I wasn't."

"I know, but I could try... We could go back home, a fresh start?"

"I'm sorry, Nathan. It's over."

He started to protest, but I carried on. "Funny, I always thought I wasn't enough for you, but the truth is, you weren't enough for me."

He looked back into the fire, defeated. I left him by the dying embers and walked slowly back to the others.

At 7am the bus arrived to take us on the long journey back to Kathmandu. Donna had left hours before to fly back to the hotel from Pokhara.

"How typical," I sighed, as we got on the bus. "I have to suffer the indignity and near-death experience of riding on this for seven hours while my bloody agent flies back in 35 minutes."

"At least Paul isn't driving, Tan," said Cindi. Apparently him driving us on the outward journey was his first challenge – but as I'd thought he was the runner, it was lost on me.

"Yes, Paul isn't at the wheel, that's something," I smiled as I climbed into my seat next to Ardash, thinking how different the journey back to Kathmandu would be – in so many ways.

I sat next to Ardash the whole way back to the hotel. I dozed, and looked out of the window, marvelling at the beauty of the scenery. It was so strange – my relationship had just ended, I'd been humiliated on prime-time television yet here I was, looking at this beautiful view, feeling like Julie Andrews in *The Sound of Music* – my mind was skipping through the mountains with a song in my heart.

We finally reached the hotel at 2pm. I let everyone else get off the bus before me and hung back with Ardash. As we sat waiting to get off, his hand slipped into mine again. Only for a split second, then it was gone. My heart fizzed as I climbed down and walked into the hotel, still in Julie-Andrews mode, I resisted the urge to dance up the steps with happiness and begin a vigorous performance of 'The Hills Are Alive' from the top step.

The others had moved quickly, desperate for a real bed and when Ardash and I entered the foyer together, everyone had gone. Wordlessly I walked to reception and picked up my keys, walking slowly up the thickly carpeted stairs, not sure what would happen next. I felt him behind me, following; surely he could hear my heart beating through my body? What was I thinking? At my door I hesitated, turned to see his face and though my head told me different, my heart said this was the right thing to do. I opened the door.

It was dark and, still groggy from the previous night and the long bus ride, I was aware of his hands around my waist, then without a word, his mouth was on mine. I pushed the door closed with my foot and let go, kissing him back, my lungs filling with...love? lust? I didn't know, and didn't care. I could barely catch my breath and had to pull away. The eyes meeting, the hand on my back, the rush that coursed through my body whenever we'd talked; I was giddy and scared and yet I'd wanted him so much for so long I couldn't wait and pulling him back towards me, we staggered to the bed. Falling in a heap we carried on kissing. He tasted of the city, past and present, tourist scent and native spices, for the second time that night I felt on the edge of the world. I tried to focus but everything was misty – I knew tomorrow when I was alone I would want to remember every minute detail. I wanted to take this memory out and look at it on cold, grey days back home, studying every second of my short time with him and reliving it again and again. Tomorrow he'd be gone, but the night would stay with me forever.

Afterwards, as we lay in a tangle of warm limbs and high-count cotton, the worry butterflies began to flutter in my chest. This was so wonderful, so perfect, why did it have to happen now, just as I was about to leave? A well of tears suddenly flooded up through my chest and into my eyes, my head rocked with a heavy aching. Ardash looked alarmed.

"Tanya, Tanya..." his voice, like the honeyed Nepali sunset, "you are OK? Please don't cry."

"It's just...too much beer...at the party" I tried to be flippant, to laugh it off. But he saw through me.

"Tanya, beer doesn't make you cry. It makes you happy. Why are you so sad?"

"Oh...I don't know, Ardash. So much has happened these past few weeks. I don't know who I am any more, I wish things could stand still...here...tonight." I was now in full blubbing mode, wiping at my damp face. I picked up his shirt, still lying on the bed and put it on to comfort myself.

"Tanya, my English rose" he said, his voice husky, his hand brushing mine. My heart almost stopped.

He was being so kind and gentle it made me sob more. "I'm not an 'English rose,' I never was. I've never been good enough and now I'm old and wrinkly and..." at this I heaved out more sobs.

He looked so confused and he was so kind and gentle. He was giving me a compliment and I'd thrown it back in his face. I was so stupid. Then I just thought *sod it*, and kissed him. His lips were warm, his skin stubbly as his eager tongue searching through my half-open lips. I felt him growing hard again as he pushed me back onto the bed, pulling open the shirt and caressing my breasts.

We rolled together on the bed, kissing and moving as one. Making love that second time was even better, I felt braver, more sure of myself, more sure of him. He gasped and we came together in a rush of heat and lust.

GOSSIPBITCH: *Whose reported five-figure sum deal to write a tell-all book on their former boss has just been cancelled? Her win in the Himalayas has turned the tide and no-one is buying negative stories on the Queen of the Mountains...*

33

The Twisted Permutations of the Spa Trek Queen

We must have drifted off to sleep, lying together in each other's arms. We stayed there for the rest of the day and all night, exhausted and happy. I was woken from this blissful slumber by the loud trill of the telephone.

"Hello?" I said sleepily.

"Sweetcakes, it's me. While you've been sleeping, your agent's been working her balls off. Get your ass into the lobby, *OK* magazine are here!" Donna yelled down the phone.

"*OK* magazine? Why are they here? What...?"

"For you, my little *Spa Trek* Queen, all for you. Oh and they want a piece of the tasty trekkie too, so bring him with you."

"But...Donna, no. I'm supposed to be going back home today..."

"Oh, but honey they wouldn't take no for an answer. Those journos are rapacious and at the mere whiff of a little 'Tanya on trekkie' action, they're offering big bucks. They said they'd fly over as soon as the show was finished and do a fabulous shoot with you. I rearranged our flights last night when they confirmed. Everyone knew you would win my love – the whole country was holding its breath."

"Why would they want to do a piece about me?" I asked, confused.

"Because, my little Drama Queen, the 'will she, won't she' has been keeping the viewers gripped all series! Highest ratings ever, they tell me. Better even than Jordan and Peter in a hammock together on *I'm a Celeb*..."

"What a high bar!" I gasped, sarcastically, feeling the familiar annoyance and irritation at Donna's mad bookings. "Ardash and I are nothing like Jordan and Peter! And what do you mean, will she, won't she?"

"Will she see the love rat for what he is or go ahead with a tragic showbiz wedding? Will she hook up with the trekkie who is crazy about her or will she ignore his big brown eyes and taut biceps and run off with the gold-digging sex addict? So many twisted permutations, my little *femme fatale*. Anyway, the flights home have been moved to tomorrow. *OK* are in the lobby now and you and the trekkie need to put in an appearance, pronto. Wake him up."

"He's not here..." she didn't answer, she knew. There was no point lying to Donna, she always knew everything. "Anyway, what would you say if I told you I don't want to do this anymore, Donna? I'm not interested." I said firmly.

"If you told me that, I would say it's not a request, sugar-bee. You are homeless and hungry and it's a done deal – that is what I would say. You're not in a bargaining position, so don't take retirement just yet."

I glanced at a sleeping Ardash and didn't answer, so she tried a different tack. "And just think what that money could do for the trekkie and his favourite orphanage. Not to mention the fact that you need to get your career back on track – you are currently poor and that's not good for you or Mama Bear. So I'll see you in five?" and without waiting for an answer, she banged down the phone.

I looked across at Ardash again and marvelled at how gorgeous he was, sleeping peacefully. I gently shook his shoulder, reluctant to wake him and allow real life into our bubble.

"Ardash, we have to go downstairs. There's... Well, there's a magazine company that want to take our picture." I didn't mention the fact there was also a rampant talent agent who would eat him for breakfast and spit him out if he refused.

He opened his eyes and looked at me. "Magazine company? For what are they taking the picture?"

"My agent says that people in England are very interested in you." I said, watching him. "And me. You and me. She also says they'll pay for our photos, enough perhaps to buy something for the orphanage."

He sat up. "That sounds good... They need a water tank, so if you wish, Tanya Travis, I don't mind having the photographs for a tank." And he smiled his beautiful smile.

I jumped into the shower, silently cursing Donna for putting me in this awkward situation. Ardash and I had grown close on *Spa Trek*, but it was early days to say the least – no romance had blossomed until yesterday and I was feeling very confused. I pressed my head against the cold shower tiles as the water gushed over me. One thing I did know was how much I had enjoyed last night and how much I didn't want it to end. I wanted to help the orphanage get their water tank, and I wanted an extra day with him – even if it did involve a magazine shoot and a large dose of Donna.

Ardash and I arrived in the white marble lobby half an hour later. I looked around for Donna and suddenly she appeared, in a full-length kaftan, pearly lips, hair all bouffant.

"Good morning lovebirds," she twittered, striding towards us on enormous wedges.

I glared at her. "Donna, I'm really not sure about this," I said, taking her to one side, away from Ardash. I sat down next to her on a seat in the lobby, I had to talk to her properly, make her see beyond the 'big bucks' and 'great offers on the table'.

"I don't know what is going to happen with Ardash, but I do know that the last time I spoke to a magazine about a relationship, it didn't end well," I started.

"Look, you can't win 'em all, honey," she said absently, checking her Blackberry. "All that matters is that *OK* are paying six fabulous figures, and you need every single one of 'em."

"I'm giving the fee to the orphanage."

She went pale. For once she was speechless.

"Donna, I don't think all this is me anymore" I said.

"Honey, I told you there's no choice; you have to take that fee if you want somewhere to live when you get back to Blighty. And as for saying 'this isn't me', it is *so* you... You're Tanya Travis and I will get you back on top, I promise. You'll have another fabulous home and all the designer gear you can..."

"What good is a fabulous home and designer clothes? I had a kitchen I never cooked in but worried about keeping clean. Clothes lined up in shades in my wardrobe that I wore only a few times. I can see now how little I did, how empty and superficial it all was. I don't need it and I don't want all the crap that went with it."

"Sweetie" she said in a low, quiet voice. "Don't think I'm not impressed by your sudden prioritising of global welfare over Prada's latest line in cruise-wear, but it's a simple equation. If you want to eat, you have to work. The only work you know is being Tanya Travis – and unlike other people, you don't have the luxury of changing your job. You ARE your job, your job is being a celebrity, so please, just do this. Once you are back in Britain, I promise you, all those things will be important again. This place has disturbed you... Jeez, you're so disorientated kiddo, just listen to Mama and all will be fine."

I opened my mouth to reply, but a team of people burst through the hotel doors and swished towards us, all smiles and cameras.

"Hi, hi, hi! I'm Chloe," said a rather glamorous, long-legged redhead in strappy maxi dress and wedges. "And this is Toby our photographer and Tim his assistant." We all said hello and sat down to outline what would be happening over the day.

"Now, guys I'm sure you have your own utterly fabulous clothes but we also have the latest pieces I'd like to put you in.," She said, batting huge fake eyelashes at us both. "They are on trend but still in-keeping with the whole 'Indian' thing."

"Nepal...she isn't India." Ardash said.

"Oh, really? Never mind, these pieces are soooo gorge it doesn't matter where they're from... and India's around here somewhere, isn't it?" She waved her arm around like India was just to the left of the reception desk. I groaned inwardly, this was just the sort of thing I didn't want to have to deal with any more.

"Now Tanya, we have some deelish saris and Ardash we've got THEE most darling loose pants and sweet little Arabian Nights separates," her voice squeaked as she held out her hands in a delicate gesture like she was describing baby clothes. We both nodded and smiled. Ardash seemed bemused. He was sitting next to me, and I kept thinking about the proximity of him and how easy it would be to slip my hand into his, the thought of which gave me little jolts of electricity.

"Ooh, you two look so good together," Chloe oozed.

"Gorgeous couple," agreed her nodding assistant, "happy too."

"Happy? They're delirious... she's damp with anticipation about their future together," interrupted Donna, staggering across the foyer in those impossibly high wedges having ordered herself a 'proper' drink at the bar. "Coffee's for pussies," she hissed at me as I gave her a warning look.

"Right, let's begin!" said Chloe brightly. "Come this way!" she commanded, getting up and leading us through the hotel and out into the stunning gardens.

"Wow, this is lovely," I said, taking in the bright, turquoise pool framed by lush greenery, all set against a breathtaking back-cloth of snow-capped mountains.

Donna staggered around, shouted 'gorgeous' a few times, ordered herself another drink, a jug of Martini for everyone and took to a sun lounger to observe. I knew my agent well and it would be a matter of time before she added her distinctive brand of running commentary to the proceedings. As we took in the view, the stylist arrived, trailing wafts of tulle fabric in her wake.

"Hey, you guys," she said in a trans-Atlantic accent. "I'm Fenella. Can I get you on the loungers?"

Ardash and I did as instructed and sat on adjacent loungers. We smiled awkwardly at each other and waited for Toby the photographer to start snapping. Chloe was wafting her hair and Fenella was wafting fabric around us, muttering to herself as she wrapped swathes round me and draped some over Ardash.

"We can't get too close... Culturally, it's not acceptable here," I said to Chloe, eyeing the fabric suspiciously. Toby was already snapping.

"Put your right leg over his and your hand on his chest," he instructed.

"Oh I don't think..." Apart from the cultural aspect, it was one thing having sex in the privacy of my hotel room, it was another wrapping my leg around him and clutching at his chest for several million readers of *OK*.

"Honey, you know you want to," came the voice from the sun lounger. Donna leaped up and strutted across the tiled floor, three sheets to the wind on Martinis and having slipped into her poolside lounge-wear of mini kaftan and turban, was looking like a 70's Tupperware housewife.

"Tanya, don't be shy..."

"Thanks Donna. I'm just working out how to do this with dignity, and without offending a whole nation," I caught Ardash's eye and we both giggled, embarrassed.

"Is this OK with you?" I whispered, as Fenella instructed us to get closer together.

"Ah, no... it is not good Tanya... My family would die from the shaming, but they will give us the water tank yes?"

"Yes, I will no doubt die from the shaming too but let's just lie back and think of the water tank." I smiled, burrowing my face into his neck.

The shoot continued on for another hour and 57 minutes with Chloe suggesting several intimate poses neither of us would agree to. She finally reluctantly conceded we could sit close and look into each other's eyes instead. Toby was re-lighting and I was just relaxing into this when Donna screeched; "Oh Tanya, you don't have to hide it, everyone knows you're both crazy about each other honey... Let's do the kissing shot next, Chloe?"

I got up from my seat, fighting off the tulle 'bondage' and marched over to her. "Donna, will you please keep out of it? God, you won't be happy until I'm straddling his naked body in the hotel lobby wearing nothing but a bloody bindi..."

"No-one would ask you to do that... yet... Mmm, naked you say...a bindi? Now you're talking."

I shot her a filthy look and she avoided my eyes by popping her oversized sunglasses on. Chloe motioned for us to go upstairs and my heart sank. What the hell had Donna promised these people?

* * * * *

Once upstairs, we refused Chloe's first request to take everything off and get in the hot tub together. She made a few urgent, hissed calls to London and eventually asked Tim the photographer to shoot some soft-focus photos of the two of us in the bedroom, while muttering about 'contractual agreements' and 'unscrupulous agents'. We stood by the window in flowing robes, looking out at the mountains, on the balcony at sunset with drinks and of course, on the bed. Through all this, I dared to think about a life with

Ardash and how wonderful it would be to wake up with this funny, wise, gentle man each morning and live a perfect, simple life.

The bedroom scene opened with me, Ardash and a hundred-weight of rose petals but in true Hollywood fashion, he kept one foot on the floor. We looked into each other's eyes and though we didn't actually touch, I swear the air sizzled and sparked around us. Without Donna's presence I felt myself relaxing against him, giggling with him, throwing my head back with laughter at everything he said and undressing him with my eyes. He was looking at me all the time and when they were all busy checking shots on the monitor and exclaiming about how 'sick' the photos were, his fingertips reached out and touched mine secretly. Everything in the room stood still – like the world had stopped and we were totally alone. I looked at his mouth, knowing I would kiss it later, my eyes swept over his slim hips, longing to caress his firm, muscular chest through the white linen shirt he was now wearing. And I wanted it all.

By sunset, the shoot was over and Chloe and the crew headed off for the nearest bar.

"As it really is my last night tonight, I thought it might be nice to eat here at the hotel," I said to Ardash as we strolled through the hotel lobby. "Would you like to join me?"

Tonight was my last in Nepal and I wasn't going to share Ardash with the city or Donna or even strangers in a bar.

"That would be good," he said; "I like to spend the evening with you Tanya. I will be sad when you leave."

Not as sad as me, I thought, looking beyond the restaurant area out onto the twilit pink mountains, the deserted pool.

We wandered into the restaurant and I ordered a simple salad. Ardash ordered a rice dish and as we ate, we talked about the shoot and I dared to ask about what might happen next.

"What will you do now the show's finished?" I said, spearing lettuce with my fork. I wasn't hungry; my stomach felt like lead, the lettuce tasted like wet paper, I just wanted him. I didn't need food.

"I will go back to my trekking company. I will be glad to return. Trekking season is now busy... So, I will begin tomorrow."

"Gosh. So soon?" I said, thinking, *wow he will just go back to his old life in the morning like nothing has happened. Like I never existed.*

"And you, Tanya... What will you do?"

"I don't know. I didn't exactly enjoy today – but I wonder if I will have to go back to that life? I mean once I'm back home, if there are offers on the table, I might be tempted. Anyway, it's not that bad, I could put up with anything as long as I have the right person by my side." OK, I was being very obvious but given the cultural chasm between us and the fact I had to leave in less than 12 hours, I felt it necessary. To my dismay he didn't pick up on it, or if he did, he chose to ignore it. He just nodded, half-heartedly.

"What would you think? About...being in that life? In Britain...could you ever see yourself living ...somewhere like that?" I asked, trying for nonchalant while sipping my wine and studying his beautiful mouth.

"Ah, Tanya it would never do. Your agent she talks of the papping and the big bucks and she shouting all the time – like she is in great pain... No, no, I could not live with that life. I belong here with my mountains."

I sighed, he was right. Why would he want to live a mountain-less life of incessant tweets and flashbulbs and Donna's tobacco-infused obscenities? No, if I wanted to be with Ardash, it would mean leaving my heart here with his, entwined in the prayer flags hundreds of feet in the air, fluttering through the mountains.

"I need to think about a different future now that I don't have my show. But I have here...and the orphanage...and you?" I ventured. He smiled.

"I'm not obsessing about marriage anymore, Ardash and I had planned to spend some time alone for a while but sometimes life has other plans...doesn't it? I suppose what I'm trying to say is, I've learned here that life is very short and we can't plan or buy a moment, it just happens. I've never wanted to spend the rest of my life alone, I always wanted to share it with another person. Once upon a time I hoped to have kids of my own too but..."

"You don't want children?"

I felt tears well up. I put my fork down, unable to eat any more.

"I can't...and it's not what people think – it's not my age. Plenty of women have babies in their forties...but I..."

And the floodgates opened. I started to cry and using my napkin to wipe at my face and blow my nose was disconcerting for the other guests. So I fled the restaurant. Apologising to him through tears and tissues I ran out to the courtyard with the now dark, deserted pool and black distant mountains. I leaned on a wall facing the huge, eternal blackness and sobbed.

Within seconds, Ardash's hand was on mine.

"Bahini... What is it? Why do you cry? Have I upset you? I am so sorry."

"No...no..." I shook my head. "It's not you. It's...it's something that happened a long time ago."

"But if it's long ago, why you cry today? What makes you so sad?"

"Oh, Ardash, you've no idea how much I've always...longed for a child, children...but..."

"But what...?"

I put my head in my hands. I couldn't talk about it, not after all this time. I looked up into those kind, trustworthy eyes and slowly my heart opened up.

"When I was a teenager I got pregnant."

"Ah...so you have child, this is what you are telling me?"

"No. I don't." I could feel my legs swaying under me. I leaned on the wall for support and looked at him. I'd never told anyone this before, well, apart from Donna.

"I was 16, it was the first time I'd had sex...a boy I thought I loved. I didn't tell anyone I was pregnant. I thought if I ignored it the problem would go away but when I told him, the father of the baby didn't want to know and I was alone...then Mum found out."

I thought back to that day, it was late August and it was too warm. I was standing in the kitchen drinking water from the tap and Mum was looking at me strangely.

"Tanya, do you have something to tell me?" she asked. I turned, saw the look on her face and cried. I wasn't crying about the fact I was scared and pregnant, I was crying at my mother's disappointment. She'd been a single mum and life was a struggle until the day she died. She didn't want the same for me or my sister.

But as much as she wanted a future for me, I wanted the baby. Perhaps that's why I'd kept it to myself, a natural instinct to protect my daughter inside me, so no-one could take her. I had no doubts until I saw what having my baby would do to my mum. "I broke Mum's heart...so to mend it, I had to break my own," I heard myself say.

This was something I'd lived with every single day of my grown-up life, yet I'd never voiced it. Even my sister Tara never knew as she'd moved away by then and Mum said we mustn't talk about it to anyone. I think Mum believed if we never spoke about it then we could put it away in her blue silk sewing box, with the bills we couldn't pay.

And every morning since, when my alarm went off, I'd thought about my lost baby. Every good review, every new designer suit, every award and every penny I earned from that great big future I'd worked so hard for amounted to nothing compared to the child I'd lost. I'd have given everything I had to get my baby back.

"Even now, all these years on I wake up in the middle of the night and know something is missing," I heard myself say.

As I spoke about it for the first time, it became more real and thoughts were crystallizing in my head. Ardash and I moved wordlessly across the empty courtyard to sit on the sun loungers. The evening breeze got up and caught a parasol, I absently watched it flapping. I stared into the pool; bright turquoise sunshine by day, it was now an empty, swirling blackness, swallowing me up.

"I pleaded with her to let me keep it. There was no-one else – Mum believed it was best for me – I never knew my dad." I wiped at my palms again and again.

"Tanya. I'm so sorry... I have no words. Your mother, she did what she thought was right."

"Yes, but right for whom? Mum wanted to save my future," I said into the water, "but ironically, what I did for her destroyed it."

"Ah... the Western World sees things in very strange light. Having a child would not have stopped you having a future."

"No, but we were all stupid back then. It was the 80's, we all wanted big hair and shoulder pads and women suddenly had their own careers – and not merely as assistants and secretaries to men. Motherhood as an unmarried teen in my culture was seen as a death sentence to success." I used my sleeve to wipe my eyes and my nose, and didn't care how I looked. "I have spent my life grieving for a child I never knew, children I never had. And when I was old enough to leave home, to earn some money and make my own decisions the first thing I did was find a boyfriend. I was desperate to get pregnant, like I owed it to myself – to my baby – but after having unprotected sex for two years, nothing had happened so I went to the doctor. After tests it seemed as the abortion had been so late and I'd been left with scarring – even if I could conceive, it was unlikely I'd ever carry a baby to term. So not only did I lose my first baby, I lost all the babies I might have had."

"Oh Tanya." He sighed and gripped my hand.

"I have never told anyone any of this. Except Donna of course, and all she worried about was the press getting hold of it. And the show that paid my wages, that made me famous was based on me criticising women who allowed their kids to get pregnant. It would have been hypocrisy... But what I should have done was use my celebrity to tell teenagers that yes, it is OK to have the baby, it's also OK to have an abortion but only if that's what *they* want."

I smiled sadly to myself, all those years telling other people to follow their hearts – yet I'd never followed mine.

"I have never been able to look into the eyes of a baby in a pushchair, or see a toddler in the street without feeling this terrible, crushing grief and guilt...for what I did," I stopped crying now and was gasping for breath in that hiccupy way when emotion is too strong for tears alone. "That is, until the orphanage. I was so scared going there. I had avoided babies and children all my life, yet on that first day I could see those little ones needed me so desperately that I had no choice... And touching them, I can't explain, but it felt like I was being healed."

Wracking sobs suddenly thrust through me and I thought my heart was coming out of my throat.

Ardash put his arm around me and I leaned on his chest gratefully.

"Tanya, you need to grieve. You need to face what happened and get on with your life."

I sobbed harder, but in my heart, I knew that he was right. It was time to face what had happened, mourn and acknowledge the significance of my loss. All my adult life I'd tried to wipe it clean, scrub it away and cover up the smell of my grief and guilt with expensive room scent, but all the time it was there.

"I will never be a mum..." I heard myself say into the blackness, still leaning on Ardash who squeezed me gently.

"Motherhood – she isn't always about the blood," he said. "You were like mother to Maya and the motherless children, if only for an afternoon."

My heart melted. I'd felt worthless and less than human, like I could never really be a 'real' mother but with someone like Ardash I could change my life. He was a shard of light to cling to in the dark and for the first time I had a chance of being whole again. I might even finally be able to come to terms with what I'd lost at 2.34pm on September 12th 1982, on that cold operating table somewhere in Manchester.

* * * * *

Later we went back to my room and he held me for a long time. No sex, no heat, just warmth and comfort and lying together on the bed. I had never felt such lightness, such a sense of deep joy and relief. "What are you thinking?" I asked.

"I am thinking I need to go now, Tanya."

"Oh, but it's my last night Ardash. It may be a couple of weeks before I can get back here..."

"I have to talk with you... I am hurting." He wasn't smiling.

"Yeah... I know. Me too. But I'm too old to play games. I don't have time to sit around waiting to be asked, I wasted too many precious years with the wrong man when I could have been happy with the right one. Do you want me to come back here? If things work out, we could live together perhaps? I know it won't be easy...but I've never felt so sure about anything in my life. What about you?" He said nothing.

"Well?" I asked, "You do want to be with me again, don't you?"

"Tanya. I should have told you before...I can't be with you."

"Why? Is it the abortion? Oh God, you hate me for it, don't you?" I said, wracked with guilt all over again.

"No, I don't hate you."

"I never told anyone because I knew it would change how they felt about me, how I feel about myself, knowing they know..." I said, feeling the tears pricking behind my eyes.

"Tanya, it is not you."

"Well, what else could it be?"

"I... I have a wife."

"What...wh... Hang on, are we saying the right words here?" I grappled in the darkness to make some sense of this. "You said 'bahini' meant sister, which also means girlfriend... 'Wife' is someone you marry – it means married in my language." I explained.

"And also in mine."

No. No. No. How could I have missed this? It was the oldest story in the book and I was one of the oldest women in the book and I bloody missed it.

"Ardash, are you teasing me?" I wanted to laugh. If I laughed loud enough I could drown out what he was saying. He was shaking his head.

"Why didn't you tell me this last night when we first slept together? You asked me to the party and I assumed you were free...we've talked so much. I've told you things I never told anyone before, yet you failed to tell me that you are *married*?"

"Tanya, I was wrong to ask you to the party, but you have filled my heart since we met. I never think you would want to be with me, and now I am hurting your heart... But I can't."

"No, you can't." I snapped, searching my brain for the appropriate words, desperately trying not to show my anger, my wretchedness.

"Tanya, my wife... I miss her so much, she died." he said, with a crack in his voice.

"Oh... I'm sorry... I didn't understand..." I instantly felt awful for doubting his integrity.

"She had the weakness in her heart... So sudden. We had only been married for five years."

"Oh, Ardash. How awful, there's me going on about my pain, but your suffering is just too much. You lost your parents as a child and now this. I had no idea... How long ago did she die?"

"It's been four years since her death. She was twenty-nine years old. I was thirty-six. We wanted children like you, but her health was always so bad...it never..." There were tears in his eyes. "I can't ever be in the love with another woman Tanya, it would disrespect her memory. My wedding was for my life," he said, head now in his hands.

My heart crash-landed into the basement of the hotel. "I understand how you feel. You must have loved her very much."

He nodded and I put my hand on his shoulder.

"But what would be sadder is if you devoted your life to her memory and didn't have a future for yourself. I can't imagine she'd want you to spend the rest of your life alone, mourning her." I said, gently.

"It's not my choice, Tanya, I can't help the feelings. The loss it is very deep." he replied.

"I understand." I smiled sympathetically and tried not to cry.

"These last two days were very beautiful, Tanya, but today, it hurts too much. It can never be – I am so sorry."

And he climbed out of bed, dressed and left, without even saying goodbye.

TWEET: @TanyaTruth Thanks 2 all who voted 4 me back home soon. So sad 2 leave #Nepal a beautiful place + beautiful people #TheLostChildrenOfNepal

34

OCD in Overdrive and Kardashians in Crisis

Four hours and 22 minutes later, he'd gone and I was packed and waiting in the lobby for Donna and our taxi to the airport.

She finally staggered down the stairs, yelling at staff and demanding help with her baggage. "Honey I arranged for a car... Where's the car?" she was in full stress mode and I didn't need another layer on top of my own. I'd already showered for a whole hour and all the tears and vigorous scrubbing had left me crispy-dry and exhausted.

I had to put this one down to experience; Nathan had left me vulnerable and I had been too willing to let Ardash in. I needed to stay closed and detached and never allow anyone to screw me (in every sense of the word) ever again. (OK, perhaps not totally 'ever again,' but I had to be wearing the emotional equivalent of a bullet-proof vest if I were to venture down that rocky road.) Despite my own talking-to though, I'd wanted the phone to ring, a knock on the door– and Ardash to be there. It was bad timing, terrible geography and the stars were not aligned, they were all over the damned place – so why did it have to be now that I'd finally fallen in love for the first time? Even as the taxi pulled up outside the hotel and Donna hurled a fag across the lawn, swearing loudly about the service, I imagined him appearing from nowhere, taking my dry, crusty hand in his and walking me back into the hotel. Into his lovely, calm, centred life.

I picked up my bags and took a final look around. The sky was its usual breathtaking blue and the white hotel building gleamed in the sun. I wondered if I would ever come back again. I'd arranged for the magazine fee to go to the orphanage and any money I earned beyond my needs I would send too. I desperately wanted to see the children again – and one day I would, but I couldn't come back too soon. At the moment my heart was too full of Ardash and I couldn't take the pain of seeing him until I felt stronger. So I reluctantly stuffed my stupid, mangled old heart into the boot along with all the bags. Donna's cases were engorged with glamorous saris and gold jewellery, she was a magpie and couldn't resist anything that glittered, but her unruly bags made me feel unclean. I never bought anything when abroad because my perfect packing would be ruined – there was a place for everything. I never carried extra stuff in my luggage as it was too messy. But this time I had one extra item, the blue elephant that Maya had given to me – I kept it close to me, in my hand luggage.

"I just need to pop to the ladies." I said, rushing back into the hotel, ignoring Donna's yells of protestation from the taxi. As much as I couldn't allow myself to be late for the airport, all the stress was making me desperate to wash my hands. I had to break one obsession in order to obey another and my head was starting to whirl as I scrubbed my hands in the hotel bathrooms, all the time fretting about missing the plane.

After a few minutes I walked out of the bathroom and I'll admit, I scanned the foyer for Ardash. I don't know why I thought he'd turn up, after all he'd made it clear the previous night that he couldn't be with me and I needed to accept that. I climbed into the taxi, telling myself this was no time for me to behave like a love-struck teenager.

The taxi shuddered and spat and set off for its ride through the crazy beeping, cow-loving, traffic-jamming city and I felt nothing but loss. I'd come here to get my life back yet now I was leaving most of it behind. I'd had my heart torn apart, mended and torn again, the remaining fragments were now swirling through the mountains.

Arriving at the airport we stood in a queue and waited. As I looked around, I caught sight of a man examining the departures board. He was standing with his back to us and he was taller than most Nepalis. It was Ardash, here, at the airport. He started to walk off, and abandoning Donna and the cases I ran after him. I called his name, but he couldn't hear me and when I caught up with him I forgot all about the taboo touching thing and grabbed him by the arm.

"Ardash? I'm here" I said, breathlessly. The man turned round. And it wasn't Ardash. I almost cried with disappointment and embarrassment. "I am so very sorry, I thought you were someone else," I said, stroking the stranger on the arm and upsetting him even more. He shook me off and I scuttled back like a naughty child to an incandescent Donna.

"What the *fuck* are you playing at? Our flight's been called!" she screamed as I approached.

"Sorry, I thought it was – someone I knew," I said sheepishly. For once she didn't say anything – I think she guessed what had happened.

The flight was long and uncomfortable but the cabin staff were attentive. Walking past with scarlet smiles in tight red skirts and swishy hosiery, they constantly offered spicy titbits and paper cups filled with cool water.

"Honey, order yourself a very large drink," was Donna's considered advice whilst prattling on in her seat. Travelling with her was hell. I endured hours of her loud 'freakin' and 'fucking' and unsubtle exclamations about the physical appearance and estimated age of every passenger walking past to use the bathroom.

"She clearly chose face over figure," she hissed, nudging me as a very made-up, plump, middle-aged woman waddled past.

I tried to close my eyes to it all, and resorted to putting on my headphones to drown Donna out. As I surfed through the entertainment channels, I couldn't even get excited about a '*Kardashians in Crisis*', headline on Showbiz News. I was the one in crisis and had to hope to God the paps weren't waiting to descend on me at the airport. I was headed towards home, towards everything I knew – but had never felt so alone, or so afraid, in my life.

TWEET: @AgentDonna Queen of Mountains about 2 touch down in UK. Press conferences, exclusives + new show TBA ASAP! #BackWhereSheBelongs #GoTanya

35

Lost Brides and Cancelled Cake

We arrived back to an autumnal Britain of rain-swept skies and leafy streets. There was a flurry of press and fans taking pictures on their phones outside the airport as I came through arrivals. Flashbulbs popped in my face and I scrambled in my handbag to find my Chanel shades. "Tanya! Tanya! Over here! Did you know Nathan's seeing a new blonde, Tanya?" one of the paps yelled, trying to get my attention. I put my head down and with Donna striding ahead and clearing the way with her big Brooklyn voice, I made it outside.

It was 5am and a grey dawn was breaking over London. "Let's find the taxi rank, Donna" I said, staring glumly at the dull sky and pulling my wrap around me to keep out the wind. Donna smiled.

"Mama Bear has taken care of it" she said and pointed to a familiar car parked in the 'pick-up only' bay. The door opened and Arthur stepped out.

"Welcome back, Miss Travis" he said, opening the car door. I had to bite my lip to hold back the tears. Donna and I climbed in, and Arthur drove us silently towards Donna's London apartment.

"You must stay with me for now, sweetcheeks, until you get back on your feet," said Donna, lighting up a cigarette and opening the window.

"Thanks Donna but I need to go home." I replied.

"Home? Kiddo I don't want to rub it in, but you may recall your house has been repossessed. You don't have a home." She blew smoke back into the car, making me cough.

"But hey, über-agent Donna is here for you, girlfriend. And when life throws me lemons...well, you know the rest. There's a silver lining up there somewhere my little diva. I can see it now; you, a cardboard box, a few ill-fitting clothes, a shop doorway – somewhere photogenic, a designer store of course. Karl Lagerfeld, probably." She sat back and raised both arms to indicate the headlines; "'*Homeless and Desperate*' scribbled blindly on a bit of old card and your wrinkled old hand reaching out to readers of *The Sun*' – '*Tanya's Tragedy*.'" She turned to me; "Is that fabulous, or is that fabulous?"

"You are kidding, right?"

She wasn't.

"Just look what bankruptcy did for Kerry and Martine, my little benefits bunny. You can't get those girls off the front pages. Kerry Katona's relationship with the prawn ring was lucrative, but what probiotic yogurt has done for Martine McCutcheon will go down in showbiz history! We will have magazine and book offers rolling in, my little cash cow'."

"I'm not interested" I said in a quiet voice.

"Nonsense sweetie!" she yelled as Arthur pulled up to her apartment. "Listen, are you sure you don't want to stay here?

I nodded and smiled.

"Then go back to Manchester and check into a hotel – The Hilton, I'll cover the costs – and call me tomorrow." She opened the car door and with one leg on the ground and one still in the car carried on yelling; "I'm thinking a warts-and-all, fly-on-the-wall doc covering your descent into true poverty... Must call Dickie and see if he's up for it. I'd say ITV? Whaddya think?" I didn't answer. "I know, I know... You're thinking BBC3, More 4 – Youth Culture? Either way, I guarantee your über-agent will milk this for all it's worth". Arthur hauled her luggage out of the car and set it down. "Speak soon, my little honey bee. And cheer up – you won the show!" she said, and in a flurry of kisses and a swish of Prada luggage she was gone and I was alone in the back of the car.

"Where to, Miss Travis?"

"Home, Arthur. Take me home." I said.

The car hurtled along empty roads. I was tired and jet-lagged and looking through the car window was struck by the lack of vibrancy and colour after Nepal. The hedgerows and trees were lacklustre, dotted tightly along impossibly straight roads framed by little, bland, uniformed houses. Fragrant spices didn't scent the air here. There was no perfumed jasmine or honeyed sunsets, just a veil of greying net curtain over Britain.

We finally arrived a few hours later outside the beautiful, white Georgian house that until recently had been my home. I knew the locks had been changed, but I had to see it one last time.

Arriving at the front gates I climbed out of the car and with a little push was surprised to open the large, iron gates. There was no electricity to operate them anymore and they hadn't been locked. The garden was slightly overgrown and my bespoke patio furniture, left out in the weather, would soon become shabby and unloved. Like me.

I walked up to the house and peered through the letter box, and despite the publicity about my cancelled nuptials, it seemed a gushing tsunami of wedding brochures had continued to litter my doormat. Tulle brides standing in front of stately homes and couples holding glittering glasses of fizz in soft-focus candlelight peered up at me from the mat, making me nauseous.

Having peered through the letterbox I wandered around the back, revisiting my past, like a ghost. I pressed my face against a window to see the sad remains of my designer kitchen. Cakes had never been baked there, Sunday dinner never cooked, no family to sit around the table. I thought of my perfect bedroom and the king sized bed that had never seen love, a living room so manicured and clinical it had looked like a private doctor's waiting room. This was my past, what I'd come home for. All the champagne, the congratulations, the awards, the press and the fans – this had always been the truth of my life: I'd been empty and alone.

I got back into the car, numb inside. Like a blank canvas before paint, it was daunting, but up to me to paint a new picture now. I had to make myself a new life. "Take me to a hotel, Arthur. Not the Hilton – somewhere less... Well, just...less."

"OK Miss" he said and we pulled smoothly away. I looked back through the window at my former home and as it disappeared from view, tears slid down my face not for what was, but for what could have been. Then my mobile rang.

"Hello?"

"Tanya, you big shit, it's me, Astrid!"

"Astrid! How are you? I am so sorry about your job, I couldn't keep you on, as you know everything's being sold. Where are you living now?"

"Don't worry about job. I have new job and new flat. I am dialling because I have your room, Tanya."

I was confused. "What do you mean, my room?"

"They let me get some of your shit before they close the house up. I told big bastard bailiffs to be pissing off and I took your clothes. I have all things you like at my flat now – and Tanya, there is a room for you. You can be living with me now, yes?"

For a few moments, I couldn't speak. "Thank you, Astrid" I finally managed to whisper. She gave me the address and said she would meet me there later, once she had finished work. It would be mad, I had no doubt, but better than being alone in a hotel room.

It was mid-morning when I arrived at Astrid's and bid farewell to Arthur. I welled up again when we said goodbye – who knew when, if ever, we would see each other again? I found the key to Astrid's flat outside under a meerkat pot, where she'd promised to leave it. I opened the door in no doubt this was the right place, as a nasty citrus blast of her signature air freshener hit me right between the eyes.

"Jesus," I sighed. The tiny flat was filled with Astrid's stuff, fluffy-soft toy cats and piles of TV box-sets strewn across the living-room rug. A Gok Wan calendar stood proudly on the mantelpiece, the perky boy smiling back just for Astrid. Lovely Gok, all white teeth, designer specs and a horribly mistaken, but well-meaning, belief he could make every woman look good naked.

I wandered into the tiny kitchen to see Martin Clunes' signed photo on the fridge (so she'd finally tracked him down, God help him!) I also saw some letters addressed to me. I'd asked the wedding suppliers to send their invoices to Donna's agency due to the current housing situation and somehow, they'd ended up here. As I ripped open the envelopes, I stared at receipts for the deposit I'd paid from Nepal only days before, on the venue, cakes and dress alterations. The very last pennies I owned spent on a wedding that now wasn't happening. I stuffed them into my bag.

There was too much going on, so I tidied the box-sets away, wiped the worktops down a few times, (twelve times to be precise, always even numbers) put the kettle on and went in search of the bathroom. On the way, I poked my head into the other rooms. One was clearly Astrid's bedroom; all pink hearts, plastic daisies and even more cuddly cats. I walked into the last room, and stopped still, overwhelmed at what I saw. A small single bed was swamped with my enormous Fenn Wright Manson duvet in café-latte and covered in my plump, goose-down pillows. My buttercream lambs' wool handmade rug took up most of the floor space and when I opened the wardrobe, all my suits and dresses looked back at me. And there, carefully wrapped and hung, was the Vera Wang wedding dress I'd had for so long. Tears filled my eyes and I shut the door. There was a bottle of Jo Malone room spray on the bedside table along with a packet of Saniwipes and under the mirror was my jewellery box. I sat down on the bed, taking it all in. I couldn't believe Astrid had gone to so much trouble to rescue my stuff. I lay down on the soft, comfy duvet and stared at the ceiling, until I drifted off to sleep.

I woke a few hours later and wandering back into the cluttered living room, caught sight of a familiar object. My huge flat-screen telly sat on an upturned crate in the middle of the lounge with a cat shaped post it note on it. '*Tanya's TV*' it read. '*Bailiff Bastards Fuck Off*'. I smiled and flicked it on, hopping without much interest through the channels. I didn't want to think and settled on *Housewives of Orange County*. It was the one where Gretchen danced with *The Pussycat Dolls* and I was just about to record it for Astrid when my mobile rang. "Tanya are you home, did you find key under meerpussy, you old bitch?"

"Hi Astrid, yes I did," I smiled, pleased to hear a familiar voice that wasn't Donna's.

"Tanya. I want to hear all about your adventures. I'm going to pub after working tonight. You need to meet with me for the drinks and shit."

"OK, that would be nice – well, the drinks anyway."

"I bring new friend with me Tanya, his name is Lars. He's a big dick's head, you will like him."

For one horrific moment I thought she was trying to fix me up with some moody Swede. I wasn't ready for another man and if he'd learned English from Astrid I feared my life would start to sound like a script from a Quentin Tarantino movie.

"Is he just a friend, Astrid?" I said suspiciously.

"Ah Tanya, you fucker, you guessed... Lars, he's my hot lover."

"Really? Well, good for you," I smiled to myself, delighted for her, she actually sounded happy.

After the freedom and openness of the Himalayas I was keen to leave the cramped flat if only for an evening and agreed to meet up with Astrid and Lars later in a small wine bar.

They were already there when I walked into the Mexican-style bar, decorated in oranges and yellows with cactus and piñatas posing everywhere. It was supposed to look Mexican, but to me it just looked messy. I pushed down an urge to start tidying and walked to where Astrid and Lars were sitting, looking into each other's eyes. Lars was blonde, handsome and clearly besotted with Astrid, who looked younger and prettier than I'd ever seen her. Lars kindly went to the bar to buy more Sol and I hugged Astrid, who had become more girlish with love for her fellow Swede.

"He's cute fucker, no?"

"Yes he is. Have you given up on Gok Wan?" I asked, settling down into a booth.

"No. But Lars will do for now," she giggled. "He's very long..."

"Too much information, Astrid," I said. "I don't need to know the size of his penis, thank you very much."

"And I'm not going to tell you, you nosy old slapper. Yep, he's a long tosser..." and she raised her hand to indicate height and I remembered it was all in the translation.

"I bloody love him and Tanya, Tanya...are you guessing what? We are engaged." She held out her hand to reveal the ring and I squealed with genuine happiness. "I know it seem quick Tanya, but I know him for many years before, in Sweden. When I come back from Nepal, I meet up with him and now I cannot live without his funny little shitface."

When Lars appeared with three lime-wedged bottles I hugged him too and demanded an invite to the wedding.

"Ah, we wait a little while, Lars is gardener and the bastards he working for don't pay much."

"Where are you working now?" I asked her, thanking Lars as he handed me my bottle.

"I am just starting work for the vets" she said proudly. "I am training to become a nurse and I will be soon taking examinations so I can make the little buggers better." She squeezed Lars' hand

and looked into his eyes. For a few moments I thought of Ardash and how his eyes had taken me somewhere else. How wonderful that Astrid had managed to capture the elusive true love that I had never been able to hold on to. She looked so beautiful and so young.

"I need to pop to the bathroom," I said, "I'll be back in a few minutes." I walked into the toilets and washed my hands. Then I called Vera Wang's office, the Cake Fairy and the wedding venue (one of the bonuses of being an ex-celebrity was that I had people's out of office mobile numbers) and went back to join Astrid and Lars.

"Where in buggering hells-bells have you been, Tanya?" Astrid exclaimed as I landed back at the table.

"I've been making a few calls. There's something I want you to have." I said, sitting down. I opened my wallet and took out the receipts for my wedding and placed them in front of the happy couple.

"I don't have any need for it now, so please make me very happy and accept my fairy-tale wedding," I said. "I have spoken to everyone involved and they are happy to make any changes you would like."

There was a silence while the two of them looked from each other and back to me. I hoped I hadn't offended them with my offer.

"You killing me, you big shit!" Astrid suddenly leaped up and hugged me followed by Lars, who wasn't sure what was happening but smiled and nodded, knowing that if Astrid was happy, so was he.

GOSSIPBITCH: *Who's been whoring himself around the tabloids promising an exclusive kiss-and-tell about life and love with a former Daytime talk-show star? And who went home empty-handed with his tail between his legs because his former lover is now the media's darling?*

36

The Bridesmaid and the Bröllop

Six weeks later I was proud to be the sole bridesmaid at Astrid and Lars' fairy-tale wedding, or 'bröllop' as the Swedish call it. She looked stunning in my Vera Wang with her beautiful long blonde hair and young, glowing complexion. Perhaps the cut of the dress was always meant for someone younger and more voluptuous.

My own dress was midnight-blue satin. Astrid had offered to buy me a 'fucking cool pink dress' she'd seen in Manchester at the Arndale Centre, but when she described the 'fantastic furry trim' I politely declined. I said as it was a winter wedding, pink (even 'fucking' fur-trimmed) might be a little unseasonal on a cold November day, especially on an ageing, spinster bridesmaid. "I will take you to slut spurt and buy bridesmaid dress," she'd insisted. This time I protested strongly; dear God, what retail mind from hell had that idea sprung from? However after much confusion, I Googled 'slut spurt' and was relieved to discover it meant 'seasonal sale' in Swedish.

I stood with Marcus and Donna in a beautiful room in the big old Cheshire mansion that would have hosted my wedding to Nathan. As the guests arrived, Donna was in full throttle. "I'm thinking, a big no to that big ass in yellow," she bitched at my side.

"Oh absolutely, the woman looks like an overripe honeydew," was Marcus's considered response.

The sniping was silenced only when the bridal music played and Astrid walked serenely down the aisle to her man. I was filled with nothing but love and pride for my friend. How lovely for her to have someone waiting like a safe harbour at the altar...it brought me out in goosebumps. I wasn't surprised to see in my mind's eye that the person I would have liked to see there for me was Ardash and not Nathan. I wiped my eyes as I thought about how beautiful Astrid looked, how happy and fresh and smiling she was, in the presence of Lars.

We moved into another room for drinks and dinner and it was clear that Astrid had enjoyed free reign in her 'decorating.' Amid the Old Masters and velvet chairs was an abundance of patriotic foliage – yellow, white and blue things sprouted up everywhere, with a two-foot tall Swedish flag on a pole in the middle of each table.

We dined on lutfisk; a traditional Scandinavian dish of cod steeped for many days in lye, until its flesh was caustic enough to dissolve silver cutlery.

"Honey, this is THE most revolting crap I've ever eaten," Donna screeched, spitting it out into her napkin.

Marcus was busy fawning over Astrid, who was circulating and had called by our table. "You sweetheart, you little darling," he effused, like she'd just come off stage. "I don't know what the bloody hell you did out there, but you were an angel at that altar. Not a bloody dry eye in the house, love."

"Aw, thank you Marcus, I was so fucking nervous I shitting all morning."

"Oh... Oh dear," he said, turning away from Astrid and towards Donna who was still being equally forthright about the catering. Astrid plonked herself down next to me.

"Tanya I want to say to you this. You stupid whore, I never knew how you sleep with Nathan," she began with a shake of her head.

"I know Astrid, he wasn't good for me but sometimes we are just blind, or don't want to see the truth." I said with a sad smile. "Anyway, enough of Nathan. This is your day."

"He giving it to all the girls."

"Yes... I can see now. It was all so painful and if I'm honest I was simply afraid of being left on my own. So I put my head in the sand."

"You crazy shit, you can't breathe with the mouth of sand!"

"Yes it was crazy, I couldn't breathe," I smiled.

"I wouldn't put my head in sand, not for sex-addict, frog-dick bastard" she said firmly.

I didn't know quite how to respond to that.

"He made me paranoid, Astrid." I explained. "I know better now, but...well, it's not the time to talk about it, but it's funny, at one point, I even thought you were sleeping with him!" I shook my head.

"You crazy shit Tanya!"" she gasped, slapping me on the back. "Do you have piss in your head?"

"No I don't have...piss... It's just, sometimes I heard giggling coming from your room and once you saw someone out of the front door and when I asked you about it, you wouldn't tell me."

She looked down, embarrassed.

"Astrid, I'm sorry, we really shouldn't be talking about this today – it doesn't matter, you don't have to say if it was Nathan in your room." I said quickly, wondering how the hell we got on to this conversation. "It really doesn't matter now."

"Tanya I have some confessions."

Oh Christ, I thought. *Not now, not at your wedding breakfast.* Marcus and Donna had stopped chatting and were now listening intently.

"Honestly, Astrid, it's not important, you don't have to say anything." I said, hot and embarrassed.

"Tanya – you right, I wasn't alone in my room... He was there all the time, the cheeky little bastard..."

She was nodding up and down and I was dying a thousand deaths.

"Please don't, Astrid. I don't need to know. Nathan's the past."

"Not Nathan, you silly cow! It was bloody Bjorn in my bedroom."

"Oh." I breathed again. "Astrid, I don't know why you kept it a secret, I wouldn't have minded if you had a boyfriend in your room."

"No Tanya, you would have been shouty bitch."

"No I wouldn't, I'm not that bad."

"Yes you are, you would have screamed about his bastard hair everywhere."

For a moment I didn't understand.

"But he sooo cute, with his little furry arse and..."

"Astrid."

"Yes?"

"Was Bjorn a pet?"

"Ya. A lovely little kitten Tanya, injured on side of road, some big fucker truck hit his little kitty leg. I kept him for a few weeks but when he gets bigger, I give him to my friend Anna. I say; 'Tanya will have a shit fit if she finds out'."

I smiled. What could I say? She had a point, discovering all that fur in my clotted-cream, pure-wool Berber would have possibly been as bad for me as finding Nathan in there naked. Oh yes, Bjorn the injured kitty would have sent me into...well, as Astrid so delicately put it, 'a shit-fit.'

The bride moved away to speak to more of her guests and I excused myself and went to sit outside for a while. I had time over the next few weeks to plan the rest of my life and despite all the lucrative offers, I meant what I'd said to Donna, I wasn't tempted. This was going to be a new and different chapter for Tanya Travis – I was starting out again with nothing. And this time it wasn't going to be about TV, designer heels or profanely-priced sound studios for men who didn't love me. This time it was about me but it was also about making other, more deserving people's lives better, more rewarding. One day I would go back and help in the orphanage for a little while, but right now it was still too raw to return, I couldn't risk the chance of seeing him. So until then, I would send what money I could, try and raise awareness about the lost children of Nepal and use what little celebrity I had left to do it.

Throughout the day I continued to think about these future plans that were slowly developing in my mind and by the end of the wedding I felt a little better. It was time for the happy couple to say their goodbyes outside and step into the wedding car to whisk them off to the honeymoon of their dreams on Richard Branson's island. I stood with Marcus and Donna, smiling and waving but before she climbed into the car, Astrid came over to me and whispered in my ear. "I will never forget what you gave me, Tanya," she said. I smiled and reached for her hand.

"And I will never forget what you gave me, Astrid," I answered. "I have been alone so much in my life, yet since I've known you, I feel like you've always been there and you never judge me. Whatever I am, whoever I may be, you always care – and that means a lot."

"You know, I lose my mother many years ago, Tanya. And I have to say to you...I love you like you are my bloody mother, you filthy bitch." And with that, she stepped into the car, looking through the back window as it drove off. I was touched to see her smile just for me and wipe away a secret tear. Always keen to hide her emotions behind her disgusting vocabulary; I realised in that moment how much we meant to each other. There was me mourning a lost child and there was one under my nose.

"Looking for light while carrying a lamp," I said to myself, waving back. And for the first time in a long time I felt loved.

It wasn't long before my reverie was broken into by Donna and Marcus hugging me and saying their goodbyes. Earlier Astrid had thrown her bouquet and having caught it, Marcus was now walking towards the car with Donna, sniffing the blooms and reminiscing. "Ah if only," he said with a dreamy look in his eye. "Darling, did I ever tell you about the lovely, lovely man I almost married? A tragedy of epic proportions..." And he was off, as they climbed into the car, both heading back to London in a flurry of pink carnations and thick Gitane smoke.

I ordered a taxi and went back to Astrid's. She and Lars were staying at a hotel for their wedding night so I would be alone. But if I still wanted to drink and not to think, there was always the series 1- 4 box set of *Doc Martin*. And if I still couldn't sleep there was the extended Christmas Special from 2006...

GOSSIPBITCH: *Which young, beautiful blonde is feeling a chill from TV bosses as they try to lure back her suddenly popular former boss and oust the new girl from her recently-acquired Daytime seat?*

37

An Unexpected Guest

Very tired, I arrived home after midnight and the minor nugget of happiness I'd grasped earlier when thinking about a more positive future had died. I opened a bottle of wine, toasted Astrid and Lars and watched the first couple of episodes of *Doc Martin*. I was just thinking about how even a fictional doctor with a blood phobia and terminal grumpiness had found love and I hadn't, when the phone rang. I just knew it would be Astrid, fretting about me being on my own and asking intimate questions about Richard Branson – I had grave concerns she would spend her honeymoon stalking him on his own island.

"Look I'm OK. It's your wedding night, you shouldn't be calling me. You should be having the 'full sex', you cheap Swedish slut..." I started.

"Tanya, it's me, Ardash."

It took me a few moments to process this. "Ardash?" I whispered. "Is it really you?"

Having thought about him all day, I wondered if this was a dream, or some kind of hallucination.

"Yes Tanya Travis. It is me."

"W...w ...? How are you?" I said lamely. So many things I wanted to say, but that was all that would come out (apart from my opening gambit about sex and Swedish sluts, which I hoped he could put behind him).

"I am well – and you?"

"Great... I'm great," I was so shocked I thought I might cry – or swear – so didn't dare say any more.

"Tanya – I can't see the Big Ben."

"Oh...no. I don't suppose you can," I smiled.

"But I'm here. In England, Tanya, I am here."

My heart leaped. What did this mean?

"I am at The Manchester Airport and the taxi man says it's short journey."

"Oh God really – you are in Manchester?" I was in deep shock.

"Yes. Tanya, I...come to see you..."

"Don't talk. Just get here."

I didn't care why he was here. I didn't care if he was back on the next flight tomorrow. He was here now and that was all that mattered. I gave his taxi driver the address, sat down with Martin Clunes and my glass of wine, and waited.

After a very long 36 minutes and 41 seconds, there was a buzz at the door.

Running downstairs three at a time I opened the inner then the outer door. And there he was, his eyes twinkling, his tousled black hair just as I remembered it. He was more handsome than ever. I noticed that he was carrying a bag – quite a large bag. I hoped with every fibre of my being that this meant he might stay longer than a night.

I suddenly became aware that the taxi was hovering behind him.

"Do you need money for the taxi?" I said, back in Nathan territory too easily.

"No. The taxi man he just wants to make sure it's the address." He waved him on and the cabbie smiled, sticking his thumb out of the open cab window and revving off into the night.

"Are you coming in?" I asked, taking nothing for granted.

"Are you convenient?"

"Oh yes... I'm convenient," I smiled, beckoning him to follow me up the stairs to my flat.

We both shuffled in, me gesturing for him to go first, he gesturing for me, resulting in awkward shuffling and embarrassed smiles from both of us. Once I'd closed the door I turned round and he was bent over, taking off his shoes. "Oh don't worry – it's only laminate," I said.

"Not lamminit – respect."

"Oh... Of course, yes. Please. Take them off... Er, come through," I'd forgotten that in Nepali homes they welcome your soul, but not your shoes.

We walked into the sitting room and stood looking at each other for what seemed like ages. Seeing my world through his eyes I couldn't help feeling ashamed of the tiny, cold, grey flat in cold grey England.

"I had to see you Tanya... I think we are in the love," he finally said.

All the pent up hurt and anguish I'd existed with in my grey bubble sprang to my eyes, filling them with tears. My chest heaved with sobs and I reached out, clutching at his arms with both my hands. He pulled me gently towards him until my head was on his chest and he was caressing my hair, mopping up all the raw pain with his lovely, lovely hands.

I looked up from his chest, dribbling and crying and he kissed me. *That's love*, I thought. And he kept on kissing me until we were together on the sofa and in my head we were back in Pokhara, the little electric fire in the cold, grey room transformed into a scarlet sunset. His soft, gentle touch and the kisses that went on forever reawakened the heat and colour of Nepal. We fell to the floor, still clinging to each other and were soon making love on the shabby little rug, all the passion and lust and hurt climaxed quickly in my head and my tummy, as a Catherine wheel exploded inside me.

Afterwards, we lay on the floor in silence, his breathing next to mine. I turned my head to him, not touching him, almost afraid of being rejected again.

"Ardash, what happens now?" I whispered into the darkness, closing my eyes in preparation for the pain his answer would bring.

Silence.

"I will always love her, Tanya."

"I know." I whispered.

"Always there will be a place in my heart for her. But as you said before I need to be moving it on now."

I propped myself up on my elbow. "Really, do you feel ready?" I said, looking into his eyes.

"Really" he replied. "Now I think of her with smiles instead of tears. You have helped me to do that."

"It's a big decision after what you've been through, to be with someone else," I said, heart in my mouth.

"Not someone else... You. Tanya, with you I am ready for forever."

I smiled so hard my face hurt.

"Oh Ardash, I feel the same way."

"You do? You are in the love too?"

"I think I loved you since I first saw you," I smiled, the back of my hand caressing his cheek. "I just didn't know it. How could I? My heart thought it belonged to someone else."

"Tanya, stop the talking now so I can ask you to be my wife," a smile broke out on his face. "I want to ask you so many times tonight but your mouth, it goes up and down and I can't get the bloody words in," he laughed.

I laughed too, glad of the break in intensity. This was the real thing, the man and the proposal I'd waited for all my life. It wasn't the setting I'd planned; there were no crystal flutes of vintage champagne, no music playing in a hotel suite filled with fresh flowers and Room Service, no rose petals on the bed – all the things I'd thought a wedding proposal should be. We were in someone else's crummy flat up North on a shabby sofa with a photo of Gok Wan peering disdainfully from the mantelpiece. *And I wouldn't have had it any other way.*

We stayed still for a few moments, just holding each other. Then I pulled away gently and looked at him.

"You know that I have nothing now, don't you?" I said quietly.

"I am not a rich man, but I have a business, enough to feed us both and I have a place to live in the mountains," he replied simply.

"You mean you want us to live in Nepal? You don't want to stay and live here with me?"

"Why would I want to live here? Here is cold and grey. Nepal has chilli chicken, momos and mountains.It's not rocket surgery, Tanya. We could have beautiful wedding, in the foothills of Sagarmatha. Please be marrying me, Tanya? You still haven't given me your answer. I can't wait forever," he teased.

"Yes... Oh yes, yes, yes..! I would love to marry you," I said, throwing myself into his arms and kissing him.

The next day I called Astrid then Donna, and they independently screamed expletives down the phone in their unique ways, both happy for me.

"Jesus, you work fast, I hope to God he's not a fucking gold-digger like the last one," was Donna's first response.

"People normally say 'congratulations', Donna, but I would expect nothing so predictable from you... And before you ask, no, he doesn't want a British Passport," I said.

"Jeez, so he doesn't want money or a passport, what the fuck *does* he want?"

"He wants me. Just me." I said simply.

"Well, there's a first time for everything – when's the wedding, honey bee? Mama needs to order a hat!"

"Well, the thing is... There are visa issues with him being here, and..." I decided to come straight out with it; "and we both want to live out there. In Nepal. Very soon. " I said, holding my breath. I waited for the barrage of abuse, but it didn't come.

"Well, it was good while it lasted. You have a lot of offers on the table, sweetcheeks, including your old job but it's your life," she said slowly.

"Wow, I expected you to be angry." I said.

"I'm furious, you have lost me hundreds of thousands in potential commission, you stupid bitch. You're fucking crazy, but then I hear what you say and it's not all about money is it? And what have I got to show for the late nights, the phone calls, and all the stress? I don't have any answers, so go find what you're really looking for babe... I mean, what the fuck do I know?"

"Thanks Donna," I said, and she was gone.

Then straight away, the phone rang again. It was Donna.

"Honey bee, I'm just thinking... If you're definitely going back to Nepal, I'm thinking weekly reality show, Jordan-and-Peter style – you and the trekkie in the mountains doing hilarious and 'life-like' stuff..."

I smiled and hung up: she couldn't help herself. I looked at Ardash. "Let's do it." I said. "Let's go home, to Nepal."

TWEET: @AstridLun On honeymoon Lars + I go 2 see virgin Richard Branson in his piss-hot house + he bring security men 2 join us #HotMillionaire

Epilogue

Hi Donna,

Thanks for your email. It's so lovely to hear news from home and I can't wait to see you and Marcus later in the year. Of course you must stay with us while Marcus brings Shakespeare to Nepal. I had a call from him last week and he says we 'shall weep' at his 'Lear'. Thanks for all your admin help with starting up The Lost Children of Nepal *too – we can do so much good with my profile and your talent: this charity will change lives. I know it's not your usual glitz and wasn't the kind of joint venture you had in mind when I suggested it but trust me, it's good for both of us.*

What can I tell you about life here? Well I feel like a Nepali-Mancunian – if there is such a thing. Ardash says it's a 'hinji-minji state of affairs' because when I was in Britain I was homesick for the mountains and now we are in Nepal I long for grey rain clouds and flat Manchester vowels. I guess I'm lucky to have more than one corner of the world to call home.

You saw Kathmandu as a tourist when you were here but when you come to see us I want to show you the real city. It's a vibrant, scary, poor, heavenly place and I marvel at the way two worlds co-exist – worshippers adorn idols with scarlet paste and marigold petals while shops on the same street sell outrageously tacky souvenirs that you would LOVE. It's like past and present, religion and tourism live in harmony and the juxtaposition of ancient shrines with 'I 'Heart' Nepal' T-shirts hanging nearby for sale never fails to amuse me! I love it here and I'm so happy but I do miss our lovely lunches, Donna. I also miss Coronation Street *and Crème de la Mer and – call me an old pedant – but a constant supply of electricity and hot running water would be nice!*

Ardash is still working as a trekking guide and for the lighter treks, I join him... You'd be horrified at me in my walking boots with no make-up on, but it's OK as there are no paps around!

You'll be pleased to know I've cut down on the ritualistic washing (I knew you always knew). I still wash too much and wipe too often, but it's so much better than it was and sometimes I can go all day without even thinking about it.

I've had to abandon my vital timings, too, Donna – you would be proud! Recently, Ardash and I went back to Lake Pokhara and threw my watch into the water. It was a symbol of the new me, as I realised after a few months of living here that 'now' can mean 'several hours from now' to Nepali people. I'll say to Ardash: "Are we going now?" and he will nod and say yes, but make no move. The old Tanya would have tried to rush him and gone ballistic at the thought of being late, but this Tanya has learned to redefine the word 'now'.

It's not just the scenery that's different here; I am amazed at how Ardash and my new family and friends don't care how my hair looks or how many wrinkles I have. Here they care about spirit, happiness, health and of course – how your dhal bhat tastes and whether your chapattis are any good. I'm working on that, but it's a messy process and I still don't cope too well with 'messy'!

There's much excitement at the moment as we're making our wedding plans (yes I am finally getting my man!) I haven't called Vera Wang this time, as Ardash's sisters are making my gown and will also scatter the flowers. We're hoping to be married during your visit so you and Marcus can be my Maids of Honour (not sure they have those here but we're mixing up the cultures – the wedding will be less vintage glamour more cultural mash-up!)

Astrid and Lars visited last month and just when I thought my life couldn't get any better, she handed me the DVD of Kourtney and Kim Take New York: Season 1. They also announced they are four months pregnant and expecting a little Astrid very soon. I am so delighted for them and look forward to lots of visits from their no doubt growing family in the years to come ... I just hope baby Astrid doesn't swear like her mother...or her aunty Donna!

I'm so happy here Donna, the only shadow being that Ardash would have been a wonderful father and it makes me sad that we'll never have a child of our own. It's a sadness I will carry with me always, but I don't let it take me over any more like I did before. I have so much to give and we spend all our spare time looking after the children at the orphanage, which is staying open along with other sanctuaries, thanks to our charity. I teach the children English and Ardash teaches them music and I'm hoping you will allow your new client to do a reprise of his 'Ugly Sister' role for the kids when you come next time (his Drusella is legendary in these parts, dear!)

Maya is still a very special little girl and stays by me most days. She feels like mine and there's nothing we'd love more than to adopt her, but it wouldn't be fair on the other children. I see her every day and make sure she has all she needs...including lots of love and cuddles. Last Wednesday she made me very proud and said my name, she's blossoming and slowly starting to become the little girl she always should have been.

Oh and I may have mentioned, I am aunty to 16 nieces and nephews, thanks to Ardash's four sisters. It's funny because considering we are a childless couple, our lives are filled with children and we love them all!

Ardash and I are still very much 'in the love', as he would say. He is an antidote to my controlling, stressing, constantly-wanting western ways; he is calm, centred, kind, gentle and non-judgemental. I've finally found my place and it isn't in front of a camera, denouncing the lives of others. A year ago, I would never have believed how much my life could change... I lost my show and my partner, everything I thought I wanted, but not what I needed... I now know the difference.

Anyway, I'd better sign off for now – the wifi can never be relied upon and I lost a whole long email I'd written to Astrid the other day which, as she would say, was very "shitting' annoying!

Thanks for everything Donna and see you soon,

Much love

Tanya xxxx

PS. I've taken a leaf out of Cindi's book and found a life quote. Don't think I've gone all 'hippy-dippy' but I just think it sums up how I feel at the end of one journey and the start of this new, exciting one. Oh, and it's not Cindi's, Kim Kardashian's, or Sharon Stone's...

"We are visitors on this planet. We are here for one hundred years at the very most. During that period we must try to do something good, something useful, with our lives. If you contribute to other people's happiness, you will find the true meaning of life."

Dalai Lama XIV

Also by Sue Watson

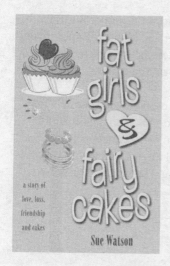

Fat Girls and Fairy Cakes

Can you really make a living from indulging in your dreams?

TV Producer Stella Weston is over worked, overweight and under fire. Having battled uphill for years to balance her career with her family life, she is repaid by being put out to pasture on a religious gardening programme – complete with a nervous vicar, his nymphomaniac wife, and 22 stone Britney wannabe gardener, Gerald.

In the past, comfort has always been found at the bottom of her mixing bowl, but when even the most delicious lemon sponge with zesty frosting cannot save the day, Stella decides enough is enough.

However, finding the courage to quit is sometimes the easy part. Can you really turn a passion into a profession? Does more time at home actually give you a happier family life? Are men truly from Mars or another universe altogether?

Stella has to roll up her sleeves and find out – when the going gets tough, the tough get baking....

A funny, well-written look at whether you can turn a passion into a profession, with lots of hilarious dates, mishaps and angst woven in...I really enjoyed it. - *The Daily Mail*

You want to devour this smart and fabulously funny read in one go! – *Closer*

About the Author

Sue Watson is a former BBC TV Producer and Mancunian now living in Worcestershire with her husband and teenage daughter.

When not writing novels on her flamingo-pink laptop, Sue can be found enjoying cupcakes, crisps and Caramel Chew Chew ice-cream while watching 'The Biggest Loser USA.'